The Blue Mexican

By

Danny Thomas Ruiz

Note for Librarians: A cataloguing record for this book is available from Library
and Archives Canada at www.collectionscanada.ca/amicus/index-e.html

Printed in Victoria, BC, Canada.

ISBN: 978-1-4269-1425-6 (sc)

ISBN: 978-1-4269-1424-9 (dj)

Library of Congress Control Number: 2009932392

*We at Trafford believe that it is the responsibility of us all, as both individuals
and corporations, to make choices that are environmentally and socially sound.
You, in turn, are supporting this responsible conduct each time you purchase
a Trafford book, or make use of our publishing services. To find out how you
are helping, please visit www.trafford.com/responsiblepublishing.html*

*Our mission is to efficiently provide the world's finest, most comprehensive book publishing
service, enabling every author to experience success. To find out how to publish your
book, your way, and have it available worldwide, visit us online at www.trafford.com*

Trafford rev. 2/24/2010

 www.trafford.com

North America & international
toll-free: 1 888 232 4444 (USA & Canada)
phone: 250 383 6864 ♦ fax: 250 383 6804 ♦ email: info@trafford.com

The United Kingdom & Europe
phone: +44 (0)1865 487 395 ♦ local rate: 0845 230 9601
facsimile: +44 (0)1865 481 507 ♦ email: info.uk@trafford.com

To my wife and our four princesses

PREFACE

It has been my extreme joy to teach and share classic literature, and sometimes not so classic, with students from the first grade through the college and university levels of education. As any educator of literature can attest, it is not easy to have the students read, much less share their thoughts about the literature in a classroom. Some literature lends itself to greatness and appreciation, but the challenge comes from the lesser known novels with its subtleties and intricate weavings of metaphors, similes, and visions of the world through the unique perspectives of the authors. Within each novel, regardless of the intent, there is life, love, loss and lessons to live by.

At times, students can lose their perspective through daydreams, i-Pods, cell phone text messages and other time stealing tricks that can often interrupt the novel under study. The challenge is to regain their attention, not through intimidation and threats of detention, but with legitimate means to recapture their interests and return to the story, and stories are the foundation of a civilized, intelligent society. Fortunately, my extensive background in law enforcement allowed for the telling of some interesting stories to my students relative to the novel under study.

During a lull in the action of a particular novel, I could sense students starting to zone out. Those were the times which allowed me to recant a particular anecdote from my varied experience as a police officer in a small town near the Bay Area of San Francisco, California, a small valley town called Tracy. The students' interest piqued and after a few questions regarding the incident, we returned to the reading of the novel. At the conclusion of the school year, I was fortunate to listen to students' comments about how interesting my stories were and how they helped enhance the understanding of a particular novel.

It was these students who provided me with the impetus to create my own novel based on my experiences. The novel is a medley of people and events which touched and shaped my life to become the man, the husband, the father and educator I am today. As a fan of novels about big city police work, Los Angeles, New York, San Francisco, I realized that even a small department can be the source of compelling stories as rich and meaningful as those in the bigger cities. Also influenced by the Romanticist element of literature and existential authors, my writing is a reflection and a tribute to those who refined the art of literature.

The names have been changed to protect the innocent, and nothing in any way can be inferred to relate to a particular individual, rather they are a conglomeration of personalities of many I have known over the years. The incidents are based on real life events, embellished in some ways for dramatic effect. Please relax and enjoy the journey.

ACKNOWLEDGEMENTS

As a baby-boomer, I am grateful to have matured during the hippy invasion and summer of love, the 60's. The philosophy and music were influential in shaping my own beliefs, attitudes and values. I wish to thank that time period and all the historical, good and bad, events that occurred. Education showed me there was life after police work and there are many within the University of the Pacific in Stockton, California, who were responsible for the resurrection of my life, so to speak. Dr. Robert Knighten for acknowledging my humanity, Dr. Diane Borden for showing me the appreciation of literature, Dr. Heather Mayne for the sheer joy of teaching, Dr. Larry Meredith for the spiritual element, Dr. John Phillips for his understanding and empathy for one from law enforcement thrust into the world of education, and Dr. Alan Ray, who showed me humor is necessary for the basic survival instinct. In particular I am also grateful to Dr. Donald Duns, God rest his soul, for instilling and supporting my desire to pursue higher education.

My eternal gratitude to my mother, my grandma and the best guy in the whole world, my Uncle Richard Lewis, my wife and four daughters who kept it real, showing me what's really important in life, my best friend Hank, who is always there for me, and lastly, my students. I am forever grateful that my life has crossed their paths, and without them, I couldn't be what I am today. We have transcended the teacher-student relationship and will remain friends forever.

Of course, the town of Tracy, California, and its people I owe much gratitude, for without them, my life would have been a complete bore.

PROLOGUE

I entered the aged building, known as Knoles Hall on the campus of the University of the Pacific in Stockton, California, and slowly ascended the creaking stairs to the second floor. I felt alone and afraid and seriously considered whether I had the courage to continue this journey. A sinister voice, hidden within the recesses off consciousness, laughed at the absurd notion of what I hoped to accomplish. Another voice strained to be heard, giving me the desire to continue climbing the stairs and bravely venture where many others had, but with a lot more confidence. To the latter voice I listened, slightly audible above the quick beats of my heart, for I had not experienced this anticipation since I interviewed for my promotional exam a few years back. I made it to the second floor and saw the door of the elderly English professor, slightly ajar, loomed menacingly before me. I hesitated. "Dr. Robert Knighten" said the sign on the door. Doctor? I hadn't known of any doctors outside hospitals in my life's experiences.

'Can I really do this?' I questioned. Of course I could. I've played this scene over and over in my mind. I've thought about the years which have passed so fleetingly, I've thought about the circularity of my stifling existence, and it came back to the same thing—a return to school in quest of knowledge in English Literature. I awkwardly entered the door and saw him, a small, hoary man amidst towering stacks and shelves of books crammed into his little office.

"Good morning, sir," I said, hiding my anxiety.

Looking up from his paperback book, he appeared to examine me. His eyeglasses lowered on the bridge of his small nose, and his energetic eyes seemed to penetrate me, to make of me the fool that perhaps I was. His demeanor told me he didn't know me and certainly could not have thought me a college student.

"Can I help you?" he sympathetically asked.

Back out now. Slowly, and simply say I'm in the wrong room or something equally ridiculous, I thought. I looked directly at him, hoping for some sign of cordiality, some approachability. I saw none and suddenly felt I was ten years old, called to the principal's office for chewing my gum in class. I had to be assertive. A sign of weakness was something I learned to conceal years and years ago, attributable to the repression of emotion necessary to survive on the streets fighting crime, fighting for "truth, justice, and the American way."

"I'd like to enroll in the English Department for my degree. I was told you could help me." What a stupid statement! My nervousness was showing. Why else would I be enrolling in college except for a degree? I saw a smile slowly steal across the kindly face of the professor, Dr. Knighten, as he sat back in his chair and looked me over. I recognized the movement as one of fellowship and acceptance and, what used to spring from my lips before anyone could actually hear what I was saying, I proudly told him, "I have a dream that I'd like to write a novel."

"You?" he laughed loudly. "A complete idiot like you dares to come in here and tell me you want to write? A book?" He laughed louder. "Do you realize how old you are? What have you accomplished in life? Take a look around you and see these kids coming in here for a real education." He cautiously rose from his swivel chair and then, with much animation, yelled: "Get the hell out of here! Go over to Sociology or Public Administration, wherever it is guys like you should be, idiots like you who try and get, what was it you said? A degree! My ass! Write a book?" Of course, this is what I imagined what was going to happen next, but it didn't. Instead, he reached out his hand and offered me a chair next to his desk. He showed me something which, for the most part, eluded me for the past eighteen years—my measure of respect.

"Relax, my good man," he told me, sensing my anxiety. "I'm certain I can help you. Tell me, you mentioned a book, what field most interests you?"

"Well, I...I don't really know. I spend the better part of my life as a cop. I've got my Associate in Arts degree in the Administration of Justice..." I felt stupid all over again. He said nothing as he looked at me, as though he wanted me to continue. "I guess I'm kind of a weird guy. At least that's the way most people close to me have often characterized me."

"Weird?" the professor leaned back in his chair. "In what way?"

Let me count the ways, I thought to myself. Hey! Isn't that from some great literature or a poem, or something? Yeah, I could do this English stuff. A silence, though not one of discomfort, eased between us. Calmness overpowered my apprehension. The professor bent forward, and his looks spoke volumes of compassion.

"This is summer. Things are fairly quiet around here and I've got some time. Why don't you tell me your tale?"

Yes. My tale. I'd be more than happy to tell him. Perhaps you'd like to listen, too.

ONE

There were two things I feared most growing up in this world--girls and fighting. Its order was of no particular importance for the thought of either frightened me to death. These perceptions, as they are to most children and however terrifying, were of little importance when I grew and learned that which caused me the most dread: my existence in an increasingly hostile universe.

My father was a career military man, so uprooting and moving frequently became the rule. My elementary school years were spent in the coastal town of Livorno, Italy, close to the American military base, Camp Darby. The American servicemen and its allies called the town Leghorn. I was about to begin my fourth year of elementary school.

For most of us boys, our first exposure to the opposite sex was usually one of a little pleasure mixed with a lot of fear. My illumination into that unexplored world came suddenly during school lunch while eating with my porky friend, Billy. He had a gap-toothed smile and a Beatle-bob haircut before the Beatles were known to any of us. Billy and I were pretty close, but I didn't know he had this dark side until that day in the school cafeteria where we enjoyed our seafood cuisine--fish sticks.

"Hey, Billy, besides baseball, what kind of things do you like to do?"

He thought about it a moment, took a bite of his fish stick and replied, "Eatin'..." then, without missing a crunch, he looked directly at me and said, "...and makin' out!" His emphatic assertion startled me. I knew what he meant, but I didn't know how to do it, I mean, I did, it's just that I never did it. He kept looking at me like he was expecting me to say something, but all I could think about was what he looked like doing this "making out" thing.

"You ever do it?" he asked.

"Do what?"

"Make out! Kiss girls! Man, what a dummy!"

"Yeah, I've done it, I mean, I do it." I was a good liar in the fourth grade, but before he asked me any more questions about something I knew nothing about, I asked him to tell me about his favorite movies.

"I dunno. My dad likes those cowboy movies with Audie Murphy, so I guess those are."

Fortunately, we never got on the subject of girls again, but from then on, I was scared of Billy, for he did things only grownups did. I wasn't scared enough not to be his friend, though, so I could stay on his side when we played football at recess. He was quite large and obesity was never a concern in those days of the early 60's, so he often finished my lunch. He was so massive; no one could knock him down playing football. Everyone was scared of him because of his size, or maybe it was because he had a way with women. We were all too scared to ask him how he did it or what it felt like because we didn't want him to know we didn't do it; we didn't want each other to know we didn't do it, part of the early indoctrination into the world of machismo. Billy was the only one we knew who actually kissed a girl.

On a crisp day early in the fall, Billy had beaten everybody at tetherball, but this one girl who resembled Peppermint Patty of the Charlie Brown comics, a girl sprinkled with freckles and a mop top of curly brown hair, was beating him. The guys were taunting him badly as he tried desperately but was quickly tiring, and she whipped him.

"Billy got beat by the freckled-face girl, ha!" yelled a voice from behind me. Billy, red faced from the tetherball whipping, got angry and started chasing the skinny kid who taunted him. His sheer size and weight prevented him from catching his tormentor as all the kids in the playground laughed at the sight. The skinny kid knew it and stopped to taunt Billy some more. "Hey fatso, you can't catch me. Come on Tubby!" One of the playground teachers heard the ruckus and came running over to intervene.

"What's going on around here," she yelled in a shrill voice.

Billy whined, "he's calling me names and making fun of me."

The teacher grabbed the skinny kid who immediately started to cry. In defense of himself, he pointed to Billy and whimpered, "Well, he kisses girls and stuff!" The teacher stopped in her tracks, wheeled around and looked at Billy.

"What? Billy? You…" she couldn't finish her sentence as Billy started running towards the boys' bathroom, shocked at the little tattletale's revelation to the teacher. It was an amazing sight to see Billy running, nearly falling over several times, while the teacher was in hot pursuit.

We never talked about that incident with Billy and he never brought it up, but judging by his confident look, we knew he was still making out with somebody. All the girls we knew wouldn't do something like that, but no one would ever ask a girl if they did.

I wasn't as experienced as Billy, but I did kiss a girl once which scared me, but felt rather pleasant. Her name was Louise, in the same grade as I and lived just down the street from me in our village in Italy. It was her birthday party and she made us play a game where she turned off the lights and made everyone hide. Louise was taller than most of the girls in our class, even a bit taller than me. She wore frilly dresses and looked ordinary, like the girls in the picture books we read in school. Her lips were pouty and her curls cropped down around her face.

For some reason, Louise hinted to me where she was going to be when the lights went out, so when it got dark, I crept to where she said she'd be, more out of curiosity, but when I found her, she grabbed me and tried to kiss me. Actually, she just put her lips on mine and kept them there until the lights went on. Was this love? When the lights went out again, she started kissing me rather arduously. I was tense but then noticed a little pencil in my pocket that was getting in the way when I was against her. I reached in my pocket to move it and was shocked to find out the pencil was me.

For the first time, I had physical contact with a girl, but I wasn't sure it was the same as what Billy did, but it was close enough for me. I thought about telling Billy about my encounter, then thought better that I shouldn't because I kissed a girl and felt grownup, but then figured that grown guys wouldn't talk about stuff like that, so I kept my mouth shut, a trait that would be of great benefit for me years later.

After that, Louise kept following me around like she thought she was my girlfriend, but I didn't like the idea of seeing her everywhere I went. It was sort of fun kissing her when no one else was around, which didn't happen that frequently anyway, but that was it for me; I wouldn't know what to do with a girlfriend. I asked Billy for advice one day during school lunch.

"What would you do if you were me Billy?"

"You know what to do when something like that happens?" He asked before shoveling a large portion of meatloaf into his mouth.

"I don't want to hurt her feelings, Billy. She's nice and all, but I can't have a girlfriend, you know. My mom would start asking questions---"

"You can't think like that," he interrupted. "You see, you got to be tough around girls, otherwise, they'll be bossing you around, and then they pass you notes in class and want you to carry their books and stuff. You know what I'd do?" He took a bite of cornbread as the butter dripped down his lip.

"No, what would you do Billy?"

"When you go back to class, you just go up to her and say, 'I hate you. I quit you',"

"Billy, I don't hate her. Why should I say something like that?"

"Just do it. You watch. Can I have your cornbread?"

"Sure. Here." I gave him my piece and thought about what he said. Why should I say "I quit you" when I wasn't even going with her, at least I didn't think I was.

He looked at me as though I knew nothing in the world. Perhaps I didn't, but it didn't seem right for me to say I hated her. But then, Billy knew all about girls, didn't he? For a guy like that to be doing those things with girls and then never having any around him, he must have them under control. Maybe he was even doing that with Louise, too.

"It doesn't matter if you're going with her or not." He put his fork down and got serious. "The thing is, she thinks she's going with you, or else she wouldn't be hanging around you all the time, right?"

"Well, yeah, I guess."

"Okay. Just tell her what I told you to tell her and she'll stop hanging around you. You'll see, you'll see I'm right," he said confidently. "Let's go get some ice cream."

I was dreading this. Louise kept hanging around me and I kissed her a couple of more times, but it wasn't fun anymore. I knew Billy was right and thought about when I'd tell her I hated her and quit her. I sat a couple of seats behind her on the school bus one morning and watched her and started to feel sorry for her. She kept turning and looking at me, and every time she turned, I was looking at her. I turned in my seat and saw Billy staring at me. He looked sternly, like our teacher when we were taking a math test. He nodded at me and I thought he meant for

5

me to go up to her and tell her now. My heart started to pound loudly and I felt like I was getting dizzy, so I looked out the window and decided I would do it today--early, just to get it out of the way.

We walked into class, and I stayed behind her until she sat at her desk. Now, I thought, while there was still noise from the chaos that starts school, the kids taking their seats, the laughter and chatter. I could say it quickly and sit down, knowing it was over. I walked up to her, took a deep breath and said...nothing. She gave me a quizzical look and then smiled.

You idiot, you complete idiot! I thought. Why couldn't I have just said it? I could feel Billy's gaze on me, I could feel the whole class looking at me, waiting for me to say something to break her heart. What was there to be scared of? Just because we kissed once in a while didn't mean I was her boyfriend, right? I didn't want a girlfriend; I just wanted to be like Billy. Maybe I really did like her, but didn't know how to be a boyfriend. I'm not really going with her, I found myself repeating, so what's the big deal?

"Louise!" I couldn't look at her. I looked down at her desk and said, "I hate you. I quit you!" There. I did it. It wasn't that hard. I quickly left her desk and walked towards Billy's to tell him when, suddenly, I heard an uncanny, high pitched sound. What in the world? Then I noticed everyone looking towards Louise's desk and this feeling raced through me that filled me with dread, as much dread as a fourth grader can feel. No, please don't let it be that.

I turned and saw the most grotesque mask I ever saw. Louise's mouth was as wide as my desk when I opened its top. She was wailing, then the tears were all over her face, her bottom lip quivered and she couldn't catch her breath. Everyone ran over to her and Mr. Rocco, our teacher, ran over and kept yelling at her what was the matter. I stood still, wondering what could have caused that woe. Through her tears and sobs she pointed at me! Everyone looked at me, and me, not used to being the center of attention, started crying, too.

I don't remember much of what happened between then and my trip to the principal's office. The class and then the school began spinning about me in a maelstrom of confusion and fear. Mr. Rocco gave me a stare that would have rivaled Dracula's. I broke her heart. Me. What did I know about girls, about love? How come Billy had everything under control and the first time I tried to dump someone, the whole world hated me? I really didn't hate Louise, it's just that I...I didn't know what. We hardly spoke after that day and I promised never, ever to break up with anyone again, a promise easy to uphold since I swore never to have a girlfriend for the rest of my life.

TWO

I began to suffer from asthma which became pretty severe while living in Italy. My parents thought it was an emotional reaction to stress, but something else told me it was one of those times to get sick again. Medication for asthma wasn't very effective from military hospitals in the early 60's, so I was hospitalized for a few days. Those hospital stays became quite enjoyable. I was usually the only kid in a place frequented by young soldiers. Plenty of rest and a vaporizer next to my bed eventually cured me, at least for the time being. I didn't have to face the kids in school, especially Louise. I was feeling blue. Billy came to see me once and brought me my favorite comic books, Casper the Ghost and Action Comics, featuring my idol, Superman, which cheered me up. He told me it was pretty neat what I did to Louise. He said he never made a girl cry like that. I wasn't sure if I had done the right thing, but I didn't want Billy to know.

"Yeah, I guess that was kinda neat," I agreed.

"Hey, guess what?" Billy asked. "I heard Monica likes you." Monica! Oh my. She was beautiful. My heart started to beat a little faster, and my breath backed up into my lungs. "What's the matter?" Billy asked frightfully.

"My asthma, Billy, that's all. I need to rest." I lay back on my hospital bed while my chest began to ache.

"OK, I better go. Should I tell Monica anything?"

"No, no, Billy. Don't say nothing, please. I have to think about this a while," I pleaded. Monica. The prettiest girl in class. I wonder why she liked me. I didn't want any more girlfriends. Too much trouble. I started to question whether Billy actually did what he said he did. I never saw him with any girls and he never had the trouble I had.

I was in the hospital for a week and when I got back to school, I was treated like a long lost friend. I felt happy. No one said anything about the trouble and even Louise said hi to me. I felt I should apologize to her, but when I started walking towards her, I saw Billy looking at me. I could tell by his face that I should ignore her and, once again, followed his lead. I walked back to my seat and saw Monica in the next row. A shiver came over me and I started to feel nervous. Maybe, I thought, if she was to be my girlfriend, I'd have to dump her the same way I did Louise and then have to go through the humiliation once again. I thought what it would be like to kiss Monica, but the thought quickly evaporated when Mr. Rocco's booming voice pierced the classroom to welcome me back. It was good to be back at my desk and a return to normal. If I stayed away from girls, things could always be this way.

It was more fun hanging around the guys anyway. I joined a Cub Scout troop during my 5th grade. Actually, my mother forced me to join so she could become a den mother, which was another way to socialize with the wives of the other servicemen stationed in Italy. It was cool having your mom as the den mother because I could act smart and boss the other scouts around, even if I wasn't the den leader. As a scout, I learned much about the country I lived. We took field trips to the Coliseum in Rome, the castle of Leonardo DaVinci, and Collodi Gardens, the literary birthplace of Pinocchio. We took hikes in the serene woods and sand hills near the Mediterranean Sea. I learned to love the sounds of the sea gulls as they soared overhead, echoing with the pounding sound of the rough surf. I watched them intently and, at times, I could see them watching me. A peculiar thought crossed my mind that maybe these were my guardian angels in disguise.

The cub scouts wore the blue uniforms with the matching caps trimmed in gold thread. Kids like me wore regular blue jeans with the uniform shirts and bright yellow scarves. The kids of the army officers, whose Dads made more money than the non-commissioned ones, had the complimenting blue trousers, complete with the shiny gold belt buckle. The yellow scarves were wrapped around our necks with the longer length draped against our backs. Some of the kids were teased when they wore their scarves backwards, reversing the B.S.A., Boy Scouts of America, initials to A.S.B., whom we then called "Apple Sauce Boys."

During one of our hikes, our troop got word that something dreadful had happened to one of the other troops hiking in the same vicinity. Everyone in my troop became scared for we thought some wild animal was loose, killing and eating some of the scouts. We were ordered to gather quickly, end the hike and return home. We later learned a major inquisition was in progress and many of the scouts were being questioned, some to the point of crying. One of the troop leaders was molesting the scouts in his troop, doing some awful things we heard. I was frightened, even though the guy was not part of my troop, but with kids rumors and falsities run rampant. We never knew the details, and I didn't quite understand what molesting meant, nor did I know one could go to jail for it, but I knew it was something horrible, something I never hoped to experience.

THREE

In Italy there were no television sets in any American household. Those who had a radio tuned in to the Armed Forces Overseas network, to which I hardly listened. My parents had a Grundig record playing machine which played vinyl discs at 33, 45 and 78 revolutions per minute. My parents owned 33 rpm records by artists I never heard of: Jimmy Durante, Nat "King" Cole, Johnny Mathis and a 45 rpm by Johnny Horton called "The Battle of New Orleans" which became my favorite. Most of the news we learned from the United States came from our Weekly Reader in school which we got every Friday. Without television, we never knew a war with Vietnam was looming, we never knew how big Elvis Presley was in the States, but we all made certain to see his movies at the army base of Camp Darby. We never knew why it was called Camp Darby until we saw the movie, *Darby's Rangers*, with James Garner.

Without television, our entertainment was the army base library and reading, and the Saturday morning kiddie matinee which played various cartoons for hours. When I was hospitalized with my asthma, I became fond of monster and horror movies, particularly the movies portraying giant insects and rodents.

Without television, the children played outside for hours, not only playing the big 3, baseball, basketball and football, but also making up games, or acting out the latest movie shown in the military base. Everyone liked the Elvis movies because of the singing and fights. He always got into a fight. We were going to act out *King Creole* and since my hair messed up the easiest, I was going to play the part of Elvis' character, Danny Fisher. Billy got his feelings hurt because I wanted him to play the character of "Dummy", who couldn't speak, the one Vic Morrow and his gang gypped out of stolen money in the movie. Billy didn't want the part so he went home, and since no one else wanted the part either, we decided to play cowboys and Indians instead.

Without television, reading was also a popular form of entertainment. *A Figure in Hiding, A Sinister Warning, While the Clock Ticked* were some of the ominous titles of the books read by the kids in class. They comprised of the mysterious adventures of Frank and Joe Hardy, the Hardy Boys, and I often dreamed of being a detective someday, unraveling mysteries and facing dangers. My dream lie implanted deep within my subconscious, surfacing at a most auspicious time in my adulthood.

We didn't play out any monster movies because most of the kids were afraid to remember the movie. I found a certain delight in those movies, for something about being scared intrigued me, something like kissing girls in the dark. There were films about giant scorpions, spiders, praying mantises, crickets, ants and even an octopus. I was terrified of *The Deadly Mantis* so much so that I remain terrified of praying mantises. I swear they're the only insects who will stare you down. The crickets weren't too scary, though, in *The Beginning of the End*. The ants were certainly creepy in *Them* and although my friends got a kick out of kicking over ant hills, I refrained, for if they ever did grow gigantic, perhaps they'd remember that I was nice to them. I vividly recalled the octopus from *20,000 Leagues Under the Sea* raising its tentacles around a bridge, destroying it. In years to come, I got lost driving around San Francisco, California, and wound up on the San Mateo Bridge, a bridge seemingly resting right on the San Francisco Bay. I drove across it as fast as I could knowing any moment an octopus could have easily wrapped a tentacle around it. My fear of movie monsters was overshadowed by a dream, a nightmare, or an ordeal which recurred more times than I wanted to remember.

I lay sleeping in my twin bed when I sensed a presence staring at me from the dark repose of the night. A figure stood against my bedroom door, a figure in white, though the white shroud or whatever clothing it was didn't extend to the floor. I pretended to stay asleep and the figure seemed to glide across the floor towards me. I lay as motionless as I could, hoping the entity would disappear. I didn't look at its face and it seemed as though in an instant, I felt its breath, a breath falling heavily onto my neck. A vampire? I was wrapped in its grip, a grip tighter than the tentacle of the octopus around that bridge. For a brief moment, I felt something pleasurable, something I felt when I first leaned against Louise as she tried to kiss me in the dark. That sensation gave way to a sharp, penetrating pain that wouldn't go away, intensifying with the obscene movement of this being, this monster. The pain slowly gave way to confusion while a dizziness swirled through my head, and then something seemed to be smothering me, stifling my every effort to move. I thought I heard a vile whisper, though I couldn't make out the words. What execution of humanity was this? What was happening to me--what sort of a monster had crept into my bed? Why couldn't I scream out? Mom, where are you? Questions which remained a mystery.

The night seemed to extend beyond the dark. I lay, unable to move, frightened and bewildered. The experience ended, though it seemed I never awoke, or maybe I never slept, I couldn't tell which and I couldn't tell anyone, that much I certainly knew. I remembered breakfast, but not what I ate. I remembered people, my family, but I didn't hear a word. The uncertainty of my dream, my nightmare, hovered around me like a spectre, clinging to my very being, taunting my soul. The dawning of the subjugation and domination of my innocence had begun. There was nothing I could do, nothing I could say. Perhaps there was one thing...

Nothing offered me escape more than my adventure into the world of the comic book. *Casper the Ghost* was one of my favorites as was the home of the friendly spirit, the Enchanted Forest. I followed Casper's adventures along with his girlfriend, Wendy, the good little witch, and Nightmare, his horse. At the end of the Casper stories, there was another adventure of *Spooky, the Tuff Little Ghost*. Spooky made me think of Billy--more image than substance. It was easy to enter into that wonderful forest where Casper and I had much in common.

That awful nightmare permeated my sleep once again. The following day, my friends and I were playing with our little toy soldiers in the high hills of the sand, the sands left by centuries of erosion and recession of the Mediterranean Sea. My thoughts drifted into my nightmare which I quickly eluded by retreating into the Enchanted Forest. Casper was in the middle of an underwater adventure and he needed some shelter from the water. His friends were making sure his venture would be safe by providing him with a diving bell with a large window so he could see the undersea riches. One of his friends led the amiable spirit to the bell:

"This way to the diving chamber Casper," I said aloud. Casper and his diving chamber had nothing to do with our little war game.

"Diving chamber? Casper?" exclaimed Billy incredulously.

"What?" I asked slowly, emerging from my other world. Billy looked at me puzzled, shook his head and pretended to blow up my army fortress with his neat, little tank. Those excursions of my mind began to happen too frequently causing my friends to think of me as a little strange. "You're kinda weird" was a phrase I heard often. I learned to hide my thoughts when I was in the Enchanted Forest, but I couldn't control my hand gestures which accompanied my thoughts. My friends ignored my gestures as long as no peculiar utterances accompanied them. Sometimes it was difficult to remember which world I was in, the world of enchantment in the comics, or the one where a demon seemed to follow me late into the night, infesting my bed with horrors seen only in Dante's world, or so I thought at the time.

The Man of Steel was my other alter-ego. Every dime I saved I spent on *Superman* comics. He, like me, was able to avoid serious contact with girls. Lana Lang, Lois Lane, the mermaid Lori Lemaris were girls he liked but never kissed, at least not in the comics in those days. Contrasted to the Enchanted Forest, Superman isolated himself within his Fortress of Solitude, where remnants of his former home, Krypton, lie hidden from the scrutiny of humanity, a secret he kept only to himself, later to be shared with his friend, Batman.

Yes, I knew of secrets and I would be like Superman, keeping my secret only to myself in the fortress of my darkest solitude. My solitude would be my purpose, my purpose my solitude. Superman solved every problem himself. He never cried or asked for help--Bizarro, Mr. Mxyzptlk, Braniac, Lex Luthor--none of his enemies prevailed. Superman and Casper were my role models. I learned the world of men whom I couldn't trust, of women whom I feared, and the suspicion of all people. The eyes of the innocent, the eyes of children and talking animals in the world of comics and fantasy, the trek through the Enchanted Forest, were my deliverance.

FOUR

The approach of night brought multifarious, absurd, and unwanted guests--anxiety, fear, dread. I was afraid to sleep, afraid the wraith in white would materialize in my room. I lay for hours until the lack of sleep oppressed me, then, uneasily, closed my eyes and gave way to a somber slumber. I knew it. There he was! I lay as still as I could, afraid to look directly at the haze of white against the darkness of my door. Slowly, ever so slowly, it seemed to glide towards me and I thought I could wait it out and it would disappear as long as I didn't show fear. Please leave. My bed sagged under the additional weight of the demon and I felt its ugly hands upon my body. Unconsciously, I was closing my eyes too tight in an effort to feign sleep. I felt dampness on my pillow and realized it was from the tears rolling down my own face. I gripped the side of my bed as hard as I could hoping it would help keep the tears away. The weight of the monster nearly crushed me and then the pain, the pain began again. Mom, please help me, I silently prayed, a prayer that always went unanswered. I awoke in a daze, feeling ashamed and alone as I prepared myself for school.

The sixth year of school was to be my last in Italy. My teacher was a pretty, raven-haired miss whose hair ran down her back ending just below her waistline; Miss Palomino. I was a quiet, obedient student who didn't take long to be one of her pets. She let me leave the class with the blackboard erasers, assigning me the duty of cleaning them. I took the erasers from class to the end of the hallway just outside the door and beat them against the ground until the pavement was covered with white chalk. I felt important.

I was captivated with Miss Palomino and stared at her continually. I sometimes felt she knew because when we were taking tests, she'd walk between the rows of our desks to make sure we weren't cheating, and then stopped right in front of me. I thought she did it on purpose next to my desk where I could admire her close up and smell the radiance of her perfume. None of the girls in class smelled like that. I think she liked me, too, for when she talked to the class, she seemed to be looking at me more than anyone else. I tried hard to be her best student and refrained from doing anything disruptive so she wouldn't holler at me.

During the second month of school, I stayed late one day so she could help me study the words for our next spelling bee. I was the classroom champion and I believed she favored me and wanted me to win, so she never turned me away. While I was going over some extra difficult words, she grabbed my hand, rubbed it gently and told me she was proud of me. It was the first time I ever held hands with a girl, and it felt good. She put her hand on my shoulder and pulled me closer to her. I smelled her perfume and started to feel a little dizzy, but I liked it. She was a big help to me and I won the spelling bee again that Friday.

A few days later, during a recess, I had to use the bathroom when I discovered a couple of my friends writing words with a marking pen on the wall.

"Look at this," I heard a familiar voice say from one of the stalls. It was Billy and he was beaming over the word he had just written, F-U-C-K, over the toilet. There were other words written all over the place and it figured that Phillip Kirby would be one of the culprits. Phillip was the biggest cusser in class. Another kid walked into the bathroom while the guys were still writing words. Everyone got scared and stopped. The kid got scared, too, because when he looked at us looking at him, he scurried out.

"Shit!" Billy exclaimed. "Let's get outta here. He's gonna tell."

"Yeah! No one say anything about this," Phillip warned. We ran out of the bathroom leaving markers all over the floor.

The next day, word through school was that there was this big investigation going on about the words written on the boys' bathroom wall. I wasn't worried because I hadn't written anything, but I wasn't going to snitch on anyone either. Who was that other kid who walked in? He wasn't in my class. I felt sorry for him because I knew Billy was going to beat him up for telling. I wouldn't want Billy mad at me for any reason.

I saw Miss Palomino approach Phillip's desk and whisper something to him, then walk him out of class. I could see tears starting to form in his eyes before he even got to the door. It seemed like he was gone for a long time and when he came back, I could tell he had been crying hard because his eyes were puffy and he was sniffling, trying to act like he hadn't been crying. Miss Palomino went to Billy's desk and he started blubbering right away. Miss Palomino grabbed him and hurried him out the door because his crying was getting louder and she didn't want to disrupt the class any further. Billy didn't return that day, and I learned he had been crying so hysterically that his parents had to be called to take him home. Poor Billy! Now I knew he had to be lying about kissing girls and stuff.

That stupid Phillip snitched on everyone and even told that I had written words on the wall. I was found innocent only because Billy saved me by telling the truth. I received a one-day detention for being there and not telling anyone what I saw. Billy and Phillip each got 3-day detentions. Detention meant we had to stay after school for an hour and then the parents had to pick us up since we missed the busses. I thought it unfair for me to serve detention because I hadn't done anything. They didn't understand why I wouldn't rat on my friends, but it was just something you didn't do. Such was the mentality of a 6th grader.

While serving detention, I was reading my Weekly Reader at my desk and then asked Miss Palomino if could use the restroom. It was kind of cool being alone with her in the classroom.

"Sure, you can go," she answered, "but because you're on detention, I can't leave you alone. I'll have to go with you." I walked with her to the bathroom. The school seemed deserted. I opened the door to the bathroom where I figured she was going to wait outside. I was surprised when she walked into the bathroom with me, which suddenly caused me not to have to go anymore. The bathroom looked enormous as I heard the slight echo of the door closing behind us. I didn't know what to do, so I looked up to her.

"Did you write those words on the wall?" she asked.

Startled and a little bit scared, I said, "No ma'am. I really didn't. Phillip and Billy wrote everything. I was just there."

"Do you know what they wrote?"

"Yes, ma'am, I knew," my voice squeaked. She moved closer to me and started rubbing my shoulder.

"What did they write?"

"Well, they wrote, you know, words, bad words and stuff." I was very nervous but I dare not say any nasty words to a teacher.

"Danny, I want you to tell me exactly what they wrote," she said more forcefully then I heard her say anything.

I don't know if I was frightened or excited, maybe a little of both. She grabbed me by my belt and pulled me towards her, making me think she was going to hit me, but then she put her hand inside my jeans and pulled my belt out a little so she could reach inside my pants.

"Tell me what they wrote," she repeated.

"Miss Palomino. I...I can't say the words. You know, the F word and everything."

I started breathing rapidly and my head felt dizzy. For a second, I thought I was going to fall down. I felt her warm hand inside my underwear. She was touching me gently which felt funny, but also felt kind of nice, too. I became very confused with a little pleasure mixed with a lot of fear.

"Do you know what the word means?" she asked, her voice sounding tender and friendly. Her hand was so soft and so warm. I didn't want to move and I didn't know what was happening. All of a sudden, Billy flashed into my mind. The "F" word! Billy wrote that word. Billy does it! Is this what he means? I thought to myself. Miss Palomino bent down to me and her face was right next to mine and her warm hand had a firm hold of me. At that age, there certainly wasn't much to grab hold of, but the sensation--I didn't know what it was, scary and pleasurable--I think I liked it.

I was scared and woozy, things were happening too fast when suddenly, Miss Palomino's lips were right in my face. I felt like crying, but she put her hand around my head and pulled my face right up to hers, like she was going to kiss me. I tried to pull my head back, but she was strong and held me there. I felt something funny against my mouth. It was her lips, larger than mine, smelling nice from the rosy lipstick. She was barely touching her lips against mine. Her hand was still on me and her mouth was caressing around my lips. My eyes were wide open, I don't think I was breathing, and I forgot where I was now. Was this the Enchanted Forest? A warm feeling engulfed me and my knees got shaky when I reached out to her with my arms to keep from falling. I couldn't talk, but I now sensed that her massaging was getting to hurt a little. She sensed something was wrong, slowly stopped and removed her hand. I was still a little wobbly and continued to hold her because I knew I was going to fall. What took a few seconds seemed to last for hours, but in actuality, lasted a lifetime. The warm glow I felt lingered for awhile and then reality set in. I was in the boys' bathroom with my sixth grade teacher. Her face was still close to mine and she looked at me with eyes of fire. I felt hypnotized, unable to take my eyes off her.

"Now, you can never tell anyone about this. Do you understand?"

I still couldn't talk and shook my head up and down.

"I mean it. You could be in big trouble and I won't be able to help you. You can never tell anyone," raising her voice a little. She stood up and put both her arms around me and squeezed me to the supple fabric of her dress. I could smell the perfume while my arms hung to my sides, still feeling the dizziness.

"I…I'll never tell," I promised. We walked out of the bathroom to the desolation and quiet of the corridors.

"You can go to the office and wait for your parents," she said. "And remember, no one!" she warned.

"Yes, ma'am."

That night, I slept well, no dreams, no nightmares, only the lingering perfume smell of Miss Palomino. I didn't know if that was sex, I didn't know that it was wrong. I only knew she made me feel funny inside and, oh yes, one more thing--I was in love with her.

When I walked into class the next morning, the butterflies flew wildly inside my stomach. She calmed them when she smiled at me and I felt that glow again. There was another incident when we were alone again, but she didn't approach me and never said anything about the incident, but I knew she still liked me and I was still very much in love with her.

Weeks later, I walked into class and saw a different teacher whom I assumed was a substitute. She announced to the class that Miss Palomino would no longer be teaching. No one asked why and we never found out why. I felt as though someone pulled my desk from me and I fell into a bottomless hole; reeling, falling, whirling into nothingness. Billy looked over at me and asked me what was the matter.

"Huh?" I looked at him but didn't see him. "Nothing, just not feeling too good, I think." I was blue.

I never saw Miss Palomino again. I never said anything about her to anyone. She remains hidden within my Fortress of Solitude. Sometimes I think it was just another of my fantasies, my escape, but when I look at the photo of my sixth grade class, I know it was real. I see me standing next to her in the class photo. When I look closely at her, I notice she isn't smiling. There is a frown on her face, but I can still smell the perfume each time I look at that picture.

FIVE

The summer of my last year in Italy, my father received orders to return to the States, specifically Columbus, Ohio. There was a distinct difference in the atmosphere in America than what it was in Italy. I was about to enter the seventh grade, junior high school. Even the school atmosphere was different. Being new, I felt somewhat alienated for awhile, but this time that feeling was more pronounced. I didn't seem to fit in. The kids looked distorted and unfriendly, especially the girls. I never saw girls my age wearing makeup--eye stuff, lipstick, even tight skirts. For a while, I thought I was put in the wrong school, but I was in the right place because here at Whitehall-Yearling High School, seventh through twelfth grades were combined. The boys looked menacing, too. A lot of them had their hair done up in high pompadours, slicked back with greasy stuff. Being in Italy for so long, we had no idea of the influence Elvis Presley had on the kids my age. I was soon to learn about American rock and roll.

The worst part of seventh grade was going to school. I always felt like I was going to get into a fight. Guys were bumping into me deliberately in the hallways, then looking at me like I was a freak. It was here I learned about my color, my ethnicity, a moot point when I lived in Italy.

During P.E. class, we were playing baseball when a hideous, fat kid who didn't dress for P.E and wasn't playing, walked up to me. He certainly wasn't friendly like Billy. "How come you're so goddamn black?" His question confused me; I didn't know what he meant. Not getting an answer, his face contorted, and he demanded, "Are you a nigger?"

Nigger? I had heard the word before and knew it was a bad word, but why was this guy saying it to me? The fat kid looked scary. His eyes bulged from his head and spit flew from his mouth when he talked. He seemed to be frothing at the mouth. I didn't know what to say, so I said nothing.

"Nigger!" he said and walked away. I hated the guy. I was flustered and scared. I learned later that he was "calling me out", meaning he wanted to fight me, but I didn't know it was a challenge to be answered for he showed me no respect. I learned about prejudice that day, or rather the ignorance prejudice brings. Being Hispanic, I tended to get very dark during the summer, and there were hardly any minorities in Columbus, Ohio in those days. I was the new kid and a Mexican, a minority, and for people like the fat, bug-eyed guy, I was the school "nigger".

At the playground of the school, I was able to get into a game of basketball, and one kid kept playing me much too close, bumping into me on purpose and no one called a foul. After another flagrant foul, I grabbed the ball and said, "Stop fouling me!" The kid stopped and came into my face.

"Are you, or aren't you a nigger?" the kid demanded. I discerned the kid was goading me into a fight. The other kids stopped and looked towards us. I was the center of attention and couldn't stand it.

"Hey nigger!" some other kid from the crowd shouted out. I felt alone. Everyone stood back from me and the kid who belittled me. Growing up in military circles in Italy, race was never an issue. We were all the same there. I hated this school.

I hated this kid. I started to tremble and the surrounding kids became a blur.

I was one of those kids who starts crying before he even starts fighting, some sort of a defense mechanism, or something like that. I started crying and the only thing I remember was a teacher pulling me off of the kid who was pinned beneath me. I was beating him up and didn't even realize it. I was crying from fear and confusion, the kid was crying from pain. I didn't know I won the fight. Talk got around the school about the fight, that the kid was some kind of a school tough and I beat him. The other kids then looked at me with some respect, as though I was some kind of a mysterious hood. I just wanted to be left alone.

I gradually made friends and, in time, the only ones who made derogatory comments to me were the older kids on the bus. It didn't matter none, though, at least no one tried to pick a fight with me and nothing they said hurt me. Well, that's not entirely true.

As my junior high school years progressed into my freshmen year of high school, I became acculturated into the American way of life. I learned to use pomade in my hair to give me the "greaser" look that was popular. I even had a pair of tight-fitting, cuffless pants, giving me the "shotgun" look that was the in thing. My father was chewing me out for something inconsequential, which was usually the case. He was doing a pretty good job of it to which I tuned him out, a feat which became easier and easier to do. He looked at my hair and said, "You look like a goddamn nigger!" There was that word again. Was I? What was I? If my own Dad said so, there must be some truth, but did that make me less than human? Did I really care what he thought anyway? Isn't he the one who, isn't he the one who…I dared not think it. I tuned him out and retreated into the Enchanted Forest.

During those high school years, my Dad and I never got along and rarely spoke, which was fine with me. The only communication we had, if it can be called that, was when he was hollering at me. I laughed silently when we watched *Leave it to*

Beaver on the T.V. when Beaver used to worry to Wally whether or not their Dad was going to "holler" at them. They call that hollering? Ward Cleaver sang love sonnets to his kids compared to my Dad's hollering.

When living nightmares and demons obscure a father and son relationship, when the delicate balance of a child's psyche is thrashed by the reality of the threatening, ruthless drive of the damaged psyche of a grown man, the purpose of one's own existence is thrown awry; the direction of one's life is going nowhere, it means nothing. It was easier and easier to descend into the hidden catacombs of my Fortress than to face the demons awaiting me in the real world. The chimeras dwelling within my soul tendered me comfort and solace from the demons of the real world. I never really understood what happened with my 6th grade teacher, Miss Palomino, in the boys' bathroom that day, but when I left Italy, I left her in the back roads of my memory, suppressed, but there nevertheless. In Columbus, I couldn't shake the nightmares which followed me at random times during my slumber, a restless slumber desecrated by the demon.

Six

The Beach Boys and *Surfin' Safari* were sweeping the nation my last summer in Ohio. There wasn't a beach close to Columbus, but the song was a hit there anyway. The song seemed to be blasting through the single speaker at the A&W Root Beer Stand where the school kids hung out and munched on the Coney Island dogs. I also got my first job selling ice cream from a little white cart attached to a bicycle seat and its rear wheel. The handle was equipped with a row of little bells I was supposed to jingle as I peddled the cart. I sold fudgesicles, popsicles, ice cream sandwiches, push-ups, and drumsticks. Each morning the boss would come to my house, count my money, give me a new load and wish me well. My route consisted of a few blocks around my neighborhood.

I made a mistake and drifted off my route one sunny afternoon and made some pretty good sales. That neighborhood was quite profitable, so I made it a habit of going off my route and often stopped at the Piggily Wiggily market for some treats, particularly Hostess Sno-balls. I was under the shade of large tree sipping on a cream soda and nibbling the marshmallow covering off the Sno-ball when another ice cream vendor came into view.

He rode straight towards me, and I noticed his cart was a light shade of green, a different company than the one I worked.

"Is this your route?" he asked.

"No, not really," I answered. "I just stopped by for a soda."

"You been selling on my route," he charged. How did he know, I thought. He stared at me through thick glasses, a kid of about eighteen. His white t-shirt sleeves were rolled up on his arms and I could see a pack of Camel cigarettes rolled up one sleeve. A tough guy. He wore the tight fitting, tapered pants and shiny shoes. He took his job seriously. His greasy hair was slicked back while the front curled over his forehead, distinctly different than Elvis.

"You better stay off my route!" His thin lips barely moved as he spoke. "Hear me, nigger!"

Man! What's with these people? It was summer and I tanned easily and was darker than I usually was. "Yeah, I hear you… and don't call me…" what's the use I thought. I hopped back on my cart and rode away, tinkling my bells in his territory as an act of defiance. He kept a watch on me as I headed towards my neighborhood, making sure I didn't poach anymore. As I headed back towards my neighborhood, another kid waved me down to buy some ice cream. I looked back and realized the other vendor was far enough back I could make a quick sale. I pulled my cart over to the curb and quickly opened the heavy door to the ice cream compartment. I peeked back and saw the kid stand upright on the pedals of his cart so he could pedal faster. He was coming after me!

"Here, quick. Take this," I said as I handed my surprised customer a push-up ice cream bar without taking his money.

"Hey you! I told you…!" I heard the tough guy vendor yell at me as his cart was now moving at breakneck speed. The chase was on! I stood on my pedals, too, to increase the force of my leg strength. I made progress. I looked back and he was just a few yards back, but I had a light load so I started to distance myself. Once I got to full speed, I again looked back, ignoring the shouts and waves from people who wanted to buy ice cream, and the kid was pedaling like an evil spirit, though he couldn't gain on me. I was now in my neighborhood which I thought I could use to my advantage. We were pedaling at the same speed; he couldn't catch up and I couldn't lose him. I made a maneuver like I was going to turn one way, then quickly straightened out my cart and went the other. He took my gambit and continued the other way. He must have had a full load, so he had to be careful. I continued on and made another turn. I couldn't see him, so I made another turn, hoping I had eluded him. Suddenly, I lost control, bounced off the gutter into a lawn and toppled over. The compartment door flipped open, scattering ice cream bars all over someone's lawn.

Neighborhood kids came running over to see if I was alright, at least that's what I thought, but they grabbed some ice cream bars and ran off. My nemesis, the other vendor, found me as he rode his cart slowly by. He pointed at me and laughed out loud. I must have given him the satisfaction he wanted as he pedaled back to his own territory, laughing all the way.

* * * *

It was time to move again. My father had orders to report to Korea for a year. My mother decided to move to Texas to be with her relatives while my father was doing his duty. It was hard for me to leave Columbus. The few friends I made were close, and when I had to say goodbye, I was fighting back tears, and I could tell they were too. I liked it here. I wish I could have stayed, but when your fifteen years old, your dreams seldom become your reality.

We left Columbus early in the afternoon. I saw the tall buildings on Main Street and passed the ballpark where I'd watch the Columbus Jets play minor league baseball. I left a part of me in Ohio; I left everyone who was important to me. I left everything, except the demon--the Wraith in White, who followed me, haunting me, hurting me.

SEVEN

Dallas, Texas, summer of 1963. Hot, parching heat. The culture here was strikingly different than up north. The Beatles made their presence known on the *Jack Paar Show*, the predecessor to Johnny Carson. The program showed a film clip of The Beatles in England, and shortly after that, well, as they say, the rest is history. President John Kennedy was making plans for his ill-fated trip to Dallas. My mother rented a house a mile from Parkland Hospital, where the President died after being shot by Lee Harvey Oswald. It was in Dallas I learned of pride and respect, I learned humility, and I learned the importance of family, and it was here I was granted a temporary reprieve from the nightmares that had permeated my sleep for far too long.

My aunt, my mother's sister, and her husband owned a Mexican restaurant in Dallas who had some of their nine children, my cousins, assist them in various culinary responsibilities. I felt at home here. The family on my mother's side was of the same skin color as I. I didn't hear any one call each other things they weren't. Two of my cousins, Bentura, Jr., and Ramona, were the same age as I and each went to a different high school. I went with Ramona to North Dallas High School, where the majority of the white students went and a few Mexicans who aspired to go to college. My cousin, whom we called Junior, went to Crozier Technical School, across town, where the majority of the Mexicans went to "learn a trade." Crozier was also notorious for its "pachukos", Mexican hoods. They had their own code of clothing identifying them to each other. They wore khaki pants with a sharp crease, white tee-shirts, and spit shined the toes of their black shoes until you could nearly see your reflection on them. The Mexicans at North Dallas dressed like the white kids; jeans tennis shoes and a print shirt. The girls wore dresses which were never tight, loose fitting sweaters, and black penny loafers with white socks. I dressed like a clown. Fashion was never my strong suit, so I wore remnants of what was left over from Ohio and whatever my mother bought me on sale from Montgomery Wards.

With my father gone, I convinced my mother to buy me some Beatle boots, of which I was very proud. When The Beatles sang _She Loves You_ on the _Jack Paar Show_, I saw how their mop top hair shook and thought it was cool. I tried emulating them by combing my hair forward, then pushed it to the side so I could like George Harrison, whom I thought was the coolest Beatle. I took a last look at myself in the mirror before school, and yep, I had it, even if my big nose and thick lips betrayed that I wasn't British, let alone my skin color.

I sat next to a kid in my homeroom class who talked very little as the school year started. He didn't seem very friendly. Before the first bell rang, he kept looking at me and asked, "What are you"?

"A sophomore," I answered, wondering why he asked such a dumb question if I was in his homeroom class.

"No, I mean, are you a whitey or what?" Up north I was called the "N" word, now here I'm being called a whitey? Recalling my experience in Columbus, I wondered if he was calling me out.

"I ain't no whitey. I'm Mexican, like you."

I then told him of my family and their restaurant and of

my cousin, Ben, Jr. My classmate, named Simon, had heard of my cousin. Junior had a reputation of being a tough pachuko at Crozier Tech. "He's *your* cousin, eh?" he asked in disbelief. My cousin had earned respect. I suddenly felt like Johnny Concho, the Frank Sinatra character from the movie of the same name. Johnny Concho lived off the reputation of his big brother in a small western town. Johnny was a wimp, but everyone was scared of him because of his brother's reputation, but if my cousin's reputation kept me from getting beat up around here, I'll be Johnny Concho.

Simon continued. "Pachukos are calling you a queenie,"

"A queenie? What's that?"

Simon laughed as though he couldn't believe I didn't know what a queenie was. "A queenie! Part girl, part boy."

"What the heck? Part boy, part...why would they think that?" I was mystified.

"It's because of how you dress." He looked down at my boots. "Especially those."

Simon was doing me a favor, but he didn't know how much he discouraged me. When I got home, I put the boots in my closet and never wore them again. But all was not lost, for the word got out that I was Bentura's cousin and no one bothered me. None of the pachukos called him Junior, he was Bentura.

My cousin, Junior, and I got to be pretty close. Although he had the reputation of a tough guy, he was still a kid and we always had a good time. I enjoyed being around him and his family. The smell of beans and flour tortillas wafted through the air constantly. There was warmth, laughter and love each and every day. Although the same age, Ben was considerably larger than I, wore his hair in a crew-cut and spoke in a slow, deliberate southern drawl. Just his essence commanded respect. Whenever he went to hang with friends from Crozier, he wouldn't take me. He probably didn't want to be seen with his queenie cousin and then have to fight them to defend me, his family. I understood and respected that. He made it known, though, that to choose between friends and family, family came first, "La Familia," even his queenie cousin.

On a lazy, humid day in Dallas, Junior took me and some of his younger brothers and sisters to one of his favorite hangouts, a place where some railroad tracks went over a bridge, a trestle they called it. Underneath the bridge was large valley. We were on one side when we noticed some pachukos on the other side. A territorial dispute was about to be begin. The 'chukos yelled something in Spanish to my cousin.

"Don't listen to them," said Junior. "They're just trying to cause trouble. They don't want us to come over to their side of the trestle." He yelled something back which I didn't understand, and then they started to come towards us. Junior turned to his brothers and sisters and said, "Let's get out of here!" We hurriedly started walking towards his house when suddenly a rock landed a few feet from us.

A rock fight! I hadn't had one these since I left Italy when we used to fling rocks at the Italian kids living outside our village. "Come on, Junior!" I yelled. We turned and started flinging rocks causing them to scatter in all directions. No one carried guns, no one carried knives. If one of us was to get beat up, no one else jumped and started stomping on them with cheap shots. No. Even at that age we had a code of honor. Once the fight was over, it was over. In a rock fight, it only took one rock to hit someone to end the fight.

Suddenly, I heard my cousin scream loudly and grab his left ear. I saw blood oozing from between his fingers. A direct hit! I looked back and the pachukos started running towards us. My younger cousins and I started flinging rocks furiously and I heard one of them yell out. A retaliatory hit! They scattered. Turning my attention to Junior, he bent over, and then threw up. "Let's get him outta here!" I bellowed to my cousins. We got him home and he seemed to be all right, a good sized gash on his upper ear. He made us promise not to tell anyone what happened or else we couldn't go back to the train trestle.

My cousin was quite a philosopher when he wasn't in his pachuko mode. Hanging out at the family restaurant, I developed a fondness for tamales, and in Texas they were humungous. They were best when moist and just out of the steamer. The corn husks slid easily off, and the red chili sauce trickled slightly from the thick corn masa. Pork filling and olives made a complete meal, providing we ate several at one sitting. A cold cream soda topped off the meal scrumptiously! After wolfing down another tamale, I commented to Junior the wonder of the original Mexican treat.

"Yep, we invented them," he drawled proudly.

"Invented them? What do you mean?"

"You didn't know?" he quizzed, almost as puzzled as my classmate who didn't know that I didn't know what a queenie was.

"Know what?" As I reached for my third one.

"About tamales! We did. We invented them," he said emphatically.

"Come on, Junior. Are you serious?" He was named after his father, but the family was the only ones who could call him Junior, because it didn't look right for a tough pachuko to be called Junior, especially at his size.

"Really. Daddy had this worker in his restaurant named Molly who worked hard for him. Well, one day she got sick and didn't make it to the restaurant for a few days. Daddy got worried, but she turned out to be okay, so he wanted to do something to make her feel good when she came back to work." I listened with fascination as I took a swig of my cream soda.

"So he made up this stuff by mixing corn meal masa, pork, chili sauce and stuff, rolled them all up and put them in corn husks to keep them fresh." He looked at me and saw my interest. "Did you know that the basis of our survival is corn?"

"No, I never realized," I answered, awed that he was also quite the historian.

"Yep. Then he wrapped them in some tin foil to keep them warm before he took them to her. He made about a dozen and then got a get well card for her." He took a large bite of his own tamale and continued. "My brothers and sisters came into the kitchen hungry and saw them on the counter. They saw the envelope with the get well card in it addressed 'To Molly'."

"To Molly?"

"Right. And Mona (my cousin and Junior's older sister by a year) said, 'What are these?' My little brother read the card and said, 'to-molly'. Well, they opened up the foil and ate a few. They loved them so much they bugged Daddy to make some more of them 'to-mollys'. So, they became tamales."

"Dang! Cool! I never knew I had a famous uncle," I uttered in complete reverence.

To this day, I think I still believe him.

After the history lesson provided by my cousin, my mother thought I should get a job to help with the family finances. In other words, I'd have to buy my own stuff with my own money. I secured a job in a corner restaurant a few blocks from the Mexican restaurant, the Maple Avenue Pharmacy. It was a small apothecary with a soda fountain towards the back. My job was to make sodas, shakes, hamburgers and simple sandwiches for the lunch crowd and do general clean-up at closing time. I was paid fifty cents an hour. I went to high school with the kid of the ones who owned the drug store, Allen Duvall, who was a junior at North Dallas. He was a white goofy guy with glasses and slightly bucked teeth, a year older than me. He was to be my boss and he treated me pretty well when we were working. At school it was a different matter. He pretended not to know me. I slowly learned of race and class distinction in Dallas. Since I was Mexican, he didn't want his peers to know he knew me, as he couldn't be seen fraternizing with "them Mexicans." It was here I entered into my abbreviated life of crime.

As I cleaned up the pharmacy at closing time, the old man, the owner who was gruff and grumpy most of the time, was in the back tallying his daily receipts. I discovered some condoms on the shelf, stopped mopping, and stared at them. As far as girls went,

I was still virginal (that encounter with Miss Palomino didn't count). I studied them closely, reading the labels, trying to figure out what "reservoir" meant and feeling the pliancy underneath the foil wrapper. As I continued mopping, I snatched a pack of the condoms and quickly stashed them in my pocket.

On my walk back home, I pulled the package out of my pocket and tore one open. I was spellbound. It was velvety soft, had a peculiar aroma and looked long, very long. I certainly wasn't ready to use one of these yet. I became rather excited when I envisioned what you were supposed to do when you had of these things on. It was sex! I knew then that sex was something that really happened, except for me. The fascination of that moment became darkly clouded by the thought of my nightmare; the Wraith in White. Confusion reigned, I felt dizzy and then threw the package on the ground. But I was safe from the wraith here in Dallas, and I then had a brilliant idea. I retrieved the condoms and kept them. The following day in school, I boasted of them, even showing them to a select few.

"Whatcha gonna do with that, Homes?" my homeroom partner, Simon asked.

"The Louie Louie, Simon, the Louie Louie," school ground code for having sex with a girl. It was taken from the popular song at the time by the Kingsmen who stirred quite a controversy over certain, hazy words that were supposedly in that song. Simon couldn't believe it and laughed out loud, causing a stern lecture from the teacher while I quickly stashed the condoms out of sight. I think he laughed at the thought of me actually using them. About a week later, I tossed the condoms in the trash and made sure my friends knew I didn't have them anymore. They begged me to tell who the girl was, but real men keep secrets. That should prove once and for all I wasn't a "queenie". As the school year quickly faded into spring, I was beginning to wonder about that myself.

EIGHT

Our modest, rented house in Dallas was situated across from a palatial estate owned by the family who also owned the major tortilla factory in downtown Dallas. There were 5 children in that family, a girl my age, two boys older than me and two younger. The older ones went to North Dallas High School, my school at the time. The girl, Graciela, was stunningly beautiful and I was secretly in love with her, but even though she went to my school, she was out of reach due to her family social status compared to mine. She had light brown skin, with flowing black hair caressing her shoulders and gleaming white teeth. She never seemed to notice me, but I attributed that to her really liking me and just playing hard to get.

I befriended one of the younger boys who invited me to his house to swim. The family owned an in-ground pool, the first one I had ever seen in the backyard of any house. Graciela was in the water, wearing goggles and swimming close to us. This was my chance! I'd show her what a great swimmer I was, learned from my younger years swimming in the Mediterranean Sea, and then she'd talk to me.

I ran and dived into their pool, not a belly flop, but a cool one of a considerable degree of difficulty. We couldn't afford real swim trunks, so I wore cutoff jeans as my swimsuit. Mine were a bit baggy since I was a pretty skinny kid, so when I dove into the water, the force of my dive caused my jeans to slide off me. Normally, this wouldn't have been a big deal, but when the girl I loved was so close, I started to panic. My cut-offs started to slide completely off me, but I was able to use one foot to cling to one pant leg before they completely escaped me. I didn't have any underwear on because I never thought about Graciella being there when the younger boys invited me to swim, but now, here she was! I was thrashing about, trying to get my pants back on, staying underwater as long as I could. I desperately tried to hang on to my shorts with my big toe, but I lost my grip and my cutoffs sank slowly to the bottom of the pool. I had to come up for air, and as I jerked my head up from the water, I caught a glimpse of Graciella running into her house. I must not have impressed her for she never cast so much as a glance my way.

My larceny from the drug store proliferated. I'd hide stuff out in back and take them when I went home after I finished cleaning up. Sodas, combs, notebooks, pens, everything was fair game. I'm sure they suspected me as I caught Allen, my boss, spying on me when he thought I didn't see him. He was pretty tricky, but I was trickier and he never could catch me. I think he was afraid to catch me cause then he'd have to fire me, and then he'd have to fight me after he fired me. He was the prototype of the nerd, and I knew I could take him, so we reached an impasse and co-existed peacefully.

President Kennedy was to arrive in Dallas in a few days, and politics was the prime subject of conversation with the lunch crowd as I cooked up burgers and made them milkshakes from the soda fountain. I didn't know much about politics, but I knew my parents were enamored with the President, so he was my guy, too. Allen's parents were Republicans, so Allen took their side as we argued after the lunch crowd left. He bad-mouthed the President and I defended him, when neither of us knew what we were talking about. He was getting pretty serious about it, so I presumed he must have learned something from his Government class at North Dallas High. He was getting mad at me when I was just messing with him about it, then he tried to talk tough and talked about "bumping him off" when he came to town. Of course, that was just mindless chatter from two ignorant kids. Or was it?

After President Kennedy was shot and killed, the town was in pandemonium. It happened during the school day, and after the word got out, I saw teachers crying, parents were there bustling about, the school was in utter confusion with no one going to their classes. I walked by the office and saw Allen there. Two men were talking to him and he was in tears, nearly hysterical. I learned Allen made his mindless threat to others, and somehow, it got to the principal's office. Lee Harvey Oswald hadn't been captured yet, so everything was magnified to an absurd degree. I knew Allen didn't shoot the President. A wimpy high school junior, afraid of Mexicans, assassinate the President of the United States? Allen never told me what was said because the principal warned him to keep his mouth shut, but with all the lunatic theories that have surfaced over the decades, I wondered if Allen did have something to do with it. Maybe he was the guy in the grassy knoll.

Things in Dallas erupted after the assassination. Though I never experienced it, my uncle warned us all to stay off the streets after dark. After Jack Ruby shot Oswald on live TV, violence in Dallas had risen to an alarming level. Fortunately, my troubles were limited to the anxiety of being asked out on a date--a real date, with a girl and everything. I was scared. A kid named Salvador lived a few houses down the street from us. He was a little, wiry guy making him a great neighborhood football player. His smile never left his face. His older sister, Ophelia, my age, went to Crozier Technical High School, the pachuko school. Talking to her was like talking to one of the guys. She was nice looking, but far from my dream girl, Graciella.

Her mother connived with mine to have me take to her a dance. "Sure, mom, I'll go," I said as casually as though she asked me to go to the store. The dance was more than a month away and I scant gave it another thought, even when I saw her on the block. The days passed into weeks when my mother reminded me of the dance this weekend. She also told me Sophia bought a new dress and I better start thinking about what I was going to wear. Sophia came to the house to discuss the arrangements, but she spoke mainly with my mother while I tried to hide in the shadows and corners. She didn't look the same. She was wearing makeup and lipstick, her hair was brushed differently, and she smiled a lot more. A dance. I was supposed to take Sophia, a real girl, to a dance--just her and I. Her in a dress and me in a suit? The honeybee was about to land on a dead flower.

My asthma suddenly erupted, leaving me weak and gasping for air. This time it was quite severe causing me to miss school Thursday and Friday. There didn't seem to be much of a chance I'd recover in time for the dance. My mother had to call Sophia's mother and tell her I couldn't go. It didn't matter if it was Sophia, or Graciella, or Miss Palomino for that matter. The thought of a date, a real date with a girl, filled me with dread. The uncertainty of an ever changing future and the possibility I might actually like Ophelia conjured up memories of Louise and her face of tears and I'd have to repeat those dreaded words, "I hate you, I quit you," forced to break another heart. I couldn't do that to her, or maybe it was the thought to my nightmares and the confusion fuddling my brain. I couldn't reach out, I didn't know love, I didn't even know "like" as I retreated into my Fortress of Solitude. I know my heart couldn't be broken--it was a heart of stone.

"Heart of Stone" was precisely it! I was struck by the appearance of a band from England, The Rolling Stones and their hit, "Heart of Stone." Their mien contrasted with The Beatles, and when I read where Mick Jagger said, "we may be ugly, matey, but we're down to earth," I immediately bonded with them and bought every single record they made. It would only take me one hour of work at the pharmacy to pay for the records, which were 49 cents. I played "Not Fade Away" over and over, but very soon, I was to fade away.

The end in Dallas came quickly with the close of my sophomore year. My father returned from Korea and announced we were moving to California. I never saw Ophelia again after our ill-fated date. Through her actions, Graciella made it known that I was beneath her class of Mexican. I was saddened to leave my cousins, especially Ben. He promised he'd come and visit us once we settled in California.

We drove the distance from Texas to California, and I was haunted by the same feeling of dread before the dance with Ophelia, which never materialized. I would have given anything to stay in Dallas. If I had any guts, I would have run away and forced the issue for me to stay in Dallas, at least until I finished high school. What's one more mouth for my aunt and uncle to feed when they already had nine?

The heart of stone one night gave way to that loathsome sensation of fear, the return of the Wraith in White. In Dallas, my development and confidence grew, each day shone brighter than the day before. My will was stronger, but in California, as before, withered under the spell of the horror of my nightmares.

NINE

We arrived in California in the summer of 1964. My welcome to this tiny town was the stench. We moved in a house not far from the sewer farm, which was not far from the Holly Sugar Plant in full operation, which was across town from the Heinz 57 factory, which was also in full production. The mixture of aromas from all was quite nauseating. I didn't see many Mexicans or Blacks, for I learned later they lived on the south side of town, across the railroad tracks which were once the lifeblood of this town decades ago. I felt lost. There was one high school whose mascot was the bulldog. Upon entering my junior year, I was clearly singled out as the new guy. It was difficult to make friends for I learned you belonged to the sporties, cowboys, or the Mexicans. I was getting strange looks from others trying to figure what I was, much less who I was.

The town was 60 miles east of the San Francisco Bay Area and 25 miles south of the county seat, Stockton. It was in the fertile San Joaquin Valley, completely flat and literally cut off from the rest of the world. Nothing but agricultural crops surrounded the town, with tomatoes the prime product. Acres and acres of tomato fields, as far as one could see. The green and white sign outside the city limits said the population of this town, called Tracy, was about 18,000. I longed for Dallas and the crowded house of my cousin. My parents bought a house in a new subdivision, just south of the sewer farm and the city's animal shelter. I walked a mile and half to my new school. Kids with cars cruised up and down the street before school, honking at each other. A lot of the cars were packed with girls who seemed to laugh at me as they passed.

As the school year progressed, it spawned more groups. You were either a cowboy, sporty, preppy, Mexican, or a "stoner." I figured since I loved the Rolling Stones, the "stoners" would be my group, but I learned you had to take drugs and drink alcohol to be a stoner, you had to be "stoned", a bit of the vernacular from the early hippy movement in the Bay Area. Drugs and alcohol were a new concept for me, a completely new world which didn't make any sense, so I belonged to a group called the "payasos," Spanish for "clowns". They were dorky new guys who didn't fit in with anyone, just a bunch of invisible kids who went to school and then straight home afterwards. Harmless. Alone.

Most of the residents grew up here, went to the same junior high school, then the same high school. If the boys weren't drafted into the army, they married their high school sweethearts and went to work in one of the factories or the major defense supply agency just outside town. Those owning the agricultural crops surrounding the town wielded the most influence, many having immigrated from Portugal years before to this soil rich area. The vast majority of the dairy farms in the outlying areas were owned by Portuguese.

I latched on to another "payaso," a tall, thin kid with slicked back hair and spoke with a slight, but noticeable, speech impediment. I noticed he didn't seem to have many friends and I wondered if he was new like me. "Been here all my life," he told me. "I'll probably get drafted and when I'm done, I'll be working at the family store." His parents owned a small produce market where he helped out after school. I also learned he had an older brother who was doing time in prison.

"Jeez!" I exclaimed. "What the heck did he do? Did he kill somebody?"

"He was making kids give him 'BJ's' ", he answered frankly.

"BJ's? What?" He explained and my jaw dropped. I didn't know what to say. I had never heard anything like that before.

As time went by, I learned more about my town and my new friend. I understood why he didn't have many friends. Legend had it his older sister was impregnated by her father. Her own father had sex with her! My mind numbed as a flashback of my nightmares engulfed my already swirling mind. The family scandal was news to the whole school for years. The little boy, my friend's brother-uncle, the product of this unholy union, was the source of cruel, local jokes, references often made to his "sister-mother", and his "father-brother." Now I also knew the sordid tale of "Cactus Jack." I learned what the word incest meant. This town was beginning to get strange.

I was scared every day of my junior year of high school. There were many other tales of girls getting pregnant and never seen again. Sometime during the year, they seemed to vanish to live with an aunt. One of the girls in my class, a junior, was even married! I stayed far away from her. Fights were frequent and happened mainly in the park across the street from the high school. It seemed most of the fisticuffs were two boys fighting over the same pregnant girl, or trying to end a rumor of who actually was the father. There was far too much sex going on than I ever remembered from my previous high schools, and I was certainly not going to partake in that.

Whenever the park was filled with people after school, it was a safe bet that a fight was taking place. A lot of them were the cowboys against the Mexicans. Typically, a cowboy was much bigger than the Mexican, so it didn't take long for the cowboy to clean house, but to make it fair, the cowboy would then be jumped if he were winning, and then other cowboys would jump in and start massacring the Mexicans who were then chased back across the tracks. The next day, a few sported shiners or a fat lip, but no one was seriously hurt and there was never a grudge. Retaliation was unthinkable. Friendships prevailed until the next imagined insult, or trivial matter was cause for another donnybrook. It was a way of life, a ritual, at this strange school.

I was able to escape high school, even graduate on time, without getting seriously hurt, arrested, or having a girlfriend. A friend I made during school and with whom I was closely attached, Francisco, was drafted and sent to Vietnam. Some of our classmates had been killed in the war, so we prayed daily for Francisco. He was an athletic Mexican, born of Mexican parents, but spoke no Spanish and was truly "Americanized." He hung mostly with the white guys and was labeled a "sporty" rather than a Mexican. His love of sports was insatiable, so we often played whatever sport was in season from sunup to sundown, on weekends and during the summer if I didn't have to work in the fields. My love and loyalty to him were going to get me in some serious trouble in the years ahead. I did not get drafted, so I was left with one of the options most of us had: work at one of the factories, the defense depot or go to the junior college, located in the county seat, 25 miles away. If none of these were open, one could always get a job in one of the surrounding agricultural crops. It wasn't unusual to see many from the high school picking tomatoes, cherries, or knocking almonds. I enrolled in the junior college and found a job for the summer picking tomatoes.

The tomato fields. Dusty, dirty and demanding. The sweat burned into my eyes while the dirt and dust from the roving tractors in the fields stuck in my throat as I threw a few more tomatoes into my crate at the end of my row. My crate was nearly full, meaning I had earned another 20 cents, and if I continued working at my present pace, I might earn three or four dollars for my day's labor, certainly enough to buy a cream soda and a double cheeseburger before I went home for supper. I glanced to the row next to mine and saw the field workers, the braceros, ardently picking the red vegetable from its vine, never looking up as they moved rapidly down the rows, a pace that me think of old movie comedies, speeded up for its comical effect, but working in the fields was no comedy.

I noticed a thin, young bracero who could have almost been my double, so much into his work that it fascinated me. His lips were a bit large which were even more pronounced as his chin receded towards his neck, his frail body hunched from spending far too much time in these hot, dry fields. Tomato harvesting was at its peak and so were the braceros, many of whom were here illegally, crossing the border and somehow finding their way to this prosperous agricultural town. I couldn't help but watch him as he furiously picked the warm tomatoes, filling his crate as fast as I had wanted. For him, this was his life. These men worked fast, all day, making as much as 20 dollars for a grueling day in these dirty, dusty fields.

It was nearing 4 o'clock when I decided I had worked hard enough. The foreman counted my crates stacked at the end of my row, then wrote the number on a piece of paper he tore from a brown paper bag. I gladly took my tally sheet to the small portable trailer where a middle-aged Mexican lady served as the accountant. She calculated our pay after deducting for social security and taxes which she wrote on another paper bag. She didn't speak much English, and I noticed she had written down my social security number wrongly. I tried to explain, but she brushed me off, and then with a hard push of her pencil, she circled my number as if this was some official act. Any further protests would be futile, I presumed. I didn't like that payroll lady. She had the air of superiority, as though she was a higher class Mexican than those who toiled in the fields, acting as if she was giving us her own money. She was a short, slightly obese woman, lightly complected, wearing a beat up straw hat pulled low over her eyes. She had at least two teeth missing from her lower jaw, from which she also had a slight, but detectable, growth of whiskers. I knew these "deductions" would not be going to the Social Security Administration or that the Tax Board would ever know how much money I earned, or that I even worked this day. I didn't know if the braceros knew that, but if they did, they couldn't object because the alternative was to return to Mexico and try to find suitable employment there. I figured the supervisors pocketed the money, or gave it back to the land owners for the privilege of working in their fields. After these deductions, I received $4.20 for my day's pay.

One of the labor trucks drove me back into town and let me off at corner where a Foster's Old Fashioned Freeze was waiting for my money. I was hungry. Shortly after, a pickup with a make-shift camper pulled into the lot and a load of field workers climbed slowly out. I recognized one of them as the young, thin one I watched laboring intently. A passing police car cruised slowly by, and the cop gazed keenly as the nervous braceros trudged unhurriedly past, avoiding any eye contact with the passing policeman. This was one of their lucky days as the police car drove away, probably deciding it was too hot to get out of his car and check them for their green cards and arrest those who didn't have one; the illegal aliens, or wetbacks, as they were disrespectfully called.

TEN

As with most of my high school alumni, I enrolled at the Junior College, Delta Community College in Stockton, 25 miles east of Tracy. My original intent of going to college was to become an accountant. Most things in high school were quite boring, but numbers intrigued me, particularly how they were measured in sports. I perused the Sunday sports pages memorizing the batting averages and statistics of my favorite players, Mickey Mantle, Hank Aaron and Willie Mays. By attending the college, I landed a job through the college's neighborhood youth plan at the local police department. Cops? I never gave it a thought. I used to lie to them and outrun them when they chased me on my bike because it didn't have a light when I did my early morning paper route. I ditched them when they tried to catch me when I broke into an outside soda machine at a service station near my house. I was scared when I reported to work my first day.

The old department in Tracy was a cracker-jack box of a building, a seeming remnant from the Dark Ages. A short tunnel led to the jail cells, themselves cold and dank as dungeons reeking of ghosts from an era long since passed when the town thrived off the railroads decades ago. It was said that the only way to tell a drunk from a rail was the rail carried a lantern. Tales of opium dens, whorehouses, and gambling halls were as vivid as the pictures of the people stored in the department's Hall of Records. I heard yarns of Hazel's whorehouse directly across the street from the Hall of Justice and men of the law who frequented the establishment after hours. I was fascinated by this history. The old records, preserved on documents created from antique typewriters, told tales of murder victims dumped near the tracks, Indians named Carlos Shot With Two Arrows found drunk and disorderly (listed as D & D, a recurring transgression on these old records), homosexual activity reported in the bathroom stalls of the Greyhound Bus Depot, and a time when the police were summoned by the glow of a red light high atop the radio tower of the "Hall of Justice," a time long before I was born.

On my first day, a jolly-looking, slightly overweight man in his 50's greeted me. He wore black horn-rimmed glasses and had thick, undulating graying hair which made him look distinguished, I thought. He was the Chief of Police. He was very kind to me as he explained my duties, which were to compile crime statistics, traffic citations, and other related duties as assigned, strictly paperwork. Adjacent to the office of his secretary, he gave me a tiny office equipped with an old desk, a broken chair and a typewriter. I was to spend two hours a day here after my junior college classes. The smell of the building told me of the mass of humanity which traversed this ancient relic since near the turn of the century, or at least the 1920's or 30's. I sat glued to that desk, scouring reports and noting in the appropriate boxes with a check mark things that qualified as a particular crime. Thefts with a value under $200, grand theft over $200, robbery with a gun, robbery with a knife, robbery with force, malicious mischief, and the like. The homicide box was never checked. I became quite efficient, and soon the Chief was piling all kinds of things on my dilapidated desk, asking me to sort and compile various things ranging from the time of day citations were issued to the average number of men worked per shift per month. It wasn't difficult to compute that one as only 1 to 4 men worked a particular shift during the 24 hour period. Policemen marched in and out of the building, talking, joking, hardly conscious of my presence. Occasionally I heard someone ask, "Who's he?" referring to me.

"He's the Chief's new butt boy," someone said under their breath, hurting my feelings. I wasn't anybody's "butt boy" and never will be. Who said that? I thought, straining my neck ever so slightly to identify the culprit. A couple of cops were standing close by, one of whom had slicked back hair and wore mirrored sunglasses, the kind cops always wore in the movies to symbolize autonomous authority. I figured he was the one. I noticed his .38 caliber revolver had pearl handled grips, when every other cop's gun had the stock, wood grips, so I knew he had to be the one. He had that arrogant demeanor that gave him permission to say things out loud to hurt people's feelings. He reminded of the high school hot shot who bullied everybody. It had to be him. I was starting to hate him already.

The department was small as one would expect servicing a population of 18,000 in the middle of nowhere, a bit larger than Andy Griffith's Mayberry. It had a Chief, one captain, a Detective Sergeant, one Detective, 3 patrol sergeants, 15 patrol officers, and a dogcatcher. The citizens used to call the police if there was an animal control problem. There were also 4 dispatchers, the Chief's secretary, who doubled as a report writer, transcribing the dictated police reports, and me, the clerical statistical assistant. As the months wore on, I kept my mouth shut and did my work. A few of the guys, usually the older ones, were friendly, making it easy for me to talk, mostly about sports and my studies. The loudest guy was the one with the pearl handled grips. He spoke with a slight drawl and I often heard him talk about "niggers, spooks and spics." I don't know if he was saying stuff about spics (a derogatory term for Hispanics) to hurt me or what, but I grew to despise him. I used to hate it when there was no one for him to talk to, so he would talk to me always about the same subject- -himself. One day when I was particularly busy calculating the red light traffic violations, he poked his head into my little office, and I thought, 'no, please, no, not this guy.' Fortunately, one of the sergeants also came in, so pearly-grips left. I wonder what I did to garner all this attention.

"You got a few minutes?" he asked softly. I was startled. Was he talking to me? I did a double take and looked at him again, and he nodded at me. Yeah, he did want me. What did he want from me? Did he know about the soda machine? Was he one of the cops I ditched when he was chasing me on my bike during my paper route? I knew I was in trouble for something.

"Uh, yeah, I mean, yes sir, sure." My nervousness was obvious.

"Come with me." I got up to follow him. "Let's go in here," he said, pointing to a small office that had "Captain" written in brass on the door. Jesus. They were going to beat me to a bloody pulp, I feared. Maybe he found out about the marijuana I smoked at Jack Carter's house, and he was going to bust me. My job, my school, everything would go to pot. Even one joint of marijuana was a major felony in the 60's.

"I've been checking you out. You seem like a pretty good guy," the sergeant said. Oh no, here it comes, I thought. "You ever smoke dope?" He suddenly asked angrily, getting uncomfortably close to my face, his eyes squinting and I could smell the nicotine on his breath. Here it is. He's going to grill me. I'm caught. The sergeant was a man of small stature, late 30's, dark complected, who took great pride in being part Choctaw Indian, with a sense of nobility that permeated his existence. He was one of the patrol sergeants who worked rotating shifts, but he also doubled as the department's only narcotics officer. I was anxious.

'It wasn't my fault, he made me do it. I was going to tell,' I thought about confessing, but my survival instincts took over. "No, sir. Never." I looked him straight into his squinting eyes.

"Good. I can use your help," he smiled and backed off.

Help him? I'm not going to jail? What could I do for him? He explained he'd like to use me to make some controlled buys from a guy selling marijuana. He said since I was in the right age group, it would be easy for me to get in, to make the "score," as he put it, then he'd make the arrest. In the mid to late 60's, the drug scene was just starting to proliferate, and many departments weren't prepared to handle it. Thus, the sergeant was appointed the department's narcotics "expert". He wanted me, in essence, to go undercover. My mind was in a haze, purple haze.

"Sure, sir. I'd be glad to help." I spoke too soon. What if the guy he was talking about was my old friend, Jack Carter? "What do I have to do?" I asked weakly. My first experience, I had never been experienced, was with Jack Carter in his bedroom when he pulled out little matchboxes full of marijuana. The trend now was to package the stuff in plastic sandwich baggies and sell them for five dollars a lid, or baggy. The sergeant, Sgt. Wolfe, was working with another officer from a nearby town to feebly combat the influx of the summer of love generation from the San Francisco Bay Area. He told me they identified a guy who hung around the Taco Bell in the other town, a town as tiny as mine 15 miles east, Manteca, as a major drug dealer. Kids in cars would flock to him, not only increasing the business for Taco Bell, but also making a pretty good living for himself. The guy was pretty slick, being able to detect undercover officers, such as they were back then, quite easily to avoid arrest, the Sergeant told me.

I was told I'd be given a small listening device to hide under my shirt and Sgt. Wolfe and the officer from the other town would be parked in a nearby car listening to my every word in case I got in trouble. Trouble? What could happen to me, I thought. It was only grass. I was supposed to report to the department on Saturday, meet with the sergeant who would drive me to the town and then meet with the other officer. I agreed. He also told me to not tell anyone about it. As if I wanted to be known as a "narc!"

I was relieved to know it wasn't Jack I was to set up. I knew he wouldn't go to that town to sell his grass. If he sold any, it would be from his home or when he was at the junior college. By now,

Jack had progressed to hallucinogens; mushrooms, LSD, and stuff like that. I thought if it turned out to be him, I was going to warn him because I knew he'd sell to me in an instant, but now I didn't have to worry about it.

Jack Carter and I went to the junior college in Stockton. Since he had the only car, he drove another friend and me to school while we paid for his gas. Jack bought into the hippy scene and was the first guy I knew who smoked marijuana. He was intelligent, much more than me, but sometimes a bit spacey. I thought he must have been under the influence of marijuana when he acted like that. After the trip home from Delta College, Jack invited my friend and me to his house to listen to his stereo. We accepted the offer.

My friend was a short, tow-headed wannabe surfer. He had sharp, lively blue eyes and slightly bucked teeth. He was one of those who was always "smartin' off", always had something wise to say. He was a load of fun but didn't take his college studies too seriously. His Grandma lived in Aptos, an ocean town south of Santa Cruz, so we often went there on the weekends and tried to take in the surf scene. We never quite made it, so my friend, Richie, was referred to by us as the fake surfer.

Jack took us to his room where he had some posters hung up and a stereo record player, the first one I ever saw. He played Jimi Hendrix's album, "Are You Experienced?" Richie and I were nervous, but even more so when he went to his dresser and pulled out a little matchbox. He opened it for us and we saw it! Marijuana! Richie was ready to make a run for it, but I grabbed him.

"It's alright," I told him. "Relax. Let's see what happens."

Jack then showed us how to roll a marijuana cigarette. He rolled two, lit one up and gave us the other. Richie and I looked at each other. We didn't know what to do. Jack lit his up and inhaled. He held it in, then slowly blew the smoke back out.

"Try it," he said.

"You go first," Richie told me, still scared. I lit up the cigarette but was overwhelmed by its pungent odor and backed off.

"Come on, man!" Jack ordered. "Like this." He took another puff. I followed suit. I took a little puff and started hacking and coughing. I gave it to Richie whose eyes nearly popped out of his head. He took a puff. He didn't hack or cough, so he took another and slowly exhaled, like Jack.

"Hey, Richie. How is it?" I asked. "Lemme try it." I grabbed the joint from his hand and tried again. This time, it wasn't so bad. After a few more puffs, I heard some strange sounds coming from the corner of Jack's room. Then I heard more weird sounds coming from the other side of his room. What the--? I got fearful. Richie heard it too and stopped smoking. Monsters! They were coming to get us and kill us!

"Richie!" I yelled. Jack was laughing hysterically.

"You guys are messed up," he laughed. "Take it easy. That's Jimi Hendrix!" For the first time we heard true stereo separation in Jimi's music. The marijuana made us paranoid and we weren't used to the music, especially Hendrix's guitar wizardry. My first experience was not pleasant, so I vowed to stay away from it, as my friend Richie did, too. Jack never asked us back.

I was nervous all day Saturday, knowing I was going undercover to make a big drug bust in the neighboring town, our school's rival at that. Sgt. Wolfe wasn't in his uniform making him look funny because all the times I ever saw him, he was in uniform. Now he looked like a regular guy. He drove me to Manteca which took about 20 minutes and I barely said a word. I had doubts I wanted to go through with this. We met the other officer in a back room of their police department. The officer was about the same age as Sgt. Wolfe, a bit gruff and smoked incessantly. He seemed more nervous than me. This whole drug scene was new to everyone, and procedures weren't quite refined then. Sgt. Wolfe then pulled out a black metal box, about the size of a pack of cigarettes, with a long wire protruding from it. He explained this was the transmitter, and I was to wear it beneath my belt. The wire had to extend up my body and be taped to my shoulder so it could be as close to my mouth as possible because this was the microphone. It felt weird because I had this tape all over my body with the little metal box digging into my skin. The officer then gave me a ten-dollar bill.

"Here. Make the buy with this," he ordered. "After you make the buy, start walking towards the school and turn the corner from Taco Bell. We'll pick you up there." This was starting to get serious now. I stuffed the ten in my pocket, and then he ordered me to stand spread-eagle against the door.

"What? What for?" I asked, confused.

"We've got to do this, son," Sgt. Wolfe answered. "It's for court. We've got to be able to say we knew you didn't have any money or drugs on you when you left so we can testify that the narcotics you have came from the suspect." He was starting to sound like Joe Friday. "That way, his attorney can't say you already had the stuff and was just loaning him ten dollars. Understand?" Jeez! All this for 10 bucks worth of grass?

"Yes, sir." Well, not really, but by now I just wanted to get this over with. The officer ran his hands all through my pockets, in my pants, shirt and socks; everywhere.

"Clean," he said satisfied. Of course I was clean, you idiot. I just took a shower before reporting to Sgt. Wolfe. They drove me two blocks from the Taco Bell giving me last minute instructions. They had tested the listening device back at the office and it worked fine. I walked down the street with the ten-dollar bill in my pocket, the metal box digging into my waist, the wire taped to my body. I had to adjust the box so it wasn't so uncomfortable. I was feeling stupid, regretting my decision to do this undercover stuff. I sat on a table outside the Taco Bell which was doing good business on a Saturday night. Taco Bell was near the end of the drag in this town. The drag is the main street extending for miles where kids cruise up and down the street for hours since there wasn't much else to do. The minutes seemed like hours as I waited. I was told to look out for a white guy about 20 years old with blond hair and drove a blue '66 Mustang.

I was getting bored when--there he was. I saw him right in front of me! I was nervous and excited. 'So this is the big time dope dealer, eh', I thought. Looked like a regular guy to me. He went into the Taco Bell, placed an order and came right back out. He walked slowly to his car and I was right behind him. I had him! My heart started to beat faster while the instructions I was given became jumbled in my mind. He got back in his car and I walked up to him.

"You got any marijuana I can buy?" I asked quickly and loudly. I remembered I wasn't supposed to use the word marijuana when I asked for the stuff, but I couldn't help it. I felt awkwardly official and phony and it seemed like the right thing to say. The guy looked me over carefully.

"Excuse me?" he asked.

I forgot what to say. I was face to face with this criminal and became flustered, feeling a little dizzy. "I…I want to make a score," I said, remembering the words of the sergeant.

"You want to buy some grass?" he asked bluntly.

Excitedly, I answered, "Yeah, yeah, some grass, I want to buy some grass."

"How much?"

"A baggy, just a baggy," I answered, relieved that I remembered to say that instead of ten dollars worth, which I almost did.

"How much you got?" He was slick. He trapped me.

"Ten bucks."

The crook looked around and said, "Okay. Give me the money and you wait here." I got him! I got him good! I jammed my hand into my pocket, snatched the ten-dollar bill and forked it over. "I'll be right back." He backed out of the lot, gave me a wave and drove away. I never saw him again.

I waited and waited; no Mustang, no grass, no bust--nothing. I noticed the unmarked police car cruise by and Sgt. Wolfe motioned for me to get away from the Taco Bell. I started walking to the "pre-designated location," as they called it, but they were right there at the corner instead. You idiots, I thought. Everybody knows the unmarked police cars in these small towns. I got in the car, afraid and anxious. I got ripped off on my first assignment.

"What the hell happened?" the other officer angrily demanded.

"I guess I got ripped off," I sheepishly answered.

"Ripped off? What?"

"Yeah. Didn't you hear?"

Sgt. Wolfe explained that they couldn't hear a thing. The wire must have come loose when I adjusted it from my waist, so I had to explain the entire incident to them. The other officer was angry, but Sgt. Wolfe thought it was rather funny. I exposed my naiveté by botching a simple grass buy. The other guy eyed me distrustfully, as though I conspired to blow his case. I didn't, but his attitude made me kind of glad it went awry. I had to be searched again before I left to make sure I didn't make the buy and keep the grass myself, or worse, had the grass and his stupid ten dollars. The way he was acting, I felt I was the crook here. On the way home, the sergeant was quite consoling, chalking it up to experience. Next time, I'd be ready.

The sergeant convinced me my career choice as an accountant was for wimps and wusses but being a cop took a real man. Made sense to me, so I changed my junior college major to Police Science. The government sponsored a program, the Law Enforcement Education Program, to educate the police with a bona fide college degree in hopes of making them more worldly, more sociologically enlightened, more human. At that time period, all that was necessary was a high school diploma, or its equivalency, be 21 years old and free from any felony convictions. I qualified in two out of three, not quite achieving "manhood", the mature age of 21.

Even working in a small town police department, I was exposed to the other side of life: the wicked, the insane, the heartless.

Those were the cops, the criminal element wasn't that bad. It was a rather simple concept, really. Crooks broke the law, cops catch them, criminals lie, then cops counteract their lies with better lies, for subterfuge was allowable when questioning suspects I learned, and then they go to court where their attorneys concoct more elaborate lies to set them free. That I could deal with. The uncertainty of insecure men wielding immense authority who didn't know how to be men was much more frightening. Witnessing the flow of human decay and despair in and out of the department was a much better learning experience than going to the junior college. I ended up quitting before I completed half of my degree requirements, accepting a full time job as a dispatcher within the department. My indoctrination into the real world was about to begin.

ELEVEN

The hippy movement swept through California, but forgot to include the town of Tracy. My town seemed to be the last to engage in the latest trend, or perhaps the movement deliberately avoided the town. Regardless, I was struck by the music played on the then not too popular FM stations, particularly, KSAN out of San Francisco. The music of the Jefferson Airplane, Cream, The Doors, Janis Joplin, Iron Butterfly, and lesser known groups as the Strawberry Alarm Clock and Steppenwolf was mesmerizing and addicting. My particular favorite, beside the Rolling Stones, was The Doors. Now that I was working full time, making $480 a month as a police dispatcher, I could afford to attend the concerts in San Francisco in venues such as The Fillmore, The Avalon Ballroom, Winterland, and even The Cow Palace, where I witnessed the mystical, mesmerizing performance of Jim Morrison of The Doors.

My small group of friends was dumbfounded by all the hippies. Their peculiar smell, a combination of patchouli oil and marijuana, was quite intoxicating, a distinct odor I liked but dared not imitate. I thought you had to have a license to be a hippy to be able to obtain patchouli oil. The concerts' light shows

59

were the happening, a radiant display of ever changing colors and images shown on a screen behind the band, an utterly fantastic experience even if not under the influence of the illicit weed. The Jefferson Airplane and the Iron Butterfly staged the best light shows. We stood in the crowd hypnotized by the conglomeration of light and strange images flashed on the screen in concert with the music. Several times, I thought I saw the image of Jesus and thought, man, they even have religion in these shows. As the image became clearer, I could see it was the face of the Zig Zag man. The air was heavy with the cannabis as it seemed to drape itself around you, like a friendly ghost.

One of my friends, Harold, was a large lad, similar in stature and demeanor to Hoss of the old Bonanza TV western. We called him "Head," not because he had a proclivity to be "hophead", a term reserved for those who smoked marijuana regularly. Head, too, was not experienced in drug use. He had a very small head for his body and he was not drafted into the army because he was classified 4-F. We never knew why he was classified as such, so we told him he wasn't drafted because there wasn't a helmet small enough to fit his head. Richie was the fake surfer of the group. His blond locks, buck teeth, and short stature made him such a lovable character; you just wanted to bounce him on your knee. He was the friend who was with me the first time I tried to smoke grass. He owned a metallic blue '57 Chevy with baby moon hubcaps. His grandmother lived in Aptos near Santa Cruz, so we often made trips to the ocean and tried to surf.

We decided to take my car during the Summer of Love to the Haight-Ashbury district of San Francisco to take advantage of the free love we heard so much about. For some reason, no one ever gave us free love, so we had to settle for the strip shows at 16th and Mission in what was known as The City, San Francisco, California. It was the first time any of us had seen a live girl actually naked. Head didn't know if he should gawk or hide his head. I could see it was making him uncomfortable. I thought he was actually blushing.

"Hey, Head! What's wrong with you? Check it out," I told him.

He took a quick look at the girl onstage and started giggling.

"What's so funny? She's gorgeous!"

"I never saw something like this. I don't know what to do," he mumbled softly.

"Don't do anything, Head. Just watch. Good grief. No wonder you weren't drafted." We had enough of this naked stuff and left to get something to eat in San Francisco, home of some of the finest restaurants on the planet. We walked to Market Street and stopped at a hot dog stand, one of many dotting the famous street. We each ordered a foot long, mine smothered in chili and onions. As we munched on the dogs, my attention was diverted to the back of the little restaurant where a handwritten sign read, "Peep shows - 25 cents." What the--? "Hey look, guys. What's that?" I shouted and pointed at the sign.

Everyone looked and Head started giggling again. With his mouth full of hot dog, he muttered, "My brother told me about those. Those are porn movies."

Puzzled, I said, "Porn movies! What the heck?"

"Come on. I'll show you," said Head, leading the way.

A dark, heavy curtain partitioned the restaurant portion of the hot dog place to the back where the peep shows were. A dark, foreign-looking guy was standing back there and opened the curtain for us. It was shadowy, and when my eyes adjusted, I saw a lot of individual booths covered with more dark curtains. A paper towel rack hung by the booths with another sign:

THESE ARE FOR CLEANING YOUR GLASSES ONLY.
PLEASE DISPOSE OF PROPERLY

Head took us into a booth where we all crowded in. He put a quarter into the slot and an image flickered on the little glass screen above the coin slot. I was stunned. This was a movie with a naked man and a woman who were doing something I had never seen. Richie gasped, I yelled, and Head nearly lost his head from his laughter. The little booth shook from our combined shock and laughter. The show didn't last long and Head started fumbling through his pockets for more quarters. Richie and I ran to the foreign looking guy demanding quarters for our dollar.

We each took separate booths and once in a while, one of the guys would yell, "Come here quick. Look at this!" It was dark, so we accidentally ran into the wrong booth and saw a creepy looking guy with a glassy look staring into the screen. This was better than the strip show! I ran back to my booth before my quarter ran out, but it was too late. The screen went dark, so I hurriedly put another quarter into the slot which fell through and dropped to the floor! 'Dang,' I thought. I couldn't see, so I bent down on the floor and felt around for my quarter when, unexpectedly, a terrifying sense engulfed me. My hand touched some wet, sticky stuff, causing me to immediately forget about my quarter. I pulled my hand back quickly, wiped it on the heavy curtain and sprang from there as fast as I could.

"Let's get out of here!" I yelled to the others. I grabbed one of the paper towels on my way out, disgusted and scared. "You know what that place is?" I asked angrily.

No one answered.

"Bunch of weirdoes, man! A bunch of weirdoes go in there and…" I couldn't finish answering my own question.

"What did you expect?" Head asked, still laughing.

"Your brother goes into those places, Head? He's a weirdo! No wonder you never got drafted."

Richie looked dazed and confused. "What just happened?" he asked.

"Let's just get out of here. Let's get back to the Haight. It's just about time to pick up Jerry."

Jerry Leary heard about our trip to San Francisco. He was our town's resident hippy, or as close to a hippy as one could be in Tracy, California. He was tall and thin, with long, straight greasy hair and a slight acne problem. No one liked him too much because he was always smoking marijuana and talking like a hippy. He said things like, "Far out, man!" and, "That's heavy," and "rapping" with people. He was close to the pothead Jack Carter, the kid who turned us on to marijuana, so we let him come along after he agreed to pay for the gas. He didn't want to go with us to the strip shows, opting to hang around Haight and Ashbury instead. We agreed to pick him up at a certain time and dropped him off in front of a humungous Victorian house off Haight Street. He disappeared into a sea of hippies and seemed to fit right in. He frequented the Haight and probably didn't want to be seen with the rest of us anyway.

"There he is!" Richie spotted him near the corner. "Let's just leave him. I don't like that guy, anyway."

"It's alright, Richie," I said. "He's paying for the gas."

"Stupid dope head," Richie exclaimed defiantly.

I looked over at Head and he was still grinning, probably thinking about those peep shows.

Haight Street was moving slowly, bumper to bumper traffic filled with tourists who came to stare at the hippies and be, in some small way, a part of the San Francisco scene, to be a part of the beautiful people. Jerry spotted us and hopped into my car.

"Look! I scored!" he shouted triumphantly. He held out his hand and showed us four, double-scored purple tablets. He called it Purple Haze.

"Purple haze? You mean, like Jimi Hendrix?" I asked ignorantly.

"Acid, man, acid," he emphasized.

"Acid?" I continued my ignorance.

"LSD, stupid, L-S-D! Look at it!" He was getting impatient.

"Jesus, Jerry! What are you doing?" We were all scared.

"Don't worry. I'll share some with you," he offered.

"No way. You think I want to jump off some building and kill myself?"

Jerry just laughed. "You dork. That doesn't happen. This is good stuff. All you need is one quarter and, like, far out!"

"Lemme try some, Jerry!" I was astounded by Head's request.

"Head? What's wrong with you? Why?" I asked. Head was all excited. I was worried. I felt like we just robbed a bank. Richie just froze, his mouth agape and eyes all bugged out.

"Richie? You all right?" I queried.

"Man, acid. We're all going to prison. I don't wanna die," he answered, his voice quivering.

Jerry laughed louder. "You guys are a bunch of dumb ass hicks. Watch." He popped a portion of the tablet into his mouth.

"Damn you, Jerry! Don't!" I was too late. Everybody got quiet. We thought he might start floating, or maybe disappear. We didn't know what to expect. After a few minutes, nothing happened. Richie kept looking around for cops to bust us. Head stared at Jerry in wonder and awe. Maybe Jerry was a real hippy.

"Come on, lemme try one," Head begged.

"Here," Jerry proffered.

"Head…!" Before I could finish, Head gulped the purple, slivered tablet down.

"Aw, man! This is crazy. Richie, what are we going to do?" I asked, looking for some sanity.

"Just get us home, man, and let's get away from them. They might try to kill us." Richie was seriously afraid.

I tried to calm down and drive carefully, fearful that the police were waiting to bust us all. How would I explain this to my sergeant? Things seemed calm enough. I turned on the radio and Scott McKenzie's "San Francisco (Be sure to wear some flowers in your hair)" was playing. I was feeling blue. We had had enough of San Francisco for awhile. Soon we were in familiar territory. We were past the foothills known as The Altamont, which would itself become notorious in a couple of years when the Rolling Stones played a concert where the Hells Angels acted as bodyguards. I felt safe when we were on the streets of our town.

Suddenly, a voice from the back seat said, "Watch it. There's a police car behind you."

Oh no! That's all I need. It was dark and all we could see were the headlights.

"Richie! Stop turning around. You're acting all suspicious and he's going to stop us for sure," I barked to him.

"All right. But that ain't no police car," he said.

"The hell it ain't," said Jerry. "Look! There's another right there." A car pulled up from a side street and slowed for the stop sign. It didn't look like a police car to me. By now, I could tell the car behind us wasn't a police car either.

"They know about us," Jerry whispered. "You work for the pigs. You told them." Jerry sounded hateful towards me.

"You're all messed up," Richie broke in, defending me. "You're gone."

"Don't be so sure," Jerry countered. "They're all over the place. They're watching every move we make. Don't you idiots understand? He's a narc!" Again, he was referring to me. Paranoia ran deep. The acid must have made him paranoid. Now what do I do? "Look!" Jerry nearly yelled. "There's cop cars all over the place!" He was freaking out.

"Relax, man, just relax," Head spoke out. Head didn't seem to be affected by the hit he took, or at least nothing noticeable. Maybe since his body was so big and his head so small, the LSD had some kind of counteracting influence, nullifying its affect.

"Let's get him out of here," Richie pleaded, "before he kills us." Now Richie was sounding paranoid, and he didn't take anything. But I took his advice and dropped Jerry off near his house and left quickly. He left without even saying goodbye or thanks.

"You all right, Head?" I asked.

"Yeah, yeah. I'm OK. Better get me home, too."

Head lived with his parents, so we dropped him off a block from his home. Richie stayed with me while we talked about the day's events. Weird stuff.

About a half hour later, Head called me. "You gotta help me, please." This sounded bad. I never heard Head sound so scared. Head explained he was freaking out. He was looking into his mirror and saw his skull. He said he then looked at his hands and he saw right through them, seeing the muscle, tendons, and bones. I told him to quit looking into the mirror, that I'd be right there.

"Come on, Richie, Head's all messed up. We've got to help him." Richie didn't hesitate and we drove to Head's parent's house. His parents were older than most who had a kid Head's age. After a few gratuitous Eddie Haskell hellos and how are yous, we went to Head's bedroom. He had his head under his pillow, shaking.

"This is bad. This is real bad. I feel like I'm going to die," he said almost crying. Richie and I looked at each other.

"We can't take him out of here now. His parents will know something's wrong," Richie wisely said.

"You're right. What are we going to do?" We were scared. We stayed with Head for the next few hours until it seemed he started to come down. He nearly became hysterical a couple of times and we thought his parents heard us, but Richie stayed calm and helped him through it. We were able to get him out of the house and cruise for awhile.

"I'm hungry," Head finally said. "Let's go to Foster's Freeze." We knew Head was alright now.

"Don't ever do that again, you idiot--never!" I scolded him.

We didn't see too much of Jerry after that. Nobody wanted to, really. Richie was still convinced he wanted to kill us. We heard he left town to join the hippy movement in San Francisco, but burned his brain out with drugs. He eventually returned to Tracy and was often seen years later walking the streets, long haired and barefooted, alone, desolate--a flower child who never bloomed.

TWELVE

I was enjoying my job as a police dispatcher. It was fun telling
the cops where to go. Not much newsworthy ever happened in
my town. The newspaper, The Tracy Press, came out only 3 days
a week. One headline story was when the town got a new traffic
light. Folks were impressed, looking at the shiny new lights and
exclaiming, "Yep. There it is. Pretty green, bright red. Look at that
yellow? Ain't that nice?" When I was hired as the new dispatcher,
I even had my picture on the front page, seated in front of the
police microphone with a caption that read: "Car 54. Where are
you?" in reference to a comical TV show about the police in New
York. The paper was usually dominated with news of the high
school's sports teams.

A girl, Shelley, who read the newspaper often called and tried
to flirt with me. At first she was a bit annoying, but then I began
to like the attention. She, too, like many others of the town, was
going to the junior college where I had dropped out. She was
getting a bit personable, confiding in me about her father dying
a few years ago, her mother working full time leaving her alone
quite often and a boyfriend who was drafted, now doing his stint
in Vietnam. Shelley later came into the department with two of

her friends to check me out. They were asking questions about police stuff, to which I was still new, and the few answers I did know seemed to impress them.

Months passed and we continued to talk on the phone along with her occasional visits while I worked. At the end of one phone call, she said, "I love you." Love? I felt funny and a dizzy feeling came over me, as though my head was detached from my body. I love you. She said that. No one had ever spoken those words to me before. I didn't say it back, because I couldn't. I didn't love anyone. I didn't even know what it was. The words left me dazed and confused. The song, "The Elusive Butterfly of Love," went through my mind, the one about a guy chasing the elusive butterfly, looking for love, except I wasn't looking for it, it was chasing me, or perhaps I was running away from it. I didn't know which.

I pondered those words 'I love you' on a quiet night at the dispatch desk. I consciously pondered my existence, my fate. I had broken from the bonds of my secret confinement, the physical and psychological terror which had entombed me for so long, yet there it lingered, a barrier to my own humanity, my fate bonded to this barrier of my passion, my passion suppressed by the loss of my innocence I never knew I had. Shuffling through the paperwork at the dispatch desk, I contemplated my fate, but why, I wondered when it's only me who can direct my fate, but I was never consciously aware of it. My consciousness never confronted my existence; it simply existed, independent of each other. There is no fate. And then this girl tells me she loves me? Fate. Twists of fate. But isn't the choice solely my own? If I choose to do nothing, then nothing is my choice. If there is nothing, there can be no choice. I am nothing. I am no one. I am surely not love. I got up from the dispatch desk and poured myself a cup of rancid coffee.

My experience with sex, as it was, skirted on the perverted side of perverse. I was never one to initiate lovemaking, or as my childhood chum, Billy, used to say, "making out." I wasn't sure what lovemaking was, except for what I saw in those peep shows in San Francisco, which I later learned wasn't really lovemaking. Things simply happened to me. I didn't cause them, nor did I want them--it just was. I didn't want Miss Palomino to take me into the bathroom, but I didn't stop her. I didn't want those nightmares to infest my childhood bed, but I didn't stop them either. My curiosity kindled, I wanted to find out more about what Shelley meant by love.

Before I entered into a journey of unknown pleasure or horrors, I knew not which, duty called. As I pondered weary and weak into the wee hours of the graveyard shift, the telephone rang. The call came in a dedicated line known only to police department employees. It was Sgt. Wolfe.

"Hey! You awake?" It was nearing 5:30 AM.

"Yes sir."

"Busy night?" he queried.

"Not really. The only action was at the El Gato Negro. Arrested a guy for ADW." The El Gato Negro (The Black Cat) was a small bar frequented by the south siders and the Mexican braceros. A fight started and someone got stuck. Typical Mexican bar fight. An illegal was arrested for Assault with a Deadly Weapon. "Other than that, it was quiet." I answered.

"I want you to hang around after you finish your shift. I'll be there around 7:15. Don't leave."

"OK. I'll be here." My shift ended at 7:00 AM. What did he want? What did I do?

Sgt. Wolfe was prompt. He motioned me to a back office of the department. "You ready for another assignment?" He asked. From his serious look, I knew it was another undercover operation. I was anxious to prove my mettle. I wanted to show the first one was merely a fluke. He explained he had this guy, a snitch he called him, who would be my "in" to another major drug dealer in the city 25 miles to the east, Stockton, the city of my former junior college. He then introduced me to this snitch, hidden in another office. I recognized him as a kid I knew from high school.

"Pablo? Hey, how ya doin' ", I asked surprised.

He looked surprised to see me, too, and then embarrassed. Most everyone I knew, except my closest friends, were always surprised to find I worked for the police department.

"Ora le," he said in Spanish. "Do you know Sergio Macias?"

"Who?"

Sgt. Wolfe intervened. "Sergio Macias. He's the guy we're after, big time."

"Never heard of him." My life was quite sheltered in this little town. After I dropped out of JC, I didn't go to Stockton, except for a McDonald's hamburger. My town didn't have a McDonald's, so a trip to Stockton always meant a stop at McDonald's. I didn't know anyone in that city.

"Good," the sergeant continued. "Pablo's going to be your in. Pablo's been making buys, but in order to protect his cover, we need someone else to take over. He'll introduce you to the mark, make a few buys, and then he'll back out. You'll be on your own to make the buys and we'll list you as the confidential informant on the search warrant." He paused. "Any questions?"

That was a lot to run by me. I was tired from working the graveyard shift and tried to absorb what he told me. I wanted to make sure I wouldn't blow this one. It sounded more important than a guy selling grass at a Taco Bell stand. But one word stood out.

"Yes, sir. I do have a question." I hesitated. "How come he's going to be protected and not me?" A reasonable question I rationalized. I glanced at Pablo and he looked away.

"In time, you're going to be what's known as a police undercover operator since you work for the department. But you have to have your credibility established to be a reliable informant," the sergeant explained, puffing on a cigarette. "Pablo's going to be making other buys, so we need to keep him from being identified, or else he's worthless...and he owes me, big time!" He emphasized, staring right at Pablo. "He won't be mentioned in the report, search warrant, nothing. You're the one who's going to be listed." And then he raised his voice a little and got close to me. "You're the cop. You'll be the one to testify."

A cop? Me? I wondered. I wasn't even old enough yet. No one ever told me before about testifying. He also told me that the dealer was a major source of not only grass, but heroin. The guy was pretty crafty, so much so that even the state agents couldn't get to him, Sgt. Wolfe explained. The cops in Stockton just started a narcotics unit and had two guys working it full time. They were pretty excited about having an "in", an informant who could get to this guy. The responsibility was then to fall on me. They made me feel important, but I was scared, too. Something about heroin frightened me--big time. It conjured up images of gangsters and guys being murdered and guys with golden arms, like in the old Frank Sinatra movie which I had seen on late night TV. Heroin was the one drug that my town and the love generation hadn't experienced, or at least that was my naiveté.

I was temporarily relieved of my dispatching duties and told I couldn't tell the rest of the employees, especially my friends what I was doing. I was suddenly sneaking in and out of the department at all hours, being driven back and forth to Stockton from Tracy, being given all kinds of attention. Why, they even bought Pablo and me hamburgers from McDonald's. I was being treated like royalty, but I had a sense of doom, of something wrong, something not quite right. At times, I was feeling a little blue.

"You want a soda? You want a hamburger? Anything you need?" I was always asked, and my reply was the same.

"No, sir. No thank you. Not right now."

Over the next few weeks, I spent a lot of time with Pablo and grew to understand him somewhat. I presumed this was my indoctrination because I had to know a lot more than I did when I got burned for my ten bucks in Manteca, the town 15 miles east of my town. Manteca. In Spanish, the word means "lard." Why would any town, I mused, name itself after the fat of a hog? Pablo explained he got busted for the possession of a couple of joints, a felony, meaning time in prison. Sgt. Wolfe was the one who arrested him and arranged a deal that if he cooperated, meaning snitch, he would help him out. Pablo was afraid to go to prison, so he agreed. He made a controlled buy for Sgt. Wolfe, and ever since, he's been doing this snitching. No one had been arrested for the sales, but we learned they were waiting to secure warrants and make the arrests all at once, thereby sending a message to the underworld, as it existed. Pablo didn't like what he was doing, but it was better than prison. He felt he already paid his end of the bargain, but they wouldn't let him go. He was afraid there were some who were starting to get suspicious.

So that was it. I was going to be his relief and then the burden would fall on me. I had a strange feeling come over me, like maybe this wasn't in my best interests. But I was in too far to back out now. I couldn't imagine myself being a "confidential reliable informant" or "police undercover operator" for long. The time came for me to meet the mark and ease Pablo out. I felt sorry for him. He was just a kid, like me, forced into this undercover lifestyle. It made me feel better that maybe this would be his last snitch and he'd be even for his crime of two joints.

The dealer's house was in the lower south side of Stockton, a run-down, two-bedroom project, known for its welfare, minorities, and drug addicts. Getting in was much too easy. Pablo knocked on the door where a young Latino woman quickly looked out and recognized him. She gave me a quick look and then opened the door. She let us in and Pablo asked for Sergio. There were two toddlers in the house, and in the corner of the tiny living room was a baby in a dirty looking bassinette. If this guy was a major drug dealer, then I was Joe Friday. This guy had to be poor, or maybe he was keeping his drug money in a Swiss bank account.

Sergio appeared from a back bedroom and greeted Pablo. "Ora le, Homes," he said. He was about 30, a bit short and lean with slicked back hair and a full moustache. Pablo introduced me, and Sergio seemed to take a quick liking to me. He was jovial and laughed a lot. He made me feel at ease. Sgt. Wolfe and the Stockton officer were parked around the corner. I had no wire this time, which made me think this was really serious stuff.

"Same stuff, Pablo?" Sergio asked.

Pablo reached in his pocket and retrieved a twenty-dollar bill. Sergio went to an old dresser next to the baby's bassinette and pulled out the bottom drawer, which was the only one that had knobs left, exposing baggies of marijuana packaged on top of baggies and more. The drawer was stuffed with marijuana baggies, dozens, maybe a hundred! He grabbed a couple off the top and handed them over to Pablo who gave one to me, which I quickly stuffed in my back pocket. Incredible! I just made my first controlled buy, well, actually it was Pablo, but I felt it was my buy, too.

As usual, we were searched thoroughly once we got back to the Stockton Police Department. Everyone was joyous that I was in. I felt nothing. Pablo just wanted to get out of there. I went with Pablo a couple of more times, as planned, and then he disappeared. He literally disappeared. Sgt. Wolfe, Pablo's family, I mean no one knew where he was. Because of my talks with him, I understood why he disappeared. He tired of his role as a snitch, feeling like he was being abused, which, in reality, he was, but that's the nature of the business of undercover work, I learned. How much would I be abused, I wondered. My mind whirled, wandering back to my childhood, to my nightmares, to Miss Palomino. How long Pablo would be gone was anybody's guess. I silently wished him well and hoped I would see him again. I liked him.

I was supposed to make the next buy alone. I was given a twenty-dollar bill, searched, and then driven a couple of blocks from the house. Before I got out of the car, the Stockton cop told me to try to get him to sell me some "chiva," heroin. As I walked the two blocks to Sergio's house, I realized the absurdity of it all. Here were two white middle-aged men, sitting in a car that obviously did not fit in the neighborhood smoking cigarettes. It's a good thing it was dark. As I passed the houses, I noticed they were not much different from where I grew up. The houses were close together, small yards, some with chain link fences, nothing fancy. No one had much. Now they want me to buy heroin?

Sergio knew I was just a pothead, or at least that was my persona in this undercover role. What did they expect me to do? 'Hey, Sergio. Can I buy some heroin this time?' 'Why sure, good buddy. How much you want?' he would reply. I was just going to buy the grass and that was it. I wondered where Pablo was hiding and thought about what would happen to me. I didn't want to get locked into this "police undercover role" like he did and end up running away. Where would I go anyway?

Sergio answered the door, smiled like he always does and let me in. He was more friendly than usual. Sales must have been good. "Where's Pablo, eh?"

"I don't know. Haven't seen him for awhile."

"Wanna beer?" he offered.

"No thanks. I'm in a hurry."

"Sit down. Stay awhile," he said. I didn't know what to say without Pablo there.

I sat at the kitchen table next to his couch, for there wasn't much separation from the kitchen and living room in these welfare projects. I looked over to his dresser, his stash, when a sense of dread came over me. Did he know how close he was to getting busted and sent to prison for years? What would he think of me, the one who betrayed him? I tried to get these thoughts out of my mind, for my dread was from the gun I saw on top of his dresser. I became weak and light-headed. Did he leave the gun there for me to see on purpose? Did he know about me? I became nervous and scared. I wasn't wired. I'm a dead duck. What if Pablo snitched me off and that was the reason he split!

My thoughts were shattered as I instinctively jumped when I heard some loud banging on Sergio's door. Somebody was knocking on his door unusually loud. Feeling like I'd been

burned, I hoped it was Sgt. Wolfe and the narcotics guy coming
to rescue me. I looked towards the rear of Sergio's kitchen for
the back door in case I needed to bust out of there, and fast. My
weakness turned into an adrenalin rush preparing me for some
quick movement. Sergio answered the door. Sgt. Wolfe? I looked
towards the dresser and the gun was gone. Two guys, a Black
and a Mexican, were yelling and laughing, obviously drunk. The
loud knocking must have unnerved Sergio, too, as he grabbed
the gun before answering the door. What if the guys were cops?
Would Sergio have used it? My sense of dread heightened. The
Mexican guy. I knew him! I had seen him somewhere in Tracy. If
I recognized him, he may have recognized me and knew where I
worked. I found myself staring at him, trying to place where I'd
seen him, but soon realized my staring might cause him to stare
back and he'd recognize me. I was this close to busting out that
back door, but then thought I might get shot in the back. Fear
gives way to fearful thoughts.

"Ora le! Give me some chiva, es eh!" The Mexican yelled at
Sergio.

"Shut up, eh?" I got kids." Sergio shot back. "You got the
money, June Bug?"

They were pretty wasted, which was fortunate for me because
they didn't pay me much attention. My heart was racing as fast as
Eric Clapton's guitar riffs. Sergio pulled something from an upper
drawer; heroin, I presumed. On their way out, the Mexican cast
me a glance and then looked at me again. He knows me, I thought!
I'm dead. The Black guy was pushing him out the door, knocking
his head against the screen. "He turned towards the black, "Hey,
June Bug! Take it easy, eh?" They stumbled out and left.

Sergio turned towards me and stared. I must have looked
like a scared clown, an amateur exposed. He took the gun from
his pocket and I felt like I was going to collapse on the floor,
until he said, "What's the matter, eh? Don't worry, those are just
some home boys," as he put the gun back on his dresser. He then
opened the bottom drawer, the one with the knobs.

"Two baggies?" he asked.

"Uh, yeah, two." My hand was trembling as I reached in my pocket to retrieve the twenty. I hated this stuff. I hated this feeling. What was I doing? This meant nothing to me. What did I have to prove? I couldn't act like nothing was wrong. I couldn't act like something I wasn't. Sergio kept looking at me as he gave me the baggies. I forked over the twenty and hurried out of there. Before I was able to get out, he grabbed me by the shoulder.

"Relax, Homes. See you next time," he smiled. Funny how he was giving me some reassurance when I was the one about to take him down.

"Thanks, Sergio." I couldn't leave fast enough.

Fortunately, the narcs had seen the two guys and got the license registration from the car they left in, the Mexican's. That's who it is! That's where I had seen him! I told the sergeant he worked at the Mexican restaurant around the corner from the police department in Tracy. He knows where I work because I had been in there in my dispatch uniform during lunch breaks. Damn! I knew I knew him. The sergeant told me I was lucky he didn't place me, probably because he was so wasted. He didn't have to tell me! He said he'd work fast to obtain warrants and arrest Sergio before the guy remembered and told him where he'd seen me, if he even remembered. I was glad Sgt. Wolfe didn't want to take any chances. I was scared of being dead.

Weeks later, back on the dispatch job, Sgt. Wolfe told me they served a search warrant on Sergio, recovered a good bit of dope, a stolen gun and a small quantity of cash. He told me I did good. I didn't feel good, though. I don't know what I felt. I know I didn't feel like I was going to die, and I didn't like playing this role of police undercover operator. I was rewarded with an extra day off, receiving no compensation for the undercover work, aside from my normal dispatch pay.

"You've got no reason to feel guilty," he said, sensing my angst. He told me to come with him for a ride in his patrol car while another officer manned the dispatch desk. We cruised the city.

He continued. "The guy is a piece of shit. He's a dope dealer. He sells stuff to anyone, kids, it don't matter to him," he continued, almost counseling me as a father to his son. "What you did had to be done. Understand?"

"Understand what," I retorted, somewhat defiantly.

"You did what the State guys couldn't do. You did what the Stockton narcs couldn't do. You made the guy--you did! You took a major dealer off the street," he said, as proud as a father whose son just scored a touchdown. Sergio's house, his children, the squalor flashed through my mind. Yes, I scored alright.

I was fighting back tears, why, I didn't know. It didn't make me feel any better, doing this great and wonderful thing. The sergeant drove the patrol car slowly around the outskirts of town, lighting a cigarette. He offered me one and I took it. I never even smoked before, but I took this one and lit it. Maybe it would keep me from crying. I choked and hacked on my first puff. It tasted harsher than the joint I smoked at Jack Carter's house when I was going to college.

"Gimme that," Sgt. Wolfe growled as he grabbed the cigarette from me and threw it out the window. "Look. Things are going to happen in this job you're not going to like, ugly things. There are people a lot worse than that guy, let me warn you," he said. "If you're going to be a good cop, you can't let these things bother you. You just go on to the next one." Next one? There'll be no next one, I thought. I didn't cry, but his words meant nothing to me.

Months later, the sergeant brought me a subpoena to testify against Sergio. "He still can't figure out what happened," he told me. "He has no idea how he got busted," the sergeant cackled. My name was concealed. In the warrant and subsequent police reports, I was referred to as the "CRI", confidential reliable informant. That made me feel better...until I got to court.

I only owned one suit, the one my mother bought me for my high school graduation, which I wore to court. I sat in the spectator area of the San Joaquin County Courthouse, felony trials. I saw the sergeant conferring with the Deputy District Attorney assigned the case seated at the attorney's table in front of the judge's bench. The sergeant walked over to me and whispered, "He still doesn't know what happened. You just answer the questions, don't volunteer anything, and don't guess. If you're not sure, just look towards me. Got it?"

"Yes, sir." I couldn't look him in the eye.

Then I saw him. Sergio walked from the prisoner's waiting area to the courtroom, accompanied by the court bailiff. I shrunk low into my seat, trying to hide myself. He looked differently in his orange county jail coveralls. He was clean shaven, except for his thick moustache and his hair slicked back. For the first time, I noticed the tattoos on his forearms. They were supposed to represent something, but I never knew what. He walked despairingly, looking down, far from the jovial man I had seen when I "scored", then cast a glance around the courtroom. He acknowledged a woman whom I scarcely recognized as his wife. He looked past me and then did a double take and looked directly into my eyes. My eyes were frozen on his, and I felt awkwardly. Not knowing what to do, I gave him a little wave of acknowledgement, as though there was nothing wrong between my neighborhood drug dealer and me. I wasn't being disrespectful, I was just saying 'hi', not knowing what else to do. I fidgeted a bit in my seat. Taken by surprise, he nodded his head in a friendly gesture, then looked to his wife again who, by now, was looking at me, seated two rows behind her. Sergio looked at me again, and then hung his head in resignation. I felt like saying, 'I'm sorry, Sergio,' but then remembered what Sgt. Wolfe told me about guys like him

Sergio sat next to his attorney, whispered something, and his attorney looked back at me. The way everyone looked at me, I felt like some kind of celebrity or something. The judge stopped the proceedings as the attorneys met for a little conference. Sgt. Wolfe walked away from them, came back to me and told me I didn't have to stay--Sergio was going to enter a guilty plea. I was relieved. I stood up to leave when Sergio turned to look at me again. Our eyes met and something in our gaze told me of a secret kinship, a trust betrayed by choices not our own, choices but for fate, perhaps, could have easily been reversed. This was merely one lesson, an awakening of a world infested by deceit, betrayal and distortion, on both sides of the law.

Sgt. Wolfe approached me again in a few weeks since the trial. No way, I thought. There was no way I was going to do any more undercover stuff. He gave me his look, the one he gives when he's about to build me up and ask me to work dope. I was ready to assert myself and tell him to find another snitch.

"Pablo is dead," he said.

I stood silent. I couldn't believe what I heard. I felt weird and that dread hovered over me again. Sergio! It had to have been Sergio who contracted him, and now he's going to have me killed!

"What happened?" I asked, afraid to hear.

"He was killed in Salinas. He was found stuffed in the trunk of a car. They found my card hidden in his wallet and called. Salinas PD said it was a hit, a Mexican Mafia hit," he said deadly serious.

"Mexican Mafia? What?" I didn't know what that was, but it sounded scary. Dammit! They killed Pablo, whoever they are, and now they're going to get me. I felt like running away.

"It's got nothing to do with Sergio," he went on assuredly. I heard what he said, but I wasn't so certain.

"Really? Are you sure?" I hopefully asked.

"Yeah, I'm sure. Pablo got himself mixed up in some pretty heavy stuff when he split. Heroin and stuff. He burned the Mexican Mafia for quite a bit of chiva, I was told, and 'bang!' Dead. They don't take that lightly," he understated.

The Mexican Mafia had its roots in the 1950's in the Deuel Vocational Institute, DVI, the prison just outside of Tracy. It was formed primarily to protect Mexican inmates from other gangs' attacks. While the Mexican Mafia was founded in part to show reverence to its Aztec and Maya heritage, its primary focus was to protect members against other prison inmates. As a response to the increase in violence, the California Department of Corrections transferred some members of the Mexican Mafia to other prison facilities, including San Quentin Prison. This action inadvertently helped the Mexican Mafia in recruiting new members in both the prison and juvenile correctional facilities in California. The gang evolved into drug trafficking, extortion and murder. Its influence on the street was immediate. How Pablo got involved, I never knew. I never knew a guy who had been murdered before.

"I knew you'd find out sooner or later, so wanted to tell you so wouldn't think there was any connection. You know, between you, Sergio and the Mexican Mafia," the sergeant asserted.

I remembered Pablo as just a kid who got mixed up in something he shouldn't have, or he just didn't know. Sgt. Wolfe was the one who made him do what he had to do. Or maybe it was me. I should have told him to knock off all that drug stuff and sneaking around when he was getting me into Sergio. We were just doing what we were told. He shouldn't have been dead. I was feeling blue.

"You alright?" he asked.

"Yes, sir. I'm okay," I lied. Death had introduced himself to me. I sensed the emergence of the grim reaper, complete in cloak and scythe, hovering about me. I hated him. He sensed a vulnerable being, confused and searching for his place in life, subservient to anyone who exerted a little control, so he decided to throw me a little tease through a startling murder. He just wanted me to know he knows I'm here. He wanted me to know so when he comes again, and he will, I cannot repudiate him. I must fear and respect him. I better be ready, he warns, for he is coming. He will come with such terrifying, unpredictable force, and he will keep coming. He will never leave my presence, and if I'm not ready, he will take me with him. I'll be ready, I thought. Will I?

THIRTEEN

It was a Sunday night in Tracy. The graveyard shift was dead. Everyone in town was home, sleeping, preparing for the week's work. My tinny, tiny portable radio was playing Suzie-Q, by Creedence Clearwater Revival. Around midnight, the phone rang. I turned the volume down. Dang! Why'd they have to call now? I loved this song.

"Tracy Police," I tiredly answered.

"Hi," a soft voice whispered. It was Shelley. I haven't heard from her in quite some time. "Can you come over tomorrow?" She timidly asked. "I think I'm going to be sick and have to stay home from school. I'd really like you to come over."

It might be nice to spend time with someone not associated with cop stuff. I thought about it a moment. "Sure, sure. I'll come. What about your mom?"

"She leaves at 8. I'll leave the door from the garage door unlocked. You can pull your car in there, close the door and I'll leave the inner door unlocked, too." She had an elaborate plan.

"Okay. See you in the morning."

"I love you." She said it again.

I couldn't say it. "Okay. Bye," and hung up. Just then, the

phone rang again. Someone thought she heard a prowler in her back yard. Time to go to work and dispatch the right beat car. I missed the rest of Suzie-Q.

The night slowly passed into dawn. It was nearing 7 AM. Anticipation grew within me as I thought about Shelley and sneaking into her house. Anticipation turned to excitement, then to fear. What was going to happen? She was a pretty girl, but I didn't love her, but I did want to be with her. I was quite shy and repressed, but she made me feel comfortable, as though I mattered. What little I did know, I stopped at the local drugstore and bought a package of condoms--just in case. Thankfully, a male clerk waited on me. If it was a female, I would have been embarrassed to make the purchase and simply left. I drove nervously to her house when Cream's "Sunshine of Your Love" played on my radio. I drove around the block of her house until the song finished. I pulled into her driveway and paused a moment. Should I do this? I got out, opened her garage door and quickly pulled in and closed the door. It was excruciatingly quiet in her garage. All I could hear was the exaggerated sound of my car creaking and settling. I quietly opened the door leading to her house from the garage. Her house was clean and neat.

"Shelley?" I whispered.

"Back here. Come here," her voice softly called from a back bedroom. I was starting to shake, trembling almost as badly as when I attempted to make my first drug buy. I followed her voice, as though it reached out and grabbed me full force. "Back here," she said again and I smelled the perfume, a wondrous odor I had never sensed before, and then I saw her. I had never seen her like this; I had never seen anyone like this. She was seated at the end of a bed, brushing her hair and wearing a bathrobe. "Hi" she said with a look that nearly melted me to the floor.

"Hi. How are you feeling?" I forgot she wasn't really sick.

"Come here," she told me, standing and holding her arms out. Obediently, I walked to her. I saw she had no clothes on underneath her bathrobe. I gasped. She drew me close to her and held me gently. The sensation of her nakedness, the perfume, the secrecy made me quiver, made me weak. I felt the warmth of her body against me, even though I had my clothes on. She was soft, she was warm, she was erotic. I was nervous. She sensed it.

"What's the matter?" her voice barely a whisper.

I knew what was the matter, but how could I tell her? Unlike Jimi Hendrix's song, I was not experienced. Never. Not like this anyway, not in the normal sense. I didn't know what was normal. "I just, I…uh, are you sure your mother's not coming back?" was all I could blurt. She laughed.

"She won't be back until after four-thirty. Don't worry." She hugged me.

"Can we watch some TV?" I stupidly asked.

She backed off. "Sure," and turned on the TV. She switched through the four channels available then, passing through two news shows and then I saw Captain Kangaroo.

"Yeah. Stop right there," I told her. I then realized we were in her mother's bedroom; big bed, TV, a bathroom to the side. I could see her body underneath her bathrobe and kept trying to look without seeming I was gawking. I had never seen a girl naked before, except for those peep shows. She told me to take my clothes off and lie next to her. I didn't like having to take my clothes off in P.E. class in high school, now here I am in front of a girl? I slowly took my pants off and the condom fell out of the pocket onto the carpet. She didn't see it land, so I slid it quickly with my foot under my pants so she wouldn't think I was there for one thing. I was down to my shorts, but I couldn't bring myself to take them off in front of her. I was feeling dizzy again and lay on the bed next to her. I felt the heat from her body without even touching her.

Mr. Moose had just hidden the carrots from Bunny Rabbit and Captain Kangaroo came in to save Bunny, as he always did. I hoped this would be the day the Captain showed the Tom Terrific cartoon with his dog, Manfred, the mighty wonder dog. I then remembered where I was.

"I love you," she said. "I really do." I looked into her eyes which seemed to pierce through me, a look that scared me even more. How could she love me? She's just a kid. She didn't look like a kid; I looked more like a kid than she did. Her face was right next to mine. Her eyes were so blue. She got even closer and kissed me. I stared at her and her eyes were closed. I closed mine too. This was it. This was the day I lost something I never knew I had, my virginity, right in front of Mr. Greenjeans, Grandfather Clock and Dancing Bear. I pulled myself away from her. I knew I had to have a condom. I was scared to death of getting her pregnant. I couldn't fancy myself at 20 married to an 18-yr. old with a child. I felt awkward and didn't know how to do it.

"What's wrong? Don't you want to?" she asked, seemingly disappointed.

"No, I mean, yes, but…don't you think we should have some protection or something like that?"

"Oh yeah," she said quite comfortably, easing my tension. She reached over to her mother's nightstand and brought out a small, pink can from the top drawer. "How's this?"

"What's that?" I had nary a clue.

"It's my mom's. It's foam that's supposed to keep you from getting pregnant."

"Foam?" I asked, incredulously.

She handed it to me and I read something about contraceptive foam and saw a little diagram which confused me.

"Do you want to do it?"

I looked at the diagram again."Uh, no. I don't think I can." It seemed pretty frightening and I knew I couldn't handle anything like that." I was losing the excitement of the moment.

"Here! I'll do it," she said, sounding a bit agitated. She grabbed the can from me and disappeared in the bathroom and returned in a jiffy. She then jumped into the bed, tickled me and laughed loudly. "I'm safe!" She held and touched me. In a flash, I was in the bathroom with Miss Palomino.

"Shelley. If you don't mind, I'm real tired. Do you mind if I just lay here for a moment?"

"No, it's OK," she cooed.

"Thanks." I lay still and quickly I drifted off into a slumber. Soon, I felt her again. She pulled me towards her. I held my eyes closed and suddenly, suddenly this sensation of passion overwhelmed my entire being. I was elevated far above the world into a distant universe, soared over the Fortress of Solitude, then entered into the Enchanted Forest. My consciousness became conscienceless, a tranquil flight which took me somewhere over the rainbow, softly brushing against the velvety sheen of a fluffy cloud. Beyond the clouds, a setting sunset splashed brilliantly against a calm, blue lake. I glided towards the lake and saw the trees of the forest brush aside for my flight as I saw the painted forest, alive with the brightest hues of the spectrum which were slowly dropping onto the soft petals of large, blooming flowers. The flowers swayed gently in the breeze as though speaking secretly to me, seeming to say, "play with us, Danny, there is no fear, there is no death for here you are eternal, here you are content."

My sensual flight moved me toward the brightest blue I ever witnessed--the waves of a dynamic sea, gently kissing the shore and near the shore sat a man in a tiny boat. I hovered over him and beheld a dwarf. My flight passed over the elf who thrust both hands upward from which a dove alighted, fluttering its velvety wings and perched on my shoulder. The dove cooed in my ear and whispered, "You cannot be hurt here, but shelter your heart against the ill wind which must never enter the passageway to your fortune." The dove spoke in tiny gasps of breath, falling warmly against my neck.

"Yes, yes," I told the dove. The dove lightly pecked me on the ear and flew away, leaving a feather upon my crown. My flight decelerated considerably as I approached another luxuriant cloud and landed delicately on its surface, its fluffiness taking my breath away. I felt a glow radiating through my body as the cloud began to move. It started to move rapidly, upsetting the balance of this eternal bliss. Stop moving.

"Stop moving," I said. "Please stop." Slowly, I felt the body of Shelley relax. Her eyes were wide open. The magic carpet ride was over. "I'm sorry, I didn't mean to...I just..." I couldn't tell her I was starting to hurt a bit. Shelley let me sleep a few hours in her mother's bed and when I awoke, I groggily found my way to her garage and left. Nothing I read, nothing I saw, nothing I did would replace those wondrous moments in flight. Though the emotion was overpowering, it was not love. Not for me. Shelley was special, never to be forgotten, but like the rest of my existence, I didn't really know what it meant, but for now, I wasn't feeling blue.

FOURTEEN

I returned to my dispatching duties on what was known as the relief shift. I filled in for the other shifts' days off. That meant working two nights graveyard, two swing shifts and one day shift. It was here I met the one the dove warned me against, the one I was to shelter my heart against, the evil one. Weekends in Tracy were a time for some old fashioned hell-raising. The town unwound itself in its haven of bars and churches. Sin Friday and Saturday, pray for forgiveness on Sunday mornings. California Penal Code 647, disorderly conduct, was the most violated code in town and the easiest to take down a drunken perpetrator. The code was broken into subsections; 647a, annoying or molesting children, 647b, prostitution, 647c, panhandling, and so forth until subsection F, drunk in public. At times, the whole town could have been booked for 647f P.C. The code was an easy catch-all for family fights, barroom brawls, and sassing a law officer type calls. If they were a problem and smelled of booze, book 'em; 647f P.C.

I felt for the winos, the losers, the men of failed hopes, broken hearts and broken dreams whose only existence was in the bottle. Kindly old men--the pensioners, the disabled and the disillusioned. Easy arrests. Every town had them, no matter the size. Some officers thought they were doing society a favor by ridding the streets of their presence. The truth was, society didn't care. Society produced the bottle, so all the wino had to do was figure out how to manipulate society to give them the bottle. And society always produced.

An old Mexican man, in his 60's, had hopped the rails in southern California and made it to Tracy, a man who should have been dead a long time ago. He hopped off the train already a 647-f'er. He was arrested soon after and booked into the city jail on a Friday night as a kicker, which meant he was "to be released when sober" instead of going to court on formal charges. The ones who went to court were the ones who committed additional crimes costing money, or for swinging at a law officer, a common occurrence. I entered his name into the arrest register and filed the report for the arresting officer. The drunk's name didn't really matter, for he was like hundreds of others who would never be seen again once they left town, a long since forgotten name on some illegible police blotter years from now.

My shift assignment had me working swing shift Friday and Saturday, then returning Sunday morning at 7:00 AM. I drug myself to work, having stayed up much too late watching a rerun of Night of the Living Dead. Sunday morning, truly a night after the Night of the Living Dead. No one was awake. The arrest register showed no one in custody. Everyone had been released. I was reading the Sunday morning Stockton Record, for Tracy didn't have a weekend newspaper, at the dispatch desk, catching up on Dagwood's latest dilemma when I heard a noise from the jail cell area. On Sundays, only one officer was on duty since everyone was in church or sleeping off their hangover from Saturday night. The on duty officer was on the street, so the noise was unusual. I turned on the monitor at the dispatch desk to listen in on the cell area. Its purpose was for the dispatcher to listen when a prisoner was being booked. If it sounded like the officer was being given a hard time, we were supposed to call for backup, then we had to go back to help however needed. It was quiet, but I distinctly heard a voice coming from the jail cells.

'What the--?' I thought. I walked back toward the cells and heard a voice weakly crying for help. Someone was still in there. 'How in the--?' I ran to the cell and opened the small, metal hinged window of the cell door and saw the little Mexican man who was booked on Friday night. He reminded me of my grandfather whom I hadn't seen in years. I couldn't believe it.

"What are you still doing here?" I asked.

"Do I get to eat?" He feebly responded. "When do I go to court?"

"Hang on," I told him. "I'll get you out of there." I went back to the dispatch desk and checked the arrest register. His name was there as I wrote it on Friday night, but in the "disposition box" someone wrote, "released 849.2 P.C.," meaning he was released with no formal charges, but he was still there. Someone messed up. I summoned the patrol officer, in police code, to return to the station.

I didn't know the patrol officer very well. He had been one of the two police detectives working the day shift since I joined the department. He had not been very friendly to me during my few contacts with him. He had just been reassigned to patrol from Detectives and was not very happy about it. He felt Detectives was his exclusive domain, but the Chief thought he should rotate the position. Gary Rendle was his name, a square jawed man in his 30's. I thought he was a bit peculiar, not only for being unfriendly, but his hair was reminiscent of guys I knew in high school. He had a crew cut on top, and it was long on both sides of his head, greased straight back forming what was known as "ducktails" at the back of his head. He had beady eyes of the strangest color, a grayish-blue, and he was immaculate in his appearance. He could have passed for a clothing store dummy, the kind who comes alive in Rod Serling's Twilight Zone television series. He gave me the creeps. We didn't converse much whenever we happened to be together, which didn't bother me. I told him of my discovery.

"I'll take care of it," he said, and went back to the cells.

I felt for the old man, so I ordered him a meal to be brought to the department. The only means of feeding the prisoners was to prepare a meal voucher for the Chinese restaurant around the corner. Usually, an officer picked up the meals and brought it to the prisoners through the metal hinged windows. A meal for the prisoners consisted of two small hamburgers with a pickle only and a cup of black coffee. For breakfast, it was an egg sandwich, no meat, black coffee and a pickle on the egg. Why the Chinese put a pickle on the egg I never knew. The waitress brought me a paper bag with the sandwich and a bag of chips and the coffee. Because it was Sunday, I guess the chips were an extra treat. I gave her the voucher and waited at the desk.

The little speaker monitor to the cells was still on. I heard a loud commotion and someone yelling. There were definite sounds of a struggle. The crashing and banging sounds were getting louder. 'Jesus! What the--,' I thought. Something is wrong, not quite right. Since Rendle was the only officer on duty, I was the backup. I ran back to the cells and saw the drunk's cell door open. I saw Rendle standing over the drunk, obviously sober by now, who lay supine on the concrete floor. The old man looked at me with a sense of loss and confusion. I looked at Rendle, who hadn't seen me yet, and he gave the old man a kick to his back.

"That'll teach you to fuck with the kid," he said triumphantly to the little old man.

'My God,' I thought. 'Come on Rendle,' I said in my mind. I could have beaten up the old man in my sleep. The guy must have said something to anger Rendle and since he was mad anyway, he took his frustration out on this old drunk. So he thinks he's The kid, does he?

"Is everything alright?" I dumbly asked.

He turned slowly to me with strange eyes, a vacant doll-like stare and ignored me.

"Now get up," he ordered the drunk. The man struggled to get up, then fell down while Rendle watched him. I wanted to rush to the guy and help him, but I knew it wasn't my place. The old man looked at me again, defenseless. I was intimidated by Rendle and did nothing. The drunk was eventually released without getting his meal. I returned to the dispatch desk forlorn. I didn't know what to do, but I did know I didn't want the sandwich to go to waste, so I threw away the pickle and ate the egg sandwich. It wasn't very enjoyable as I thought about what the old guy could have said or did to justify a beating, no blood, no visible bruises, but a beating just the same. I thought about my grandfather. Rendle never came back to the dispatch desk, nor did he say a word to me. He left the department and resumed his patrol duties straight from the cell area. I resumed reading the Sunday comics. I was disturbed, feeling blue. I knew that Rendle and I would not get along. I just knew it.

FIFTEEN

The hippies, the love generation, the peaceniks, the dope-smoking long haired freaks slowly infiltrated my town. Members of this generation were often seen on the outskirts of town hitching a ride. Whenever one was actually in town, at a restaurant or market, he was the object of ridicule and often resulted in calls to the police, even though no laws were broken.

"Tracy Police," I answered the phone officially.

"Yeah, could you come down to The Mart? There's one of them longhairs hanging around," the caller said.

"Yes sir. What's he doing?"

"Doing? He's outside my store…he's there. He's ruining my business. Just send someone," he ordered.

"Yes sir, but I need to know what he is doing besides being there. Is he drunk, is he causing a disturbance?" Official questions I had to know before dispatching the beat car.

"Look! Send someone, or I'll call Jerry!" He threatened.

Jerry was the first name of the Chief of Police. I didn't want to get in trouble, so I dispatched the beat officer. The Mart was a clothing store in downtown Tracy, owned by a guy I assumed was a close friend of the chief. The officer I sent was the one

I remembered from my first day, old "pearly-grips," who used to drive trucks for a living. He hassled the hippy and sent him on his way. Pearly-grips returned to the department for a coffee break a short while later and gave me his field interrogation card, a small, blue 3X5 index card indicating the name and identifying details of the person in question. It disgusted me to have to work with this man. He delighted in talking about "niggers," "spics (Mexicans)," even though I was one, hippies, and anyone who didn't fit into his depraved world. He bragged about hassling the hippy.

"He started giving me that 'man' shit," he said. "I showed him who the man was. I showed that little bastard, dope smoking, long-haired freak. Give me that 'man' shit will he? I should have busted his dumb hippy ass."

"Man," I said. "He must have been something. Lot of freaks, man!" I stressed the word freaks, parodying a line I heard from Arlo Guthrie in the movie "Woodstock" which I saw 10 times. I loved the movie. If I hadn't been stuck here, I would have been a hippy. I thought the officer might get angry over my deliberate use of the word 'man', but it passed over him because I wasn't a hippy, although in my heart I was a "wannabe." The field interrogation card he gave me, which I had to file as part of my dispatching duties, had the name Richie Fritchse (pronounced "frichee), living in San Francisco. The officer wrote on the back of the card "subject was causing a disturbance and ordered to leave town." I wondered if he told him to leave by sundown.

I was intrigued by the hippy movement. I dug the music, the psychedelics, the dress, the whole sense of something new and refreshing. I particularly liked the anti-establishment attitude, but since I worked for the police, there was a dichotomy at work. There was something at work in my soul which I did not understand, but I wouldn't let the restraints of my job stop me from trying. I had just bought Janis Joplin's new album, and the words flashed through my mind from her song "Ball and Chain." 'Yes, Janis, ' I thought. *'Someday some weight's going to come on my shoulders,' and it's going to be like a ball and chain.* Maybe it was already here.

Prior to my swing shift, I stopped at the Westside Market on the corner, a half block from the department. I stocked up on Hostess Sno-Balls, Cheetos, a Cream soda and bought the latest issue of Mad Magazine for when it got quiet and I was bored. I saw a "hippy-type subject" in front of the old apartment building next to the market. Whenever a call was received by the police, a complaint report had to be initiated by the dispatcher and the nature of the complaint had to be completed, such as a disturbance, burglary, vandalism and the like. One of the other dispatchers conceived of the title of the complaint, "hippy type subject", whenever anyone called about a hippy. I guess he thought it was a crime to be a hippy. This hippy fascinated me; just hanging around. He looked at me and did a double take. I had on a dispatcher uniform with police patches on the shoulders, but I wasn't a cop, so he wasn't sure how to take me. He gave me a friendly wave and I returned the favor.

Shortly after my shift began and I was already munching on my Cheetos, beginning to read Mad's satire of Stanley Kubrick's "2001: A Space Odyssey," called "Space Oddity", someone entered the front door, jingling the warning bell, and coming to the counter separating the dispatch area from the small lobby. It was the hippy.

"Hey. How ya doing?" he amiably asked.

I covered my Cheetos with the Mad Magazine. "I'm fine. How can I help you?" I asked, wiping the Cheeto crumbs from my hands.

"I'm thinking about renting one of the apartments across the street and was wondering if there may be any problems." He saw my magazine and smiled.

"No. It's quiet really. Mostly pensioners and restaurant workers, but it's pretty safe," I offered.

"Good. I'm just moving here from The City (San Francisco) and was looking for a quiet place. You dig Mad Magazine? Far out!" He introduced himself and put his hand out to shake mine. I made sure there were no Cheeto crumbs on my fingers and shook his.

"What was the name again?" I asked.

"Richie. Richie Fritsche." I knew the name. I heard it before.

He looked around the dispatch area and saw I was the only one there. He struck up a conversation about music, the law and life. He seemed quite nice and as he left, I wished him luck. Then I remembered. He was the one who was rousted downtown, the one the mean cop bragged on. He didn't use the 'man' word too much to me. The odor of patchouli oil wafted through the lobby after he left. Hippies! Kinda cool, I thought.

As the weeks went on, he was a frequent visitor, seemingly picking his spots when he knew I was alone. We got along famously. He invited me to his apartment one day after my swing shift, which I accepted. He seemed like a regular guy to me. If there was such a thing as a stereotypical hippy, Richie was it. He was in his mid 20's, a few years older than me, a bit thin, wearing a floppy hat, beads, bell bottoms, and reeking of patchouli oil. When I got to his apartment, I was blown away. There were bead curtains, black light posters, candles and an aura of freedom, complete freedom. I liked it. He introduced me to his girlfriend, about the same age as he, wearing a loose fitting blouse which I could see she was not wearing a bra. She was very pretty.

"Have a seat," he said. I sat on a soft couch and marveled at his place. He put on the first Iron Butterfly album on his small stereo and sat next to me. His girl pulled out something from her blouse I recognized; a joint. He must have felt comfortable and trusted me, for we were of the same generation, and lit the joint and offered me a toke. I politely refused. Had I known him better and not felt so uptight, I might have accepted. We talked and philosophized about life and then the Butterfly's In-a-gadda-da-vida came on his stereo. Man, this was far out! What a life! I wanted to be a hippy. As we talked, he told me he had to get away from San Francisco for awhile because there were some people causing him problems, so he wanted to cool it. The drum solo of In-a-gadda-da-vida came on and we remained silent. It was a given that when the drum solo began, no one could talk. Homage had to be given to one of the greatest drum solos in the history of the world. His girlfriend was really into it, swaying her head back and forth to the pounding drums, and I was digging it, too.

When it was over, I asked, "Cops giving you bad time?"

"No, not the cops. Just some friends I thought were my friends. But there's no reason to get into it. It's pretty mellow over here, except for the cops hassling me." I knew what he was talking about.

"Yeah, I know. Sorry about that."

"You know about that?"

"I was on duty. I sent the cops after you."

He was getting pretty loaded by now and laughed loudly. "Far out! It was you?" He laughed some more. "Far out," he repeated. I visited him a few more times, but when he had some friends from The City with him, I figured I better leave. It was best I didn't know too much.

My limited association with Richie Fritsche caused some discomfort within the department, and, soon, Sgt. Wolfe approached me and cautioned me about my acquaintance. He said no good could come from my friendship, as he believed he may be involved in selling drugs. The sergeant confided in me he had information Fritsche was dealing grass and reds, sodium seconal, a depressant similar to the effects of alcohol. The sergeant alarmed me, so I curtailed my visits, which bothered me because he was a pretty cool dude. I was confused between what I was and what I wanted to be, but the drug scene was a turn off. I didn't judge Richie, but if I wanted to keep my job, I knew the friendship was doomed.

The sergeant approached me a day later and asked if I thought I could get Fritsche to sell me some grass. Without thinking, I told him I thought I could. He told me he wanted me to do another undercover operation. Of course, I didn't have to go undercover, I was already there. Richie knew I worked for the police and I knew he was a transplanted San Francisco hippy, and never the twain shall meet, as much as I wanted it to. Sgt. Wolfe told me this would be my chance to show the rest of the guys I wasn't a "doper," that I could prove I was going to be a good cop by having this guy busted.

I was bewildered by his comment. Sgt. Wolfe revealed some of the perceptions a few of the guys had about me. The labeled me a doper behind my back. Me? A doper? Okay, so I had smoked a few joints with my old chums when I was going to the junior college. But, a doper? The sergeant wasn't through. "Is this yours?" he asked, pulling a 3X5 index card from his shirt pocket.

I examined it and smiled. "Where did you get that?" I asked astonishingly. "Yes, that's mine, but…." before I finished, he interrupted.

"What the hell are you doing?"

"Huh?" I was confused. "I ain't doing nothing. And I certainly am not a 'doper'!" The card had the words of a song by Jim Morrison and The Doors called "Horse Latitudes" from their second album, Strange Days. Morrison was a master poet on par with my hero, Edgar Alan Poe. I loved the dark and mysterious lyrics, the drug laden metaphors and the awesome music of Ray Manzarek, Robbie Krieger and John Densmore. I played their albums over and over. "Horse Latitudes was a poem within the album without a musical accompaniment. I was fascinated by it.

When the still sea conspires an armor
And her sullen and aborted currents breed tiny monsters,
True sailing is dead.
Awkward instant, and the first animal is jettisoned
Legs furiously pumping their stiff green gallop.

And heads bob up, poise, delicate, pause, consent.
In mute nostril agony, carefully refined and sealed over.

(The Doors: Horse Latitudes)

One particularly boring graveyard shift at the dispatch desk, I mindlessly typed the lyrics on a 3X5 card. Morrison was quite a poet. After this particular piece on the album, it would then kick into the next song, my particular favorite, "Moonlight Drive." I then crumbled up the card and threw it into the waste basket. Someone found it, retrieved it, and kept it, convinced I must be high on drugs to write such jibberish. The absurdity of it all! I deduced whoever found it jumped for joy and ran to the sergeant. 'See? I told you the guy was doper. Did I do good?' I imagined. But who? Rendle, I thought. The psycho cop who beat up the old man in the jail cell. I knew he didn't like me.

"Do you drop acid?" he suddenly asked, point blank.

'Come on!' I thought. He suddenly looked so absurd to me, like an old guy trying to be young using hippy lingo. I started to get nervous. "No, I never have," I calmly said.

"You ever smoke grass?" He turned serious, as he looked me dead in the eye.

He had me. No sense denying it, I thought, but then that feeling of dread enveloped me, like a ball and chain heavily weighing on me. Possessing even a joint of marijuana was a felony then, and if I admitted to it, I'd be admitting to a felony. He must have forgotten that he asked me that before when I lied the first time, but maybe he was just trying to trick me. Or maybe he made the whole thing up. Maybe the other guys never thought that, only him. Maybe it was he who found the lyrics and was setting me up. Maybe it was just he who thought I was a doper. He did help me in my young career so far, or was it I who helped him? Maybe I should just confide in him and tell him the truth, but if I did, what would he do? These cops were pretty tricky. I hope they never find out I saw The Doors in concert in San Francisco.

"No. Never did that either," I lied again.

"Then here's your chance to prove it," he said emphatically. "Buy some dope off that guy, we'll bust him and you're in." "In" meaning I'd prove my worth to be a real cop in the department.

How could I refuse? So that's what it's going to take! Just do Richie Fritsche, the guys won't think I'm a doper, or whoever thought that, and I'll be accepted into the inner circle.

"Sure." I gave in. "Just tell me what I have to do." He gave me my instructions which weren't much different than what I had done before. He said he wanted me to try to buy some reds, which carried a more severe penalty than buying marijuana. I had avoided Richie after the sergeant warned me, which made me feel badly, but now I had to be his buddy again to have him arrested; to betray him, I figured. I didn't just want to barge in and make a buy, so I hung around him a few times to regain his confidence. The plan worked

I quaffed on a beer listening to the Jefferson Airplane's "White Rabbit" on Richie's stereo. "Do you think I can get some reds from you?" I asked, as Grace Slick sang in the background:

And if you go chasing rabbits
And you know you're going to fall
Tell 'em a hookah smoking caterpillar
Has given you the call

It was Richie's move. He hesitated a moment and looked at me.

"For you?"

"Yeah. Well, not exactly. A friend of mine needs them. He just got back from 'Nam' (Vietnam)…and he's pretty messed up." I pulled off the line just as instructed.

When men on the chessboard

Get up and tell you where to go...
When logic and proportion have fallen sloppy dead...

"Yeah, I suppose. I can get some for you. You sure?" he asked quizzically.

"I'm sure. Don't worry. I ain't 'narcin'," I lied.

Remember what the dormouse said,
Feed your head...
(Jefferson Airplane: White Rabbit)

I didn't like this. I didn't like it at all. I had nothing to prove. So what if they called me a doper? So what if they had Jim Morrison's "Horse Latitudes" as evidence? This guy was my friend. He never pressured me to do drugs and didn't judge me for working for the police. He let me be myself and now I'm supposed to have him jailed? I should thank him for letting me by myself. Being a cop lost its meaning to me. It meant nothing. If my life regressed to betrayal, deceit, and ignorance, it wasn't worth it. I failed to realize my life couldn't regress to that point, it was already there.

I went back to the department and told Sgt. Wolfe that Fritsche agreed to sell me some reds, and I could probably save the department money because I was sure he would sell them to me at his cost.

"You did good, kid," he said happily.

Did I? I didn't feel so good. I felt rather blue about the whole thing.

A week later, the sergeant summoned me to his office. "Alright. Here's what you do." He instructed me to take the marked money and when the quantity and amount was agreed upon, to pay him with it. I had to sign a receipt for the money.

"How come the money is marked?" I asked, never having it done this way before.

"Don't worry about that. Just do your part," he ordered. It

must have been a new technique to prove the case in court, I assumed.

I walked across the street to the Marguerite Apartments, dreading my role. Wait a minute. Marked money! Why did he give me marked money? What difference did it make? I then realized I was being set up, too. Once I made the buy, they'd have to arrest him on the spot and the money he had on him, beyond a reasonable doubt, had to have come from me. It would front me immediately. Instead of making the case and obtaining a warrant, it would be a "buy and bust," and the sergeant didn't even tell me. What is this? Why give me up so soon? What was he trying to prove? To put an end to any doubts anyone in the department may have had about me? Lucky for Richie Fritsche, the department didn't repair the old listening device I tried to use in Manteca at the Taco Bell.

Richie and his girlfriend greeted me warmly, as usual, offered me a beer and we sat on the floor. His stereo played the Youngbloods tune, "Get Together".

"You still want them reds, bro'?" he asked.

I paused. A painful silence followed.

"Richie," I said slowly. He looked at me askance. "You better leave. You better leave as soon as you can," I said with much relief. "Don't give me those reds. They know what you're doing. If you stay, you're going to get busted. Trust me." He looked at me with some confusion, not knowing if I was serious or joking around. I didn't smile. His look turned solemn.

"I hear you," he finally said.

"I have to go. Take care of yourself," I told him with all sincerity. "Good luck to both of you." He shook my hand and his girlfriend hugged me, pressing her body close to mine. Ah! That patchouli scent!

I strolled back across the street, wondering if I could pull it off. I had to. My face gave me away. The sergeant squinted at me sternly, smoking a cigarette. I couldn't look him in the eye. "Did you get them? Did you score?"

"No. Something was different...something spooked him. He said he couldn't get any." I felt like I was stammering my words. He kept squinting at me. "I don't know. He just treated me differently. I don't think he trusts me anymore."

"You don't think so, huh?" He asked, blowing smoke.

"No, I really don't." I didn't like having to lie to him. Outside of making me do these undercover operations, I liked him. I thought he was a compassionate cop. "What now?"

"Don't worry about it now," he said, smashing his cigarette forcefully in an ashtray. "You did what you could. I'll let you know."

Before he left, I asked him, "what about the other guys? What will they think of me now? What about 'Horse Latitudes'?"

"Hell with 'em. What do you care? Just keep doing your job, and everything will work out," he smiled at me.

My head became a swirling maelstrom, like a light show in a rock concert. What was he pulling on me? Did those guys really say what he said they said, or was he using a psychological ploy and those were the thoughts he wanted me to think. A while ago, it mattered that I prove myself to the guys, and now he's telling me to hell with them, their opinions mean nothing. But he did have "Horse Latitudes," but wait--maybe he was the one who found it and kept it to manipulate me. The sergeant didn't know everything, but even with his limited experience as a narcotics cop, he did know human nature, he knew my naiveté and capitalized on that to control me. But to what end? Now it started to make sense. The kindly Police Chief was soon to retire and imminent promotions were a source of much brutality from those jockeying for position. If he could use me to nail this guy from the Bay Area, the publicity he would receive in a small town would put him at an advantage. He was using me to use Fritsche, exploiting my friendship, but also exploiting my loyalty and respect I had for him as my sergeant, my mentor, to the point of perhaps lying to me. But then I exploited my own respect and loyalty to him by warning Richie. Who betrayed whom?

The next day, Fritsche's apartment was empty. He even took things that didn't belong to him. I was glad for him, but I was more confused about my role within the department. I withdrew and became more reticent, then thought that might be taken as a sign of drug use. I couldn't play this game, but I knew I couldn't quit, either.

Sixteen

With Richie gone, things became a little more normal. Working the graveyard shift, my portable radio softly played Van Morrison's "TB Sheets." The phone was quiet, hardly any radio traffic except for the officers checking out for a break at Reb's Donut Shop. My paperwork was done, so I thumbed through the package of arrest warrants. Another dispatcher was assigned the task of processing incoming warrants, mostly traffic, and then filing them in brown, manila envelopes near the dispatch desk in case an officer asked for a warrants check on someone they had detained. This was still the Stone Age as far as police technology went. I liked looking through the warrants because occasionally there was one for someone I knew, someone I went to high school with who didn't pay their traffic fine and now it went to warrant, meaning they could be arrested.

Thumbing through them, something did look familiar--my home address! What was my home address doing on a traffic warrant? Looking closer, I saw the name was exactly like mine, except the first letter of the last name was off, an "S" instead of "R", therefore, it was filed under "S". This was odd! I opened the envelope and found the arrest warrant was for me! My heart stopped. Sgt. Wolfe did this! He was going to have me arrested because he found out I had smoked a joint a couple of years ago, or that I tipped off Richie Fritsche. I better run! When reason took over, I perused the warrant and read it was issued by the San Francisco Municipal Court, Traffic Division. What the--?

I checked to make sure no one else was in the department. The warrant was for a traffic violation I committed when I visited The City a few months back with my friends. I turned right at a "No Right Turn" sign and forgot all about it. The bail was $69, which I could forfeit as the fine, or post it and contest the ticket in court. There was another option. I couldn't afford the $69 and I didn't want to go to San Francisco to fight it. I kept the warrant, shoving it back in its envelope and stuffing the envelope in my pants. I then took the corresponding index card with my misspelled name and tucked it in my pocket, thus destroying all the evidence the warrant ever existed, at least within my own department. With the millions of warrants San Francisco issues, who would miss one little traffic warrant? It could have been misfiled, which it was, or lost in the mail. Who knows?

This quiet night seemed to last forever and finally, the daybreak began to beam. I went out the front door of the department, propped it open with my back and watched it rise. The birds chirped relentlessly, as though welcoming the warming sun. I enjoyed their clatter, and in the distance the sound of a garbage truck moaned. From the other side of town on a still day, the smell of the sewer farm mixed with the smells from the Holly Sugar plant and the Heinz 57 factory wafted through the air. I loved the smell of my town in the morning. It smelled like...no other town in America: Tracy, California. There was something mystical, something majestic about this time of day, the period between darkness and the first dash of day. Not a soul around, a great time to feel the wonderful openness of being alone, a time to have my own soul experience:

Be yourself and live a little,
Don't be afraid of the people who belittle our lives;
Your fellow man may surprise you
(The Iron Butterfly: Soul Experience)

Better not write that down. My soul was ripped by a repressed desire to be something, to do something I knew not what. The truth was like love to me, elusive and frightening. Though I stood in the open air, freed from confinement, my soul recessed deep within my Fortress of Solitude. A stray cat ran across the street chased by another. The whir of a passing car engine caught my attention, and when I glanced to the corner, I caught sight of the familiar light green and white van of the U.S. Border Patrol passing by. Probably heading towards the fields. What business did I have of being a cop? I was guilty of a felony because I smoked some grass, I transported a controlled substance across the county line when my friend bought the purple haze in San Francisco, I obstructed justice because I told the hippy to go back to San Francisco, and now there was a warrant for my arrest stuffed in my pants. I belonged in jail. I was a disgrace to the uniform, even though it was only a dispatcher's, but the symbol of its veracity meant the same, and the Republic, for which it stands, expected nothing less than integrity.

Yes, I was worthless, I was nothing, but then my ears heard a tune by my favorite band radiating, barely audible, from my tiny portable radio. I rushed inside to turn it up so I wouldn't miss it and returned to the dawn. Yes, that was it. I had an epiphany! The Rolling Stones was my salvation. Music was my deliverance. I could be a cop, and a good one, too.

Just as all the cops are criminals
And all the sinners saints,
As head is tails, just call me Lucifer,
For I'm in need of some restraint
(The Rolling Stones: Sympathy for the Devil)

I was ready to take the oath. I heard the rumbling engine of a patrol car pull into the lot, shattering the sounds of silence. It was nearing the end of my shift; I better go make some coffee for the oncoming day shift. I returned to my dispatch console, enlightened by the music of the Stones over my little radio. I better turn it down before anyone hears it.

SEVENTEEN

The summer of my 21st year was quite eventful. Two friends from the department, another dispatcher and an officer, spent a weekend at the Santa Clara County Fairgrounds in San Jose, California. The Northern California Folk Rock Festival featured some of the biggest names in rock and folk music. It was a three-day event similar to the Woodstock Festival back East. Jimi Hendrix, Led Zeppelin, Jefferson Airplane, Muddy Waters, The Animals, Santana and many others all in one weekend. We must have been in heaven, man! My two friends shared similar tastes in music and the style of the times. The times, yes, they were a-changing.

We spent the night in sleeping bags, enjoying the people, music, vibes and culture. There were plenty of drugs, but none of us indulged, opting for beer from a nearby tavern. During one of the nights, our peaceful slumber was disturbed by the sound of heavy metal thunder, the roaring of Harley Davidson motorcycles as members of the Hells Angels drove through the fairgrounds, checking things out. There was talk amongst the concert goers that the Hells Angels were there to act as security, which puzzled my friend, Mike, the police officer, since he knew the reputation of the outlaw motorcycle gang. When the concert resumed, the Hells Angels were nowhere in sight, which drew a collective sigh of relief from us. If there was an incident, how would at least 3 police employees from a small town have reacted? Fortunately, the question never arose.

Being of age, I also passed the department's police exam and was placed on the eligibility list, meaning within 2 two years, if an opening came up, I would be hired as a full time police officer. I continued work as a dispatcher and even tried to take a class here and there at the Junior College. I was excited to hear that the Rolling Stones were going to have a concert at the Altamont Speedway just outside my town and I tried every which way to attend, but my shift assignment was the graveyard shift, so it broke my heart not to see the Stones who were so close. I drove out to the Altamont just to check things out, but the flow of traffic nearly caused the freeway to shut down. The town was in an uproar as many of the hippies attending the concert came to Tracy for food, gas, and relief. There were hippies all over the place, generating an influx of calls of "hippy type subjects" hanging around, but not much could be done about it. Cool!

I was disturbed to hear the concert ended in tragedy when what should have been a rocking good time resulted in the death of a young man by a Hells Angel, who were providing security for that concert. It was the beginning of the end of the love generation. The trial and convictions of the Manson family for the gruesome Tate-LaBianca murders put an emphatic end to that memorable period in history. Seeing its demise made me blue.

As history passed, so did the people of my life. Richie, the fake surfer, moved to Roseville, outside of Sacramento, with his parents, met a sweetheart and married. Shelley's boyfriend returned from his military obligation and a tour in Vietnam, but I'll never forget my voyage to the Enchanted Forest. Head was just Head. He got a job at the Holly Sugar Mill and we stayed in touch, often going to concerts and to the Oakland Coliseum when the Yankees were in town.

I graduated from the police academy in 1971, the same year San Francisco's Fillmore Auditorium shut down. I attended the last show featuring Credence Clearwater Revival and Santana. I was particularly fond of Santana, for a rocker with my heritage made it big in the music scene. I never told anyone in the department of my attendance at the San Francisco rock shows, fearing being further labeled a hippy, a doper--everything but what I was, a young man exploring and enjoying life.

My first official night as a policeman was a blend of pride, fear, anxiety and little bit of confidence. After all, I had spent six weeks at the Stockton Police training academy. I went to the underground, cavernous basement of the old police facility to change into my uniform and noticed a note taped to my locker. I was startled when I read, "Affirmative Action hire" and "Mexican!" underneath it. I then became conscious that no other officer was of color, not a Black or Hispanic amongst them. Not to be intimidated, I simply tossed the note on the ground and dressed.

Swing shift. The sergeant, two other officers and myself were given a briefing and I took the usual jokes and putdowns afforded any rookie on his first night; some good natured kidding. I thought what if one of the other patrol officers put the note on my locker, but I didn't say anything. I was assigned my beat, the South side of Tracy, populated by minorities and businesses. Anxious to prove my mettle, I was eager to make my first arrest. The South side usually generated the most calls and activity, so a nice, easy arrest would calm my nerves. I looked for a drunk, easy to find on the South side. Sure enough, a drunk fell from a doorway from one of the many cantinas south of the railroad tracks.

I reported a 647f (drunk) on my radio and checked him out. I helped him up from the ground.

"You alright old-timer?" I asked. Before he could answer, I

told him, "Looks like you've had too much to drink. Come with me." I led him by the arm to my patrol car and was about to tell him he was under arrest for public intoxication, when I noticed he reminded me of the old Mexican drunk who was beaten up in his cell when I was a dispatcher. I looked back and saw some his partners had come out of the bar to check on him, but when they saw me, they quickly ducked back, hoping I didn't see them.

I changed my mind. "Can one of you guys get your partner home before I take him to jail?" I asked no one in particular. "Unless you guys want to join him."

Two sober men stepped forward and grabbed him, leading him back inside the bar. I cleared my call and continued patrol duties in the South side of Tracy. The dispatch radio crackled with my call number and sent me to a theft report in the welfare projects. A couple got into a beef and the boyfriend, a fiancé, took off with her diamond ring, or at least she said it was diamond.

"That little bastard! That's my ring. I want it back. I want him arrested!" A large, hysterical white woman shouted. I recognized her as "Shotgun Sally." She was notorious around these parts for an incident when she leveled a shotgun at an old sergeant during a confrontation at her house a few years back. She was arrested and served her time, but she was still volatile.

"Relax, mom. Let me handle this," a younger, petite woman told her. "Officer, Julio pushed me and took my ring. It was my mom's. Can you get it back? She's going crazy."

"That little bastard...I'll kill him!" The mother shouted again. Knowing her reputation, I had no doubt she just might.

"Relax, Sally. Calm down, please," I ordered her. "Just tell me what happened." I got the story, the description of the ring and a description of Julio, while she was still yelling.

"Goddamn ring cost me a two-hundred and fifty dollars. I want his ass in jail!"

"Yes, ma'am. We'll take care of it," I assured her.

"Well you better, or I will!" She was serious.

"You don't have any shotguns, do you Sally?" I asked, trying to smile. She just flipped me off and walked away.

"Where do you think Julio might go?" I asked the daughter.

"He's probably down by the schoolyard, playing basketball with the home boys."

A short while later, I saw Julio walking down the street. I recognized him as a guy I went to school with. I stopped the car to detain him, not arrest him. You have to make that distinction for court so you don't lose the case, which I learned in the academy. To detain someone meant you simply stopped their movement temporarily while you questioned them. They were free to leave of their own accord. Once you prohibit their movement or usurp their freedom, it's technically an arrest causing other dynamics to come into place. I greeted him, and he was surprised to see me in a uniform driving a police car.

"You're a cop?" I heard that often my first year.

"Duh!" I sarcastically responded. "Julio. Your girlfriend, Maureen, tells me you've got something of hers that doesn't belong to you. Is that right?"

He looked me up and down. "Hey! Aren't you supposed to give me my rights or something before you can ask me questions like that?"

"Oh, a sidewalk lawyer, eh?" The guy was a wimp, but he was right. He kind of ticked me off, which I shouldn't have let happen. "Yeah, okay, I suppose you're right," I acquiesced. I read him his rights and then almost started laughing because I sounded so phony, like I was on TV or something.

"That's good," he approved. "Now you can start the questions again."

"Now wait a minute. I'm the cop here. I'll give the orders, dig? I mean, you understand?"

"Okay, okay. Don't get uptight, man," he countered.

"Hey! Don't you 'man' me," I said, raising my voice. I think he was starting to sass me, but I paused. I was letting this uniform and badge stuff consume me already. I felt myself acting and talking like those guys I didn't want to act and talk like. I remembered the lesson of Sgt. Wolfe. Just be yourself, he counseled.

"Let's start over, Julio," I said. "Okay?"

"Fine with me. You're the one starting to use police brutality."

"Police bruta--what? Julio!" I was getting frustrated. "Julio! You been watching too much TV. Look. Let's start from the beginning." I tried again. "Maureen says you stole her ring and pushed her. Now I didn't see any marks or bruises on her, so you may be okay with that, but the law says if I have reasonable cause to believe a felony has been committed, then I have the right to question and search for evidence of that crime." I sounded pretty official. "You understand so far?"

"Yeah."

"Now I have reasonable cause to believe you committed a violation of section four, eighty-seven P. C.; Grand Theft, in as much as the ring has a value in excess of $200. Now--"

"Okay, okay," he interrupted. "Stop the Joe Friday routine. Here!" He reached into his pocket and gave me the ring.

This was easy. "I'm sorry, Julio, but you're under arrest."

"Okay. I know."

I opened the back door of the car and he slid in. "How long you been a cop?" he asked, as I drove him to the department for booking.

"One day," I answered. "This is it. Six weeks in the academy, first day on the street.

"That's cool. You like it?"

"Yeah, it's okay. I spent the last couple of years or so dispatching..." Suddenly, I remembered something. "Guess what, man? I forgot something," I said, pulling over to the side of the road. I stopped the car, got out, and opened the back door.

"You have to get out. I have to search you."

"Search me? I already gave you the ring," he protested.

"I know. But I have to search you for weapons and stuff."

"Weapons? Me? Come on, you know me. I ain't got no weapons."

"I know, I know. But I have to follow policy. Besides, it's a good habit for me to get into. You never know."

He got out and assumed the position. I patted him down according to procedure. Clean. I retrieved my handcuffs from its holder at the back of my gun belt.

"What are you doing now?" He asked, fearfully.

"I gotta put cuffs on you. I forgot that, too."

"Now come on! This is getting ridiculous. What am I, some sort of a criminal?" He started to back away. "You know me. I ain't going nowhere. I ain't fighting."

"Look, Julio. I know and I'm sorry. But I have to. It's, you know, procedure." I was starting to feel stupid because I could have had him ride in the front seat with me, drove him to jail and booked him; no problem. "I won't put 'em on tight and I'll take 'em off as soon as we get there. If I don't, my boss will yell at me for violating policy."

"You promise?"

"Yes, Julio, I promise. Now let's get this over with!" I clicked the cuffs on him while passing people slowed and watched. This wouldn't have been such a spectacle if I did this when I first arrested him, but it was almost like giving a guy I knew in school a ride home rather than arresting a felon. My first felony arrest. Pretty uneventful.

At the police station, Julio gave me a full statement admitting his involvement and saying he was sorry, that he didn't mean to push Maureen down. He had nothing to hide. His girlfriend decided not to press charges as long as she got her mom's ring back.

"Okay, Julio. You're free to go. Maureen's not mad anymore. Just stay away from her for awhile," I warned him.

"Can I sue you?" he asked.

"Sue me? For what?"

"False arrest."

"False arrest? That was no false arrest. Look, I had probable cause…just get out of here, Julio, before I find something to book you on!"

"Okay. Can you give me a ride home?"

"Julio! Just go home! Bye!"

"See ya," he said, finally leaving.

This police stuff was going to be easy.

After completing my paperwork, I went back to my car, but before getting in, I noticed the back seat had become dislodged where Julio had been sitting. How did that happen? I wondered. I opened the back door to replace the seat and noticed something underneath it. What? I retrieved a baggie of marijuana. Why that little son-of-a-bitch! He ditched this on me. I got a bit queasy. Had I handcuffed him when I was supposed to, he wouldn't have been able to ditch it. When I got him back to the department, during the booking search, I would have discovered it and had a righteous charge. He got me. It was my own fault. Deep inside, I had to laugh at myself. I was still that naïve idiot who got burned at the Taco Bell on my first undercover buy. I made it a point to tell Julio he got me this time, but next time, I'd be much wiser. No one knew of my blunder except Julio and me, and Julio wasn't about to say anything. I ditched the baggie in the trash and resumed my patrol duties.

EIGHTEEN

The streets of the city slept as my car slowly prowled the back alleys, business districts and tranquil residential areas. I loved the stillness of the night, the few who were out after midnight, the muggers, buggers and thieves, but they're cool people because Tracy was my home. "Dirty Water," by The Standells, resonated through my mind. The south side bars were busy tonight. Mexican music blared through the cheap loudspeakers placed outside the bars to attract customers. Beat one was my comfort zone, where my people lived, thrived, played and died. The town was divided into two sectors, called beats, with an officer assigned a particular beat. On weekends, it was divided into three beats. I was usually assigned beat one, mainly because my shift sergeants thought because of my heritage, I could relate to those across the tracks. South side was predominantly comprised of Mexicans and Blacks, with a sprinkling of welfare projects and the demon that thrived in the area of economic depression and despair: heroin.

I did relate well with the South side, for I grew up in areas not so dissimilar. Everyone deserved to be treated with dignity and respect, regardless of their ethnic or socio-economic standing. My hippy ideals held fast. Nicknames, derogatory and otherwise, were common within police cultures, so it didn't surprise me when I heard myself referred to as "nigger-lover" or "Mexican sympathizer."

Mr. Sun hadn't made its appearance this warm summer morning when I spotted the familiar green and white vans of the United States Border Patrol sneaking into town. I hated it when they came, for it meant a raid! The illegal aliens, those south of the border, down Mexico way, the ones who toiled in the surrounding fields, washed dishes and cleaned the toilets in the city's restaurants, and worked long and hard in the tortilla factories were fair game. They had no rights. They were not citizens of the United States of America. They were the easiest arrests for tough guy cops, even easier than public drunks. Just walk into any one of the town's Mexican taverns and start asking for green cards, or "tienes papeles (do you have your {immigration} papers)?" Gone! You're outta there. To jail, to the Border Patrol and a free ride back to Mexico.

One slow evening, one of my sergeants ordered me to walk the area of beat one catering to the Mexican clientele, near the south side tracks, and start checking for green cards and arrest those who didn't have one. He needed to show some activity on his watch. He wanted the arrest register full of names, regardless of the charges, so the brass would be impressed and he would be seen as a motivator of men. Sound management philosophy.

There were two cantinas across the street from each other, the Guadalajara Club and El Gato Negro (The Black Cat), blaring Mexican tunes from their tinny speakers. These were the lively spots for the laborers; plenty of cold beer, good, cheap authentic Mexican food, hot chicas and fights. When there's lots of beer and Mexicans, fights will surely follow. It's in our blood. The fights were generally harmless, but occasionally someone gets stabbed and the guy who did the stabbing, if he wasn't arrested, fled to Mexico until he thought the heat died down, if his victim didn't die first. If the knife wielding perpetrator happened to be at the scene when the police were called, he'd be arrested and charged with section 245 P.C. of the California Penal Code; Assault with a deadly weapon. The charges were invariably dropped once he was released to the Border Patrol for being an illegal alien.

Following the sergeant's orders, I flipped a coin, which he didn't order, and went to the Guadalajara Club. The music was lively, cute girls were in abundance and once a cop was spotted, everyone tried to act like they were invisible. I chose one at random who, not surprisingly, didn't have his green card. "Let's go," I ordered, and he meekly complied. I brought him to the station for booking.

"I see you got a wetback, eh?" the sergeant said smiling.

"I no 'wetbock' " the alien said in broken English.

"No se, es hombre muy tonto," I said to the alien in broken Spanish, meaning, 'Don't mind him, he's a stupid man.'

The sergeant, named Dumas, didn't understand Spanish, but with a dumb grin he asked, "What did you tell him?"

"I just told him to be respectful," I answered.

I took the alien to the booking area for processing and emptied his pockets. Of course he didn't have any identification, but he did have five-hundred dollars in cash. He told me he'd let me have the money if I let him go, probably remembering how things were done with the police in Mexico. It was early in the summer and there was plenty of work to do in the fields. His family back home desperately needed the money. He wasn't playing on my sympathy, he was telling the truth.

I told him I had to go to the bathroom and I'd be back in shortly to complete his booking. Before I left him, I motioned with my eyes towards the outside, then looked at his pile of cash and nodded my head to indicate he better pick it up. His eyes told me he understood, but he seemed hesitant. It's a little known secret that Mexicans are masters of body language. He knew what I meant, but he seemed afraid that if he tried to escape, I might shoot him in the back, or something. I gave him one more sincere look, nodded my head and walked slowly from the cell area, through the tunnel leading to the department's main lobby.

There was no one else in the proximity, except for the dispatcher. The sergeant was downstairs reading a newspaper in his favorite reading place, the toilet.

I walked into the dispatch room and chatted with the obese dispatcher Karl. Karl wanted to be a cop in the worst way, but his weight prevented him from getting hired, so this was as close as he could get.

"How's it going Karl?" He was busy processing traffic warrants. He was the one who goofed up on my traffic warrant, misspelling my name and misfiling the warrant.

"Fine, fine," he said, busily. "When you get done, will you pick up my dinner?" The officers had to pick up his dinner every night and bring it to him at the dispatch desk. There wasn't much variation in Karl's dinner--hamburgers, hamburgers and more hamburgers. On paydays he would splurge and order hamburger steak. With his size and weird looking moustache, I could have sworn Popeye's Wimpy was modeled after him.

"Sure, Karl. Is there any coffee?"

"I think it's gone. Want me to make some?" he asked. The only thing bigger than Karl was his heart. He tried to please everyone and just loved policemen.

"That's okay. You look busy. I'll do it." I walked around the corner to the hallway leading to the storage closet housing the coffee and made a fresh pot. Oh, yeah. My prisoner. I walked back to the cells.

"Hey, what the...? What happened?" I yelled, knowing Karl had the audio monitor on at the dispatch desk. "Where'd he go?"

Karl came lumbering back towards the cells. "Who?"

"My prisoner! He's gone!" I pretended concern.

I heard more footsteps pounding up the stairway. Sgt. Dumas was putting his gun belt back on. "What happened?" he screamed.

"His prisoner's escaped!" Karl bellowed.

"What?" asked Dumas, incredulously. "Where?"

"Yeah. He's gone," I said. "I stepped out for just a moment and he split."

Dumas ran from the building, jumped in his car and screeched towards the street to search for the escapee. He radioed the other officer of the escape and they combed the downtown area with, as police lingo goes, "negative results." I sipped my coffee and told Karl to phone his order and I'd pick it up. "Order me a hamburger, too, Karl. I'm kinda hungry myself."

After his fruitless search, Dumas lectured me for not following procedure and allowing a prisoner to escape. He told me it would be noted on my evaluation.

"I understand. I'll be more careful in the future," I told him with remorse. "But I suddenly had to go to the bathroom. How was I to know?"

"You should have just locked him in a cell until you were through and then you could have finished the booking procedures," he counseled wisely.

"Yeah. I never thought of that. Thanks, Sarge. I'm sorry." He smiled, knowing he had successfully completed an employee counseling session, which he would make known to the brass.

On this morning, there were two Border Patrol vans. They were going to clean house, I surmised, because of the stealth they employed sneaking into the South side. Usually, they check in at the police department as a courtesy, but today they must have been serious as they just rolled in ready to do business. Normally, they come to town, check in then go to a few places on south side, grab a couple of them before they woke up and head back to the main office in Stockton with their catch--non-tax paying, economy draining, society burdening outsiders, not worthy of respect and propriety. I saw one of the vans parked in an alley between the bars and the tortilla factory.

Knowing they were sneaky, I turned off my headlights and quietly cruised up to the van where a Border Patrol Agent was standing outside. His function was to nab anyone who ran into the alley while the others made their raids in the basements of the homeowners. The homes on the south side had large basements and the owners would partition them off with plywood making individual living quarters, if they can be called such, charging exorbitant prices. Others were more sympathetic to their underground status and gave them a fair deal, but they were still making good money off the illegals, none of which was reported to the IRS.

"Big raid, huh?" I asked the agent. I recognized him as being here on previous raids, a balding, pot-bellied, middle aged man. I always thought it funny that these white guys spoke much more fluent Spanish than me, but before he could answer, I heard shouting and commotion coming from the basements next to the tortilla factory, Mi Ranchito. A breakout! The agent took off running in that direction while I drove back into the street, keeping my lights off, and parked a block down the street. I saw Mexicans running every which way, some still in their shorts. I then saw the squatty agent running from the ally into the street towards my car.

"You see any?" he asked, panting for breath.

"Didn't see any come this way."

"If you see any, grab 'em and let us know," he said and disappeared back into the alley.

"Sure," I said as I drove off. I saw a couple of shadowy figures duck behind a car in another alley and thought about my summers in high school when I had to work the tomato fields for a job.

My shift ended at 7 AM. On my way home, I saw the Border Patrol van in front of me as it stopped at a red light. It was full of brown-skinned, weather-beaten laborers, the illegal Mexicans. A successful raid. I hoped that the guy I let go, I mean escape, wasn't among them.

NINETEEN

My graveyard shift assignment ended, and it was my turn to work days, 7 AM to 3 PM, the shift I dreaded. The older guys liked it because they could live normally for a month or two, but I hated having to get up so early and nothing interesting ever happened. Cold burglary reports, enforcing traffic laws and writing accident reports were not my idea of police work. Sundays were the worst. The town nursed its collective hangover in churches which were about equal in number to the bars and taverns, people were in the park picnicking with their families, many were in Lake Tahoe for the weekend, not much going on here, so one officer and a dispatcher were usually assigned Sunday day shift.

The radio sputtered and my friendly dispatcher sent me to a house on south side as the occupant reported a drunk passed out on his back lawn. I pulled into the alleyway bordering the house and recognized it as one of those with the basement made into makeshift rooms for illegal aliens. A guy was lying flat on his back, and as I got closer, I saw he wasn't drunk--he was dead. He had that ashen grey look the dead popularly wear when in this condition for a while. His lifeless eyes were half-open. For a moment, I thought he was looking at me. His right hand bore laceration wounds on each of his fingers as though someone slashed a knife across them. A puncture wound was clearly visible over his heart, but very little blood had coagulated, meaning he must have been stabbed somewhere and made it this far before he collapsed to the reaper.

Death made itself known to me. He hovered near, watching me. The eerie stillness became oppressive as I breathed deeply for air. I looked at the dead man and blessed myself; maybe I was blessing him for I was still alive, poor soul. I saw droplets of blood leading from the corpse to the to the small, squared cement walkway at the basement of the house. Yes, this appeared to be a murder, I deducted. The word 'appeared' is the most overused verb in the police culture. I learned I couldn't make judgments by what you see, you can only report what you see, or else a defense attorney would make you look like a babbling idiot.

'I saw blood on the body,' I might say.

'Officer. How do you know it was blood? Are you a forensic specialist? Are you a doctor? Did you take samples?'

'No sir.'

'Then I ask that the statement be stricken from the record,' the attorney would say, and the judge would agree.

'Refrain from making statements of which you have no expertise.'

'Yes, your honor.'

Then I would say, 'I saw *what appeared* to be blood on the body.'

'Then what did you see, officer?'

'I saw a hole in the shirt of the dead man...' but before I could finish,

'Objection, your honor! Again, officer. Are you a doctor? Are you in a position to pronounce people dead?'

'No, sir. I'm not.'

'Then I move to have that stricken from the record. Your honor, please...' the attorney would plead.

'Sustained. Officer?' the judge would peer at me over his glasses.

'Yes, sir. I saw a hole in the shirt of *what appeared to* be a dead man.'

Yes, this man appeared dead; he appeared to be on the lawn of a house on what appeared to be a sunny day. He appeared to resemble the man I let escape from the illegal immigration charge, and I appeared to know what I was doing. Of course, I didn't because I never investigated a homicide before; therefore, I had the dispatcher summon the off duty Detective Sergeant, who worked Monday through Friday during the day.

The Detective Sergeant, Charles Guevara, arrived shortly. He was a short, meticulous man of Hispanic descent, but he was lighter complexioned than me. He spoke fluent Spanish, in his 40's and had been at the department much longer than I. He also began as a dispatcher and was then put directly in charge of the small Detective unit. He spent no time on patrol. He was resented by others because he lacked patrol experience, but I liked him because he treated everyone with dignity and respect, particularly those who didn't speak English. I felt that was the true reason he was disliked. He was a Mexican, a spic, a greaseball, a wetback. I figured I would learn something from him.

Because I was working days, I was able to work with him as he investigated the murder. I came in on my days off without charging the city overtime, because I wanted to help and learn from him. I felt an obligation, too, because this was the guy I had arrested and let escape. I felt a sense of guilt for had I completed the booking and turned him over to the Border Patrol, he might be alive today. I expressed my sentiments to the Detective Sergeant.

"I wouldn't fret over it," he told me. "Enough time has passed that he would have found his way back here anyway and ended up just as dead."

"You really think so?" I asked with hope.

"No doubt. The Mexican version of the Underground

Railroad is alive and well, so it doesn't take them long to get back." I felt reassured. "Let's try to give this guy some history and maybe we can get a clue as to what happened."

The Sergeant was a whiz at Mexican culture in Tracy, California. He had many contacts, not only in town, but throughout the state. In no time, he identified the murdered Mexican manual laborer as Diego Ruiz from Culiacan, Mexico. He was thirty years old, had a wife and two children. Sgt. Guevara learned that his wife stayed with her mother while he worked during tomato harvesting season was over, usually late September, early October, depending on Mr. Sun. Work was good in the summer with thousands of dollars to be made for the illegals, who worked from sunup to sundown, every day. They may take an occasional Sunday off, but work was all that mattered. I went with the Sergeant to where I had found the body. It was a house near the tracks bordering the south side, on 6th Street, the same street as the cantinas and cheap hotels catering to the braceros. Diego Ruiz lived in a partitioned section of the basement, small rooms separated by thin plywood sheets. There were eight rooms, four on each side, separated by a thin walkway running from the front of the basement to the back with a single hanging light bulb midway, the only light shared by the brown, ghostly occupants. Makeshift doors with a cheap padlock on the inside were the only security. The owner charged each occupant $80 a month, cash, always cash. At the back where I found Diego was a small toilet and a basin used for washing, shaving, and drink water.

Diego's room was tiny. An old mattress rested on the floor, a calendar from the tortilla factory hung at an odd angle on the wall, five years old. Diego couldn't have known what day it was when he died, for all the days fused into one for these guys. In a corner behind his mattress was an old coffee can. Sgt. Guevara learned this was Diego's bank, where he kept his money after each day's pay. A friend of Diego's told the Sergeant he often kept as much as a thousand dollars there. He knew because Diego expressed fear of being robbed. We couldn't establish if robbery was the motive for his death and the killer took the money, or if the money was taken by one of the other tenants after he died. Perhaps the homeowner himself took the money. The laborers dealt strictly in cash, for they could not get a bank account, credit card, or any luxury afforded U.S. citizens.

A thousand dollars was a lot of money for these guys, the Sergeant told me. I remembered working in the fields during the summers of high school and how hard it must have been to earn that much, even after the exploitive farmers deducted for their so-called taxes, as they did me when I picked tomatoes. That much would have gone a long way and provided much for Diego Ruiz's family. His family must have been proud and missed him terribly as he worked obediently in the dusty fields surrounding my town. I remembered his death pose and imagined him a good husband, proud father and a hard worker, but here in the United States he was nobody--nothing. He couldn't be anybody. He worked anonymously and paid his taxes, but he paid them to nobody.

After his daily toil, he flitted in and out of the local bars, bordering South side, like a ghost looking for its meaning, looking for its soul. He mingled amongst the other brown ghosts, invisible to the rest of the town, the side of town the rest of the community ignored, ripped off, disrespected, exploited, or any combination thereof, and, in this case, murdered. Diego died a nobody. It was some time before he was identified, so he was initially listed as "Juan Doe," an unknown, unidentified Mexican male. He was given an indigent burial by the county, no one to recite a eulogy, no known relatives, a life unknown. I prayed that he was able to at least mail his money to his family in Mexico before his killer, or anyone else, had a chance to steal it.

I was impressed how Sgt. Guevara conducted his investigation. Many potential witnesses were reluctant to come forward, fearing deportment to Mexico, but when he assured them that he wasn't concerned about their legal status, they began to tell what they saw. He talked to them almost as a friend, rather than a cop talking to witnesses. Not only that, but I was able to accompany him to the bars where an adjacent kitchen fixed meals for the laborers, authentic, homemade Mexican meals. I discovered an elderly Mexican cook who made tamales and each time we were there to talk to witnesses, she couldn't give us enough. The sergeant was more professional than I, so he politely refused, but he didn't mind if I imbibed, which I greedily did. Man! These were fantastic. Thick with masa, meaty and juicy, almost like I remembered them at my uncle's restaurant in Dallas. I thought I might enjoy being a detective someday.

I heard much resentment from other officers that the sergeant was "milking" the investigation, that he was catering to "them" because he was a Mexican, and he had his little Mexican sidekick, meaning me. Diego wasn't a citizen, hence a non-contributing, non-productive member of society. Who cares about the death of a nobody? Why waste any more tax-payers' money to investigate a crime no one cared about anyway? If Sgt. Guevara cared, then so did I. I felt kind of cool because I fantasized that he was the Cisco Kid and I was Pancho, his sidekick, from the old TV western, and we were solving crimes for the good of all people. Actually, it was the sergeant who solved the crime.

Sgt. Guevara was able to identify the killer and secure a warrant for his arrest, but it was all in vain. The guy split to Mexico shortly after he plunged a knife into the heart of Diego Ruiz. In police circles, Mexico was like a celestial black hole--you were sucked into it and ceased to exist. There was nothing. Sgt. Guevara identified the killer as Manuel Munoz, himself murdered years later in Salinas.

The farm laborers, the braceros, were receiving a lot of attention these days, and not because of an anonymous murder, but because a courageous man felt it was time they were recognized as human beings. Caeser Chavez formed a union to represent the interests of the field workers, the United Farm Workers. Health insurance, working contracts and other rights afforded most workers were obtainable, much to the chagrin of landowners who exploited the laborers for decades, fattening their crops and personal wealth in the process. For the first time, the workers had a shared sense of dignity; they had an outlet for their fears, concerns, and even hopes. They just wanted to be treated with the respect and worth afforded any human being who toils for another.

Since my town was always the last to join the latest fad, fashion or farm labors' movements, it was also true for the UFW. A major part of the economy was in the fields, so a strike would be devastating. Indeed, a strike was called against the farmers who employed the Mexican laborers. Caesar Chavez appeared and gave a speech, riling the emotions of his people. The philosophy of the UFW was based on the principles of non-violence championed by Mahatma Gandhi and Dr. Martin Luther King, Jr., so when I was called to assist in crowd control, I felt secure that violence would not prevail.

The city proper had no farming, however, we were called to assist the agency having jurisdiction, the San Joaquin County Sheriff's Department, in the event of disturbances and conflicts. We were issued riot gear, wore face shields, and wielded our batons in threatening gestures against the dueling factions. News reporters and television cameras were in abundance hoping for acts of violence for the evening news. I stood on the borders of the fields ready to advance when the signal was given and contemplated on the absurdity of it all.

It wasn't long ago when I worked in these very fields amongst these very people while they labored intensely, while I did it for fun and a little spending money rather than an actual need to make a living. Now I was supposed to bash their heads in if they made any overt action to assert their previously disregarded rights. These weren't vicious people, I knew, but I was more worried that the us versus them mentality, inherent in police work, would rise to an uncontrollable tidal wave of hostility. Just one person had to make a wrong move and the justification was there to quell the disturbance, meaning a full scale riot could erupt.

Mr. Sun was not very nice today, sending his sizzling beams

into the dusty fields, causing beads of sweat to stream into my eyes, while the odor of warm lettuce, the crop at issue, made me nauseous. I looked along the line of Sheriff Deputies, California Highway patrolmen and us, Tracy Police officers, all hot and bothered. I saw some of their faces gleaming with sweat, under the strain of Mr. Sun, face shields and helmets, furious, frightened, and frenzied, armed with clubs and ready to strike at the first Mexican who gave them the slightest provocation. In this heat, it wouldn't have taken much.

Thankfully, the confrontation ended without conflict. In time, the UFW and Caesar Chavez prevailed, as well they should have. The guys in the department made jokes of a "Mexican uprising" and were hoping to "bash some beaners." Beaners, wetbacks, spics, greasers, names I heard and was identified with. I recalled my first day on the job when the note was found on my locker, adding a new moniker to the rest--"Affirmative Action Hire," or as I was later referred, the token Mexican.

TWENTY

Many of my former schoolmates were thrown in jail for the felony possession of a single joint, one marijuana cigarette. In the late 60's and early 70's, drug use was becoming more fashionable in high school, more of a continuing experimentation and curiosity than a drug epidemic, as many would have us believe, Sgt. Wolfe included. Of all the laws I had to enforce, marijuana possession was the most difficult. I had friends who smoked grass, and I didn't see them as criminals, as long as they kept it from me. The town was small enough that many of the officers knew the families of the kids they stopped for minor traffic violations. As long as the kids weren't drunk and cooperative, it was not uncommon to confiscate the booze and send them on their way with a stern warning. It was effective. The practice was called discretion. I was taught the police had a tremendous amount of discretion when I arrested a county supervisor for drunk driving.

"Sir, would you slowly say your ABC's," I ordered him after I stopped him in residential area and had him perform field sobriety tests. He displayed the "obvious signs of intoxication" fumbling for his license and registration.

"A-B-C-D-X-Y-Z," he slurred, hurriedly, as if I wouldn't notice he missed the entire middle of the alphabet.

"Now, watch me." I demonstrated. "Close your eyes, tilt your head back, extend both arms, and with the index finger of either hand, touch your nose."

He watched attentively, and then did as I asked, as he weaved back and forth. He did fine until he tried to touch his nose, then suddenly reeled backwards, trying to catch his footing so as not to fall, but he continued backwards and fell into the rosebushes of the house. This was too funny. He was gone. I helped him out of the bushes and took him into custody.

At the police station, he blew into the intoxilyzer, the breath machine used to measure the alcohol content. He blew a .22, twice as high as the legal limit back then, which was .10, or one percent of alcohol in the blood, rendering one legally impaired to drive. I completed the booking procedures and allowed him to make a phone call. I had no idea who he was, except a drunk driver.

Less than an hour later, Sgt. Wolfe showed up at the department.

"What are you doing here," I asked. "Can't sleep?"

"I need to talk to you now," he ordered. He pulled me into an office and explained who the drunk was, a county supervisor working on a grant to give the department some government funding. I had to let him go into his custody.

"What about the intoxilyzer record?" I asked. The machine recorded the results and printed it in triplicate.

"Give it all to me, including the dispatch record and don't say anything to anyone."

The drunken supervisor with the government grant left with the sergeant, never once looking at me. So that's how it is, eh? Discretion.

I used the same discretion when I stopped a teen and discovered alcohol. Dumb idiots, I thought. I used discretion when I confiscated their beer and saw marijuana seeds, and roaches, the bare end of a marijuana cigarette, on the floor, pretending not to see them, because that would have given me probable cause to search the car and arrest everyone for a felony.

"You guys better get you butts home before I call your daddies," I commanded. That quickly ended their night.

I identified strongly with the young generation, sharing many of their values, which was often at odds with members of my department. The only means of showing it was by letting my hair grow as long as I could, which was often too long by conventional police standards.

"Get a damn haircut!" Sgt. Wolfe would often yell. My hair was my only remaining means of identifying with my peer group.

"Just who is your peer group?" an officer asked me after a swing shift briefing where we were discussing the change in marijuana laws. He was quite stodgy, in his early 30's, accompanied by another officer assigned the same shift. This one was of the same age, slightly bucked teeth and frog eyes. He thought he'd be cute and answered for me.

"Heads," he said, referring to the slang name given those of the drug culture.

They were publicly challenging me, a clash of values and generations, and since officers my age group were on other shifts, I was left to take up the challenge alone. I felt a bit intimidated, but felt my job performance exceeded theirs, which was muddled by ignorance and the sense of superiority by the oppression of the weak and insignificant. I answered meekly, "anyone who's cool."

"What is cool supposed to mean?" the stodgy one asked, turning towards me as if we were going to go one on one.

The confrontation was on. "Well, it may hard for a couple of dinosaurs like you two, blind to the wave of change flooding our society, to understand, much less cope with." Good answer I thought. The frog-eyed one turned towards me, too. Tough guys, eh?

"Who are you? The new philosopher, the Timothy Leary of the department," he cackled, impressing the stodgy guy.

"No, I'm not. But it would probably be a better department if he were running it." Timothy Leary was the guru of the love generation, the one who advocated LSD use and coined the phrase, 'tune in, turn on, drop out.' I didn't turn on or drop out, but I sure did tune in to the music and good vibes. I could tell that got to them.

"You think the marijuana laws should be changed?" Frog-eyes asked. There was much debate at the time over the marijuana statutes, whether or not they should be decriminalized. The issue would soon result in a major change in legislation. Of course I thought they should be, but do I dare express my opinion? An absurd thought crosses my mind as I was being grilled. A record album called "Have a Marijuana" by David Peel and the Lower East Side, a band out of New York, flashed through my mind. It consisted of raunchy music and explicit lyrics satirizing the rift between the old generation and the new, drug literate generation. It was hilarious. They would probably arrest me just for owning that album!

"Why shouldn't they be?" I boldly asserted. "Do you actually believe an 18-yr. old kid with a joint should share the same jail cell with a guy who killed his wife, or a guy who molested his niece?"

"Sure." The stodgy one answered. "They probably smoked marijuana before they did their crimes." They both broke up with laughter. I could see my argument was going nowhere.

"There's that ignorance I talked about," I asserted as I shook my head. Frog-eyes took offense, but before he could say anything, the intercom blared that the silent alarm had been triggered at the Bank of America, my beat. I ran to my car followed by the other two, who were to be my backup. False alarm, which it usually was. We never finished the argument, but I think I made my point. The times were indeed 'a-changing'!

I co-existed peacefully enough with the other officers, and

the subject was never broached again. We interacted only when necessary to do the job. Professional courtesy, nothing more. The only other problem I encountered during those years had nothing to do with the job. I never learned the value of a dollar and spent whatever I could whenever I could. Life was carefree, until one night changed that forever.

My classes at the junior college were going well as I pursued my associate in arts degree. I had walked to my evening filmmaking class held at the local high school as my car's battery had gone dead. Two of my high school chums were in the same class, and I asked for a ride home after class. Miguel, a lean, athletic Mexican, joined the army from high school and served a tour in Vietnam. He landed a job with the military police at the defense depot, a major employer of Tracy citizens, just outside of town. The other had been a local high school football hero who didn't quite make it on an athletic scholarship at the University of California, Riverside, a powerfully built Portuguese lad named Jorge. He was now driving tractor for a local farmer while attending the junior college extension classes at his old school, Tracy High.

Miguel drove his car out of the parking lot and I noticed a police car near the exit. As we passed it, the car pulled behind us and followed. Then a familiar sight illuminated his car; the patrol car's red lights. He was being pulled over. I knew Miguel and his girlfriend fought, often quite viciously, necessitating a call to the police. I was fortunate not to have had to respond to one of those calls, so I presumed that was the reason for the stop. He couldn't have broken any traffic laws as we had just pulled from the lot. It looked like the patrol car was waiting for him.

"What'd you do, Miguel? Slug Marianne again?" I sarcastically asked him, knowing he would never physically hurt her. He ignored me and pulled over. I recognized the cop as old frog-eyes, but he was in civilian clothes. He leaned over and told Miguel to get out of the car. Another officer was on the passenger side of Miguel's car, an officer I didn't recognize, but I knew he wasn't one of ours. This officer motioned for Jorge to get out. I was still in the back seat, confused, more that they hadn't even seen me yet. I was about to let my presence be known when Frog-eyes reached in under the driver's seat and pulled out a plastic container, the kind used to store a bar of soap. He still hadn't noticed me when he opened the container. I thought I saw a quantity of small, clear plastic bags, each filled with little white tablets. Frog-eyes then saw me and flashed his light in my face.

"Hi, there. What's up?" was all I could think of saying. He turned towards the patrol car and motioned for someone to join him. I looked back and saw it was Sgt. Wolfe, but now he was Lt. Wolfe. His eyes were squinted and he looked sternly, much more than I had even seen him.

He stuck his face to mine. "What the hell are you doing in here?" he demanded.

"I'm just getting a ride home from class." I was starting to get nervous now. "What's all the fuss?"

"Get the hell out!" he shouted. "Do you know what you just did? Do you know what you've done to every officer on this force?"

By now, Frog-eyes had the trunk of Miguel's car open and retrieved a standard sized briefcase. He opened the briefcase and I freaked out from what I saw. It was full of plastic baggies, neatly packaged with weed, obviously to be individually sold. The last time I saw such a sight was in the house of Sergio Macias when I was doing undercover work. I had no such excuse here. Frog-eyes looked at me and smirked. "Your peers, huh?"

Lt. Wolfe walked me to the sidewalk, obviously upset. I saw Miguel and Jorge handcuffed and put into the back seat of the patrol car. "Do you know what you've just done?" he repeated himself.

"Jesus." I implored. "I was just getting a ride home...I had no idea." I was scared and angry. "Ask them!" I nearly hollered, pointing to my two ex-friends by now. "Go on! Ask them. I was just catching a ride home. My car's broke, and I was just getting a ride," I repeated nervously.

Lt. Wolfe walked to the patrol car where I saw Miguel say something to him. Miguel looked at me, apologetically, and shook his head. The Lieutenant walked back to me. "You're coming with me." By rights, I could have gone to jail, forced to explain my innocence later and hope to be vindicated. But clearly, Lt. Wolfe had information on my two drug dealing friends which I knew couldn't have included me.

"You've put me in a real bad position," he said. "I've got no choice now but to call the Chief." My lesson in politics was about to begin.

TWENTY-ONE

The old chief, the one who had given me my first job at the department, retired a few months ago. The department was in transition from the "old" Tracy to the new one. A new city manager had also been hired who considered himself a progressive, so in order to modernize the police department, he went outside the ranks to hire himself a new chief, one from a suburb of San Francisco, Marina Bay. The choice caused much dissention. The chief brought a big city mentality to this town of 20,000, and growing slowly. The chief was young, in his 30's, and had a lot of innovative ideas of law enforcement. Only he thought them innovative, the rest of us laughed, but the chief laughed last. The chief was a Caucasian, thin, with close cropped hair and a neatly trimmed moustache and protruding teeth. We nicknamed him "Willard," after the movie of the same name where the protagonist befriended rats. The chief looked like a little rat. There was fear amongst the troops as the belief was the chief wanted to get rid of all the old-timers who were there before him, including me, and I wasn't even 25 yet. One of the modern things he did was to divide the operations of the police department into two categories and appoint a Lieutenant to head each. One of the positions was filled by an old crony of the chief from another Bay Area city. Sgt. Wolfe was appointed the other Lieutenant in order to appease the local citizens and the department employees who were getting increasingly paranoid of change.

Lt. Wolfe walked me into the double back doors of the police department, and it seemed the whole department was there to watch a public execution as I trudged in. I could hear the voices of my friends from the booking area as the sergeant led me to an office just outside the jail cells. I was bewildered and feeling blue over the contents found in Miguel's car. Selling drugs? Smoking a joint now and then was one thing, or maybe a few things, but pushing the stuff…I couldn't complete my thoughts as I looked into Lt. Wolfe's face while he dialed the chief's phone number.

"I think you better come down here," he said into the phone. He looked dejected, like a father about to spank his only child. "Yeah, we found the stuff, but something else turned up. I think you better get down here," he said, finishing his call.

"What's going to happen?" I asked.

"If you're telling me truth, it might not be so bad. If you're involved in this thing, I don't know. I really don't know," he trailed off, puffing on a cigarette. I was becoming nauseated.

"Involved? You don't really think I was involved…"

"I don't know what to think," he interrupted.

"Sarge, I mean Lieutenant." I wasn't used to his new position. "Listen. You know me. You know I wouldn't be selling that stuff. I just want to be a good cop. Maybe I messed around when I was younger, but…"

"And I told you! Keep messing around and this was going to happen. I told you, didn't I?" he insisted.

"Yes. And I heard you. I wasn't messing with anything. I was just getting a ride home."

Then he got to the bottom line. "You know the chief would like to get rid of us all. You've given him all the ammunition he needs to toss you right out of here, you dumb ass."

"So that's it," I said. "You know I'm not involved, don't you."

"I want to believe that more than anything. You know that. I've seen you grow up here. You're doing a great job, but this... this is beyond my control. My ass is on the line too."

I was pensive. "So, as far as the chief's concerned, I'm guilty no matter what, right?" He couldn't look at me. "So what do I do?"

He now looked at me with sincerity. I felt he believed me. "Look. Just level with him. Don't be nasty, don't be sarcastic. No matter how you feel about him, you just answer his questions, and you answer with 'sir', got that?"

"Yes, sir."

"I think he's here. I'll be right back." He left me in the room, alone. I looked around for an escape. A small window leading into an alleyway behind the department looked pretty inviting. Time passed. I looked to see if the window was locked. I hadn't done anything, though. I knew I hadn't and he was going to have to prove I had. If my friends told the truth, what did I have to lose? I decided against trying to escape. The chief was the only one who had a college degree, so he was revered by the city administration. He looked like a college nerd who stayed a nerd, only he was able to grow a moustache. His attitude was he was a big city boy, an educated man who came to this hick town to show these cowboys how to be real cops. He was staunch supporter of the chain of command, thereby, avoiding face to face confrontation with those he disciplined. Gone were the days when the chief would call you into his office and chew you out for doing something idiotic, like making a mistake. Now it was documentation and memos, meaning everyone had to watch their backs, everyone had to be suspicious, for if someone screwed up, someone else was going to write a memo. I thought the chief was just a clown, but now he was the ringmaster, and I was his buffoon. The door opened and a little rat peered inside. It was Willard.

I started to get dizzy. Was he going to fire me right now? The chief seemed a little nervous and shook my hand lifelessly. He clutched a yellow, legal sized pad. "This is now an internal affairs investigation, and I'll be the one handling it," he said officially. Police officers had no rights when it came to these investigations. The Police Officers' Bill of Rights did not exist then, so I was entirely at the mercy of the administration, but there were still some procedural requirements. "I want you to start from the beginning," he ordered.

Oh, that's good, Chief. Where else do you start except from the beginning, I thought.

"Just tell me everything you did and how you got started?" he said looking at his pad, ready to begin writing.

How I got started? He thought me guilty and assumed I was going to tell him everything he wanted to hear, about how I got started selling drugs on duty, fronting my buddies. I told him what I was doing before I went to class, how my car had broken down, and that I had simply asked for a ride home.

"What was your association with these two men?" he asked about my friends, Miguel and Jorge.

"Just my friends. My friends since high school."

"Were you aware of the conspiracy to transport and sell narcotics?" He was pretty efficient.

"No, sir. I wasn't aware."

"Have you previously participated in the consumption of a narcotic in their presence?" Though scared, I almost laughed at such a stupid question. Now if he'd have asked, 'Did you ever smoke dope with these guys in the past?' I might have told him the truth.

"No, sir. Never." I remained stoic.

"Your friends are going to be charged with the possession of dangerous drugs and narcotics and the possession of said drugs for sale. What do you have to say about that?"

"Nothing sir. I was not involved. I told you..." he cut me off.

"Consider yourself on administrative leave," he said forcefully. "I know you're upset. Are you going to be okay?" he asked, feigning compassion. I knew he could care less about me.

"Yes, sir. I'm fine, thank you." I feigned politeness.

"I don't want you going back to your apartment. I don't want you to be alone. Do you have a place you can go until tomorrow?"

"Yes. I can go to my parents."

"Good. I'm worried about you. Consider this an order; don't go back to your apartment. Tomorrow, I want you here at 2 o'clock."

"Yes, sir. Why?" Was he going to fire me then?

"I'm going to schedule a polygraph for you in San Jose. I want to do this investigation properly. Do you understand?"

A polygraph. An investigation. This could not be real. The air grew heavy around me, his voice trailed, echoing like cymbals throughout my mind.

"I...I understand." I started to show some weakness, but quickly regained my composure. "2 o'clock. I'll be here."

"Now come on. I'll drive you to your parents."

He stopped in front of my parents' house. "Is there anything I can do for you? Do you want me to come in and explain this to your parents?"

No way, I thought. "No, sir. Thanks, but I'll manage."

"Remember, don't leave your parents and don't do anything you'll regret." Regret? It's already been done. What more could I do, kill myself? Over this? He really wanted me to think he cared about me. I knew what he had in mind. Ever since he got to Tracy, he was real publicity hound. Now he has this cop in trouble and he's going to do everything he can to prove my guilt and then the headlines in my 3-day a week newspaper, The Tracy Press, would show what a righteous guy he was. He would say he did a fair, thorough investigation on a bad cop and he won't tolerate a bad cop in his department. A bad cop doesn't deserve treatment any better than any other person who breaks the law. He'll fire me and bring charges.

I started to walk up the driveway to my parents' home, wondering what I was going to say, and then it hit me. It hit me harder than the first wave of marijuana smoke when I entered the Avalon Ballroom in San Francisco for a rock concert. He wasn't concerned about my welfare, he was going to search my apartment. No wonder he was so adamant, even to the point of ordering me not to go home. That little rat! Let him, I hadn't anything to hide. Then the image of my younger brother flashed through my mind.

Joey! My little brother. I had given him a key to my apartment. He lived with my parents but he was often there when I worked, even had a few parties. What if he left something there? I ran back to the street to make sure the chief left. Clear. I then ran back to my apartment, about a mile and a half from where my parents lived. I ran as fast as I could, talking back roads, avoiding the main streets just in case, ducking behind trees whenever I saw headlights pretending it was the chief's car so I wouldn't make a mistake and get caught. I climbed the back fence, adjacent to an open field, leading to my apartment and slipped through my back door, which I always kept unlocked. My brother wasn't sneaky and never tried to hide anything from me, even though I told him to keep it away from me. I knew if he left something there, it'd be easy to find--just as easy for the chief if he had beaten me here.

Joey, you idiot! I found a small baggy with enough grass to make a joint or two, enough to have sealed my doom. I stuffed it in my pants and was about to leave when I heard the rumbling of a car engine nearing the front of my apartment. I knew the sound of a police car constantly in need of repair. I darted for my back door, but suddenly thought to quickly search some more. I cleaned out some seeds and a couple of roaches, marijuana cigarette butts, from the living room when I heard the slamming of two car doors. Another minute and the chief would be inside.

I heard a key turning the lock and I quickly and quietly slid through my back door, hiding out of sight. Not daring to breathe, I deftly peered through my kitchen window.

I was right. It was the chief. I threw the baggie over the fence in case I got caught. There was someone else with the chief. It was Lt. Wolfe. The chief took him with him, knowing full well the relationship I had with the Lieutenant, the only person I would listen to in the department. Although we had our differences, I still respected him. I didn't know whether to quietly scale the fence and run, or keep hiding, hoping they wouldn't come to the back patio area of my ground level apartment. I hid.

They were there for quite awhile. I knew the chief knew what he was doing was illegal. I later learned he had the Lieutenant tell the apartment manager they were conducting an internal investigation and that I had given a consent search of my apartment, therefore, the manager provided a key. Even if he did find my brother's stuff, he couldn't use it against me in a criminal trial, but it would be enough to have me fired. The chief had no intention of filing criminal charges against me. I knew he couldn't because I was confident my friends would tell the truth. He was hoping to find anything to justify firing me. All he could find were some black light posters, hippy-type bead curtains, lights that flashed to the sound of my stereo and a poster of Alice Cooper with a snake draped around him. I was influenced by my old San Francisco friend, Richie Fritsche. When they left, I waited a full hour before entering my apartment.

My near arrest was the topic of conversation throughout the department the next day. I showed up at 2 and was treated like a criminal or a saint. I went to the chief's office and pretended I followed his orders, while he pretended he hadn't done anything out of the ordinary after he dropped me off at my parents. I pretended to express remorse, acquiescing to his superior intellect and leadership, while he pretended to care for me as a human being. The drive to San Jose took 90 minutes, but it seemed as though we were driving to Anaheim, except there would be no Disneyland in San Jose. On the way, the chief told me what a disappointment I was; he told me how I had lost respect of my peers, or at least the other men in blue; he told me how I had set law enforcement back a hundred years. I stared out the window and said nothing, imagining I was going to Disneyland, my favorite vacation spot I shared with a few close friends, but when we got to the Santa Clara County Courthouse, I didn't see Sleeping Beauty's castle.

At that point, polygraphs were not used to screen police applicants, so I had never seen one. This was my worst nightmare, well, almost my worst. I was strapped in a chair in front of a large mirror and told I'd be given a series of ten questions. I was instructed to answer 'yes' first to each question, and then answer 'no' to each one, and then the questions would be reversed. Before those questions, I was asked a series of personal questions and instructed to answer those incorrectly, too.

I had not the benefit of representation, no rights, but if I wanted to use the bathroom, that was allowable. I was more nervous than I had ever been about anything in my life, including that morning with Shelley when we went into the Enchanted Forest. My asthma started to act up and I did not have my inhaler, so I tried my best to control it. The polygraph operator told the chief I was trying to foul the machine up with my erratic breathing, as if I knew that would work. One lie, just one and the chief had what he needed to get rid of me.

The test took nearly two hours to complete. I was asked the same questions over and over, in different order, with different voice inflections by the operator.

"Have you ever ingested marijuana?" was one question.

"No," was my answer.

"Do you know if the other parties ever ingested marijuana?"

"No."

"Did you know of the other parties selling or in any way distributing marijuana?"

"No."

"Did you ever sell marijuana while on duty?" This robotic session was getting monotonous, not to mention the complete absurdity of it all. Did they really believe...?

"No."

"Did you ever ingest marijuana while on duty?" Where is this guy getting this stuff?

"No."

"Do you know anybody who ingests marijuana?"

Again, a trite "No."

At the conclusion, I felt like I had gone 12 rounds with Muhammad Ali. My stomach was in knots. The chief told me he would have the results in a couple of days, but I was to remain on leave until further notice. Even though my stomach was churning, I was still hungry, but the chief drove straight back to Tracy, not offering me anything to eat.

My apartment seemed enormous and empty. Things were too quiet, no parties, no people, nothing. I was afraid to leave my apartment, for it seemed everywhere I went, people were pointing at me, talking about me. Yeah, I was the one they read about in the papers, the one who didn't go to jail, the one under investigation. One morning, I was watching the Watergate hearings on television when someone knocked on my door. Lt. Wolfe.

"Chief wants to see you."

It must have killed the chief to tell me I passed the polygraph exam. Nothing showed that I was involved, nothing was conclusive about me being a crooked cop.

"Because of your association with the two who were arrested, I am going to have to suspend you from duty without pay." I had no rights to appeal and resigned myself to do the time. The charges against my friends were dropped as the informant refused to testify once she learned I was in the car. I knew who it was, but kept my mouth shut. In a small town, news and gossip spread quickly, so I knew how to separate the two and learned it was the girlfriend of Jorge, the football hero.

The local newspaper printed my story on the front page with the headline, "Cop on scene of drug bust suspended," a story I had to live down for a long time afterwards. Coincidentally, a San Francisco police officer defied the marijuana laws by smoking a joint on the steps of City Hall. Due to the times, it created quite a sensation and the San Francisco cop was dubbed "Sgt. Sunshine." When my 30 days were up, it was difficult to put the uniform back on and do my job. I was often greeted with shouts of, "Hey, Sgt. Sunshine!" or, "Doper cop! Let's get loaded." They were just having fun. I simply smiled, flashed a peace sign and continued on. In time, my town forgave and forgot. Even in this conservative, blue collar town, the collective consciousness understood the changing times. I proved I could do the job with professionalism and empathy, even if my hair tended to get a little long.

TWENTY-TWO

During my enforced vacation, the suspension for being the cop on the scene of a drug bust, I had two frequent visitors, two who believed in me, who knew I didn't deal in drugs and betray the oath I had taken. The two were kids, high school kids who were part of the fledgling Tracy Police Cadet Corps. In an effort to bridge the generation gap, high school kids were initiated into the police department to learn about police procedures and assist in non-violent, non-threatening situations. I was an advisor to the corps and related well to the youth of my town. The three of us became lifelong friends. One of the cadets, Hank, was given a fulltime position of dispatcher while he was attending high school. He dug the music, the hippy scene, and, most of all, police work. He was very efficient for a high school kid, very intelligent and very caring. He decided to enlist in the navy after high school, but wrote often and visited whenever he was on leave. He always let me know when he was in town on leave. Being in the navy on leave made one want to party, and when he was in town, that was first on the agenda. He was also a real prankster, one who often pulled what we called "clown jobs."

The other was a thin, rather frail lad named Jim, whom we

nicknamed "Stiggy." Why we never knew, except he looked like a guy who should be named Stiggy. He had been a cross country runner in high school and, like Hank, hoped to be a real cop someday. His hair was combed straight back, a bit greasy, with a slightly pock-marked face from prepubescent acne, piercing hazel eyes and an infectious laugh. He resembled Shemp of the Three Stooges, the one who replaced Curly Joe. I liked Stiggy because he never took anything too seriously. He was willing to learn, but after the lesson, he was able to laugh at what he had done to prompt the lesson. Hank was of the same character, only a bit more intellectual. They were always at my apartment and we soon saw ourselves as the Three Stooges, our heroes.

After Hank sailed off to serve his country, Stiggy became old enough to become a part of the police reserve unit. The reserves were an auxiliary to the regular force, comprising common citizens, bankers, factory workers, educators, and people from all walks who felt it their civic duty to help the local constabulary. They were provided with cursory training and then took the oath, the same as regular policemen. They were non-paid volunteers but a valuable asset to the department. As long as they were with a certificated policeman, they had the same powers of arrest and responsibility. Many could handle it and often obtained positions as a fulltime police officer. Others were a joke, a burden, power-hungry weaklings who felt empowered with a badge and gun. Most were weeded out quickly. The weekends were usually filled with reserves seeking an assignment with a regular patrol officer.

Stiggy was an exception. He had what it took to be a good cop, but one night, he was found passed out in his cadet uniform near the jail cells. Fortunately, he was revived by one of the patrol sergeants, a kindly, fatherly type named Vern. Vern provided first aid and sent him to the hospital. Stiggy suffered a diabetic seizure. Aside from the diabetes, he was fine except for his heart. It was broken when he learned that being diabetic meant he could never become a full time police officer with any agency, ever.

He was a tough kid and accepted his disability, content with being a reserve police officer. He obtained a full time job at the Heinz 57 cannery and often accompanied me as a reserve. I trusted him with my life, my secrets, and my wife, if I had one then. When he was with me, I often tossed him the keys to the patrol car, confident he knew how to patrol a beat, how to treat citizens with respect, how to handle his authority, and, most importantly, be my friend. Stiggy loved to frequent the Mexican restaurants in town and I teased him about being a closet Mexican.

He was a cool guy, but he had this strange fixation on older women. He seemed to always date women who were at least 20 years older than him. He ended up dating an older Mexican girl, named Amelia, a waitress at Chaparro's restaurant near downtown. Amelia spoke broken English, but she sure could cook. Stiggy often brought her to my apartment where she would fix up chili rellenos, cheese enchiladas and tortillas. Being a frequent guest after duty hours, she was quickly becoming Americanized. The police crowd grew fond of her and whenever one visited Chaparro's Restaurant, she gave them first class treatment, serving larger meals for the police than normal. What a woman! She adored Stiggy.

During a sound sleep after a graveyard shift, I sensed someone was in my apartment. My door was intentionally left unlocked for I hated to wake up, particularly during graveyard shift, to answer the door. Anyone I knew had access to my apartment. Never once did I get ripped off

"Stiggy?" I groggily asked, knowing, of course, it was him. "What's up buddy?"

"Not much. What are you doing?"

"What am I doing? I'm sleeping, you idiot! What'd you think?" He looked distant. Something was wrong.

"Stig. Sit down, man." I ordered my friend. "Want something to drink?" I fixed him a gin and tonic, his beverage of choice. I knew he was troubled. "What's wrong, Stiggy?"

"It's Amelia," he said, dejectedly.

"Amelia? What?" I knew she couldn't have dumped him. She

absolutely loved him. We had both been dumped before, but no one was worth being depressed. "Whaddya mean? Did she dump your dumb ass? Figured you were too young for her?" I asked, hoping to alleviate some of the tension.

"No. She's gone!" he replied, matter of factly.

"Gone? What do you mean gone? How could she be gone?"

He looked at me with loneliness in those hazel eyes. "I mean, she's just gone. I went to her house, she wasn't there. I went to Chaparro's and they hadn't seen her all day. What am I going to do?"

"Stiggy! She just can't be gone. This is ridiculous. Let's go find her," I said, putting my shoes on. We got into his VW bug and drove to the south side. We looked in bars, in restaurants, checked in at the police department. Nothing. Vanished into thin air. We went to her house, a tiny one-bedroom shack near the tracks. Nothing seemed amiss. Clothes still there, food in the cupboard. This was weird. "Stiggy. We've got a Scooby-doo mystery on our hands. What do we do now?"

"I don't know."

Death be gone! I didn't get that sensation whenever death hovers near. She had to be alive somewhere. "Not much more we can do, Stig," I told him. "She has to show up sooner or later." I was hopeful.

"I hope you're right," he sighed. "I hope you're right," he repeated. I had to work graveyard that night, so I had to get some sleep.

"I'll see ya, Stig. Let me know when you hear something."

The next day, Stiggy came back over. The mystery had been solved.

"Border Patrol?" I asked, incredulously. "You mean she was wet? No green card? Nothing?"

"I guess not," he answered.

"Get out of town, Stig. That's outrageous. You can't be serious," I said, nearly laughing at the absurdity of it all. "The Border Patrol. Unreal!" I was still stunned. The Border Patrol picked her up at her house, right there. No phone calls, no goodbyes, no rights, no nothing. Taken forthwith to Mexico.

Stiggy saw through the absurdity of it all and began laughing, breaking out of his depression. There was nothing he or I could do now. His girl was gone, just like that. No kisses, no goodbyes, no promises to write, no hopes for a reconciliation, nothing you'd expect in a normal relationship. But then Stiggy wasn't normal. He never saw her again. His plight was right for mean spirited jokes, and we laughed about it for days.

He got over Amelia rather quickly, and a cute, tiny girl, 25 years older than him who drove an MG and had money, latched onto him, totally crazy about him. We could never figure out what his attraction to older women was. I couldn't imagine my life without Stiggy. He was one of those rare individuals, a friend, a true friend who loved you for just being.

TWENTY-THREE

I survived the so-called turbulence of the 60's which disappeared into the softer, mellower 70's. Things began to change rapidly within the department. The new chief, angered by my "victory" continued his vendetta against those who were here before him and made many strategic mistakes. He disciplined a young officer, a handsome Armenian lad named David Davidian, for failing to properly complete an investigation. It was the chief's final act, for the members banded together and urged the officer to file suit. Procedurally, before a lawsuit, all administrative remedies had to be exhausted. A hearing was scheduled in the City Council chambers to listen to the appeal. The Police Officers' Bill of Rights had been passed by the legislature, so the officer had more rights than I had. Fortunately, he used them. A majority of the officers had been subpoenaed to testify on behalf of the officer.

When the chief arrived at the hearings and saw the assembled multitude, he nearly fell over and quickly conferred with the city attorney to postpone the hearing. In the following days, revelations over the chief's tryst with the City Manager's wife surfaced. Befitting a true bureaucrat, the City Manager sold the chief out, and the chief resigned and moved from town faster than my old hippy friend high-tailed it back to San Francisco after I ratted out to him. Such were small town politics.

Many of the town's citizens, many of them influential landowners with kids, expressed resentment over the chief's hiring outsiders to enforce the law. The department had lost its down-home atmosphere, so in an attempt to rectify it, the City Manager appointed my old mentor and friend, Lt. Wolfe, as the new chief. He resolved to hire home grown applicants which, in a small town, was the way it should have been. A feeling of great relief permeated the department. The other Lieutenant the old chief hired left town also, knowing his days were numbered. Many promotions were due, and I was in line to be a sergeant. I passed the exams and Chief Wolfe proudly handed me my stripes and offered advice on how to an effective supervisor of men.

All was not rosy, however. One of the officers I beat out for the promotion complained to anyone who would listen that the department wanted its token Mexican. He whined how a partying doper like me could even make sergeant, much less be a cop, referring to the drug bust a few years back. He was a typical whiner who blamed the world for his problems, how society and the department continually screwed him. The officer who beat up the old man in the cell when I was a dispatcher was promoted to Lieutenant, Gary Rendle, who always signed his name "G. R. Rendle." He frightened me, not because of what he might do to me once the honeymoon period was over, but more that he seemed to be psychologically imbalanced and he might go off one day. His crazy doll-like eyes had no color, no life, as if he lacked a soul. Others were wary of him, too, thus, his nickname, Lt. Psycho.

The hardest part of being a supervisor was pretending to care about the slugs I didn't respect, those with poor work habits who did as little as they could, only what they had to do, yet still drew their paychecks. The hardest part of being a supervisor was listening to whiners who thought of every excuse why they shouldn't be held accountable for their actions. The hardest part of being a supervisor was having to make simple decisions for those who could think just as clearly, who had every bit of knowledge as I but were afraid to take action, for if it was wrong, they could blame someone else. The hardest part of being a supervisor was hearing about those who second guessed me behind my back, but kept silent when their input was solicited before a decision was made. The truth was, none of this was very hard, it was just an absurd part of wearing the stripes.

My previously 'slick sleeves' suddenly had on what seemed to be huge blue and yellow chevrons, designating the rank of sergeant. The bright yellow hue kept distracting my vision causing me to continually look to see what it was and then realizing they were my stripes. Advice came from everywhere on how to be an effective supervisor.

"Congratulations on your promotion," said a fellow supervisor, Sgt. Dumas.

"Thanks. I appreciate that," I cordially responded. The sergeant had been my supervisor when I was a patrolman on rotating shifts. He was a corpulent man, about 6-3, a big behind and even bigger ears. He wasn't very bright, having a brain the size of a peanut, thus causing us to refer to him as Sgt. Peanut-brain. He had a reputation of getting more delight in finding "parkers", amorous couples in cars who thought they found a nice hiding place in the outskirts of the city, than finding real crooks.

"Just remember," he offered. "You know you're doing a good job if the men hate you."

"Hate you? What do you mean?" I genuinely wanted to know. I waited for the punch line, but none ever came. He was serious. He actually believed it.

"Yeah. You're never going to please everybody, but you've got to make decisions and take action which will cause resentment amongst the troops, so they end up hating you."

Wow. What advice. "Gee, Sarge. Then you must be doing a terrific job," I complimented. "Thanks for that." The sarcasm of the remark went completely over his head.

"Anytime. Good luck," he said as he waddled off.

I took to heart what the new chief told me, Chief Wolfe. He told me the hardest part was for me to break my relationships with the men I befriended, for I had to make objective decisions and couldn't be swayed by old loyalties, something I clearly remembered from my old high school chums. The chief was wise. He knew my weakness was my loyalty, a trait that got me in trouble and would continue to do so, a source of heartbreak for me.

My hope for success was to influence those who truly cared about humanity and felt they could learn something from me. I hoped I wouldn't do anything to let them down. I hoped I wouldn't let them down they way I was let down by those I once held in high esteem.

TWENTY-FOUR

The town continued to grow, and soon that little, dilapidated building known as the Hall of Justice in the 30's, 40's and through the present regressed into a relic, forcing its closure. Modern times came to Tracy, California. An updated, state of the art department was here. It was complete with humane jail cells, TV monitors, a weapons room, and a self contained, computerized dispatch module. An era passed from the love generation, the disco ducks and into the "me" generation, the 80's. Younger cops from outlying areas were being hired, many with a drug literate background more sophisticated than mine, but just as innocent, a curiosity, an experimentation as our youth has done for centuries.

The years passed blending into one cycle of repetition as I battled to keep the constrictive world of law enforcement from stifling my existence. With experience comes knowledge, and with knowledge comes power. With what little power I was perceived to wield, I was cast into the role of a subversive, one who undermines the authority of the administration. I didn't attempt to undermine anyone, but as a "homegrown" I knew my authority; I knew my town, my people and my department.

I only wanted respect, not subservience. My naïve rebelliousness was mistaken for contempt and disrespect; except for the one I respected the most, Chief Wolfe.

I was a sergeant answerable to the two Lieutenants, the gentle, fatherly type, Vern Fuller, and the other, the one I dreaded, the one we nicknamed "Psycho", Lt. Psycho. Ever since his beating of the elderly Mexican man in the old jail, I was leery of him. The image of the old man floundering on the floor of the cell and the unsettling look in Psycho's eyes remained within my consciousness. I abhorred his utterances, his perception of his self worth heightened whenever anyone of any status or importance was near enough to be impressed by him. He was one of those administrators who tried to make you believe you were an insider to information he was privy to. He would pass useless, outdated information, as though it was confidential, hoping you'd buy into his confidence. It was though you were supposed to say, 'Gee. Thanks for giving sharing that with me. I respect you for respecting me by giving me that privileged information.' I hated his guts.

The single life as a policeman was a double-edged sword. I was a fan of the Joseph Wambaugh novels, the Los Angeles police officer turned author and was particularly intrigued by his stories of "choir practice," the LAPD term for drinking parties after duty hours. Many of the officers in my department were single, so we initiated our own choir practices at a local tavern near downtown Tracy. The problem was with a small department, most everyone knew the off duty officers. We were either being bought drinks by other patrons as a down payment for future considerations, threatened and challenged by some we had arrested, or complained about by department straight-arrows who deplored drinking and carousing. Occasionally, a sincere citizen who respected our work showed his heartfelt gratitude by buying a round of drinks without any considerations. I felt there was nothing wrong with the local constabulary mingling with its citizens, getting to know one another, simply being amiable. It was a fine line. The chief didn't mind. The Psycho resented it, but couldn't do much to curtail the frivolity of Tracy's finest.

To ease the tension, I moved to the city of Stockton, commuting to Tracy for my shift work. Choir practices were now held at my residence in Stockton, away from potential problems within the city and in relative privacy. Stiggy was nearly a roommate of mine as he would often ride his newly acquired Harley-Davidson to my place after his shift at the Heinz Cannery in Tracy. A loyal, dependable friend. It was a shame he had diabetes for he would have made an excellent police officer. A bachelor party was staged for one of the officers soon to be married. It turned into a choir practice Joe Wambaugh would have been proud. Booze and women flowed throughout the house. One officer brought his girlfriend, a waitress in one of the restaurants on the main drag through town, a petite woman named Tina. Cops and waitresses went together like hot dogs and sauerkraut, tacos and hot sauce, Mexicans and moustaches. Tina knew most of the guys, having met them while working graveyard shift at her restaurant, always ready to pour a free cup of coffee. She was a good, caring waitress, a graveyard shift cop's dream. Every cop put the moves on her, but she was loyal to the one. Most cops who ended up marrying waitresses didn't see their marriages last long. It's just the way it was and probably still is.

As the hours went well beyond midnight, the party started to get out of control. Tempers flared, petty grievances escalated to the point of absurdity and a fight broke out between two of the newer officers. In a back bedroom, Tina and her boyfriend cop were getting a little too amorous, so it was time to end it.

"Let's hit the road everybody! Bar's closing!" I announced. "Drive careful. Stockton PD is cool, but those CHP guys will nail you," I warned. There was an unwritten rule, a professional courtesy that cops wouldn't bust other cops, unless an extreme situation, but the CHP didn't quite adhere to the rule. Some had the attitude they were God's gift to law enforcement. Stiggy had too much to drink and I wouldn't let him ride home on his

Harley. He passed out on my couch for the night. A good time was had by all. Sometimes it was good to let off steam and raise issues and yell at each other to clear the air, something which couldn't be done during the strict regimen of shift work. No one harbored any ill feelings the next day.

Days later, the department received notice that a paroled rapist would be released to the city of Tracy. It was a certainty he would rape again, so a twenty-four hour surveillance was put on the guy, a psychopathic hardened con named Graveyard Nelson. He was given the name Graveyard because that's where he forced his victims to submit to his brutal, violent will. The California Department of Corrections assigned a parole officer to supervise the others to continually watch him. I had to sit with one for eight hours to watch his apartment, but Graveyard made no suspicious movements, no overt actions to warrant an immediate revocation of his parole. We loved Parole Agents. To the con, the Parole Agent was God. To us, the agent was the best tool in law enforcement, a true knight, the ultimate defender of the preyed upon and the most victimized of society. The Parole Agent could violate one of his charges for spitting in public if he wanted to. They had the ultimate power and the cons knew it. Whenever we called an agent to assist us in the enforcement of the con's conditions of parole, the con knew he was gone--six months back in the joint for violating parole, no matter how trivial the offense.

Weeks passed and Graveyard seemed to be rehabilitated. Maybe there was something to this rehab thing after all. The overtime allotted to pay the agents was used up, so all we could do was force a parole search on him from time to time. Graveyard knew the routine and complied. He must have found Jesus, I thought, just like every prisoner claims to have done when they have to appear remorseful and rehabilitated, just another of the games cons play. Remarkably, there were many officials in the system who actually believed and fell for it, but with Graveyard, it was just a matter of time before he would rise again. His apartment was just a block from the new police department, so he knew he had to be careful. He knew he was being watched, but old habits are hard to break.

Just when we thought he was left for dead, Graveyard rose and struck again. He lie in wait behind the 7-11 store at the north end of town, and when a woman left after a purchase of beer, he forced her into his car, beat her nearly unconscious and drove her to the cemetery south of town. She was raped, sodomized, beaten again and then dumped near a headstone, one with an angel on it. The brutality of the crime was his fingerprint. Since the victim was found staggering near the cemetery just outside city jurisdiction by a passing motorist, the Sheriff's office was notified who then summoned an ambulance where she was taken to the hospital in town. The sheriff's deputy learned the crime had originated in the city, the kidnapping, so he notified us, Tracy PD. I met the deputy in the emergency room of the Tracy Hospital.

"Oh my, God! Tina! What the hell…?"

"You know her?" asked the deputy.

"Yes, and so do you. That's Tina from the Horseshoe Café," I told him. He did a double take then recognized her through the bruises and blood.

"Jesus Christ! Tina." The deputy frequented the restaurant when he worked graveyard and enjoyed the free coffee she served. "She doesn't know who did this," he told me.

"No, but I do." The deputy looked at me quizzically. "It can only be one guy."

"Christ! Graveyard?" the deputy remembered.

"Yep. Graveyard Nelson. He's been paroled here a couple of months, and now this." The deputy and I put out an all points on Graveyard. Since he was on parole, there was no need for a warrant or even a positive I.D. from Tina, at least not at this point. The department already had a photo lineup assembled with Graveyard's picture, for it was that much of a certainty he would rape again. She picked him out immediately.

"It's gonna be alright, Tina," I told her, as if I knew. It would never be alright for her. "I'm going to have an officer meet you at the county hospital for some evidence." I summoned for an advocate from the San Joaquin County Women's Center to assist in the investigation and to offer Tina some support. They provided invaluable assistance in rape and battered women cases. The last person a raped woman wants to talk to at that most vulnerable moment of her emotions is another man, even if he is in uniform.

"That son of a bitch," the deputy fumed, referring to Graveyard. "Maybe this time he'll do some real time."

"No," I said. "I'm gonna kill him." The deputy looked at me, not sure if I was serious. "Thanks for your help. See you around." I left the deputy at the hospital. The sheriff guys were okay in my book. I had a lot of respect for them. If I did kill Graveyard, I knew the deputy wouldn't snitch me off by revealing my threat, for he knew it'd be justice to put him out before he was sent through the system again, but I didn't get a chance to. A stakeout of his apartment put a nail in the coffin of Graveyard. He was held at our jail, where he invoked his rights, until parole picked him up and put him back in the joint for parole violation and to await his trial for the abduction, rape and beating of Tina.

All the guys felt for Tina, but she recovered and eventually went back to work at the Horseshoe Café. Seeing her smile again made the coffee taste even better.

TWENTY-FIVE

After Tina's ordeal, I was assigned the 3-11 PM shift. Most of the calls were routine. Kids acting up after school, throwing rocks, fights, nothing of much consequence. Swing shift bored me, except there was time for choir practice afterwards.

"The psycho wants to see you," the off going day sergeant informed me when I appeared for roll call. 'Now what,' I wondered. After the swing shift briefing, I trudged the hallway leading to the lieutenant's office.

'Probably wants me to change someone's evaluation again,' I surmised. As a sergeant, it was my responsibility to complete annual performance evaluations on those of my shift, an assignment I hated. I felt rather than a learning and training device, it was more often used as a tool for discipline, or a time to get even with those who didn't please the supervisors doing the evaluations. You should have seen Sgt. Peanut-brain salivate when it came time for him to evaluate someone he didn't like. Lt. Rendle had a separate evaluation form designed for me with performance objectives he personally set up. I didn't know it at the time, but the practice was unethical and illegal, but it didn't matter to me none.

An elderly woman had been hired and assigned to the police department on a Senior Citizen's incentive program. It was designed for senior citizens to become involved in the community and give them a sense of purpose while making some extra money to supplement their retirement income. Doris was assigned to the police department, a gentle ruby-lipped, red-haired grandmotherly type who resembled Aunt Clara, the forgetful, stumbling aunt of Samantha, the charming witch from the television show "Bewitched." Because the department was small, Doris had to sometimes act as a matron to assist in searching female prisoners, a job she did with much disdain, and sometimes filling in at the dispatch desk, another task she didn't care for, but she tried her best as she wasn't trained as a full time matron or dispatcher. She was shocked to learn what went on in a police department more by what she saw went on between employees rather than what crooks did. I had to evaluate her and felt stupidly doing so. I liked Doris and spent time talking with her, drawing from her life's experiences. How could I possibly evaluate someone as old as my mother and whose life wasn't contingent on her menial job at the police department? I was a softy anyway, but I still had to give her the evaluation. She was cordial, tried hard, and for what she was hired, filing paperwork, she was efficient. I evaluated her as such.

They psycho didn't like it that I used the term "above reproach" when I described her work habits. "I don't believe anyone is 'above reproach'," he chided me.

This was ridiculous, I thought. Challenging my evaluation over that old woman. He pointed out some other comments he disagreed with, and I remained quiet, dumbfounded over the absurdity of it all. I watched him reading over the evaluation, carefully looking.

Finally, I said, "If you feel that strongly about it, why don't you call her in yourself and evaluate her? You seem to know her work habits better than I."

His lips got tight, as they do when he's about to lose control. "Because that's your job. That's what you're paid to do."

"Well, that's what I did." What was I supposed to say? "I'm not going to change it now. What good would that do?"

"You're not running this damn department," he shot back.

What the---? Where did that come from? "I never said I was," acquiescing somewhat. He was still my supervisor, so I had to be careful. "I gave her what I thought was a fair evaluation for what she does…" He interrupted me.

"Other employees have complained about her. What about that?"

"What about it? Look. She's doing things she hasn't even been trained for. It's not even in her job description," I pleaded in her defense. "She's an old lady. What good is this going to do her?"

"That's not the issue," the psycho responded, raising his voice. "The issue is your objectivity as a sergeant." This was getting weird. He started to remind me of peanut-brain and his feeble counseling sessions. I decided to play along and end this farce.

"Perhaps you're right. Tell you what. Let the evaluation stand. I'll keep a close eye on her and the next time, even if she's not my responsibility, I'll give her a stricter evaluation. Fair?"

He leaned back in his chair, somewhat puzzled by my proposal. Seeing he was about to bite, I continued. "Alright. Maybe I was a little soft. Old Doris. Can you blame me?" I shook my head. "I'll keep a sharp eye on her," I promised.

"Okay. I'll let it slide this time." He acted as though he gave me a reprieve from the gas chamber. I got up to leave his office when he said, "Remember. You've got her next time. I'm going to document this."

"Yes, sir," I respectfully said as I left his office. What an idiot, I thought. I wasn't worried about the next time. I didn't have to. Doris got fed up with the lunacy she witnessed daily, quit and went to work for the Emergency Food Bank, a non-profit agency which provided meals to the poor. I wondered how she was evaluated there.

I walked into his office to find him leaning forward in his chair with a grim look on his face, his hands shading his eyes as he rubbed his forehead. This looked more serious than a performance evaluation. "I had a meeting with the District Attorney this morning," he said looking up. There was a pause. So? Was I supposed to congratulate him for meeting with the D.A. or something? Is the D.A. reviewing our evaluations now? I told a silent joke to myself.

"There's a problem with your case, the kidnap and rape case," he continued. "Big problems."

"Problems?" I echoed.

"She doesn't think she's going to be able to prosecute Nelson," referring to Graveyard, the one who beat and raped Tina.

"What? You've got to kidding?" I exclaimed in fear and anger. "What the hell happened? Why not?"

The psycho dropped the report on his desk and glared at me, the same empty glare I saw when he beat up the old prisoner years back. He leaned back in his chair. "Because of YOU, that's why," he said, his voice quivering.

"Me?" I was dumbfounded.

"Yes, you! You and your damn choir garbage...practice, whatever the hell you call it!" He was getting into a rage.

"I don't understand." I really didn't.

"You and your drunken parties!" He threw a pencil on his desk for emphasis.

"I don't know what you're getting at. What does my personal life have to do with any of this?"

"Don't give me any of your liberal bullshit routine. You think I don't know what's going on?" His eyes were glazing over. This was getting very bizarre. He was totally in the twilight zone, and I wasn't liking it.

"You had that girl as a prize at one of your parties. How do you think that's going to sound when it gets to court? All you drunk cops banging that girl, and then she gets raped! Do you know what you've done to this department?" He started shouting.

I was letting him get to me. He was making me angry. I heard that phrase before. It meant nothing to me then, and it didn't mean anything to me now. "Don't you yell at me! You want to yell, I'll yell right back!" I warned him. Damn him. I think he was the one who put the note on my locker when I was a rookie, the one that said 'Affirmative Action Hire.'

"I'm going to put an end to these ridiculous parties if it's the last thing I do. You and your goddamn liberal lifestyle--." He was out of control now.

I tried to reason. "Look, Lieutenant. Calm down. I really don't understand any of this. What does this have to do with Graveyard not being prosecuted?" The question eluded him, totally.

"I'm damn sick and tired of hearing about these parties! Now it's going to cost us a major case. Do you know what you've done?" He was too focused on his anger at me to reason. It was time to go on the offensive.

"You better clean off your own doorstep, Rendle." I shot back. That stunned him and he stopped. He suddenly looked like a mannequin as only his mouth moved.

"Don't you threaten me! You don't know what the hell you're talking about," he fumed as he started to stand. The look in his eyes scared me a little. I was not going to be that old man in the cell. I remembered him brushing himself off after the old man was on the ground, triumphantly blurting, "That'll teach you to mess with the kid." Now the psycho's messing with the real kid! Come towards me, just come towards me, I hoped. I would knock him on his posterior harder than he did that old man. Unfortunately, an old-fashioned butt-kicking was a thing of the past. We were civil, we were sophisticated. We now fought with memorandums, documentation and policy violations.

"Come on, Rendle," I said with much disrespect. "You think everyone doesn't know? Who are you to tell me how to live my life? I'm a single man. I don't care what you think about my liberal lifestyle. You're a married man, you're in a position of leadership, and you think you've got a right to tell me how to live?

He backed off. "What the hell are you talking about?"

I hit him right between the eyes. "Donna, Lieutenant. I'm talking about Donna." Donna was the Chief's married secretary, married as in adultery.

"What's Donna got to do with this?" He feigned innocence. His meek protest told me he was going down.

"Like I said, Lieutenant. Sweep off your own doorstep." I turned and walked out, hardly aware of the people gathered at each end of the hallway, clearly trying to eavesdrop on the contentiousness.

It's people like him who, in the end, screw themselves because they think everyone "below" them in rank is dumb--they think we're all ignorant. People who have affairs get all wrapped up in the lust of the moment and make critical mistakes, failing to be aware of other people who are aware of them. Did they really believe that everyone thought it a mere coincidence when Donna came back to the office after hours to complete payroll and then Rendle showed up shortly after to complete his work? A couple of times, maybe, but with successful deceit comes confidence in further deceit. Did they really think no one noticed when they were scheduled to attend conferences out of town together? And did they really think everyone believed them when they openly joked about attending the conferences at the same time, but warned each other to keep their distance from their respective motel rooms? Did they think no one noticed when every time the Chief left the department, Donna high-tailed it to the psycho's office and closed the door? Yes, that's exactly what they thought.

Since the beating of the old man, I never respected the Lieutenant and never trusted him. I'm sure he sensed that, thus, his paranoia for me. What I later learned made me downright despise him. I was concerned about the case with Tina. This party became so distorted and out of proportion, and she didn't deserve to be denied due process, particularly for the brutality she suffered. At least with Graveyard, I knew what he was, and he was what he was, a psychopathic criminal. With people like the psycho, I never knew who he was, and I don't believe he knew either, making him just as dangerous without the violence. I made it a point to talk with Tina and see what I could do to help.

I stuck around after my shift was over and rode with another officer on graveyard shift until it was time for his break. We stopped at the Horseshoe Café where Tina was working.

"How's it going, kid?" I asked. Kid? She was nearly the same age as me, but she looked so young.

"It's all good. I met with the D.A. about my case. She seems nice and told me what to expect. I'm kinda scared."

"It's only natural. Somebody from the Women's Center going to be there?"

"Oh, yeah. I couldn't do it without them." I told her about my "conversation" with the Lieutenant. She laughed.

"Prize? I only wish!" she teased.

She told me the D.A. wanted to know the last time she had sex, and she told her it was with her boyfriend at my house, at the bachelor party. She resented the characterization of being a prize. The D.A. didn't seem to make a big deal out of it she said, so the trial was still scheduled.

The Lieutenant lied to me. I sensed something wrong when he seemed to make a bigger issue of the parties than actually losing a rape and kidnap case. He thought he'd be able to use the information he got from somewhere, distort it, and use it as a hammer to quell the choir practices. It certainly wasn't to any degree described in the Wambaugh novels, but in a small town, it may just as well have. A few days later, Chief Wolfe called me into his office.

"Lieutenant Rendle wants to bring insubordination charges against you." he calmly told me. Apparently the Lieutenant felt he had to save face for the argument became pretty heated, falling onto some eager ears.

"If he wants to do me, let him," I responded defiantly. I explained to the Chief my side of the argument, including the perceptions of his secretary, Donna. I put the Chief in an uncomfortable position. He knew I was right, but by backing me, he would further alienate himself from his Lieutenant. The administration has to have at least appearances of being unified to be effective.

"I understand, Chief. Do what you have to do. I can accept whatever. But you know I'm right, right?"

He simply grinned. "Let me handle this. Just do your job and don't rile anyone."

"Yes, sir."

"I'll take care of it," he assured me.

He did, to some degree. The Lieutenant recommended three days off for insubordination and "involving other members of the department," his girlfriend, the Chief's secretary. She was upset, fearing her reputation had been impugned by my ranting. If she only knew! As long as they could deflect responsibility to a whacked out Sergeant, their tryst was safe. I was going to appeal, but the Chief talked me into accepting one day off if I dropped the appeal. I did it for him, thereby pacifying Rendle a little longer, the second suspension of my career. I lost a day's pay for speaking the truth, although angrily, and did nothing wrong, but it was worth it.

The rapist, Graveyard, was sentenced to a million years. The parties continued and Donna treated me with contempt. The Lieutenant, to his credit, decided to co-exist peacefully with me--at least for now.

TWENTY-SIX

The intrinsic danger of police work is its autonomous authority, often granted to people unworthy of its might. For the betterment of society, those few are in the vast minority. Those behind the badge are ordinary human beings thrust into an extraordinary world of victims and suspects, the losers, disillusioned, downtrodden, and demented. It's often an absurd world where nothing seems to have any logic. The solitude of one's existence can be multifarious when you're battling wits against your own. The isolation can be impregnable and has driven more than one sane person to the edge of dementia. I wanted to be sure that my sanity didn't stray outside the boundaries of the societal expectations I was sworn to uphold. Chief Wolfe often counseled me of the impassioned threats to ourselves by ourselves, thus the suicide, alcoholism and divorce were uncommonly high for those in the profession, even in a small town. My anger needed to subside before I took it out on an innocent public, a far too frequent occurrence which departments keep secluded behind bureaucratic words like, "a struggle ensued," or, "I saw a furtive movement," and, "he attempted to resist arrest," although frequently legitimate, conversely often abused.

Most cop fights occur during what's known as domestic disturbances, a euphemism for a drunken coward who takes his frustrations out on his spouse, more commonly known as a wife-beater. They are desperate to assert their dominance and the wives or significant others are frightened and frustrated enough to go to any means to escape their hostile existence, often risking further violence if they have their mates arrested.

A husband's and wife's disagreement, fueled by alcohol, intensifies to such a degree that the rules of protocol and logic have no meaning, not to mention the laws of society. A drunken husband decided to thrash his wife whose screams caused the neighbors to call the police. When the officer arrived, a scuffle ensued in the living room and the harried husband was arrested. The officer was squeezing the culprit into the backseat of his patrol car when I arrived.

"You alright, Howard?" I asked. He was one of the candidates I beat out on the Sergeant's exam. He resented me for that, but mostly because I was a Mexican and he didn't like anyone not his color. He was a snake in the grass who badmouthed everyone behind their backs. He questioned decisions made by superiors, including supervisors like me, but only when they weren't there to defend themselves. He had a mediocre following with a few others who shared his warped perception of the world and the subsequent frustrations responsible for his plight, such as being passed over for a Sergeant's position. He was in his 40's, meaning the window for advancement was rapidly closing in on him. He saw himself as a hardened, wisened veteran, but most saw him as a whiner, thus, earning him the nickname of "Boo-hoo."

"Don't worry about me," he replied scornfully. "Take more than this scumbag to hurt me." Scumbag was a popular name cops used for anyone who broke the law.

"Fuck you, motherfucker! I ain't drunk. Take these cuffs off and I'll whip your ass clear to next Tuesday---son-of-a-bitch!" slurred the drunk to either or both of us. He was mad.

"It's OK," I said. He was a regular visitor to the jail cells.

"He'll calm down. Always does. Just hold him till he sobers up and call his wife. She hasn't pressed charges before and probably won't this time. She needs to keep you working so you can buy her that cheap whiskey. Ain't that right, pal?" I asked the drunk.

"I ain't your pal! Stinkin' cops. Get these cuffs off me. I know the mayor. I'll have your badges for this you mother--"

"Shut the hell up and get in there!" Boo-hoo interrupted, shoving him awkwardly into the back seat, quite agitated.

The realization of another weekend in jail calmed the drunk down when Howard got him back to the cells. He wanted to get him booked as quickly as possible so he could get back to the coffee shops. It was just another tussle, not enough to justify a charge of assaulting a police officer or resisting arrest. The District Attorney frowned on too many of those, so a cop had to have some righteous bruises and blood to justify the charges. Howard was still miffed when he led the wife-beater to the booking area.

"Everything cool?" I asked both. Howard didn't answer.

"Yeah, I'm cool. Sorry about this," the drunk said with genuine remorse. Comically, he was the stereotyped, pot-bellied, middle aged man wearing the "wife-beater" tank top t-shirt. I'm sure he was the one to set the style for other women abusers to follow.

"Don't worry about it. No harm, no foul," I said as I left Howard to handle the booking while I went to the dispatch desk for a cup. No sooner had I left, I heard the sounds of another struggle. 'C'mon Howard,' I thought as I went running back to the jail cells. 'You can certainly handle this clown.' I then heard the distinct sounds, the blunt thuds. Boo-hoo liked to wear sap gloves, the black leather gloves with weighted knuckles, legal for police officers on duty. I went into the cell where Boo-hoo was standing over the drunk seated on the lower bunk who was leaning forward, seemingly trying to keep himself from falling to the cold, concrete floor. A thick torrent of blood was streaming from his nose and mouth. His head was buried into his chest as soft moans emanated from his liquor paralyzed throat. Boo-hoo hovered over him, fists clenched at his sides, breathing heavily.

"Jesus Christ! What happened?" I asked, afraid to know the truth.

Boo-hoo nearly beat the drunk senseless. My concern turned to horror when I saw the drunk's hands still cuffed behind his back. In police parlance, Boo-hoo rationalized he made a furtive movement, therefore, justifying enough force to overcome his resistance. He wasn't beating up a drunk, he was beating me, the administration, society, the world--the world which repressed what he felt he was entitled. He was certainly entitled to what he achieved in this, his conquest; nothing. And nothing is what became of this incident. A resisting arrest charge was added and no one became the wiser. No video cameras, no audio, no word from the prisoner, just another coward amongst the ranks of Tracy's finest, a coward who resented me more because I knew that's what he was.

I stormed back into my patrol car. Get me out of here! My patrol car became my haven, my fortress of solitude. In here, my soul rested in kinship with my shotgun, my siren and emergency lights. Here I was impenetrable. I fled the controlled chaos of neurotic, psychotic men swaggering through police buildings, men empowered to enforce their will and domination on the rest of humanity. Here, in my car, I'm insulated from the latest fabrication of our culture's ideal, itself a façade, a barricade we hide behind to classify, organize, and systematize ourselves from knowing our own meaning and our true purpose. I preferred the uncontrolled pandemonium of the masses, itself shielded behind the wall of crime and degradation. I am a rock; I am an island, as Simon and Garfunkle would agree.

The streets of my town are my blood. They flow, full of life, full of dreams broken, full of loves lost equal to promises broken. They flow with the people I love and some whom I hate. They flow with memories cherished and times lost, and they flow with the hopes that this is my Enchanted Forest. Feeling a little blue,

I cruised the main street of my town, lost for a moment in my displeasure over people and events which should have meant nothing to me, when my vision detected some hurried movement on the sidewalk outside a tavern. Men fighting. I reached for the microphone and radioed in a "415 in progress," then did a double take at the combatants, recognizing one as my friend, Stiggy.

Stiggy frequented these bars after his shift at the Heinz cannery when I wasn't assigned the graveyard shift, but he was never one to cause trouble, realizing his position as a reserve police officer. I requested a backup, then made a u-turn and jumped from my car as Stiggy was clearly on the losing end. My backup arrived and we broke them apart. The other guy was strong, fighting us off while still taking swings at Stig. A "scuffle ensued" and we finally subdued him. We had no choice, really, but to beat the guy into submission, nothing brutal, nothing unfair, unless you want to call two on one unfair, just a street fight because in this town, that's often the only way the law can be enforced. We got the guy handcuffed and were stuffing him into the patrol car when Stiggy ran up and gave the guy a cheap shot to the back of his head.

"Hold off, Stig," I warned. "We got him, now back off!" Stiggy was bleeding from his mouth, nothing serious, just enough of an ass-kicking to render him a near maniacal lunatic. He reared back to take another swing and I lunged forward and pinned him against the patrol car.

"Take it easy, Stig," I pleaded. "People are watching. You're a cop, you don't need witnesses." He listened and calmed down. His sanity quickly returned and he erupted into crazy laughter, realizing he'd been acting like an idiot. The other guy was a known barroom brawler, Virgil Hayes, known in these parts as Okie Hayes. Okie drove truck for a living and often stopped in town for some libations and loose women. If he couldn't find a woman, he always found a fight, and Stiggy was his choice this night. If I hadn't stopped by, Stig would have taken more blows, more than Moe, the Stooge, gives to Shemp.

"It's Okie Hayes, Stig. You want to press charges?"

"Nah. Hell with 'im. He's just drunk." He thanked me and headed back towards the bar.

"Come here," I told him. "Let me see your face." I examined his mug closely. "Little bit of blood, a bruise here and there. Nothing some good whiskey won't wash off. You'll be alright."

"Come on by when you get off," he offered.

"Might just do that. Keep the peace, will ya?" I returned to my patrol car and headed back to the jail to help book Okie Hayes.

The other officer removed Okie's property from his pockets, a proper booking procedure. Okie was a big, strapping truck driver, 6 feet, two inches, 250 pounds of solid man. He didn't say much, but he was certainly drunk.

"S'matter, Okie? What got you in a bad mood tonight?" I jokingly asked him. I removed one of the tightly manacled cuffs from his massive wrists and then lost all sense of time. A brilliant splash of light exploded before me, and cartoon stars circled my head. I felt myself ricocheting off the wall of the booking room then felt the crashing thunder of his other fist against my cheek. What the---? Okie hadn't had enough fighting and caught me with two quick cheap shots He was about to land another when I regained my senses and saw him swing the hand with the cuffs still dangling from his wrist. I managed to lunge back and felt the metal graze against my forehead. The other officer was stunned by Okie's attack and was slow to react. I bull rushed Okie, him knocking him to the ground while the other officer finally reacted and came to my defense, pummeling Okie with blows. Okie pushed me off and bounced me against the wall like a pinball, which caused me to fall on top of him full force.

This was all the justification we needed. Assault on a Police Officer, section 243 of the Penal Code, which was cause for a righteous beating. Another officer heard the ruckus and came rushing in to join the fray. We were bouncing around the booking room, rumbling, stumbling, fumbling, fists flailing, cussing, screaming. I thought I felt someone bite me, but it could have been one of my own. The scene was reminiscent of the best Bugs Bunny and Yosemite Sam fights, only the blood was real. Okie was one tough dude. We knew we had finally won when,

"Oh, God...oh, God, help me!" Okie blurted out, blood smearing his face and mouth.

"God ain't going to help you now," said one of my partners as he landed the finishing blow and Okie submitted. "Okay, I had enough!" he whimpered.

"Let's clean him off and get him booked," I ordered the other two. "Anything broken, Okie?"

"I don't think so. You guys ain't gonna charge me are ya?" he seriously asked.

"You gotta be kidding, Okie. What do you think? You draw blood and you've crossed the line." I was only bleeding a little. "Get your ass in the cell and we'll think about it."

I didn't like having to beat a guy that badly, but this was a righteous assault, and I could probably get Stiggy to file a complaint against Okie to justify the use of force. I tried to limit assault against a police officer charges as too many can give one a bad reputation, one who can't control his temper, or of being a brutal officer. In this town, fights between cops and drunken citizens were commonplace. Most cops didn't file charges as long as they weren't seriously hurt and their uniforms weren't damaged. The thought of having a lawsuit filed for administering street justice was unheard of in those days. As long as the drunk could go back to work the next day, he was fine with it, sort of an unwritten rule, the law of the jungle.

"I got a long haul tomorrow. I can't afford to go to court," Okie implored.

Chief Wolfe taught me a cop must always be in control of a situation, for if the situation controls you, objectivity is lost, and, thus, professionalism. If he could have seen the donnybrook in the cell, professionalism was certainly dubious. The chief also taught me that a good cop leads with his reserve, but my reserve, Stiggy, was taking a pounding himself. He can't do me much good if he's not in my car protecting me instead of cleaning the city's sidewalks with his face.

Okie passed out in the cell, breathing heavily. I checked to make sure there wasn't any blood to clog his air passages. Okie was okay. I decided to release him when he was sober, hoping he learned his lesson the next time he stopped in for a good time. The brawl became the topic of much conversation the next day, while we tried to downplay it for fear of too many questions being asked. The psycho Lieutenant was in charge of Internal Investigations and I knew he'd welcome it if I was involved, but he also knew drunken brawls were not my thing, at least not on duty, so he never pursued it. He also never asked if I was alright. I was hurt.

TWENTY-SEVEN

11:00 PM couldn't come fast enough; the end of my shift. I dressed hurriedly and made a beeline to where I hoped Stiggy would be. He earned his respect as one of the top members of the reserve policemen. Efficient, dependable and more loyal than a German Shepherd. He became like a brother to me. I was worried about him as he took to drinking more. The reality of his dreary existence as a Heinz cannery worker took its toll on him. He could never become a full time police officer because of his diabetes, and it depressed him. He kept it inside and was always the jovial character I loved.

"You buying?" I asked as I pulled up a barstool next to him. "You don't look so bad for a guy who went toe to toe with Okie Hayes."

He smiled. "Good thing you came when you did. I was about ready to dust him," as he laughed at the notion. I could tell by his look and sarcasm he was getting toasted.

"I think you had enough. We got a shoot in the morning. Better get your ass to bed," I scolded him.

"Yeah, yeah. Who are you my mom?" He laughed again.

Sitting and drinking with Stig was always a good time. For as young as he was, he possessed much wisdom, or at least I always thought that until he was about to misjudge his own wisdom, and I bought right into it. He talked about a girl his own age he met where he worked, the Heinz Cannery. I thought it unusual because he had a preference for older woman, at least 20 years, but now he's talking like a normal guy. The beating must have knocked some sense into him. He wanted to go see her and asked if I'd go with him. The problem was, she lived in the welfare projects on the South Side.

Her name was Bianca with whom I was familiar. She had sister a couple of years older than her and a brother, who was the oldest of the three. I arrested the brother a short while back on a burglary charge after he broke into a wig shop in the business district downtown. I ended up chasing him for blocks. His partner got away, but I always suspected his partner was his sister, the older one. It seemed nearly everyone on South Side was arrested for burglary at one time or another—the have-nots taking from the haves.

Their mother received welfare and was often suspected of turning tricks in the bars near the city's main thoroughfare, but nothing was ever proven and she was never arrested. She was an attractive woman in her 40's with gorgeous legs, as I often saw her in a mini-skirt when patronizing the bars, but she had a problem with alcohol. Her children were just as gorgeous, but welfare and alcoholism was the only life they knew. Their singular goal in life mirrored their mother which, essentially, was nothing.

Bianca lived with her mother and older sister, named Mary, in the South Side projects. They were fiercely loyal to each other. The brother steadfastly refused to tell on his partner the night I chased him down on the burglary. We tried every trick known to cops, cajoling him, offering him leniency, threatening him because he never lawyered up. He was a stand up guy who would take the rap, never thinking of snitching off his own sister. His sister had guts, too. She came in later to inquire about his bail and I was struck by her beauty, which nearly left me breathless.

She knew I didn't see her when she split, and she also knew her brother would never give her up. She had spirit! She could have been a center-fold model, she was that dazzling. I don't think she ever conceived how beautiful she was, either, sort of a Cinderella who, unlike the story, could never leave the clutches of poverty and despair, the projects. In her environment, her prince was to become the Dark Lord of the Golden Arm—heroin.

It was near bar-closing time, 2 AM, and Stiggy consumed enough courage to go the South Side to see Bianca, conning me into going with him. We poured into his cherished '67 VW bug and slowly drove to the cul-de-sac where the single and two story housing projects crammed into each other, known as West Court. He parked in the red zone, shut off his engine, lit up a smoke and contemplated silently.

"What are you going to do?" I brightly asked. He puffed, his eyes a little glassy, and stared straight ahead. "Well, what are we going to do?" I asked again. "Sit here like dorks?"

Without answering me, he opened his door and said, "Be right back."

"Stiggy. Wait—I...I'm scared." I wasn't really, but I didn't know what else to say, his actions so startled me.

"I won't be long," he said and then made a beeline to Bianca's hovel.

I waited and waited. No sign of Stiggy. A patrol car drifted by, slowing near the opening of the cul-de-sac. Aw, come on! He's not going to ticket Stig's car for a red zone violation this time of the morning, is he? I thought. The patrol car idled, then turned its lights off. No movement. Come on, Stig, hurry up. I didn't want anyone seeing me here. The patrol car lingered at the end of the street. A dim light emerged from the interior. Someone lit a cigarette. The glow of the match illuminated a familiar ear, the ear of old peanut-brain, Dumas. His ears were quite prominent and since most of the town knew the officers, it gave them a level of comfort if they knew who was stopping them, or who arrived to handle their call, things like that. With Dumas, you could tell it was him because his ear, the one closest to the door, flapped in the wind when his window was down. What's he doing there, I wondered.

I sat in Stiggy's car uncomfortably, and after a few moments, Dumas drove off. I hurried out of the little bug and walked to Bianca's place, knocking quietly on the door.

"Is Jim here?" I politely asked at 2 in the morning. I wasn't sure if she knew him as Stiggy.

"Oh, hi. Sure he is. Come on in," she said, her voice barely a whisper.

The place smelled familiar. All the welfare projects had that some odor, not a stench, but a peculiar odor that accompanied indifference—the indifference of a society that could care less about the welfare of the welfare people. This was the side of the city the rest of the town refused to see. It made for interesting reading in the local paper when they were arrested for narcotics offenses, robbery, and burglary, but for the most part, this side of town was non-existent—there was nothing here.

Stiggy sat on a little sofa between Bianca and her sister, Mary, holding a can of beer. "You forget about your buddy?" I asked him, somewhat perturbed.

"I was coming to get you," he answered. "The girls want to party. Can someone give my pal something to drink?" he asked no one in particular. Bianca went to the small refrigerator and brought me a beer. People on welfare can't afford good liquor. If they manage their money, which is an amazing task in itself given the paltry sum they are allowed, beer or wine was about it. I wasn't going to complain as I popped the top and took a sip, although beer wasn't my choice of beverage.

Being here made me a little nervous, not because I judged them, for choice is often something we can't choose, rather, I was worried about Dumas and the rest of the department's judgment if they knew we were here.

Mary wore loose fitting pajamas which clung to her provocatively, something which I'm sure she had no consciousness.

Her beauty captivated me as the beer circulated through my body, a bit distastefully. If only I wasn't a cop and she wasn't on welfare, I fantasized. She was a wisp of a woman, maybe 21, with flowing auburn hair, prominent teeth and smooth skin, but it was her eyes that were her most striking feature.

"Come sit by me," she said with such a serene voice that may or may not have been contrived. Did she have designs on me? Stiggy cuddled next to Bianca, his hand resting on her leg. She gave me a look of disinterest, but Mary's was definitely centered on me. I took a small swallow of the beer and accepted her offer.

"You're different from the rest," she started.

"Different? What do you mean?" I was puzzled.

"You know, the other cops. You're different."

"I don't think I'm much different. I have to arrest people and stuff, so I don't know about that."

She laughed. "Yeah, you are. You're here, aren't you? Who else would be here in my house on South Side?" She had a good point. What was I doing here?

Bianca had her arm draped around Stiggy who gave me a look of confidence. You phony chump, I thought, and smiled at him.

"Well, my goofy friend over there, he wanted to come, so I couldn't let him come here alone, could I? We know about you guys," I told her, hoping she wouldn't be offended by my joke.

"We know about you, too," she countered, half jokingly, half seriously. In fact, the South Side knew almost as much about the cops as we knew about them.

"Yes, I'm sure you probably do."

"So!" She announced, moving closer to me. "How come you're a cop?"

Time to philosophize. I looked at her and she seemed to sincerely want to know. "I didn't start out to be, I just needed a job when I finished high school, so I went to work there and pretty soon, it seemed like a good profession to get into. Maybe

I thought I could save the world, you know, the shining knight and stuff. Or maybe if I didn't, I could have ended up in jail."

Mary laughed at the notion. "Right. I could just see you in jail. Maybe you'd be next to my brother." She opened the door for me. I had to know.

"Mary, I'm going to ask you a question. You may find it disturbing, and I don't mean to do that, but there's something I'm dying to know." She looked inquisitive.

"I won't be offended. Living here, it's pretty hard to do that. What do you want to know?"

"Listen. I just want to know. You tell me the truth, and I will leave it right here, right now. Honest. I wouldn't lie to you in your own house."

"Well, I'm waiting."

"You talked about your brother, Robin. You know I'm the one who busted him for the Wig-Wam rip-off (the name of the wig store)."

"Yes. He said you were pretty cool," she answered.

"Mary, you were with him that night, huh? I know it was you, so you can tell me. I'm not going to bust you. You got away. You're pretty slick." She laughed nervously, which told me I was right.

"You think I'm going to tell you? Get real!" I wasn't sure if she was angry or faking it. She was good.

"Come on! It was you. I can tell. I knew it."

"You said you ain't gonna bust me?"

"Swear to God!"

"You got me," she confessed. "But I know you didn't get any prints or even see me, and I know Robin wouldn't tell you."

"You're right. Well, now that we're being honest, what about---?"

"That's it!" She interrupted. "No more questions. You wanted to know, so I told you."

"OK. I'm sorry. I appreciate your honesty, but I have to tell you, you could be a smooth criminal." I liked Mary. She was honest when she didn't have to be. I looked over and saw Stiggy trying to kiss Bianca. She felt uncomfortable with her sister and I sitting there talking about the trials of life. Stiggy was in a zone, the twilight zone.

"You know what they say about you?" The "they" she was referring to being the criminal element on the South Side—the "they" with whom she was much too familiar. I was intrigued.

'No, what do they say?" I took a small sip of the beer.

"If they get busted, they hope it's by you." I was taken aback and didn't know how to respond. She was complimenting me, and I wasn't sure whether to thank her or move on. I looked at her, her beauty, her eyes, and heard the sound of a siren—a siren which seemed off in the distance, but gradually grew louder. The sirens came closer and now sounded like they were outside her door, and then many more. The welfare residents were awakened by something happening, running to see the action.

'Damn,' I thought. 'Everyone's going to know we're here.' Stiggy jumped up, as did Bianca and Mary. Mary motioned for us to stay put.

"I'll be back. I'll see what's going on." She closed the door, keeping us out of sight. She didn't put anything over her pajamas. Seconds later, she ran excitedly back into the house.

"You guys better come here," she yelled. Carefully, we walked outside, trying to be as obscure as possible. It looked like the entire neighborhood was aroused outside Mary's housing project. Stiggy's eyes flared as he saw his car engulfed in flames. The flames were jumping higher than the second stories of the projects as the fire department personnel fought desperately to contain it. I could only look on in dumbfounded outrage. His '67 VW bug, on its way to becoming a classic, burned in the red zone, the casualty of an irascible arsonist. As we stood with the crowd, hypnotized and horrified by the deed, Dumas appeared out of nowhere, behind me.

"Isn't that Stiggy's car?"

Stig was clearly upset. "You know it is, Dumas," the anger in his voice clearly evident.

"What are you guys doing here?" Dumas asked, looking at me. What was I supposed to say; we're trying to make it with a couple of welfare chicks. We're here to score some heroin? I had to think fast, for this was sure to be reported to the brass tomorrow.

"I got a lead from an informant," I answered. "It's a case I've been working on for a while." I didn't actually lie. Mary had informed on herself for the wig shop burglary. "The informant was in a bit of trouble and wanted me to meet him here right away." Now I lied, hoping he wouldn't smell the beer on my breath. "Stiggy was over so I asked him to drive me here. You know, safety in numbers."

"Your informant calls you at home?" He was suspicious. What an idiot, I thought. A valued informant can always call the cop at home, but, of course, Dumas didn't know that because he had none.

"I haven't got time to explain, Dumas. I felt I had to get over here, but this…" I motioned to the still flaming VW, "this is something totally outrageous. We never anticipated this."

"Got any ideas?" Dumas asked.

"I think so. I'm betting it's a cohort of my informant. Saw us going in and torched it. I'll be working on it." Mary turned away before she started laughing. Stig knew my style and played along.

"My car! It's all your fault, dammit! My car!"

I kept it going. "Stig, I'm sorry. How was I to know?"

Dumas bought it. "I'm sorry, Jim," he said. He wasn't close to Stig, so he had to call him by his first name. "This is an obvious arson. We'll do all we can to find out who did it." He then left to confer with the on-scene fire captain.

"You guys are too much," Mary offered. "We couldn't have pulled it off any better. You should be living on South Side." She gave me another compliment which I knew was sincere. We achieved an invisible bond, something I knew could develop even more, but it wasn't to be, not under our present circumstances. I was sick to my stomach for Stiggy. He loved and took great car of his little bug. Those jerks. Someone must have recognized his car belonging to someone from the department and exacted revenge. Any romantic inclinations for Stiggy had burned up, along with his car.

"Can I get you guys a ride home?" Bianca offered.

"No, thanks. Dumas will give us one. Thanks just the same. We better get going," I said.

Mary was looking at me with those eyes, eyes that brought back memories of Faline, Bambi's consort from the Disney movie. "Come back again." I wanted to, but knew I couldn't. She had the look that held the answers to life's mysteries, and only she could provide the answers to the universal riddle of existence. I wanted to discover the secret to that mystery.

"What case are you working," Dumas asked on the way home.

"I'm not allowed to divulge that information at this time," I officially told him, an inside joke for the benefit of Stig, glassy-eyed and quiet in the back seat.

"Must be something pretty big for you to come out at this time of the morning," he kept prodding.

"It is. Just be patient and I'll fill you in at the right time. I don't want to sound so mysterious, but it's just one of those things I'm trying to develop early. You understand."

"You sure you don't need any help with anything." I wasn't sure if he was sincere, or playing me, figuring he'd been the victim of a clown job to cover our tracks for being in South Side. If I was really working a case, he'd be the last guy to know about it. He was one of those guys who didn't mind stealing your information, developing it and taking credit for himself. That is, if he even got anywhere with it the first place. Dumas was a puzzlement. Sometimes he could be a regular guy, cracking jokes and having a good time. Other times he could be surly and abrupt, a real pain to be around.

He not only had humongous ears, but everything about him was big, especially his hind end. He was 6 foot 3, about 240 pounds, but not really fat or muscle bound, just big all over. It was difficult to communicate with him. If it wasn't about police work, there was no conversation, no sports, politics, world issues, nothing. As patrolmen, our responsibility was the city proper, everything beyond the city limits was off limits, unless you were Dumas. While us peons were beating the bushes, looking for bad guys, Dumas was beating the bushes, literally, in the outskirts of town, looking for local kids parked, making whoopee. We often thought he got a bigger thrill finding two adolescents in compromising positions rather than interrupting a burglary in progress.

It was an unwritten law amongst us that if we happened upon a car parked surreptitiously in a darkened corner of town, to light it up with our car's spotlight for awhile, giving the kids time to get dressed before embarrassing them any further. Not Dumas. If he came across a parked car, he'd sneak up to the occupants with his flashlight, then get as close to the window as possible and shine his light within hoping to see as much as he could. Strange man. Per procedure, he always radioed it in when he was going to check out a "suspicious vehicle," and before any backup arrived, he'd call it off, seeing all he could before anyone else got there. No one ever hurried to back him up whenever he radioed it in, for we all knew the routine. Pervert!

To his credit, however, aside from checking out local neckers, he was a straight forward policy wonk. He was by the book, no deviation from policy, no variations in his routine. I never got past the "forward" in the same book, and I knew that some of my supervisors wanted to throw that same book at me! I knew well he'd tell the brass, first thing, about my trek to South Side. If he detected the alcohol on my breath, that would be reported as well.

"Thanks for the ride, Dumas," I said as he dropped us off at the bar where I met Stiggy.

"If you need any help with your case, let me know."

"Right. Thanks." I drove to my apartment for some good spirits as the beer from Mary's didn't set well with me.

Somebody really had it in for cops, not Stiggy or I necessarily, just cops in general. We tried to figure out who, but it didn't really matter. It was us versus them, cops versus criminals, cops versus the world; that's the way it always was, that's the way it is, and that's the way it will always be—but then, nothing really mattered in this bizarre existence. I fixed Stiggy and myself a drink while we tried to relax to the Rolling Stones' album, <u>Flowers</u>. A song came on called "Backstreet Girl," where Mick Jagger sings about British aristocracy and a lower class girl who becomes the secret lover to a higher class gentleman, one with whom he cannot be seen in public. She is his backstreet girl. I thought of Mary. Could she become my "Backstreet Girl?"

"Come on, Stig. We got a shoot in the morning. I better take you home."

"Wait…just one more. Wait until the album's over."

"I think you had enough. You been drinking too much lately anyway. If we leave now, we'll get a few hours sleep. Let's go."

"Who are you? My mom? One for the road, then." I felt for him. He had a rough night. First getting his clock cleaned by Okie Hayes, then his car torched. Poor guy.

"Alright. One for the road. And that's it! Dig?"

I drove him home. He finished his drink and left. "Thanks, mom. See you in the morning."

"G'night, Stig. I'll be by around 9."

The department had its qualifying training shoot at the pistol range every four months. The officers had to shoot a certain score to maintain their proficiency, which often became an unspoken competition. Loser had to buy breakfast. The reserves also had to shoot a certain score in order to maintain their eligibility to ride patrol. Anyone who didn't qualify could not ride until the next shoot. In the unlikely event deadly force was ever used, meaning an officer had to kill a bad guy, the issue would be tantamount in the event a civil lawsuit was filed by the family of the dead crook. Many reserves were crack shots, including Stiggy. His cross country prowess as a high schooler gave him much stamina and calm nerves. Our scores were close each time, so our breakfast tabs were nearly even. After every shoot, the routine was to devour huevos rancheros at Chapararro's Restaurant then take a nap before the swing shift.

I groggily awoke to the 8 AM alarm, hit the snooze button and finally woke up around 8:30. I rushed over to Stiggy's to wake him up in time for the shoot. I knocked on his apartment door; no answer. I knocked louder, still no answer. I knew he was home because his motorcycle was parked out front. He lived in a quiet apartment complex next to the Catholic Church and across the street from an elementary school. I walked around to the back of his apartment and forced open a window and crawled inside. One of the nuns from the church saw me, so I stuck my head back out the window and yelled, "I locked my keys inside." I felt guilty for lying to a nun, but figured it was easier than explaining the situation.

I found Stiggy still in his clothes passed out on his couch, dead drunk. A melted drink was by his side. "Stig. Wake up!" He didn't respond. I yelled louder and shook him violently, I mean violently. I couldn't believe anyone could sleep this deeply. I couldn't wake him, so I poured some water in his face. "Stiggy, you jerk! Get up. We got a shoot today. You miss it you don't ride patrol. Get up!"

"Huh? Who the...? Lemme alone." The words dripped from his mouth.

"GET UP!"

Slowly, he opened his bloodshot eyes, his mouth dry from a night of drinking. I got him a glass of water and waited until he was cognizant of the world. We were able to stop for some coffee on the way to the pistol range. "You alright?"

"Yeah. Thanks for waking me. I was gone."

"You're telling me. For a minute, I thought you were dead."

He just laughed. "Nah. I'm too cool to die."

A moment of silence followed. "Stig. You're drinking too much. You ought to cool it for a while."

He didn't answer, taking a sip from the hot coffee.

"I'm serious, Stig. You been driving home from the bars drunk and stuff. What if you got in a wreck, or one of the guys stopped you? You'd be done."

"OK, mom."

"I should be your mom. No. I will be your mom. You're grounded!"

Stiggy laughed, and then got serious. "Yeah. I suppose you're right. I'll watch it. Just don't tell my mom, alright?"

Most of the officers were already at the range, waiting for stragglers like us to show up. Stiggy fixed his target and nearly shot a perfect score. "Sheesh! You shoot like that when you're hung-over, I can't imagine what you'd shoot sober. Maybe I was wrong about your drinking," I kidded him. He just smiled his wry smile. He was really starting to worry me.

After I bought his huevos rancheros and took a nap, I checked in for the swing shift. It was a bright, sunny afternoon. The wind was stirring a bit which would become a bit fiercer as the afternoon wore on. The town was infamous for causing hay fever and allergies, besides its smell. After briefing, I headed for South Side. As the wind whipped my hair into a frenzy, I pondered the night's occurrences. The criminal grapevine travels faster than any office gossip system. It didn't take long for Mary to find out who torched Stiggy's car.

TWENTY-EIGHT

The wind picked up causing me to sneeze incessantly. I cruised through the cul-de-sac where Stig's car was torched, West Court. Mary was walking near, saw me and gave me the high sign. I waited until she was away from the projects, then drove next to her as she walked, then stopped.

"Jose Lopez? Who the hell is he?" I asked Mary.

"Just a chump trying to make a statement," she answered.

"I'll say he made a statement. He's got a target on his back now," I told her, figuratively of course.

"Don't take it personal. He doesn't know you guys, but somebody recognized Jim's car as belonging to a cop and told him. He's trying to prove himself, so he torched the car thinking it would make him a big man," she explained.

"We'll see how big he is when he finds himself in the joint," I said in anger.

"He's just a nickel and dimer. Money in the bank for you guys. He'll mess up soon and you guys can nail him, for sure." Mary knew our clientele better than we did. She meant he sold a little drugs now and then but wasn't very careful. It would just be a matter of time before he got busted. The easiest criminal to get is one who likes to flaunt his stuff, and it sounded like Jose Lopez fit that group. I wanted him badly.

"Can you set him up for me?" I asked Mary without thinking. She looked perturbed. I knew I hadn't the right to ask her that just yet. She trusted me but didn't know how far, so she didn't answer. "I'm sorry," I said, which I really meant. "I didn't mean anything; it's just that Stiggy's my buddy. That guy's got to pay for what he did." Her reply surprised me.

"I wouldn't mind setting him up. He's a real jerk. I just don't want to get burned. I have to live here," she said, meaning South Side.

"I understand. I been here too long talking to you already. Better leave before anyone thinks anything. Do me a favor. Don't say anything to Stiggy about what you told me. Let me handle it." It went against my gut to do this to Stig, but if I didn't, he's the kind who would go after the guy himself by retaliating and setting his car on fire, and probably con me into helping him. I didn't think that was too hot of an idea.

"I won't say a word to anyone. The only one I'll talk to is you." I looked into her hypnotic glance, her eyes so intense, so big I nearly swooned. "You get off at eleven?"

"I plan on it, unless I can kill Jose Lopez."

"I'll be at the bowling alley. Why don't you stop by? I'll buy you a drink."

Eleven o'clock couldn't come fast enough. Something about her intrigued me. Maybe it was the criminal element, or maybe she was just a genuinely good person, I didn't know. Maybe I was a criminal myself, trapped inside the body of a cop, waiting for my deliverance. The music of Lou Reed, formerly of The Velvet Underground, had a powerful effect on me, particularly "Walk on the Wild Side." The lyrics of his music touched the boundary of decadence, despair and human imperfection—the addicts, the queers, the losers, the transvestites—the side of life I, through some fortune, escaped yet completely empathized. They were humans, too, struggling as best they could for their piece of dignity, a dignity which could be defined only in and of themselves.

Tracy had one bowling alley consisting of thirty lanes, a small restaurant situated at one end and a bar in the middle, accessible from the bowling alley and from the outside, in case one didn't want to bowl. It catered mostly to the middle-class clientele on the opposite side of South Side, and you didn't find too many Mexicans there, unless it was a night a live band played. On occasion, Tracy Bowl hired a live band, enforcing a slight cover charge, so it was open to anyone who could pay the modest fee. Tonight, the band was there. The bouncer knew me and waived the cover charge. He figured it an investment to have a cop in the joint, just in case.

Good band, good crowd. I had to be careful. This looked like one of those nights when one idiotic drunk could start a major donnybrook. Some of the mentality of the crowd hadn't changed since they were in high school when the "Cowboys" fought the Mexicans in the park after school and chased them back to South Side. On band night, everyone was fair game, but the Mexicans were still outnumbered. Still, the people had enough respect for each other to never bring weapons. It was the cowardly thing to do. I responded plenty of times here while the band played on and the whole joint was engaged in fisticuffs. Bob Seger's "Old Time Rock and Roll" seemed to spark some primal consciousness evoking a fighting instinct. If the band played Seeger's song tonight, I resolved simply to slink out the back door.

Mary saw me scanning the crowd and motioned for me. Smart girl. She had a table adjacent to the back door.

"Thanks for coming. I didn't think you would," she smiled bashfully, barely audible over the sound of the band.

"Why wouldn't I? Someone offers to buy me a drink, I'm there." She looked kind of hurt. "I'm just kidding. If it weren't for you, you think I'd be here?"

Some in the crowd looked hard at me, as though they were trying to place me. Others definitely made me for a cop and were "mad-dogging" me, that is, staring at me to provoke me into some kind of confrontation. Those few mad-dogging me were overshadowed by the rest of the folks who let me be, figuring I had the right to some kind of life. They seemed to respect the idea that I didn't hold myself above them, sharing enjoyment in the same bar as them. It didn't take long for the cocktail waitress to bring me drinks bought by people who were trying to buy me off as a cop, in case I ever stopped them for a speeding ticket, or simply a way of telling me thanks for the work I did. It mattered as I hoped for the latter and tipped my glass in appreciation and swallowed. I loved the people of my town. The band was in fine form, raucously playing "Heartache Tonight" by The Eagles. The crowd moved as one, swaying, singing, swinging; a fight erupted but was quickly quelled by many. Some looked to me, but by the time I realized what was going on, the combatants had cooled it.

> *"Somebody's gonna hurt someone, before the night is through,*
> *Somebody's gonna come undone, there's nothing we can do"*
> "Heartache Tonight" – The Eagles

I then realized Mary was shouting something at me, trying to be heard over the music. She leaned forward and yelled again.

"Let's get out of here," she proffered.

That was fine with me, but I knew I wasn't going to her place. I couldn't afford to have my car torched.

"You want to go to another place? Or, if you want, we can go to my apartment," I sort of yelled, not wanting to be heard by anyone near.

"You going to bring me home?" she asked.

"How did you get here?" I asked, but she couldn't hear.

"What?"

"How did you...never mind...it doesn't matter. Let's go!"

I never experienced a freer, more untroubled evening with a woman in my life, at least not since that day with Shelley when

I was barely an adult. We drank, we laughed, we danced to the music of Alicia Bridges' *"I Love the Night Life,"* which sort of became our theme song. I hated disco with a passion, but I tolerated this one song for Mary. We talked at length and she confided to me the times she had been molested as a child, the suffering, the indignation, the loss of esteem. I empathized with her and held her tightly.

She was a wisp of a woman, an unreal vapor of life with radiantly flowing hair, punctuated by the dim lights of my apartment. Her eyes looked into mine, transcending my being as she spied into my dreams and peeked into the hidden regions of my existence. I could only allow her the outer region because of what lay inside, that being which exists in the lair of my Fortress of Solitude, was better left undisturbed. It was better for her to not know things which didn't concern her. Her lithe body fused with mine and we immersed ourselves in the music of David Bowie's *"Always Crashing in the Same Car,"* and soon my flight into the Enchanted Forest began.

I felt myself rising, then soaring into the depths of a remote island. She seemed apprehensive, letting go for a moment while I held her and brought her to me, to share a stolen flicker of contentment, a splash of time free of pain, free of doubt, free from the consciousness of our troubled worlds. I winged high amongst the birds, through clouds laced with the spirit of my passion. She allowed herself the freedom, the daring to explore the heights of a secret world, clinging to me with the intensity of her essence. We drifted beyond the sphere of earthly existence, into a tunnel, the tunnel of enchantment fusing the spirits of disparate beings into one meaningful instant within the eternity of discord. She clung to me tightly, fearing her voyage with me may somehow be an illusion, illusions of hope which permeated her existence causing her to tread the thinning line of desire and despair.

It's difficult to explain the convergence of our worlds which, upon departing, was again alienated into absurdity; one of confusion and chaos, the other one the reality of my existence as a cop—a thing, a robot, void of humanity and emotion. I worried someone might see me when I dropped her off in front of her welfare projects as she rushed inside. We couldn't plan on being together, it was just something that seemed to happen spontaneously. I'd spot her in a bar during a routine check, or she'd come to the department with others to see about bail for one of "their kind" who had just been arrested. I identified strongly with her, for she was as much an enigma as I thought I was. She was able to circuitously part from the crowd to talk about meeting later, or give me information she thought would be helpful to my job. She never asked anything in return, or perhaps she was already receiving it: a genuine measure of respect for her as another human being.

TWENTY-NINE

Supervisors changed shifts every month, whereas the patrolmen were assigned three month shift assignments. I was already bored and tired with swing shift as I trudged myself into the locker room on a weekday. After changing into uniform and checking the daily briefing log, the chief summoned me to his office. Now what, I thought.

"Sit down," he said, firmly.

"I didn't do it, whatever it is. They're framing me," I protested before he could accuse me. "If you haven't got fingerprints or photos, talk to my lawyer. You ain't got nothing on me."

"If I wanted your skinny ass, I would have had it a long time ago," he bantered. "You're lucky I'm here to cover for your ugly mug, you closet Iranian," he joked, referring to my skin color.

"What's up, Chief?"

"I'm going to announce my retirement. Before I do, I'd like you to take over the Detective Unit." I didn't hear what he said after retirement, startled by his revelation. It blended into a string of senseless words.

"Why?" I quietly asked.

"Because I think you'd make a damn good Detective Sergeant. You work well with people, and you've got something to offer."

"No, I mean, why are you retiring?"

He had enough with the small town politics, about having to appease those he couldn't stand, and facing difficult positions between being a cop, administrator and politician, ills inherent in a police chief. Chief Wolfe had been my mentor, my friend, my detractor, enemy, father figure, trusted advisor and, now, heartbreaker. No matter how I may have felt about him at various times, he always had my respect, one of the very few to have actually earned it. He took his work seriously, but not enough to forget the people who worked under him were human beings, each unique in their individuality. He had the unique ability to joke about things on the job no one dared approach. He poked fun at our weaknesses without offending, and he found humor in everything, except when he was righteously angered, for which I was often at the receiving end. But even so, I knew he cared because, well, because you could just sense it. There were a few who resented his style, including the psycho Lieutenant.

"When are you leaving?" I asked again.

"I don't know, maybe I'll hang around another six months, burn up some sick leave and vacation, and then I'm outta here."

"You serious about me working detectives?"

"You better make me look good my last few months here!"

"Yes, sir. I'll do my best," I promised.

"You better do better than that."

"I will." I reached out to shake his hand and fought back a tear. He grabbed me and hugged me, and I'm sure he did, too.

"I'll make you look so good, you won't want to leave," I said with more hope than reality.

"One more thing," he ordered before I left.

"Yes?"

"Get a haircut!"

* * *

Detectives, huh? I never thought much of the current unit, supervised by Sgt. Dumas, old peanut-brain. But then, I never thought much of the unit at all after my old mentor retired, Sgt. Guevara. Dumas would be rotating back to patrol once I was assigned as the supervisor. Dumas was like a guy who jacks up his point total at the end of a blowout basketball game, the one who keeps tabs on his statistics, taking cheap shots instead of passing the ball to open teammates. The supervisor assigns the detectives cases necessitating follow-up and then bring some kind of closure. You either identified a suspect and filed formal charges, or exhausted all leads and then suspended the case.

Dumas measured success by the percentage of cases cleared by arrest or what was called 'exceptional' clearances, meaning the case was solved even though no charges could be filed. Dumas always assigned himself cases where patrol clearly identified a suspect, or the victim merely had to come in and sign a formal complaint, thereby assuring him a nearly ninety percent clearance rate, far above the other detectives in the unit. He felt it showed he was an effective supervisor, but Chief Wolfe didn't buy that routine. He knew the other Detectives weren't motivated to work for him, and I knew it wouldn't take much effort to work circles around his regime. I asked the Chief to allow me to pick the guys I wanted to work with, and since he cared less about perceived favoritism due to his pending retirement, he agreed.

The department hired a local kid, a popular athlete who had quarterbacked the high school football team and whose parents were successful in business within the community. He liked his job and possessed a high work ethic, so I figured he didn't have any bad habits or bad attitude. The officer, a Portuguese youngster named Kevin Vierra, was apprehensive about working detectives without much experience on patrol. I told him it was a mystery to me, too, but we'd learn together. The other was a red-headed, freckle faced young man from the neighboring town, the one named after pig fat, Manteca. His name was Tim Heskett, a free-spirited, aggressive officer with a charming personality. Maybe I chose him because he reminded me of one of my favorite childhood TV characters, Howdy Doody, the marionette. Together, we were about to change the image of the Detective Unit, much to the consternation of a certain department administrator after the retirement of Chief Wolfe.

While waiting for the transition into detectives, the comfort and solitude of graveyard shift beckoned. A drizzly, wet and chilly February shift was uneventful as most. The town slept while temperatures dipped into the 30's, a night not fit for a thief, drunk, or even a cat. I nearly dozed relieving the dispatcher for her lunch break, playing the Jumble, the scrambled word game, in the newspaper while the young football hero turned cop read the sports pages. The other officer, the cowardly Boo-hoo, was lollygagging in a donut shop. The 9-1-1 emergency phone line blinked red, then rang.

"9-1-1 emergency," I answered. No one said anything. I heard a commotion, or rather, what appeared to be a commotion in the background. "9-1-1 emergency," I repeated.

"Hurry. My son-in-law thinks vampires are after him. He took a shot at my daughter...please hurry. He's crazy!" She gave her address in the county, the jurisdiction of the county sheriff.

"Hang on, ma'am. I'm connecting you the Sheriff's Office." The 9-1-1 system was relatively new, so all calls in the area come into the police department, then routed to the appropriate agency. I monitored the conversation to the Sheriff's dispatcher. The caller explained her son-in-law had taken a drug called PCP, phencyclidine.

In the 1950's phencyclidine was investigated as an anesthetic, but due to the side effects of confusion and delirium, its development for human use was discontinued. It became commercially available for use as a veterinary anesthetic, capable of putting a horse down. In the 1960's, it was declared illegal for human consumption. However, it soon became accessible through the manufacturing in clandestine labs. Its street names include not only angel dust, but supergrass, killer weed, embalming fluid and rocket fuel. It was typically sprinkled on a marijuana joint. PCP users experience extreme feelings of aloneness, lack of emotion, paranoia and the inability to control their thoughts and actions. Chronic users show signs of severe anxiety, depression and hallucinations. It was relatively rare in Tracy at the time, but its effects were well known throughout the department as anytime a person under its effects was encountered, it took several officers to control and arrest him. It gave the user super-human strength and nearly impervious to pain.

I listened in as the sheriff's dispatcher received enough information to send the deputies. I recognized the name of the woman's son-in-law as one who had a minor record ever since he was young, all drug related offenses in and around Tracy, but I didn't recall any acts of violence. Before the dispatcher hung up, I asked if she needed any assistance as I knew it often took a while before the deputies arrived at the scene, since their area of responsibility was the entire county of San Joaquin.

"Hang on, Tracy. Let me check with my supervisor," she responded. Law enforcement agencies within the county referred to each other by the name of the city, such as Stockton, Lodi, or Ripon, or in the case of the Sheriff's Office, San Joaquin.

The department also monitored the Sheriff's radio frequency, and I then heard the supervisor: "That's affirmative. Go ahead and have them send a couple of units until we get there."

"I heard that, San Joaquin. We're on our way," I told the dispatcher.

"C'mon, Kevin. Let's go." The rookie officer threw down the newspaper as we ran from the police facility into a patrol car. The other on duty officer, Howard, or Boo-hoo, the cowardly wife-beater beater was still in the donut shop. I ordered him to respond as well.

We drove the desolate, winding county road to the farm's entrance, a couple of miles from the tiny town of Banta, an artifact from the days of the Wild West. The town had one general store, a small fire department, a matchbox of a post office, a restaurant combined with a drinking establishment, a few houses and many mobile homes. Rumor had it the bar was haunted by a ghost of an infamous cowboy of ill repute, and many eerie sights were reported. Banta was seven miles east of my town with railroad tracks running through the center of it. The sheriff's department asked us to wait at the entrance of the farm. We parked and waited. The rain skipped softly off the windshield, a stillness aligned with the quiet of the night, and then that sensation, the familiar horror of its nature deadened the darkness of the day. The hideous nature of death flitted by. It was about to reveal its awesome power; there was no mistaking its presence. Perhaps it hovered behind a nearby haystack, or swooped outside the farm house, or perhaps it descended in my car, but where ever it was, it would leave its calling card this strange hour.

THIRTY

I was barely conscious of the blur of two sheriff patrol cars whizzing by, into the entrance of the farm. Boo-hoo was right behind, so Kevin and I joined the parade. By this time, the woman called again and reported her son-in-law had jumped onto a tractor with the gun he fired at her daughter. I thought I saw a death mask reflect off the rear window of the car ahead of us, Boo-hoo's. Suddenly, and seemingly without reason, back up lights illuminated the road in front of us, causing Kevin, who was driving, to do likewise. The backup lights seemed unusually bright as they came close to us while Kevin flipped the gearshift into reverse, backing rapidly to avoid a collision. Our back window had fogged up making it difficult for him to see the road. I rolled down my window as a splash of rain greeted my face, hoping to get a better view to guide Kevin away from the oncoming cars while keeping him on the road.

I turned forward, horrified to see a dragon, a monstrous dragon with one eye barreling towards us. It was the tractor with a bright headlight heading on a bead to our reversing car. "Jesus Christ, Kevin!" I yelled, realizing the tractor was going to run us down. "Look!" Kevin looked up, saw the oncoming tractor and floored the gas pedal as we spun and were thrown off the roadway into the muddy fields bordering the thin roadway. The tractor followed us into the field, hell bent for metal. We flung the car doors open and leaped from it as the tractor collided into the front of the car, hesitated then lurched forward with its over-sized humongous tires climbing our car, crunching and twisting metal as though it was a mere aluminum can. We watched in shock and awe as the tractor, like a mighty dinosaur about to devour its weaker prey in one gaping bite, continued its slow, deliberate velocity, pulverizing the overhead light bar under its massive weight. The tires of our car exploded and flattened, even in the mud, in concert with the distorted metal giving way to the size and tonnage of the tractor. After devouring our car, it turned its appetite and seemed to commandeer itself to the Sheriff's patrol car, a few feet behind us in the muddy field.

The bright headlight of the tractor obscured any vision into the cabin, making it look as though it had a life of its own. The Sheriff's car became its prey as the two Sheriff's deputies took refuge behind a haystack as death watched. I heard the distinct, sickening sounds of gunfire, its brilliant flames absurdly visible in the night air from the Sheriff's deputies' duty weapons as they fired at the monstrous tires, which dwarfed the men and their useless patrol car, rendered to scrap metal by the dragon tractor. More shots rang out which didn't come from us nor the deputies. The unseen guy in the tractor was firing at them, or at least into the direction of their muzzle blasts. Everybody hit the mud, face first, as though the soft earth would protect us from a madman's bullets or, if struck, provide a temporary grave. The vast openness of the sky suddenly squeezed itself and swooped upon my shoulders, stifling me. I acknowledged Death's presence and vowed he wasn't going to take me. Perversely, the melody of the song by Kansas, "Dust in the Wind" infiltrated my mind---*"all we are is dust in the wind."*

The tractor paused, mollified by its devastation and continued slowly forward. The abandoned deputies, Kevin and I became aware of each other, standing and dirty in the muddy fields, awkward and confused, like a bunch of Barney Fife clones. The deputies ran to the safety of their brethren, the other deputy's car. Kevin and I spotted Boo-hoo, a look of utter confusion on his face, then ran to his car while the dragon carefully, tantalizingly slithered away from its lair, the farm, towards the tiny town of Banta. After having a car destroyed and shots fired, we had to remember this was the Sheriff's turf, so they were still calling the shots. We followed the remaining car which was following the tractor when suddenly, the sheriff's car pulled to the side of the road. Four deputies piled out and ran to the trunk, donning heavy, armor protected flak jackets. We watched and waited for what seemed like far too long. Finally, they hopped back into their car, but were going nowhere fast. In his excitement, the deputy who was driving pulled too far off the road and his tires were stuck in the mud, spinning and slinging the wet earth onto the pavement.

"What the--? I can't believe that!" I yelled. "Hell with 'em, Howard. Follow that tractor before it gets away."

We passed the deputies who were jumping up and down and yelled for us to stop. Sorry guys. We were already looking pretty stupid, so there was no way we're going to pile four more cops into a car which already had three. We'd look like a circus car where an endless stream of clowns emerges. The demon-tractor was smart, familiar with these country back roads as it kept a distance in front of us. We followed the red eyes of its taillights, and then lost sight of them, and then they opened again, inviting us into its descent into Hades.

"Damn," said Boo-hoo with trepidation. "He's turning his lights off and on! He's messing with us!" We kept a safe distance behind, fearful of more gunfire when we monitored the Sheriff's office who have the "940-A" call, officer needs assistance, meaning all available cars were dispatched. We lost sight of the dragon in the tiny, ghostly town of Banta. Howard stopped the car by the diminutive post office, near the tracks. We waited and listened.

Nothing. Not a sound. Not seeing or hearing the demon tractor, we waited for the Sheriff's instructions.

"Where do you think he went?" queried Boo-hoo, quietly.

"Oh no!" Kevin moaned.

"What's wrong?" Boo-hoo asked. "See something?"

"There's the Banta Inn," he pointed behind us. It was the haunted restaurant-tavern.

"So?"

"I hope the ghost doesn't jump out and compound our problems," Kevin reasoned. I wasn't sure if he was serious or not, but the levity helped and I couldn't help but chuckle.

"That's ridiculous," Boo-hoo whined. "Ain't no ghost. Think there's a ghost, Sarge?" he asked me.

"Well, I tell you what. I don't not believe it." My double negative answer confused him.

"We ain't got time for no ghost. Where did that son-of-a-bitch go?" Boo-hoo asked defiantly. Do you think he went towards the trailer park---Jesus Christ!" He was interrupted by the sudden sound of the dragon's roar, the diesel engines of the tractor revved up and it suddenly appeared from behind the post office, lumbering towards our car. Boo-hoo tried backing from its path, but found himself a sitting duck, if dragons liked duck, as the tires were spinning on some loose gravel on this unpaved street of Banta

"Fire, Kevin!" I hollered. "Start shooting or Howard's dead!" For the first time in my career, I was about to draw my service weapon and shoot at a human being, or was he? Kevin had the acumen to grab the car's shotgun before jumping from it. He fired the shotgun into the tractor's cabin, the glass breaking and the dull thud of metal struck by the shotgun's pellets clearly audible above the roar of the engine. Unthinking, I took a point shoulder stance, as taught in our qualifying shoots, and fired four rounds towards the cabin, unable to see the wraith wreaking havoc. Kevin's shotgun emptied, which he threw to the ground and in one motion that would have made John Wayne proud, drew his revolver and fired more shots into the dragon. An old Banta resident, a hundred yards from this bizarre action, was on the toilet of his mobile home when an errant bullet from Kevin's gun crashed through his window, splatted against the bathroom wall and landed harmlessly at his feet.

The tractor stopped inches from Boo-hoo's car when the patrol car's tires finally engaged and spun out of harm's way. The tractor paused, its engine idling. A deadly calm followed. Did we shoot him? Was he going to give up? The devil on his mission will not be denied. Astonishingly, the engine revved up, made a u-turn and disappeared into the backstreets of this Lilliputian town. The street had only one way out, and that was to the main thoroughfare leading into our town. We ran to the patrol car.

"Howard! You okay," I asked, genuinely concerned.

Clearly shaken at his flirtation with death, he answered, "Yeah. I'm good. Let's get that son-of-a-bitch!" Even in the dark, I could see my widened eyes reflecting off his glasses. "Damn! I'm almost out of gas!" I glanced at his fuel gauge and saw the red arrow resting on "E".

"You idiot! You're supposed to gas up at the start of shift. What the hell?"

"Ain't got time to worry about that now. Let's get another car." Kevin hopped in the back seat with the empty shotgun. In a firefight, it's easy to lose count, so on the way back to the department, we regrouped. I thought I fired 4 shots, but one of my 6-shot speed loaders was empty. My revolver had three live rounds left, meaning I fired a total of 9 shots. Kevin unloaded four rounds of buckshot from his shotgun plus four rounds from his revolver, and we still weren't sure if we even wounded the driver. We monitored the Sheriff's Office on our police radio and learned the tractor was on its way to our town with a contingent of their patrol cars following. The Sheriff's commander ordered his deputies to take the driver of the tractor out since he was shooting randomly at the cars following.

At the department, Howard grabbed an assault rifle from

the weapons room and another car. Kevin and I grabbed more ammunition and jumped into another car. "Let's avoid the highway to the edge of the night and take the back route, Kevin," I told him. Because of the slow pace of the tractor and the following deputies, we were able to race ahead of them and park at a corner service station near the Heinz 57 plant. Kevin parked the car a distance from the street and an absurd sight was visible. The tractor slowly climbed the overpass by the Heinz plant and crept into our town. A stream of patrol cars flashing its red and blue lights kept its distance, fearful of the gun wielded by the maniacal driver. The scene looked like the crawling king snake immortalized in The Doors' lyrics, *"I'm the crawling king snake, and I rule my den..."* It then slithered off the overpass onto the flat street nearing the service station. Without hesitating, the tractor veered off the road toward our patrol car. Stupidly, we took cover behind two gas pumps, but it was the only cover available.

"He's not going to do it again, is he?" I asked incredulously.

"Yes he is! Shoot!" Kevin bellowed.

The tractor ran over, scrunched and munched another patrol car, then went back to the street. I looked at my disabled car, steam misting from the broken radiator. "What the--? Jesus! Kevin!" I was befuddled, but not enough to run towards the tractor firing more shots with Kevin firing from his gun. Then reality struck.

"Get away from the gas pumps in case he fires back, Kevin." He hightailed it as fast as he ever did on a football field. Before we realized it, the tractor stopped in its tracks. "I think we got him." No sooner did the words escape my breath, it revved up again and continued. A shot rang out, echoing off the buildings of the empty street, startling us as we realized the driver fired another shot in our direction. Death be gone! I had given it a premature burial. It lurched forward and continued its deranged odyssey into the city limits. I watched it leave and swore I heard its demoniacal laugh.

A procession of black and white cars slowly followed as Kevin and I jumped up and down, yelling for one of the deputies to pick us up. They ignored us until finally the last car slowed, then stopped; the California Highway Patrol who had joined the uncanny chase. I recognized the driver as one from the local office. "C'mon! Let's get him." The driver turned and looked at me, his eyes big as doughnuts, hesitant, fearful. "Let's go!" I reiterated.

"We...we're going to stay behind and direct traffic," he said meekly.

"Direct traffic? What the--? Direct traffic?" I found myself repeating. "Ain't no traffic here except cop cars. Come on," I yelled. He didn't flinch and kept his slow pace well behind the pursuing Sheriff cars. Howard's voice garbled over my portable radio, which I grabbed from my gun belt.

"Yeah, go ahead, 23," his radio call numbers. The tractor was now out of our sight, but Howard continued his observation.

"He's taken a side street by the Safeway Store. I'm going to get out and wait till he comes by and try to take him out." He was on our turf now. He was dead meat.

"10-4. Be careful," I radioed, a needless piece of advice. The Safeway Store was on the west end of town leading to the Bay Area. Howard hid by the main entrance of the closed store which was decorated with rock facing. We didn't know if the guy had been shot or what his condition was, but he maneuvered the tractor capably and seemed aware of his pursuers. He drove past Howard's hiding spot, and by some sheer incalculable, incredible, perhaps instinctive comprehension saw him lying in wait and fired two shots in his direction, the shots ricocheting off the rock facing sending shards of hot rock onto Howard's head. Unnerved, he took steady aim and fired the assault rifle. The .223 caliber round blasted through the metal door of the cabin and tore away the drivers' left side, blood and flesh splattered against the other side of the cabin. The shot would have been enough to incapacitate any normal human being, but this was the devil, this was the effects of PCP.

Howard watched the guy stumble from the tractor onto the

street and limp wildly to a side street under cover of darkness. "I think I got him, but he's still moving. He's out of the tractor," he radioed. I thought a scene like this existed only in the movies. A guy full of bullet holes shouldn't possibly be alive. He was surreal, a phantom flittering through the city's streets, mocking the local constabulary, defying the laws of nature--damn that PCP! At least he was out of the tractor, though still armed. The squadron of patrol cars encircled the demon tractor, like vultures swarming to a macabre death. The CHP car with us in the backseat was the last to arrive.

"Get us out of here. Hurry!" I yelled to the CHP officer who opened the rear doors, allowing us the freedom to search and destroy. We ran to the direction of the tractor and heard another shot ring out. A shroud of a figure ducked behind a car parked across from the Safeway Store. The figure arose from his cover, taking aim in the direction of the patrol cars when the inferno erupted. The ensuing shots sounded like a string of firecrackers on Chinese New Year. A bullet burst through the specter's head, proving he was human after all, jerking his head obscenely back, throwing him full force against the pavement, bouncing like a frenzied rag doll. His weapon had fallen a safe distance from his body, and the officers carefully approached him while I ran up to take another shot, if another was even necessary.

The last time I heard breathing like that was when I had to tend to a stray dog call which had been run over by a garbage truck. Its head and body crushed into itself while it desperately took its last gasps of breath. This guy's breath was usurped by the gurgling, gagging sound of blood draining into his throat as his body convulsed, then quivered its last movement. He lay dead. A sheriff's deputy checked the body and called for an ambulance. No one knew what to say, perhaps because each was saying a silent prayer that no other lives were lost. The Sheriff's commander then pulled up to the scene, ordering everyone to return to Stockton except those directly involved in the initial call. Unlike the movies, a shooting leaves one's body and mind exhausted, dazed and confused when you understand you're alive but in awe of the tremendous power of death. Boo-hoo puffed furiously on a cigarette while Kevin paced anxiously, uncertain if what happened really happened. I suddenly remembered I had to call an administrator and asked dispatch to summon the Chief or one of his Lieutenants.

"Are you guys okay?" The Sheriff's commander, a Mexican Lieutenant named Max Benitez, asked.

"We're fine," I assured him.

"You guys did what you had to do. Don't sweat it," he said as he patted me on the shoulder.

"Thanks. You going to be around? One of my bosses will be here shortly and---", he didn't let me finish my sentence.

"You tell Chief Wolfe to come see me. I'll be here." From his demeanor I figured he was an old acquaintance of the Chief's, so I was confident he'd assure the Chief everything was done to procedure. I looked down the street and saw the Highway Patrol directing traffic away from the tractor and body. I walked to the officer who was driving the car and apologized for yelling at him.

"Don't worry about it. I been there," he smiled. Yes, he understood in the heat of the moment, especially in law enforcement, things can get testy, nothing personal, just professional angst.

On of our unmarked cars drove up to the scene and I expected to see the Chief. 'Damn! It's the psycho lieutenant,' I thought. He surveyed the scene, walking towards the tractor and the bloodied pavement. He saw me looking at him then walked towards me. "I understand you wrecked two patrol cars," were the first words from his taut, thin lips.

"I wrecked two patrol cars?" I asked incredulously. I pointed to the tractor. "He ran over two patrol cars and tried to kill us. How can you even ask such a dumb question? You don't even know what happened!" I protested. Just then, Lt. Benitez approached us and our Lieutenant's demeanor quickly changed, putting on a false smile.

"Your guys did what they had to do," the Sheriff's Lieutenant said in our defense. Rendle kept that glued smile as he turned towards me. I walked away in disgust, embarrassing him in front of his peer, Lt. Benitez.

Any time an officer involved shooting occurs, an inquisition is certain. After daybreak, District Attorney Investigators flooded the scene and the department, arranging interview sessions with all involved. The rookie, John Wayne's protégé, Kevin, was the first to be interviewed, followed by Boo-hoo. I gulped coffee by the cupfuls awaiting my turn as it was nearing noon. Kevin looked harried and harassed, so he hung around until my interview was over. Boo-hoo, the hero of the day, disappeared. At this point, and without firm commitment, the D.A. said the shooting appeared to be justified. There was that word again, 'appeared.' The local press had shown up after taking pictures of the bullet-riddled tractor hoping to get an interview with the Chief explaining the bizarre occurrence. Chief Wolfe was ducking them until he got a firsthand report. He saw me and quietly waved me towards him.

"What's up, Chief?"

"Look. I hate to do this, but I want you to understand. I have to do some political posturing," he explained.

"What in the world does that mean?"

"I have no doubt the shooting was clean, I mean, between you and me."

"And?" I waited for the punch line.

He looked hesitant. "I'm close to retirement. There's a slight chance this may not go down the way we'd like it to. There's a chance the issue of you guys overreacting may be brought up."

Well this was a fine how do you do. I was astonished. Appreciative of his honesty yes, but bewildered just the same.

"Chief. How can anyone say we overreacted? We answered a call to help from the Sheriff's Office...I..."

"I know, I know," he interrupted. "I know all that." He

explained the political connections of the dead man's family. He was a relative, the nephew, of a wealthy, influential man, making a fortune in real estate. His name was nearly synonymous with our town. The family would exert extreme pressure to find any fault, anything that could be interpreted as an overreaction by zealous officers. The dead man was estranged from his family, primarily because of his drug use. Once the press got hold of the details, the family would want to keep their name from being smeared, even though the ones who intimately knew him privately said he was not a very good man.

"Until the D.A. rules formally on this, I have to make a low profile statement. I can't publicly back you until then. I'm sorry, but that's life, that's politics in a small town. I hope you understand," he explained in earnest.

"So what am I supposed to do? What do I tell the other guys?"

"You don't have to tell them anything. I won't say anything to make you look bad, but when the statement comes out, I don't want to hear anything about how I don't back them. That's bullshit and you know it. Do what you can to defend me. Can I count on you?" I was worried. Sure, he'd be retiring soon, he'd be gone. What if he sold me out from all the pressure he'd be receiving? What then? I never thought the incident could be construed any other way.

"Sure you can, Chief. Just don't wimp out on me. You know we're right." I looked at him for a sign of reassurance and felt further troubled when I didn't get one. 'I'll do what you ask." As I left his office, he called me again.

"Yes, sir?"

"Get a haircut!"

In a small town, police shootings are extremely rare. We were treated like some sort of celebrities. Stiggy came to the department wanting a detailed, firsthand account which I told him for what seemed like the hundredth time. Guys wanted to be close to the ones who battled death and lived to tell about it. I was getting sick of all the attention as the thought of the bullet riddled body stuck in my mind. The war against drugs seemed so absurd when I thought about the possibility of his stray bullet striking me in the head and killing me. What would it have mattered? Who would have cared about a dead cop years from now, or the next day? I could just envision drug use dropping dramatically because of a maniacal shoot out with the drug induced hallucinations of a suicidal man. Indeed.

All this political posturing, threats of lawsuits, an "appearance" of justifiable homicide, and hero worship because a man was shot to blazes, again and again until a bullet ripped his brain rendering the rest of him meaningless, nothing more than a husk of a human being who once loved, laughed, and lived a more purposeful existence at some point. Damn that PCP!

THIRTY-ONE

Tracy was a tough town. It was the modern version of Tombstone, a lawless watering hole no one cared about, a blip between the beauty and history of San Francisco and the fertile flatlands of San Joaquin Valley leading to the state capitol, Sacramento. Men were tough and the women tougher. The cops were Tracy's finest and had to be the roughest, toughest hombres in the west. No one took stress leave; no one was off more than a day if they were injured in a brawl or tossed by buckin' bronco, which was a tussle amongst ourselves. As such, post traumatic stress syndrome was laughed at, having no credibility whatsoever. Anyone who dared claim stress was teased relentlessly about being assigned to the rubber gun squad. Our department psychologist was the nearest bar.

I fretted waiting for the decision by the D.A.'s office's ruling of justifiable homicide. True to the Chief's analysis, the family was exerting pressure, showing the deceased to be a troubled, non-violent, disturbed young man who didn't deserve to die so barbarously. They were able to recite the number of bullet holes in his body, but failed to mention his level of PCP toxicity, far beyond human tolerance. My stress level was nearing human tolerance, but I didn't want to be a part of the rubber gun squad, meaning being assigned a desk job until things were back to normal. I kept my worries to myself which surfaced during sleep. Listening to "*Gimme Shelter*" by the Rolling Stones, I dozed off into dreamland.

I stood alone at the peak of a mountaintop, its descent plummeting beyond my vision. I felt a strong wind fiercely whipping behind, as if it wanted to push me down the descent, and I fought to keep my balance, avoiding the abyss. The wind stopped suddenly and my eyes caught the brilliance of a radiant being hovering above me. 'What manner of creature is this?' I dreamt. I saw feathers. A huge bird? Delicate, velvety feathers from top to bottom covering an upright corpse? Slowly, the feathers moved, beginning to unfurl. 'Heaven, help me,' I cried in the dream. Wings! That's what they were; wings! I saw three sets of wings, one large pair at the center of the being complemented by smaller sets of wings at its head and base. The wings at its base slowly unfurled, revealing tender human feet. The larger wings gracefully unveiled, showing a slight body wrapped in a shroud, arms folded across its chest. The head was still covered with a smaller set of wings which dramatically opened, exposing a face, a face from the ancient gallery, beautiful in its solemnity, brooding as if in grief.

A seraph! I stood arrested, gazing in sheer awe and wonder. Nothing existed in the universe but the seraph and I. A timeless silence followed when her soft eyes looked downward at me and spoke. "It's about time," she delicately said.

"You speak of time. Tell me of time," I whispered back.

"Humanity is the carcass of time. Time is the soul of existence. Existence is the essence of death."

What did she mean? What was this riddle? Why is time thematic in my dream? In dreams, there is no time. There is never a reference to time, day, night, years. Time cannot be measured within our subconscious; it is oblivious to that which our conscience reveres. My subconscious traversed time, space and infinity. It knows no limits. I felt myself falling, falling forward. My conscious wanted to awake, but my subconscious kept me in the dream, a conflict within my soul. I continued falling when the seraph's outstretched arms cradled me and kept me close to her heart. I felt the force of her wings as they fought the air, the whooshing sound of her massive, silky feathers clearly audible as I ascended above the mountaintop. I felt the sensation of flight in my sleep, a pleasurable journey of which I did not want to wake.

In dreams there is no timely logic, and the next instant, we were descending on a flat terrain adjoining a seashore. The sea seemed endless and frightening in its calmness as I saw a chair, a lone chair faintly visible at the ocean's edge. I sat in the chair facing the mesmerizing flow of the waves. All was serene until the world seemed to suddenly crack in two--the sea waves raced to the sullen shore, screaming high above my chair. A fragile thunder danced in concert with the turbulence of the suddenly rising waves. With savage impact, the wave crashed against me, engulfing me in the swirling, laughing maelstrom. My head was thrown back against the chair as the water annihilated the air, quickly replacing the oxygen in my body. I moved my head violently, gasping for the breath that would never come. I gasped and fought between the two pillows on my bed, waking and gulping precious air, drenched from the force of the waves when in reality it was the sweat from my body.

I continued to have variations of the dream some time after. What did it mean? A premonition of my own death? From the depths of the darkness of slumber, I saw faces, faces of people totally unrecognized swinging into my view. Their faces were clearly distinct--men, women whose faces were contorted in horror. As soon as one face passed from view, another one followed, each turning more hideous than the one before until they frightened me from sleep. Now who were these? Beings from the land of the dead? The dead warning me of danger, or the dead foretelling my doom? Was my sanity leaving me? These were puzzling questions, leaving me in a quandary. I told no one, except my friend Stiggy. He just laughed at me and told me I had to drink more. That would cure me. Cure me from what? I had to leave here, I had to go somewhere, anywhere but here. I felt stifled with a wave of uncertainty looming.

In the weeks that followed, I took a day off and fled to my version of the Enchanted Forest. A few short hours' drive away and I was in the charming Monterey Bay, the most magnificent city on the planet. The ocean's brisk air, the laughter of the sea lions and the flight of the gull titillated my very being, and I felt relaxed and peaceful. I walked the sea shore for miles detouring to the cragged rocks jutting from the coastline, as though God tossed his jewels there to emphasize the beauty of His creation. I drove the serpentine highway of Monterey's 17 Mile Drive and paused at Point Joe, The Lone Cypress, Seal Rock and The Ghost Tree. I marveled at its breathless majesty. I climbed the rocks and crannies of these diamonds of the earth which led to a natural, erosion caused tunnel where the waves danced solely for my pleasure.

"This way to the diving chamber, Danny," I thought I heard a voice from long ago say. The sea began to crest as the tide rolled in near sunset. The memory of my dream clashed within my brain and I instinctively moved to higher ground. The absurd thought of a rogue wave grabbing me and pulling me in forever sent a chill through my body, so it was time to leave. I drove to the quaint nearby city of Carmel to find my hero's establishment. Dirty Harry, also known as Clint Eastwood, was my role model. I found the Hog's Breath Inn, which he owned, and decided to see if I might get lucky, a Clint Eastwood sighting. The bar and restaurant were itself enchanting. I felt I had been here before, though I know I never had. There was something comforting here, something spellbinding. There was nothing like this in Tracy. I grabbed a seat at the bar and ordered a cocktail and soaked in the atmosphere. I must be dead. This was pure heaven.

Oh my! This can't be. I know I'm dead now. A woman sat

at the other end of the bar and I couldn't take my eyes off her. I didn't want to be obvious and have her think I was some kind of a weirdo, but I couldn't help it. Is that...can it be? She looked amazingly like Evelyn, the psycho woman who stalked Clint in his movie, "Play Misty for me," portrayed brilliantly by Jessica Walters. She caught me staring and I awkwardly tried to look away. It wasn't her, but she could have fooled me. I think she was now looking at me, but I was scared to look again. What if she was a psycho? What if Clint was right? Life often imitates art, doesn't it? The bar was nearly empty except for us two. She walked towards me and sat at the stool next to mine.

"You look like you lost your best friend," she said. If her name turned out to be Evelyn, I was going to run out the door. Fortunately, it wasn't.

"No. He couldn't make it. He stayed at home, so I came just to get away," referring to my best friend, Stiggy.

"Where you from?" she queried.

"Tracy."

"Tracy?"

"Yeah. A little town about 60 miles east of San Francisco."

"Oh." she replied, disinterestedly.

"Well. It looks like you could use a friend." I missed her cue entirely.

"Not really. I come here a few times by myself. It cleanses the soul." She looked at me like I was some kind of small town hick.

"You know what they say," she said.

Huh? Who? Maybe she was a psycho. I didn't hear anyone say anything.

"Who said what?" I asked her.

"If you want a friend, be one," she answered.

"Oh, really?" I didn't know what to say. "That's nice. What do you mean?"

"I'd like to be your friend," she offered.

Oh. Now I got it. Yes, I could use a friend. Here in this magical spot, in this bar, in this time, I could certainly use a friend.

After an enchanted evening, it was time to head back to Tombstone.

The District Attorney's Office officially ruled the tractor shooting 'justifiable homicide,' an incongruous term if ever there was one. The atmosphere around the department was like an emancipation, with all the smiles, handshakes, and political posturing. It meant nothing to me. A label applied to a deadly action whose aim was strictly measured in monetary terms-- the prevention, or at least the defense against, a wrongful death lawsuit. In the end, the guy's death came down to the basic law of nature, the process of natural selection; better him than me.

My partner, Stiggy, came in to ride as a reserve with me. I never hesitated to turn the keys over to him. He was dependable, astute and as good as any regular on the force. He was now taking medication to control his diabetes, but he would never achieve his dream to become a regular, sworn officer. Swing shift on weekends was quite busy as the town wound down from its week of labor. We were engaged in deep discussion of our favorite television show, reruns of the Three Stooges. We argued whether the pie fights or the spooky house episodes were the most hilarious. The argument was interrupted when a call of a shooting was dispatched to the beat officer. Stiggy activated the emergency lights and we sped to the scene, to what's referred to in police parlance as a "lower income, economically depressed area" on the city's north side. The street, bordering an open field, comprised of a series of cheap, cabin type dwellings occupied primarily by migrant field workers, pensioners and the poor.

Strategically approaching the house, in the event the shooter was still there, we found the residence empty. The front door had the window pane broken out, but other than that, nothing out of the ordinary was apparent. We learned the occupants were at a Mexican dance on south side, so we left a note to have them call the department if anything was unusual or missing. Stiggy and I resumed patrol and heard nothing from the occupants.

Weeks later, the Sheriff's Office retrieved a "floater," a dead body found floating in the water of the Calaveras River. The body was that of a young Mexican male, shot in the head, whose time of death was approximated as the time we received the call of a shooting in the unoccupied cabin. A few days later, the Sheriff's detectives identified the corpse as one who had rented the cabin, along with other farm laborers.

The current Detective Sergeant, Dumas, ole peanut brain, argued the murder could not be established as having occurred in the cabin; therefore, we had no jurisdiction. The Sheriff countered, and rightfully so, that the call of the shooting in the cabin meant that Tracy had jurisdiction, and that the killer, or killers, had dumped the body in the river as forensics showed the man was dead before he hit the water. Clearly, after the shooting in the cabin, everyone split before the police got there. The broken window pane could have meant someone forced their way into the residence. In typical peanut-brain logic, Dumas reasoned the illegal laborer, the murder victim, the passage of time since the murder and discovery of the body, and the lack of physical evidence did not prove city jurisdiction. In police circles, this is known as the royal kiss-off. The only real evidence was the tape of the 911 call, the mysterious female caller who reported the shooting. Due to the lack of substantial leads, Dumas put the case in the suspense file.

THIRTY-TWO

My time on patrol was getting short as I anticipated my transfer to detectives. There was one problem with the assignment--my wardrobe. I still owned one suit, bought when I graduated from high school, the same one I wore to court when I was called to testify against the major drug dealer years ago, Sergio Macias. Style was never my strong suit, so Stiggy helped me pick out some duds suitable for business attire on a daily basis. A trip to K-Mart and another friendly police reserve my height, a local businessman, threw in some of his old suits, and I was ready. Stiggy was a jeans and t-shirt type of guy, but I was impressed with his knowledge of fashion. He told me what to wear with what, ties, socks, things like that. He said never to wear a printed tie with a printed shirt, or a solid tie with a solid shirt. If I got the two confused, I'd end up looking like a clown. Sound advice. Before he retired, Chief Wolfe gave me more advice.

"Don't be thinking just because you're wearing fancy suits and stuff that you're smarter than everybody else around here. You start primping like some kind of prima donna, all impressed with yourself, everyone will know it. Understand?"

"Yes, sir." I gathered he saw what the rest of us saw in the current unit.

"Don't be concealing vital information on a case you're working and act like you're the only one with any investment in it, know what I mean?" he counseled.

"I'm not sure," I answered.

"Information is the heart and soul of working investigations. Information can come from all sorts of people, people you arrest, people who work in all night places like restaurants and service stations, secretaries, janitors, people who patrol the streets night and day," he continued.

I was beginning to understand. Inherently, many departments experience a rift between the Detective Unit and the patrol division, often out of professional jealousy. Cops are fiercely competitive by nature and see it as a victory if they can outdo each other, except for the obligatory whiners and slugs. It can become counterproductive when the victory becomes more important than the competition, because victory means being number one, and striving to be number one means putting oneself above the effort of the competition.

"Oh, and one more thing. Don't forget patrol," he continued.

"How can I forget patrol?" I asked him. "I'll always be a patrolman at heart."

"We'll see. Just don't leave them out. You share information with them, they'll beat the bushes for the information you need,"

"I understand, Chief. Thanks."

"One more thing." He was starting to sound like Columbo now. "You treat the people in jail with a little respect; you'll be surprised how much they're willing to share once you ask." I already knew that. I did have respect for the criminal element. They knew what they were. The played the game within their rules, which we both knew didn't exist.

The chief made sense to me. Usually does. We often joked

about guys going into Detectives who became too full of themselves, seeing themselves as TV cops, meaning they would emulate whatever TV show was popular at the time. Every cop watched Joseph Wambaugh's "Police Story" each Thursday on TV, including me. The "John Wayne Syndrome," cops battling against the justice system seemingly in favor of criminals, and cops more dedicated to their departments than their families were worn out themes and didn't apply much to small police departments like ours. Some guys thought they were supposed to act on the streets what they saw on TV once they left the academy. Stiggy and I called them "TV cops."

At the far west end of my town was an old wooden framed, tiny beer bar called the Shady Inn, which also had some small one room cabins behind it. The bar had a large, oversized window at the front affording a view into the entire place from the street. It was called Shady because the tall elms surrounding it offered much shade during the hot summer months. Peanut-brain thought it was shady because shady things were going on there, like drinking and sex. The woman who ran the bar was an old high school acquaintance whom I used to have a crush. She was always in her red, 1965 Thunderbird convertible packed with girls. My crush dissipated when I learned she was lesbian. She kept her sexuality hidden until well after high school, but I was still fond of her. She was friendly and funny, a nice combination to run a beer bar. Actually, her mother owned it, but she had taken ill, so Linda became the caretaker of the Shady Inn.

Whenever she sensed impending trouble, she called the department to ask for an officer to simply conduct a walk through. Usually, the sight of an officer making a check was enough to quell a potential row, thus saving Linda a bit of trouble and cost. I enjoyed making the walk through when I worked her beat, often stopping to have a soda and chatting with her. One Thursday before my graveyard shift, I watched Police Story to get fired up, to see how the big city boys did it. Peanut-brain was my supervisor for the shift. After our briefing, which simply consisted of reading the day's incident reports, he assigned me beat one, which was south side and the business district, incorporating the Shady Inn.

"I want you to make frequent checks of the Shady Inn tonight," he ordered me before I went to my patrol car.

"Sure. Is there a problem?" I wondered.

"There may be a problem with prostitution," he proclaimed.

"Prostitution? At the Shady Inn?"

"Yeah. Truckers hang out there, girls, and everything. I think there might even be drugs. Truckers, girls, and bennies; makes it ripe for a prostitution ring."

"What do you expect me to do?" He was getting bizarre again.

"Check it out. Make walk throughs, stake it out, whatever. I don't want it to get out of hand."

Here we go again, I thought. The Police Story show aired earlier portrayed vice cops working prostitution and drugs. Peanut must have watched it, too, and concluded we had a similar situation at the Shady Inn. There was no foundation, no past history, no complaints, just a beer bar frequented by truckers and, occasionally, loose women. Big deal! Linda ran a pretty clean operation.

"All right, Sarge. I'll check it out," I humored him.

I stopped by the bar, had a soda, and chatted with Linda. The pool table between the bar and the front plate glass window was vacant. Not many customers on a Thursday night. "Not too busy tonight, are you Linda," I smiled, quaffing my soda.

"Not busy at all, Danny-boy," she called me. A couple of locals sat at the bar, sipping their beers and giving me furtive glances. An old whore sat at the end by herself, puffing on a long cigarette. Peanut was right. This whole thing was suspicious. That must be her, I thought, glancing at the old whore--the prostitute. Maybe I ought to shake her down, question her and throw the book at her. Or maybe I should just run her out of town. Totally absurd!

225

"Take care, Linda. Thanks for the soda," I said, leaving. She walked up close to me.

"Thanks for coming in." She then whispered. "Is there anything wrong?"

I felt stupid. "Nah, just bored out there. Not too many friendly faces. I saw you working so figured I'd bum a soda and chat," I lied, sort of.

"Anytime. Be careful out there," she smiled and winked, parroting a familiar line said by the shift sergeant at the beginning of each episode on Police Story. I figured she must have watched the show, too.

Later in the shift, Peanut-brain asked for a meet.

"Is there anything to it?"

"To what?" I knew what he was talking about.

"The prostitution ring. You know, the Shady Inn and everything." I looked at him in amazement. In his mind, he actually believed what he saw on TV was occurring in my little town, at the Shady Inn, at Linda's place. Such is the power of television. Such is the power of stupidity.

"Oh, yeah. You know, I think there might be something to it. People were pretty uptight when I checked it out. Looked pretty suspicious." He looked pleased. "I'll make a memo to the vice guys and they can follow it up."

"Good job." He smiled and drove away, satisfied with his night's work.

We didn't even have vice guys. Whatever vice we had was assigned to one of the detectives to work if they had the time. I made a mental note to check out next week's TV Guide to see what further adventures I'd be assigned, courtesy of Police Story.

I learned a lot from guys like Sgt. Peanut-brain and Lieutenant Psycho. I learned how not to be. I was fearful, for if these men, contemptuous examples of the species itself, were representatives of the state of law enforcement, society was in trouble. I continued to have an idealistic point of view of my career, fostered by men who were men, like Chief Wolfe, Kevin, and my friend Stiggy.

Historically, police departments maintain archaic, rigid, but often necessary, lines of communication, a system beget by the military which, except for technology, hasn't changed much since the days of the first militia.

If you thought for yourself, if you made your own decisions, you were labeled; marked a troublemaker, one who "didn't conform to authority," or, worse yet, "marches to the beat of his own drum", a phrase the Psycho used on one of my evaluations to downgrade me. He also used the phrase, "too pro-employee" which made me understand the Peanut-brain's "if the men hate you, you know you're doing a good job" philosophy. Had I been "anti-employee", I might have warranted a good evaluation.

The men of respect were a dying breed, I worried. Or maybe it was me. Perhaps those strange faces I saw in my dreams had a definite purpose. Perhaps they were the dead messengers of life, former policemen doomed to an existence such as the one I was in, faced with a shallow existence whose only living members were victims and suspects--victims and executioners, black and white, no in-between. Or maybe it simply meant nothing.

A man I much respected, the old Detective Sergeant Guevara, was ridiculed because of his heritage and empathy for the human race, called a "Mexican sympathizer." Sgt. Wolfe survived against nearly insurmountable odds in the absurd world of city politics, yet kept his humanity and gained respect by being a good chief. But, he wanted out. Even though he had a few good years left in him, he was retiring, and his leaving foretold my destiny.

THIRTY-THREE

Graveyard shift in the middle of the week was usually quite dead. One had to drum up action to stay awake and make the night pass quickly. I stopped at a late night market and stocked up on Sno-balls and Cheetos, then cruised the business district, protecting the local merchants from would be burglars. From the corner of my eye, I caught a furtive movement of a figure in the shadows. I continued until I turned the corner, made a U-turn, turned off my headlights and waited. If I didn't see the figure come into view, my plan was to approach the area on foot, hoping to surprise a would-be thief. Soon, the figure appeared in front of me, walking slowly. I waited until he passed, then started the car to observe his movements, unseen by me, a trick I learned from Chief Wolfe when he was my patrol sergeant.

I was about to radio that I was going to check out a suspicious person in the business district when I recognized the figure. It wasn't a he, it was Mary. What is she doing down here this late and by herself? She looked forlorn. She wasn't much for self-pity, often acting out her feelings in irrational behaviors, such as petty thievery, writing bad checks, or drug use. I pulled up next to her.

She looked surprised upon seeing it was a police car, until she saw it was me.

"Come on in," I invited her. "Not a safe place to be out by yourself. Let's go for a cruise." She looked around carefully, then sat in my patrol car and quickly brightened up. She ran her fingers up and down my shotgun, sensually feeling the trigger.

"Is this thing loaded?" She asked.

"Hey, watch it!" I warned. "You wanna blow the top of my car off?" I kidded, knowing the trigger guard was locked. I hoped. "You want a Sno-ball?" I offered.

"No thanks."

"Coffee?"

"That'd be great. Thanks."

I couldn't stop in one of the all night restaurants for fear of being seen publicly with her, so I stopped at a 7-11, bought two coffees and continued patrol. Mary appeared to be rather melancholic. I munched on my Sno-ball and sipped the coffee.

"What's going on, girl? You looked bummed. Something bugging you? Man trouble?"

"Yeah, right. Ain't no men in this town."

"Hey! I resent that."

"Oh, you know what I mean," she laughed. "I have to be in court tomorrow. Checks."

"Oh, no. I'm sorry to hear that. A lot of money?"

"Forty bucks is all, so I'll probably get nailed for three times that, and I can't afford it right now."

"The judge is cool. See if you can make payments," I suggested.

We cruised the west side projects and she pointed out a house to me. "Know who lives there?"

"No."

"Juan Solorio. He's starting to deal in heroin now. A little, but he's making some good money."

"Juan Solorio, huh? I heard the name before. So, he's dealing stuff, is he?"

"Uh-huh. And over there?" She pointed to another house. "El Toro. I don't know his name, but they call him El Toro. He's fronting stolen property. He's got a lot of stuff in his garage."

"Dang, man. I'm in the wrong business."

I continued driving around while she gave me a pretty good lesson of the underground; some I heard of, some were newcomers. She even took notes for me while I drove. We drove around a couple of hours and she compiled nearly two pages of notes. She was sufficiently tired enough to sleep, so I drove her home, parking a few yards away under a large tree so no one could see her exit a police car. I didn't think it mattered to her if anyone did, but I wanted to protect her just the same.

"Good night, Mary. Good luck in court. Just look at the judge, smile that smile and you'll be okay," I hoped.

"Thanks. See you around some time. Stay out of trouble." She started to leave, but then stopped. "Oh. You got any more Sno-balls left?"

"Sure. Here ya go." I tossed her my last package.

"Thanks. Take care."

I drove back to the department to compile the notes she left me and type them in a confidential memorandum for our narcotics officers. The department now had two officers assigned to narcotics full time. As arrogant as most officers working narcotics in the 70's were, they were no different. They envisioned themselves as super sleuths, and since one had dark hair and the other a blond, they called themselves Starsky and Hutch, after the TV detectives of the same title. I nicknamed them "Snooper and Blabber," after two television cartoon private eyes, a cartoon dog and cat who wore trench coats and hats.

I prepared an inter-departmental memorandum addressed to Snooper and Blabber with the information Mary provided, keeping her name out of it. The list contained each name, address, and activity of about twenty people. Since I worked graveyard shift, I didn't see them much, but they left me a note thanking me for the information, impressed by the knowledge of a beat supervisor.

A few weeks later, Snooper and Blabber served a search and arrest warrant on a murder suspect who was also a drug dealer, one of the names Mary provided whom I had listed on the memorandum. When they brought the suspect to the department for booking, they inadvertently left their notebook in the house after their seizure and arrest. My memo was inside the notebook. It was found by another person who came to the house to buy some dope but found something much more valuable. The finder made copies of the memo and distributed them to anyone who wanted one, those of the criminal underworld, of course. Out of embarrassment, or some other reason, Snooper nor Blabber blabbed about what happened, about leaving their notebook behind, or worse, they didn't even know they had.

I didn't find out about it until an officer arrested a guy for being under the influence of heroin. During the booking search, as the officer accounted for the crook's property, he found the memorandum, wadded up and stuffed in the crook's back pocket. The officer summoned me to the booking cell and showed me the memo; my own.

Shaken, I asked the druggie, "Where the hell did you get this?"

"What's it to you," the addict answered. Wrong answer.

I grabbed him by the collar, yanked him towards me and said, "You little punk. I'll show you what it is." I lost my composure, more out of fear that if this clown had the memo, then Mary would surely know of its existence and feel as though I betrayed her. I cocked my fist back to slug him when I noticed the officer staring.

"Sarge?" he said, softly. I quickly realized I was about to act like those I despised and quickly regained self-control.

"I want to talk to you about this," I said to the addict. Aware of my reaction, he knew he had something pretty important.

"What's in it for me?" He had me. I blew it in front of him

and the officer, so I had better come up with something suitable, and fast.

I conferred with the arresting officer and he agreed to help by dropping the charge to a simple drunk in public to be released in the morning. The addict accepted the offer, knowing an under the influence of heroin charge carried an automatic, minimum 90 days in the county jail, more if they were on probation.

"I went over to Ricky's to buy some stuff," he explained. "No one was there, so I just walked in and looked around and saw this notebook on the table. I didn't look like it belonged to him, and when I opened it, I knew it belonged to a cop. I got scared and grabbed that," referring to my memo, "and saw a bunch of names of people I knew and how much the cops knew. Figured I could make some money off it." Crooks! The original entrepreneurs! "I ran out before the cops came back. Pretty good, eh?"

"Yeah, real good," I agreed. "What did you do then?"

"I took it to the library, made a bunch of copies and sold some for 5 bucks each. Some guys on the list even gave me stuff (heroin) for it."

"That's just great," I whined. "How many did you make?"

"I dunno," he slurred. "Maybe twenty, maybe more. You want the rest?"

"You got more of these?"

"Yeah, Homes, I figured I could jack up the price, you know?"

"Yeah, I know," I answered, resignedly. "I'd appreciate it if you gave me the rest."

"No problem. You did me a big favor."

"Well, I'm real happy about that," I sarcastically responded.

I'll be go to hell, I thought. Twenty! Mary's gonna kill me, if she even ever talks to me again.

The addict's friends came in to inquire about bail. Mary was among them. She was fuming when she asked the dispatcher to see me. I took her to a back interrogation room dreading this.

"Look, Mary, I…" before I could finish, she started in.

"You son-of-a-bitch! How could you do this to me?" She was frantic. "I trusted you. I'm dead. Dead!"

"Mary, I know how you feel. I…"

"No you don't. You don't live on South Side. You don't know anything about how I feel!"

"You're right, Mary. If you'll just calm down. It wasn't my fault. You know I said I'd never burn you, and I didn't. I'm truly sorry. Believe me." I never felt worse about anything in my life.

She looked at me patronizingly. I explained to her what the addict told me, that it was the narcotics guys, Snooper and Blabber, who screwed up. I assured her I wrote the memo in a way that it sounded like a male had given me the information, rather than a female, as a means of protecting her identity, more from the department personnel than the crooks, although the crooks weren't much smarter, so I thought they wouldn't figure it out. They didn't.

"I'm more pissed than you," I went on to explain. "Those idiots had no business leaving that where every doper, crook, jerk in town could get a hold of it. Wait'll I get a hold of them!" She calmed down and forgave me.

"I didn't mean to go off on you. I should have known you wouldn't do that deliberately." She looked at me with those eyes. "Can I make it up to you?"

I was the one who had to make it up to her. I was relieved that I made the memo sound like it came from a man. There weren't many women in the underworld who knew as much as Mary. It would have been easy to figure out who the informant was, and I hated to think what could have happened to her.

"Look. It's almost eleven. Here's the keys to my car. Sneak back to the parking lot when you can. Wait in my car and we'll take off as soon as I can get out of here."

"OK. Let me ditch the ones I came with and I'll be back. Give me some time."

She was there waiting for me. "Let's go have a late dinner. I can drive to Stockton, find some decent place where no one knows us, I hope, and come back to my place and relax," I offered. "What do you think?"

"Drive."

It took me about 20 minutes to drive to Stockton and another 20 to find a decent place to eat. I couldn't go to South Stockton for fear there were some who lived there might know her, so we drove to the North end and settled for a pleasant, affordable place, Denny's. I ordered the breaded veal while she ordered a hamburger and fries. She was such a pretty woman. I watched her take small portions of her dinner and thought about her future which was, essentially, nothing—a dead end. She lived one day at a time, uncertain of her deeds, uncertain of her direction, uncertain of her destiny. I wondered whether these few moments I spent with her were her only escape, her flight from the harsh cruelties of her world. I thought mine with its deceit, quest for power and betrayal was difficult enough, but hers...

"Why are you looking at me that way?" She caught me mindlessly staring.

"You ever think about leaving, Mary? I mean, you know, the South Side, the welfare, and all. You could get a decent job."

"Where am I going to go? What am I going to do? You gonna take me away from there?" I think she asked half jokingly and half seriously. I just smiled.

"Can we go to your place and listen to some music?"

I was feeling benevolent, or perhaps a bit of pity. "I got an idea. I'm off tomorrow. Why don't we just drive to San Francisco, spend the night, take in the sights, get lost and stuff?"

"Would you really do that for me?"

"Of course. You want to?" I eagerly asked. I loved the Bay Area, another great place to get in touch with my receding humanity and a reminder of my joyful days as a youth during the summer of love.

"I'd love to, but I've got court in the morning. I can't miss it," she sighed.

"Court? Again? What the---?"

She looked down at her hamburger. I didn't ask her why. That side of her life was blind to me, I'd rather not know. I knew it couldn't be serious, or else she would have told me. She was probably embarrassed to tell me it was more checks. I sent a couple of memos in the past to the local judge, a former public defender who as a righteous, fair guy, Judge Grande, requesting to consider her value as an informant for consideration of a lighter sentence. She never asked me to, nor did I ever tell her. He often granted my request, only wanting my assurance she was, indeed, helping law enforcement. Sometimes I didn't see her for months at a time, figuring she was paying her debt to society. I made sure she was home in time to make her court appearance.

The futility of Mary's life took its toll on her. What she wanted and what she was clashed violently within her. Her imminent life of crime and welfare, of despair and disillusionment, of horror and shame, induced her to a life of drugs and prostitution. One brisk, fall day, my dispatcher slipped me a note which said for me to meet with an informant under the overpass east of town. Mary had called the dispatcher and asked to have me meet with her but to keep it off the police radio. I was glad the dispatcher, good old "hamburger Karl," had the thoughtfulness to oblige her. I drove to the East end of the city limits, the road leading out of town which crosses over the tracks adjacent to the Heinz 57 cannery.

I drove under the overpass and saw an old faded blue Pinto. Mary looked horrible. She was haggard and worn with more makeup than I'd ever seen her wear. Her fake fingernails were long and deep red, with some broken. I figured she was hooking somewhere.

"Hello, kiddo," I greeted her.

"How are you doing?" she asked.

"I'm fine, Mary. No complaints. Same ol', same ol', you know. You don't look so well."

"You're not supposed to say that. How long's it been since you seen me?" Her smile looked fake. The life, the mystery was gone from her eyes.

"You know I didn't mean that. What's up?" For the first time since I first met her, I felt a little awkward.

"I hate to ask, but I did you a lot of favors, didn't I?"

I felt embarrassed. "Mary, you don't need to keep score. You just name it. What can I do for you?" She helped my career more than she would ever know.

"I need a hundred dollars. And I need it like—soon?" Now she looked embarrassed.

"Can you wait here? I'll be back as soon as I can. Don't leave." No way could I afford a hundred dollars right now, no way. But what could I do? I went to the bank and cashed a check for the money. I'd have to be late with the rent, or something, but I couldn't turn her down. She never asked for money before, so I knew she really needed it. I didn't want to think she might use it to buy dope. I wanted to believe she had too much respect for me to use the money for dope.

She was still there under the overpass, smoking, something else which was out of her character. I handed her the money.

"I'll pay you back as fast---"

"Don't worry about it," I interrupted. "I'll get it back one way or the other," I smiled and winked, trying to make her laugh a little. "I'll see you whenever."

"I'll see you soon. Thanks…I, well, thanks." She drove away and I didn't see her again. Months later, I received a letter she wrote from prison. She never explained what she did to land her in the joint, but she wrote she had about a year to go. There was one thing I was certain---she didn't kill, maim, or hurt anyone. I just knew that wasn't her nature.

A perverse thought crossed my mind as I headed back into the city limits a hundred bucks lighter. She was the most honest person I ever knew, honest in the way she treated me as an individual. Sure, she was a criminal what with her petty thievery, writing bum checks, welfare fraud, and all, but then everyone on South Side knew how to do welfare fraud. She existed tenuously on the wrong side of legislation enacted to protect us from people like her. Just the same, she behaved in her society, doing what she was expected to do to survive in her world and to keep people like me employed. A survivor she most certainly was for which she earned my respect. I will miss her. The information will come from somebody else, it always does. The secret moments with her when I felt exceptional and detached from the madness, that will be hard to replace. Little did I know that our paths would cross again during one of the most tenuous times in my life.

THIRTY-FOUR

Whenever a promotional opportunity arose within the department, it was amusing to see the candidates jockeying for position, but it was also a time for cutthroat survival. A sergeant's opening spawned many "wannabe" sergeants. Guys with time in rank were suddenly taking their jobs seriously, barking orders to their underlings, strutting their supervisorial potential to each other while impressing themselves. I often thought an effective management tool would be to announce fake promotional opportunities and then see how the efficiency of the department improves. Rendle, sensing his opportunity to become the chief after Chief Wolfe's retirement, jockeyed better than Willie Shoemaker.

The chief's retirement opened the possibility for the department's two Lieutenants to take over. Rendle and the other, Vern, the kindly, fatherly one, competed against each other. Normally, the position is announced to outside candidates, but since the last choice from Marina Bay proved to be a disaster, the City Manager decided to play it safe and keep it in-house. The contrast between the two Lieutenants made it a foregone conclusion who would be the new chief. The Psycho lowered himself to being the sweetest, nicest, understanding boss one could ever have. He hated Chief Wolfe but felt he had to carry on his legacy, to some degree, until the job was formally his.

My fellow sergeants ran around acting like Lieutenants hoping to impress the Psycho enough to promote one of them to his vacant position. I was a candidate as well, but it was a foregone conclusion I wouldn't be promoted to work under the new chief, all which turned out to be true. I continued to do my job as before, wary of the sharks circling the water, biding my time, pondering my existence. It was time for me to retreat to the waters, the waters of Monterey Bay. "Stig. Why don't you come with me? We can golf; go to the beach, the aquarium. You can even bring your girlfriend, if you want." I figured it'd be fun for my friend to come along.

"I'd love to. But why bring her? There's some far out women down there."

"OK. Cool. Let's go!"

"I can't. Have to work. The season ends soon, so I need to make all I can now."

"OK, buddy-boy. See you when I get back." The cannery was about to layoff some employees once the tomato season ends, so I went alone, cleansing my psyche from the intensity of the frenzy of promotions.

Returning to swing shift, I pushed the secret code button at the rear employee entrance of the department. It seemed unusually quiet for a swing shift, not the usual hustle and scurrying one normally sees. I glanced at my watch to make sure I was here at the right time. Mickey's big hand was on the nine and his little hand was on the three. Yep, 2:45, right on time. I suddenly saw the little dispatcher coming down the hall, moving quite rapidly. She was Mexican, very short and a bit heavy, but had flawless complexion and large, cow eyes. I had much fondness for her, seeing her as my little sister. She kept her gaze on me, and I noticed it was much too serious.

"Stiggy's dead," was all she said.

The words penetrated the pith of my being. They crashed and echoed around my brain, then crushed my heart. I heard the words, but didn't understand the meaning. I stared at her, and she stared back, her radiant face a mask of anguish and grief. Nothing came from my mouth as my emotions became paralyzed. I felt the world spinning around me, then found myself leaning against the wall. The dispatcher, Drina, rushed for me before I continued my fall.

"One of the guys is over there now, but he's dead," she finished. At that moment, Kevin rushed from the locker room, still putting on his gun belt in preparation for the shift.

"Did she tell you?" He asked.

I could finally speak. "Dead? What do you mean he's dead. I just saw him a couple of days ago." My mind and body rejected the reality. "How can he be dead?"

Drina said, "Kevin. You better take him over there." I felt weak and dizzy as I followed Kevin to the key cabinet where he grabbed keys to a patrol car, then pushed me out the back door. He nervously lit a cigarette while fumbling to put the right key in the ignition. He was trying so hard to fight back tears, he could hardly speak.

"Is it true, Kevin? Is Stiggy dead? How? What---?"

"I don't know. Drina told me as soon as I came in and I knew you were coming, so I got dressed to find out what happened."

"He ain't dead; this is some kind of clown job," I said, trying to convince myself. A clown job was a phrase between us whenever a practical joke was successful on the other, making the victim looking like a clown. Kevin pulled into the lot across from Stiggy's apartment next to another patrol car, the first officer summoned to the scene. I started to get out of the car, but pulled back and shut the door.

"I can't, Kevin," was all I could say.

"What's the matter? Come on, let's go in," he said anxiously.

"I can't. I don't want to see him dead. I can't let my last memory of him being dead. I'll wait here." Kevin left me and ran across the street. I attended too many funerals of friends of mine, an inordinate amount from the police department. Far too many died young, many from self-inflicted wounds. I saw them lying cold and lifeless in their coffins. I hated that image. I tried to erase that memory by thinking of what they were like when they laughed and joked, but the image of death always prevailed. No matter, I never wanted to imagine what Stiggy looked like dead. His life would live forever in me. There was no time for death. Kevin came back to the car, and I knew it wasn't a clown job. An ambulance then pulled up in front of Stiggy's apartment.

"Get me out of here, Kevin. I don't want to see him," I weakly said to Kevin. Then I had a thought. "Wait a minute! He ain't dead, he's just dead drunk. He's passed out. You have to yell in his ear. You have to shake him hard and pour water in his face. I know, Kevin, I know. I've had to do that. Go tell them, Kevin. They don't understand. He'll wake up. He can't be dead…he can't be." I was near hysteria in disbelief. Kevin continued to drive.

He was dead. I finally gave in. My tears refused to hold back any longer; they rushed forth uncontrollably and nothing I could do could drive them back. Kevin drove to the country away from people, away from my town, so no one would see me. Please stop, I pleaded. Please make me stop crying, please don't let this be real. I've witnessed death, I've encountered death in all its ugliness, but death never struck me a blow this severe before. It never clutched me by the throat and shook me, then took something that was a part of me, part of the essence of what I was--my best friend.

I regained my composure, somewhat, and Kevin drove me back to the department. The other Lieutenant, the fatherly one, Vern, met me at the back door, his eyes red and swollen. He understood my relationship with Stiggy and told me to take the day off. He told Kevin to take the day off, too, and stay with me.

I don't remember much of what else happened that day. Sleep denied me solace, cruelly throwing me various visions of death.

The faces came again in the night, but even their hideousness couldn't wake me until I saw the familiar face of Stiggy. He lie, supine, grinning, his face wooden-like, rising straight up resembling Dracula's rise from his coffin. Before he was fully upright, he became an apparition fading from view as another one of him rose from the coffin, again wooden and grinning, rising and disappearing, over and over again until I awoke.

I learned he died of a diabetic coma shortly after his thirty-first birthday. I never saw him dead. Although he was only a reserve police officer and wasn't killed in the line of duty, the department had a full honor guard funeral for him bestowing the honor and respect he deserved. His older sister, who looked just like him, was there and her husband, Stiggy's brother-in-law, kept trying to talk to me, kept bugging me during the funeral. I knew very little of him, but he seemed to want to offer me sincere condolences since Stiggy often spoke of me and the things we were involved when he was riding as a reserve with me. He knew how close we were.

After the funeral, he said he wanted to meet with me and talk. I gave him my home address and told him to come over whenever he wanted. I was pleased that the family wanted to stay close to me, even though Stiggy was nevermore. Nice gesture. I figured they wanted to keep his memory alive through me.

A few days later, his brother-in-law came over carrying a brief case from which he pulled a yellow legal-sized pad of paper. I offered him a can of cream soda and we sat on my sofa, prepared to talk about Stiggy and some of the things we did. He took out his pen and started writing a bunch of figures on the pad, then circled the figures and made more circles, pyramiding out from each other. What the--? He was talking fast, making the figures larger than the previous ones, circling them, too, and drawing dollar signs. In trying to make sense of what he was doing, I realized he was trying to get me involved in his Amway business, showing me the riches I could accrue if I let him sponsor me. He never talked about Stig.

"Get the hell out!" I threw him out of my apartment and slammed the door behind him.

With Stiggy's death, I got closer to Kevin. He often worked my shift and I found myself riding with him during his patrol duties. I didn't want to drive, and I didn't want anyone riding with me. I wanted to preserve Stiggy's legacy and his value to me by not having a reserve ride with me ever again. Death clowned me.

THIRTY-FIVE

I had assumed my duties as the supervisor of the Detective Division, answerable to the Lieutenant, Vern, my friend. After all the jockeying and manipulation were over, the victors, those promoted, celebrated, while the losers lamented their luck, blaming it on everything but themselves. As expected, the Psycho was the Chief, and the junior sergeant of us was promoted to Lieutenant, a former truck driver, an aggressive, obnoxious, slightly overweight man named Shultz. He was nearly 40, getting a late start into the profession, wore heavy black framed glasses, and had the kind of personality where you could like him one minute, and the next minute you couldn't stand him. We weren't friends, but we respected one another. I respected him because he was old school. He would just as soon throw blows with a suspect as arrest him. I was surprised he got the job, but it wasn't until much later I understood why he was promoted. Before the promotions became effective, duty called.

In a quiet residential corner of my town, a small combination liquor store and market was owned by what's known as a 'mom and pop' operation, long time residents of the town and their son. It was a regular stop for the officers to stock up on Cheetos, coffee, doughnuts, the standard police lunches. One serene late summer evening, the owners, their son and his wife were tending the market when two men, strangers, stumbled in. They walked the small aisles of the store, the larger one of the two keeping his face hidden. Unseen, he tied a blue bandana around his head, covering his nose and mouth, and then pulled a large caliber gun from his pants and stuck it to the faces of mom and pop. They froze in fear for they had never been robbed before, never even saw a gun. The smaller bandit reached over the counter and grabbed the cash from the till. His face was unmasked.

"More money, more money," the masked one demanded, in quick, harsh tones as he waved the gun menacingly in front of their faces.

"Th...that's it," cried the son, his voice quivering in fear, "that's all we have. We're a small business---" The masked bandit cut him off.

"The whiskey! Gimme the whiskey!" The son reached up to grab a fifth of Four Roses when the bottle shattered, glass and whiskey showering all over his head and face. The clerk recoiled and ducked under the counter, fearing another shot. The bandit ran around the counter and grabbed armfuls of Black Velvet, apparently his brand of choice, and handed them to the younger crook who ran out the door, dropping one of the bottles, fracturing it on the ground.

The big guy pointed his gun at the clerk.

"I'm going to kill you, motherfu--" as he fired two shots just over the clerk's head, causing his wife to scream and rush towards him, fearing he had just been killed. The bandit cackled demonically, grabbed another bottle, and ran to the waiting car which sped to the city limits, lost on the frenzy of the freeway, Interstate 205 towards the Bay Area of San Francisco.

Being a small department, we didn't have specialized detectives. The patrol division handled the initial call and filed their report for approval which was then assigned to the Detective Division. The assigned officer wrote a good report, getting minute details of what the witnesses could remember. Most victims only remember the size of the barrel staring them in the face, praying it won't go off. The most accurate victim was the wife of the owners' son, the clerk who was nearly shot. Though panic-stricken, she remembered the scars on the big guy's forehead, the crows' feet wrinkles around his eyes and the stench of whiskey from his breath.

I grabbed the report from the Detectives "in basket" the following morning and scoured the report. It didn't seem to fit any locals or anyone on parole that we knew of. We figured it had to be out of towners since the market was a small, friendly establishment one of those places that has stuff you need when the regular stores are closed. Even the local addicts wouldn't rob the place as dear as it was to the neighborhood. The market was about a mile from the freeway. Those service stations near the freeway were often targets of "highway bandits", but the crooks had to know about this market to brazenly rob it during the day, fire some shots and head back to the freeway. Unless a Highway Patrolman or Sheriff's deputy was in the immediate vicinity, there was little chance of apprehending them, much less identifying them.

My town had less than two dozen armed robberies a year and our clearance rate was pretty high, considering they were usually perpetrated by local druggies, but this one had us baffled; no leads, nothing. Weeks later, we got a break, not from anything we did, but from a source which is the lifeblood of investigations; snitches, informants, rats, finks, or as we called them as children, "tattletales." It is a misplaced, absurd code of honor when people think they are nobly protecting the code by saying, "I'm not a rat." If they only knew the code didn't exist. Patrol busted a local for driving under the influence of a narcotic, and his past record meant he was looking at some hard time. He wanted to deal. We had him brought to our office from his cell and gave him a cup of coffee.

"What you got, Chago?" Kevin started. He was a local, petty

criminal, a small time user and thief named Santiago Chavez, known in the streets as Chago. He wasn't even twenty yet and spent a large part of his time in the county jail. He had not yet been convicted of a felony, which meant prison time, so he hadn't become too hardened by the prison system.

"What you dudes gonna do for me? I'm looking at a long time, eh?" Kevin offered him a cigarette, which he accepted.

"Depends. You give us something good, we'll talk then," Kevin told him. You never give a snitch the first offer, or else he'll deal to his advantage, give up something petty and then make it sound like he's giving up Jack the Ripper. Then he walks.

"That market robbery?" He piqued our interest.

"Yeah. What about it?" Kevin asked. "You do it?"

Chago laughed. "Come on, Homes. You know I don't do guns. Besides, the dudes were white, right?"

Kevin looked bored. "So what? That was in the paper. You ain't telling us nothing we don't know. You gonna give us something, or do we put you back in the cell?" Kevin was doing all right with this interrogation stuff.

"Hold it, Holmes. Relax, dude," Chago pled. "I know one of the dudes, the little guy. He used to live in the projects when he got out of the joint. He robbed a place in Sacramento and just got out a little while ago, I hear."

"You gonna give us his name?" Kevin asked.

"His name? Sure, Homes. I give you his name and then you put me back in the cell. You got to give me something. Get me out," he insisted. Smart guy.

I butted in. "You give us the name. We'll check it out, and if you're right on, we'll get you out.

"You think I'm stupid, eh?" Chago took a long drag from his cigarette. "You gonna let me sit and then hang a jacket on me. I know how you guys operate." Yes, he'd been around, alright. He thought we'd burn him. Make the deal, leave him in jail and then tell the guy who it was who burned him, which is called having a snitch jacket put on you, a sign of dishonor amongst criminals. The funny thing was, most all of them wore the jacket, unbeknownst to each other. We haggled back and forth then negotiated a deal. We'd have the arresting officer issue him a citation to appear in court rather than book him, and then release him. If the information paid off, we'd ask the D.A. and judge to dismiss the citation, labeling him a reliable informant, and then he'd never have to appear in court. He agreed and gave us the name.

"Ned Kelly? Never heard of him," I told Kevin.

"Me neither," he said. "I'll check him out with parole."

So far, the information paid off. Kelly had been paroled for armed robbery in Sacramento but failed to keep his appointments with his parole officer, causing the agent to put a parole hold on him. Parole Agents are to convicts what God is to the rest of us. His is the ultimate authority. You upset your Parole Officer--gone! In the slammer, six months guaranteed. Get accused of a crime, forget it, don't matter if you're guilty or not, you're just about gone forever. Parole agents were great to work with, knowing full well that 99 percent of those paroled should still be in jail. Ned Kelly was an addict and a dope, a real dope. He had slightly more intelligence than Peanut-brain and was a known whiner. We nail him, he'd finger his accomplice, the big guy, at the drop of a hat, or a glove, or your pants for that matter. Since he was on parole and a parole violator, we didn't need the burden of obtaining an arrest warrant.

Chago was good on his word. He later phoned to tell us Kelly was staying in a trailer park east of town, not far from the prison, Deuel Vocational Institute, DVI. He submitted to his parole agent and couldn't talk fast enough. He told us the gunman was a tough ex-con named Elzie Ray Ward, known in the prison system as "Baby-Ray" due to a strong attachment to this mother. Ned Kelly was deathly afraid Baby-Ray would kill him if he knew he snitched. We promised he'd never find out from us. Kelly was heavily involved in criminal activity and drugs, so he agreed to work for us or any law enforcement agency in exchange for his freedom. His parole agent told us he was good for his word, just a wimpy guy, actually, and could probably turn a bunch of other crooks, so we allowed him the deal.

Baby-Ray scared us. We talked with his parole agent named Stan Rhodes, a burly, no-nonsense, loud talking guy with an even heartier laugh. He loved his job and enjoyed putting them back where they belonged. Stan was a local, a graduate from the same high school as us. He went to college, got his degree and was now working for the state. He met us in our office.

Ray spent more than half his life in the joint, amassing a record of rape, assault with a deadly weapon, robbery and attempted murder. He had been involved in a shootout with the Los Angeles police years ago where he'd been shot and wounded. He was now living in Modesto, a town south of Tracy.

"Los Angeles, huh?" Kevin mused. "Well. He's messing with the big boys now," Kevin bragged.

"He'll kill you as soon as look at you," said the agent. "He's a mean, don't give a damn about nothing except his momma, whiskey drinking right out the bottle, no-good son-of-a-bitch. You better have plenty of firepower," he warned.

"Uh, hee-hee," Kevin sheepishly laughed. "I was just kiddin', you know, just kiddin' around."

"You're scared, ain't you?" I asked, taking advantage of his sudden vulnerability.

"I ain't scared."

"Yeah you are, you're scared. Scared of a guy named Baby-Ray. What a wuss!" I teased.

"Oh yeah? Well, I won't be like those L.A. dorks. When I shoot him, I ain't wounding him. Right between the eyes dude," he boasted, putting his hand on his little 2-inch snub-nose revolver.

"Baby-Ray will shove that right up your ass," the agent joined in the taunting.

"Well let's go find out," Kevin responded defiantly. I think he was serious. We devised a plan to arrest Baby-Ray in Modesto, but a surprise awaited me.

THIRTY-SIX

"The chief wants me to go with you guys," Lt. Fuller quietly informed me.

"What?"

"This is a big case, so he decided it best if I tag along." He tried to downplay it. I was just disrespected. The Lieutenant knew it. The chief knew it, and my men knew it. Never before had we taken an administrator to serve an arrest warrant. I figured this was a message to let me know who was in charge. I knew who was in charge, but apparently the chief didn't. I had no respect for insecure men. As angry as I was, I had to make the most of it to get the job done.

The plan was to take two cars to Modesto, myself, Kevin and Tim in one, and for backup, Lt. Fuller went in another car with the two officers who were assigned to juvenile, kiddy cops, but they were good policemen and we enjoyed their company. The Lieutenant grabbed a sniper rifle with a scope from the munitions room and we were on our way to Modesto, about a forty-five minute drive at the speed limit.

We were pretty loose on the way, considering the possibility we may have to kill a guy, or get killed ourselves. If you dwelled upon the extreme possibility of a situation, you might get too uptight, over thinking it and then doubt enters. We had to stay focused and not lose the edge to doubt or fear. We needed the advantage, not only in firepower, but the mental state. We checked in to the Modesto Police Department, a courtesy afforded all agencies to effect an arrest outside one's jurisdiction. Modesto offered us one of their radios to let them know when we were in position and that they would cover the back of Baby-Ray's house whenever we gave the word.

"OK, guys," I announced to all. "It's set. Let's go take Baby-Ray down." We found his house easy enough, a shack-like dwelling on the outskirts of Modesto, an area known for its "Okies" and "white trash" element. We cruised by his house, not seeing any lights on as it was nearing dusk. We parked three houses down behind a dilapidated trailer on the street, giving us protection, but not a clear view. The Lieutenant and the kiddy cops took a position two houses behind us. I hoped Baby-Ray was home. If he happened to drive by and saw two cars with three men in each, he might be a little suspicious.

"I'll go see if the owner can move the trailer a little," I said, opening the car door quietly and stealthily moving behind the cover of trees in the yard. The house was an anomaly in the neighborhood with a well maintained yard and a curving walkway from the street to the front door. Trees lined the walkway, concealing me to some degree. The owner must have won a lawsuit against the city, or something, I figured. Enough to improve his lot, but not enough to move out of the neighborhood. The walk was unusually long, or maybe it was just my nerves as I approached the door which had a glass partition at the top with light beaming through. Someone was home. Before I got to the door, I saw a large, black dog lying lazily near the doorstep. The dog pricked its ears up upon seeing me. I hesitated, looking back at the dog. A Mexican standoff. He reared up, growled and came towards me, slowly, as I backpedaled gently, not certain if it was a friendly old hound, or a fierce watchdog. The chase was on. I decided discretion was a better part of valor and hightailed it, running as fast as I could while the dog was yapping and snapping at my feet.

"Open the door!" I yelled, hoping Baby-Ray didn't hear me. They didn't open the door fast enough, for in my fear and haste, I ran full force into it, doubling over into the open window. For some reason, the dog stopped in its tracks, looked at me, then trotted back to its house, satisfied with his job. I jumped further into the car in the event it changed its mind as the guys were howling with laughter.

"Shut up, man," I hollered, relieved but embarrassed. "You want to alert the whole neighborhood--look!" I pointed in the direction of Baby-Ray's house. A light went on behind the curtains of his house, meaning he was home.

"He's there," Kevin blurted.

"Damn! What are we going to do now?" Tim asked nervously, quickly ending his laughter.

"What kind of a question is that? You want to call the police?" I mocked him. "Let's go get him. You guys ready? Ain't scared now, are ya?"

I radioed to the Lieutenant we were going to move in, then I used Modesto's radio asking them to take up their positions as "the target was home." Baby-Ray's front yard was full of junk, rusted car frames, old refrigerators, tires, boxes, something right from a Jeff Foxworthy redneck joke. It was cool because it gave us stuff to hide behind as we snuck up to his house. Kevin, Tim and I inched towards the front door while the Lieutenant and the others stayed behind outside their car. The Lieutenant had his bullhorn at the ready.

I could feel my breath accelerating in concert with my heartbeat, the anticipation welling through my body, my nerves and muscles flexing, alerting me for action. I had to get into the kill zone, when suddenly, I saw a bright red dot on Kevin's backside. The red dot then moved quickly to Tim's backside and then on his face as he looked back. He saw the dot, too.

"What the hell...?"? He exclaimed. The red dot was now moving all over the place, including Baby Ray's front door.

"That damn Lieutenant!" Kevin nearly yelled, remembering to stifle it so Baby-Ray wouldn't hear him.

The Lieutenant had the assault rifle with the laser beam, trying to fix its sight on the bandit's front door. The dot was the laser beam, meaning the bullet would fire in its direction, a relatively new weapon that not many in the department knew about. Apparently, the Lieutenant wanted to be the first to try it out, but he was having trouble trying to steady it and hanging on to the bullhorn at the same time. It was an excellent weapon depending on who was operating it. None of us felt comfortable seeing the beam bouncing off each one of us. We frantically waved at Fuller to put the weapon away as we had plenty of firepower in the event Baby-Ray wanted to shoot it out.

"Ward! Elzie Ray Ward!" a loud voice boomed, echoing throughout the street and off the neighboring houses.

"Jesus! Now what?" Kevin asked. "He could have given us some warning," he said, looking at me. The Lieutenant's voice broke the quiet peace of the evening. Giving up on the laser-beamed sniper rifle, he opted for the bullhorn.

"Elzie Ray Ward. This is the police. You are under arrest. Come out of the front door with your hands up!" The Lieutenant commanded. Good job. Sounded official, crisp, authoritative, and everything. We waited. No movement. No door opening. Nothing.

"Ward!" He repeated. "You are under arrest!"

"Oh no!" Kevin said, wide-eyed. "What if he isn't there?"

"He's got to be there. We saw a light go on, didn't we?" I assured him. Still nothing. Eager and full of apprehension, we inched ever closer to his front door. That damn red dot again. Now it was on my backside and on my body. I tried to brush it away, hoping the Lieutenant would see me and put the stupid thing away before he killed one of us. Kevin saw the dot and started laughing.

"This ain't no time to laugh, Kevin. We may have to kill a ---." Before I could finish, a crashing sound from the rear of Baby-Ray's house startled us, coupled with a deafening shot and a dog barking.

"What the hell's going on?" We ran to the back of the house, wary of the snarling, vicious sound of a large breed dog. Baby-Ray was face down on the grass, a Doberman Pinscher, teeth flashing and barking wildly, was being restrained by a Modesto officer holding an enormous chain. It was over. Baby-Ray tried to make a run out his back door but was swiftly apprehended by Modesto P.D.'s canine unit. They took him into custody while we searched his house.

We learned something about this career criminal. He was a tough guy alright. There was 55-gallon cardboard drum full to the brim with empty Black Velvet whiskey bottles. He lived in squalor and gloom. Prison would be a move to the high rent district compared to this. Garbage was piled up in his kitchen, dishes strewn about and I dare not look in his refrigerator. He was a shell of his gangster self for he couldn't have made much profit from his liquor store holdups, risking years of his life in prison for Black Velvet. I wondered if their sales might plummet now that the notorious Baby-Ray's drinking days were over. The guy was living in the wrong era, or maybe it was me--I was in the wrong era. We recovered his gun in plain sight on his mattress. On his nightstand was an old black and white photo, a picture of a slim, dark haired woman with her arm around a chubby child, a boy of about 13. It was Baby-Ray and his momma.

He didn't kill us, so that was good. His gun was loaded and we were glad he didn't try to shoot it out, knowing he was looking at hard time. Maybe he was getting old, tired of it all and didn't care anymore.

"Of course he didn't want a shootout," Kevin said. "He's messing with the big boys now. He knows I would have killed him." He pointed his finger like a gun and placed it to his forehead. "Bang! Right between the eyes," and then he laughed, reminding me of the Lee Marvin character, Liberty Valance, who said the same thing about wanting to kill Jimmy Stewart, the "pilgrim" lawyer in the John Wayne movie of the same name.

"Sure, Kevin," I agreed. "Let's go take him back." We left his house and secured it, although who would want to break in and steal anything? "Wait a minute." I went back and retrieved the old photo of his mother and him.

"What are you going to do with that?" Tim asked.

"Don't worry about it," I said, ending it there.

We picked up Baby-Ray at Modesto P.D. and took him back to Tracy for court the next morning. He reeked of whiskey, his eyes bloodshot and he could have used a good shower and a shave. Although there were three of us, we were still scared. He was a burly guy, mid 40's, who stared you right in the eye without blinking when he talked. The archetype of anti-social lived and breathed here in our car. Ordinarily, we would have taken the handcuffs off once we established some rapport, but the words of his Parole Agent rang in our ears: 'He'll kill you as soon as look at you.' We left the cuffs on. We decided to question him on the way back, remembering not to mention his partner, the one who snitched him off. Tim was in the back seat and questioned him first.

"Tell me, Elzie..."

"Tim." I butted in. "Don't forget to advise him first."

"Oh, yeah. Almost forgot." Tim then read him his Miranda rights. "Elzie, my friend. We know you didn't do the robbery alone. You can help yourself if you tell us who was with you," Tim began.

He didn't answer, looking straight ahead.

"Look. It'll go easier if you cooperate," Tim continued. "You want to take the rap yourself?" Good, Tim. That was good so far. Still no response. He acted like we weren't even there.

I hoped Tim wouldn't press him on the issue, fearing Baby-Ray may sense a bit much interest and figure out we already knew and that we were gaming him. He then might figure out who snitched him off. Tim read my mind.

"OK, Elzie. Maybe you don't want to say, but we know you had a partner. We'll figure it out. You want to cleanse your soul and cop to any other robberies we can clear up?" Baby-Ray looked at me.

"Is this guy for real?" he muttered. "He ain't nothing but a chump." He caught Tim off guard.

"Huh? What do you mean?" Tim asked.

"You disrespect me," Baby-Ray said, matter-of-factly.

"I did? How? What did I say?" He caught us all off guard. Tim was perplexed. He didn't cuss him, he wasn't sarcastic.

"You ask me these stupid cop questions, and you expect me to sit here and answer them? You expect me to rat on my partner, and then you expect me to rat on myself? You're a chump!"

"Uh, well, uh, I mean..." Tim was a bit taken aback.

Baby-Ray went on. "You guys checked me out before you took me down, right?"

"Yeah. So?" Tim answered.

"You know how much time I done, you know my record. I know you talked to my P.O. (Parole Officer)."

"Yeah, we did, Ray, we did. What's your point?" I chimed in.

"So how come he disrespected me?"

"We're small time, Ray," I said. "Just cops in a small town doing what we have to do. You're going to have to explain yourself, well, you don't HAVE to, but it would be nice. I know time isn't your enemy, and it isn't your friend. You know what I'm talking about." I seemed to have struck up some semblance of rapport with this hardened criminal.

"He wants me to rat," he said. 'He thinks I'm going to rat on my partner. I don't do that. You think I'm a rat, you disrespect me." We sat silent for a moment. People of all sizes, all races, all backgrounds, even drunks and convicts want the same thing;

their measure of respect. I needed to diffuse the hostility. I pulled over to the side of the road and turned to face him.

"It wasn't meant to be disrespect. You're a complex person, Ray, more so than most, I'm sure. Right?" He nodded in agreement. "We're just small town cops from a little hick town, you know? We wouldn't show you disrespect on purpose." Even though cuffed behind his back, I felt he could have beat the hell out of the three of us and left us for bloody pulps on the side of the road. It didn't matter to me what he thought if I downplayed our seriousness and joy for what we did. His respect for us at this given moment was just as important as ours was to him, and he knew I knew.

"I understand. Can I have a smoke?" Kevin lit one up and put it into his bandit mouth, taking it out every so often to flick the ash. "You know I ain't no rat. I'll do ten, twenty, thirty years, don't mean nothing to me. I'll do the time standing on my head, but I won't rat and you guys know that!"

He certainly would. I did respect him. He was a stand up, no nonsense guy, grounded in reality and his reality meant nothing to no one and he could care less. He'd a made a great police chief. We booked him into our jail, and Kevin threw his cigarettes into his property drawer. I looked at the picture I took from his house before I put it into his property. The photo, worn and faded from decades of exposure, revealed the face of a happy, little guy, his arm around the waist of his mother.

As expected, Baby-Ray faced the consequences of his actions, never revealing his partner and not cooperating as far as confessing to other crimes, even though he was promised immunity. He pled guilty and was sentenced to eleven years in prison. Lieutenant Fuller was ecstatic by the way the incident was handled, even though our part was minimal. A dog affected the arrest. The Lieutenant bragged to anyone who would listen, except the chief, referring to us as "his boys." Chief Rendle didn't want to hear about that, he just wanted to know we did what we get paid to do. The facts, nothing but the facts.

THIRTY-SEVEN

The town was relatively quiet, no major crimes left to solve, no one getting murdered, just routine domestic stuff. The lull in activity caused some unrest, so I perused some of the old inactive and suspended cases in file and stumbled across the murder of the farm laborer case, the one where the woman called and reported a shooting on the 911 line. I was the supervisor on duty, and when we arrived, no one was there; nothing. I was surprised to see such little documentation on the case, since it was a murder, but recalling the supervisor, ole Peanut-brain and the clientele, Mexicans, I wasn't surprised.

I carefully reviewed each page of the report, viewing the little drawing of the medical examiner who concluded death was caused by a gunshot to the head. I retrieved what little evidence was stored in the evidence room, stored indefinitely since the statute of limitations never runs out on murder. The San Joaquin County Sheriff's Office report was there since the initial call was that of a "floater" discovered in the Calaveras River. I found the tape recording of the 911 call and listened to the scratchy, barely audible voice on the calling end.

"911. What is your emergency?"

Scarcely audible in the background were men's voices, mostly in Spanish and undecipherable, clearly excited. Loud, heavy breathing drowned them out when I heard a woman yell, "You gotta come quick. Someone's been shot!"

"Calm down," said the dispatcher. "What is the address?"

"Clover Road, it's on Clover Road. Hurry. I think he's dying." It then sounded as if someone grabbed the phone from her and more voices speaking Spanish could be heard.

"What's the numbers, the number of the house?" The dispatcher yelled.

"Oh, my God, hurry!" That voice. I knew that voice. I've heard it before, but where?

"The numbers! What's the address?" the dispatcher prodded.

"Two-twelve, it's 212. I think he's dead!" she screamed. The line became disconnected.

My heart stopped. Of course, I knew that voice. It was Mary! I'll be go to hell, that was Mary, I thought as my body shivered.

"Kevin! Come here quick," I yelled from my office.

I played the tape over and over, and he was also convinced it was Mary making the call. We looked at each other, dumbfounded. All Peanut-brain had to do was have everyone in the department listen to the tape. Someone might have been able to place that voice, someone like me. "It's been two years, Kevin. Two years! Can you believe it?" He said nothing, just shook his head. All this time, I assumed she was in prison. She must have witnessed the killing and called. She could at least have told us everyone who was there. My God, I thought. Dumas, you indisputable idiot. All we had to do now was find Mary.

I got worried every time I checked the papers and read about an unidentified woman found murdered, or pulled from the slough. I just knew it had to be Mary, but then I remembered she was a survivor, a true survivor, so no matter what she became involved in, she wouldn't let herself be murdered. I wasn't concerned about her because she may be a witness to a murder, but more for herself, the person she was. We learned she had been paroled for drugs and check writing. She was wanted by her Parole Officer for failing to submit to urine testing for drugs. I was upset with her P.O. when he came to the department for his weekly meeting with his parolees.

"How come you didn't notify us Mary was paroled?"

"Why should I?" he answered, defensively. "She wasn't paroled here."

"What difference does that make? She used to live here!" I argued.

"Look. We didn't want her here because of her ties to the criminal element. You know how that works."

"Oh, that's great logic, just great!" I said, becoming argumentative. "She's still involved and probably over her head. How do you know she's not dead? She witnessed a murder for Christ sakes." I was becoming frustrated.

"So what? One less loser I have to worry about. What's the big deal?"

"She's not a loser..." I caught myself become too defensive for her. I couldn't tell him she used to be my informant. He didn't know her like I did. "Never mind. You're right. It's no big deal." I dropped it.

I had to find her. I knew she was alive somewhere. I knew in my heart the reason she went underground was because she saw the murder. She knew who did it. I just knew it. I did some checking around and learned Mary had gone to hell, literally, since I last saw her. I was not surprised when I found she dabbled in heroin, but I didn't think she would resort to turning tricks for the farm laborers to support the habit. Though I heard it, I refused to believe it. I didn't want to think she became addicted to it. Goddamn the pusher man! From there, she must have degenerated into the seamy world of drugs, the ninth circle of hell where no one escapes. Dante's ninth circle is for the worst sinners, the betrayers. Nothing but betrayal, lies and deceit infest the drug circle. Mary couldn't be there, I prayed. It was just a matter of time when she would suffer subterranean homesick blues. I would see her again; I sensed it.

In the meantime, I was fighting to keep the darkness from drowning me, but the light was getting dimmer. The new Lieutenant, Shultz, the former member of the infamous "Snooper and Blabber" narcotics team, had jumped aboard the Psycho bandwagon. His name fit, I thought. Out of respect for Snooper and Blabber, Schultz reminded me more of the bumbling Nazi from the television series, Hogan's Heroes, of the same name. The word throughout the department was the chief wanted a yes man, a "go-fer" which Schultz readily filled. Under the chief's influence, he developed a dislike for me and engaged me in a series of "memo wars." He began writing me up for meaningless transgressions which contained tinges of sarcasm. I responded in kind but there is usually no winner in these wars, but the new Lieutenant had the wild card; the chief.

The development of informants is the most vital element of working investigations. Kevin was a personable, humorous Detective, often trading barbs with those we arrested. They liked him, but more importantly, they respected him. Thus, it became easy to build informants. A certain amount of conniving and manipulation helps, but the key was to not let the informant know they were being conned or manipulated. As such, our clearance rate was high, particularly in the burglary rate, a most difficult crime to solve. Someone, out of professional jealousy no doubt, spread the word that my unit was engaging in entrapment, hence, the high clearance rate. Okay, so we offered a deal to a thief for a recommendation of leniency if he would tell us when the next planned burglary was going to happen. Nothing illegal about that.

A local thief really got into this informant thing. When his first information given to us resulted in an arrest, he got to feel like a cop and liked it. Clearly, he had no loyalties to anyone but himself, a good trait to be an effective crook and snitch. To help him, we told him to call on the Crimestoppers Hotline with the information of crime and criminals for which a reward was given. We were able to pay him with merchants' money, which sponsored the program. The informant was Chago, the same guy who turned us on to the mom and pop liquor store robbery.

Chago was slick. If he wasn't a crook, he'd have been an outstanding police officer, which I think was his latent desire, but he was trapped in his life on the South Side. We struck up a pretty good trust and rapport with him, never burning him and never sharing him with anyone else. He respected that. The only thing we did that was probably questionable was to use Chago to get us out of those boring bi-monthly training sessions, the ones where someone from the department read new laws from a book or talked about hazardous materials or sexual harassment.

Chago would call about an hour into the training session, ask for Kevin or myself, and tell us something important was going down and he had to meet with us in a hurry. We'd leave the meeting, make up some bogus information and then go to our local watering hole, The Old Douglas Market, until the swing shift guys met us there after training. One of the newer, younger officers, Les Garcia, started to get suspicious and confronted us after he ordered his beer.

"How come you guys always get called out whenever we have training?"

"Do we?" Kevin innocently asked.

"Seems like it," he said after taking a swallow of his beer. "Say, is that some phony stuff? Are you having your girlfriend call or something?" He smiled. "If you are, it's working, so I'm thinking about having my wife call." He was another one bored with the training.

"Look," I said, leaning over my barstool and looking him in the eye. "That's not entirely true. With informants, you never know when something's going to happen. They don't work 8 to 5 like we do. We get called out seems like every night. You only see it when you're with us, like training or something. Being a cop, you know you shouldn't jump to conclusions, right?"

He thought about it a moment, quaffed his beer, and said, "Yeah, I suppose you're right. I never thought about it that way." Kevin couldn't stifle his laugh, so he left for the bathroom.

The next training session, a mundane public relations update taught by the chief, the call came just a few minutes into the meeting. I answered the phone and motioned for Kevin to leave in a hurry, something big was about to happen. The dispatcher asked me to come to the dispatch center post-haste. The young officer, Les, just looked, smiled, and shook his head as we slipped out the back door.

THIRTY-EIGHT

"Wait a minute, Kevin." Something was wrong. "It's too early for Chago to call. Something's up." We went into the dispatch room where Hamburger Karl was waiting impatiently.

"What is it Karl?" I asked.

"Some broad said she needs to talk to you right away. She's on line 51."

I pushed the blinking button line. "Hello."

"Hello, stranger."

Mary! I'll be go to blazes, it was Mary. My heart skipped a beat. "Mary?"

"How'd you guess?" I was thrilled. She was alive--I knew it!

"Where are you? How are you?" I asked, unable to contain my joy. "You're still alive I see."

"You gonna buy me a drink?"

"Just say when and where." She told me she'd be in the parking lot of the Old Douglas Market. She didn't want to go in for fear of being seen. I grabbed Kevin, drove to the bar and saw her in the car she described parked amongst the others. Kevin pulled up next to her.

"Get in," Kevin told her, opening the back door. She looked good, almost the way I remembered her.

"You guys ain't going to turn me in, are you?" She was still wanted by a parole agent for violating the terms of her parole, arrestable on sight.

"Damn straights," Kevin said. "Our totals are low this month, we need to jack up our stats."

She looked at him in earnest, fearing he was serious. He smiled. "How you been, Mary? You're looking good." The tone of his voice greatly relieved her.

"You liar," she answered. "I'm okay, I guess. My P. O. wants me, I got some checks hanging. I'm broke, the usual. Other than that, I'm great." We made small talk as Kevin bought a six-pack of beer and we drove around town. She never spoke directly of the things she was involved in, and we never asked, but I could see she was in over her head. Her natural, relaxed manner was missing. I hoped to ease her tension.

"They promote you yet?" She asked.

Before I could answer, Kevin piped up, "Yeah, they made him Chief Asshole," and then broke into laughter.

"You ought a get out of there," she said. "You're just wasting your time in this town."

"The town's okay, it's...it's the department, but, yeah, you're right. It's pretty messed up."

"How long you been there."

"Ever since I got out of high school, seventeen long years ago," surprising myself with the realization of how fast the years went by.

"Yeah, you better leave," Mary sighed.

"I'm starting to think that way. I really am," I confided to her, or anyone for the first time.

"You go, I'm going with you," said Kevin, his loyalty never wavering.

We decided to take Mary to my apartment. Kevin took the car back to the department, making sure he didn't leave any empty beer bottles behind, then getting his own car, met us back at The Old Douglas Market. I fixed us a late dinner, my specialty, tacos. She never was much of an eater, but she wolfed them down, apparently not having eaten for days.

I watched her and thought about a time long ago; knowing she never knew her innocence. Like mine, it was lost a long time ago, too. Here we were, absurdly in my apartment, worlds apart, but closer than ever. So many what-ifs entered my mind, and I'm sure she thought the same thing. She caught my gaze and I knew, I could see it in her eyes. She loved me. She could never tell me, but she did. Why else would she have done those things for me, why else would she keep things hidden from me that she thought would lessen my opinion of her? She risked her life and her reputation by informing on people, making me look good, always playing the game that we were on opposite sides, but we shared a secret world, a world where she never told anyone she loved them, for I never could either. I could never say 'I love you' to anyone. I gave her money now and then, but it was never out of pity or payment for her information. She never asked, but I knew it would help her, at least for awhile. Maybe I loved her, too, but I didn't really know. I didn't know what love was. But I knew she loved me, but it could never be--ever.

I couldn't resist any longer. I had to ask her. "Mary?" I paused a moment. "How come you never told me about the killing?" She was startled, nearly choking on the bite of her taco. "You were there, weren't you?" You saw what happened." I shouldn't have pressed her so soon. She washed down the taco with a swig of cream soda, my favorite carbonated drink.

"What did you expect me to do? I couldn't say anything. They'd kill me, too. You don't know him, you just don't." She began to cry. Kevin sat silently by.

"I'm sorry. I didn't mean to upset you." I told her, sincerely. "I just found out about you being there by accident. I heard the tape of your call just a while ago."

"You got that on tape? Jesus!"

"Yeah. We're getting kind of modern, you know?" I tried to ease the tension.

"It was horrible," she said. "I never saw anyone killed. He just put the gun to his head and...the noise, it was awful. I couldn't believe it. I tried to call, but they took the phone away." She was reliving the scene in her mind.

"Who did it?" I asked her pointedly.

"Don't do this to me. I just wanted to see you and say goodbye. If I'd known you knew, I never would have called you. Please don't...can't we, you know..."

"Come on, Mary. Help me out." She ignored me.

"...can't we, for old time's sake, just have a good time, like we used to?" She pleaded.

"Mary. A guy's dead. He's dead! Killed! Murdered, for Christ's sake. Tossed in the river like garbage, like he was nothing. His family, no one knows what happened, no one cares. Not our department, not the Sheriff's Office, no one. You can't ask me to pretend like I don't know or that nothing happened."

"Well that's it then," she said in anger. "Nothing happened. I didn't see nothing, I don't know nothing." She started to cry again.

"Just tell me, Mary. Just tell me what you saw. You'll be gone, nobody will know. I never burned you before--never! You know that!" She remained obdurate, which angered me. "It isn't fair. Just another dead Mexican, right? Just another worthless greaser, a wetback..."

"Stop it!" She yelled. "You know that's not it. You know I ain't that way. Kevin, tell him to stop," she implored him. Kevin stepped forward and put his hand on Mary's shoulder while she cried in her hands.

"Mary," he said softly. "You know he's right. Nobody seems to care about nothing. We don't want to hurt you, but you can't ask us not to do our job. You can't ask us not to care."

"Oh, I know, I know," she whispered, barely audible above her sobs. "Goddamn you. Goddamn both of you. Why did you have to find out? They'll kill me! I know they will...you just don't know." I backed off, feeling badly for her. I never thought she'd react this way. She was really scared. Kevin lit up a smoke and offered Mary one. "I feel like I'm being questioned. Why don't you just take me to your office, you bastards?"

"Please, Mary." I took her hands in mine. "Let us get those guys. I don't know who he was, except now he's a dead man, but you did. He didn't deserve to die, to be treated like that. What did he do? Why was he killed?"

She looked into my eyes and I saw their beauty, still striking, still mysterious. She stood up and embraced me tightly, and I felt her slight body fighting back the sobs. Kevin walked into the small kitchen of my apartment.

"Please don't let them hurt me," she whispered in my ear. "I love you." I held her closer. "Please, I know what I'm talking about. You have to promise."

"Mary, if I had kids, I'd swear by them. You've got to trust me." Her words echoed in my ear. She said she loved me. Even if she did, nothing could ever come of it, and we both knew it. "They'll never know, never. Believe me."

She told us the victim was just a typical farm laborer, up here when the crops were in harvest where he could make some good money working hard. He was one of those who wanted to stay here, so he tried to Americanize himself for acceptance. He bought the flowered shirts and platform shoes popular a few years before, but these guys were always a bit behind the times, and he grew his hair trying to imitate the now defunct disco dudes. Mary said it was funny how they thought Americans were, even to the point of experimenting with drugs, marijuana mostly. He spent a lot of money on her, she said, and treated her with respect, of which she felt some reciprocity. She didn't say how she hooked up with him, and I didn't ask. I didn't really want to know.

He soon found out how fast he could make money by selling drugs, and was transporting some, not for himself, but as a mule for the dealers who used cheap, Mexican laborers as readily as the crop owners. Mary told us the Ortiz family, owners of a restaurant and Mexican market in Stockton, was heavily involved in the smuggling and selling of heroin. Our department was familiar with the family because they had relatives in my town who were involved in narcotics to a small degree, or so we thought. The youngest son of the family, Raul, recruited the guy to transport small amounts of heroin until he could prove himself.

The dead guy, Juan Cortez, was eager to please and did well. He picked up American styles and customs, passing himself as a legal, one with a green card, granting him identity to live and work in this country. Raul Ortiz answered to his older brother, Jaime, who lived in Sacramento, the mastermind behind the drug operation. Jaime lived affluently, making no efforts to conceal the profits of his enterprise, claiming the lucrative restaurant and market bore the fruit. He did not escape the scrutiny of the Sacramento Police or the State Bureau of Narcotics Enforcement, the BNE, but they were powerless without an informant, and no one would snitch for fear of being killed. This was bigger than anything we thought.

Mary's boyfriend, Juan, succumbed to filthy lucre—the power of money: greed! He began ripping off small amounts he sold on the side for pure profit, thus incurring the wrath of the kingpin, Jaime. In these drug circles, the players are more familiar with the system and flow of illegals than any law enforcement agency. A swift, clean murder of one who betrayed or went beyond the rules was a safe bet. The killer, sometimes a hired illegal, simply fled to his home country until the heat died down, knowing the ineptness and unwillingness of local law enforcement to spend time and resources on "wetbacks." That was certainly the case in my town.

Mary further said she was with Juan when Jaime and his brother, Raul, came to town to execute Juan for ripping them off. She said she never really knew the extent of Juan's involvement, nor that he was targeted for the killing. I didn't know how much of what she said to believe. She wasn't about to admit heroin use, but there didn't seem any reason to press the issue. Maybe I didn't want to know of her drug use, at least not from her. She seemed clean and sober now. There was no doubt in my mind she was dependent on Juan for the drug, but that was then. This was now and I only saw the Mary I used to know.

"We were going to go to the Mexican dance on South Side," she went on. "Me, Juan and the other couple who lived in the house. As we were about to leave, a car drove up and it was the Ortiz brothers. Juan got real uptight, wanting to leave or hide, or something. I knew he was scared. He wouldn't open the door for them and wouldn't let us either. I knew something was wrong." She paused a moment, not sure if she really wanted to say more.

"It's okay, Mary. You're doing fine. Take your time," I reassured her.

"Then they broke a window and opened the door. Jaime and Raul forced their way in, and then everyone started yelling in Spanish…" She stopped again. I could see she was about to break down. "It's…it's just…" I went to hold her, but she pushed me back, gathering the strength to continue. "I'm alright, I…I'm ok," she said. "Can I have a cigarette?" Kevin lit her up one.

"Relax, Mary. There's no hurry. We're not taking notes, there's no tape recorder. Just chill," Kevin told her as he handed her the smoke.

She continued. "Then the older one, Jaime, he just pulls a gun from his coat, puts it to Juan's head and shot him…just shot him, like that," she snapped her fingers for emphasis. "Shot his ass right in the head."

I looked at Kevin, who picked up on it and said, "Shot his ass in the head? How can that be, Mary? I'd like to see that?"

"Oh shut up. You know what I mean." I chuckled a bit at the image, but she continued. "That's when I tried to call. I was scared to death. Jaime was yelling to his brother and the other guy who lived there. They wrapped Juan up in some blankets and then Jaime grabbed the phone from me. I thought he was going to shoot me, too…it was, it was awful." She couldn't hold back anymore and started crying. We gave her some space and mixed ourselves a stiff drink.

"Hey, Mary," Kevin yelled from the kitchen. "How about a big stiff one?" He winked at me.

"If I wanted one, I wouldn't ask you," she smiled, ever so slightly.

"Aw, come on," he said. "I'm just talking about a drink, jeez, can't even be nice to someone…" he trailed off, smiling.

Seeing her smile made us feel a little better and helped her mood a little.

"Since you're the one asking, better give me a small one then."

He gave her a glass of cream soda with a little V.O. mixed in. "You gonna be alright?" he asked.

She sipped the drink. "Yeah. Thanks. I'm sorry, but the memory, the…it's just that, everything is so clear in my mind."

"You don't have to apologize for anything," I said. "You're doing great. What you say stays right here."

"I just couldn't believe he killed him. I saw his head jerk back, back like…like I don't even know, like he was a rag doll, or something."

"You saw Jaime draw the gun and pull the trigger?" Kevin asked.

"Yes. I saw him! They wrapped Juan up in some blankets and just threw him in the trunk of their car. They dragged me and the other couple with them. We started to drive away when Jaime heard sirens, so he pulled off the road and made us all duck down. We saw you guys, or whoever it was that came. We saw another police car and Jaime made us stay down until he was sure they all passed. He drove the back roads out of town and stopped on the bridge."

"You talking about the bridge at Heinbockle's, the back way to Stockton?" I asked.

"Yes. Then Raul and Jaime got out and threw Juan in the river. I heard the splash and everything…." She paused again.

"I was one of the guys that passed you," I told her. "You mean you were right there? Still at the house?"

"No, no. We already pulled out of the driveway. Jaime had the lights off when he heard the sirens. He drove down the road a ways and pulled over until you guys passed."

"I'll be damned. I'll be go straight to hell," I muttered.

"What are you guys going to do now?"

I looked right at her. "I don't know. You're the key witness. You could put those guys away—"

"Now don't," she yelled. "You promised. They'll kill me. If they don't, someone else will. I'm…"

Kevin interrupted her. "Take it easy, Mary. It ain't going to happen; but it's true. You are the only one. You know we won't burn you."

We didn't know who was more exhausted; us from listening, or Mary from telling us. We had to take Mary back to her car while we pondered our next move. We didn't want to part, but our worlds clashed, and our hearts broke. Kevin and I hugged Mary, and she gave me a kiss. I thought I was about to cry, but I didn't, at least not then. "Don't worry, Mary. Don't worry about nothing," I said as she left.

Why do things like this happen to me? I wondered. A young man's dead. I have an eyewitness, someone who can put these guys away, away for life, or even death row, which is what they deserve. Who is she anyway? Should I give a damn what she thinks of me if I burn her and officially report what she told me? Isn't there something like a witness protection program where she can hide? I hated this. Shouldn't this have been solved years ago? Hell with those guys, the Ortiz brothers. Big deal! Little cowards. I'll take them out myself. Yeah, that's what I'll do. I'll do what the state and the system hasn't the nerve; I'll kill them myself. Wait. I'm going insane. No, I wasn't. There isn't a cop alive who hasn't thought about exacting his own justice over someone they knew deserved it. Not a one. That's it. Me and Dirty Harry. Take it easy, I told myself. Act too hastily and I'll blow it, then I'll be the one to fry. I had to think this over, formulate a plan, a plan to avenge the death of someone no one gave a damn about, someone who became nothing. I remembered my old mentor, Sgt. Guevara. The victim was a person, a human being with a soul, someone who mattered to someone. I will kill them.

Death mocked me. He was going to take me, and soon if I didn't act first. He was flittering all over the place, taunting me, showing his stuff—someone dies there, someone dies here. Someone dies who is a no one. A nobody dies who is someone, but it doesn't mean anything to anyone anyhow. Chief Wolfe was right. Posturing. It's all posturing. What's right doesn't matter; unless it's wrong to someone who wants it to matter, then it doesn't matter because someone else thinks nothing of it. It was all so absurd.

Dare I be honest? I tell Mary, 'Look, here's the plan. You're my witness, plain and simple. You'll get protection, I guarantee it. Just say what you have to say when you have to say it, and you're gone. Deal?' She'll say, 'Sure, I'll tell what I saw and that's it. I'm gone. I'm protected forever from the family.' You bet. Then I tell Chief Psycho, 'Look, I got this eyewitness to a murder. She'll testify, put two punks away, and we look good. Case closed.' He'll smile, put his hand out and say, 'Put 'er there, pal. Good job.' And we'll be friends forever.

Wait a minute, just hold it there a second, I told myself. The guy, what was his name…Juan, yeah, that's it, Juan. He was killed over two years ago. He was nothing then when we fought over jurisdiction, each agency not wanting to claim him as a murder victim, each side refusing to deny his existence in death when his existence truly ceased. And now I had this other nobody, this Mary, who lived underground, a sub-existence, telling me this nobody was somebody to her, but she couldn't tell who the somebodies were who killed the nobody because nobody cares anyway about somebody who doesn't exist, unless that non-existence means somebody will really be a somebody, somebody like a psycho Chief, who will acknowledge the existence of the somebody he wished didn't exist, namely, me! STOP! The circle seemed endless, a maze of nonsensical, meaningless drivel, a big black hole where everything jumped into its own nothingness and became just that. That did it! I am mad, I am totally insane. A lad insane, Aladdin Sane. Which way to the Enchanted Forest? Mary?

The next day, we sat in our office, drinking coffee and perusing the cases requiring follow-up. The Econo Gas Station had a drive away, somebody who filled their tank and left without paying, a time long before payment was made with a debit or credit card, a time the attendants trusted their customers to pay. The attendant was astute enough to obtain the license plate which patrol checked and found belonged to a local. I was about to give it to Kevin, but hesitated, absorbed in thought about the night before, wasteful thought.

"What's our next move, boss?" Kevin asked.

"We go find the Ortiz brothers and kill them."

"Sounds good to me," he agreed.

"Something really bothers me about this," I said. "Say everything Mary told us is true. There's no way the Ortiz brothers just drive up to that house without knowing the guy's going to be there. If they're bent on killing him, they have to know when and where he's going to be with a minimum of witnesses, right?"

"Yeah. So you think Mary may have something to do with it?

"No, not her. The couple with whom her and Juan were going to the dance. They had to have set him up. How else could they have known, if we believe Mary, and I do."

"You're making sense, for once, Sarge," Kevin mocked. "That makes two of us. I believe her, too. But this is turning into a Scooby-doo mystery."

"Good. So we find who they are, put the squeeze to them and, whoa Nelly, there's our witnesses. Cool, huh?"

"Sounds too easy," Kevin protested. "You think their names

are going to be on the gas and electric files, phone files, cable TV, and stuff?"

He was right. If they were illegals involved with the Ortiz's, they're a long time gone. Without Mary, we had nothing, leaving us with one choice—keeping it in the dead file. I handed Kevin the gas station drive away report. "Get a hold of the registered owner of the car. See if he wants to pay for the gas, or go to jail." He read the case, and then put his jacket on to leave.

THIRTY-NINE

I was becoming detached from the department's administration, partly from disillusionment, partly from contempt. The supervisor's meetings were a bore while I sat and listened to Peanut-brain, Psycho, the new Lieutenant and others professing their knowledge and superiority over all they reigned. The nit-picking and the memo wars continued, but I refused to yield, refused to be something I couldn't; a robotic yes-man, blindly fulfilling the self-serving desires of my masters. I was feeling blue. I often thought that those in management should be required to spend two weeks a year back on the street, back in patrol so they'd remember who the real criminals were.

Tuesday afternoon in Tracy, California. The swing shift had arrived so us Detectives assembled with the officers in the briefing room to share information, what little there was. I left without much input walking back to my office followed by one of the newer men, the young Mexican officer, Les, the one who was wise to our training session disappearances. He just made a significant bust and asked me about the proper penal code sections for meth charges.

"What'd you nail 'em on, Les," I asked.

"Possession of meth, possession for sale and under the influence," he said proudly.

"Cool. Nice going." I was about to tell him, but thought better of it. "You better go check with the Lieutenant. Dope is his domain, if you know what I mean," I said with an impish grin. "Let him make a decision." He walked down the hall to the Lieutenant's office, Lt. Schultz.

"On my arrest, Lieutenant, what code sections should I use?"

The Lieutenant glanced up at him, peering over his glasses and hesitated. "What are your goals? What are your objectives?"

The officer wasn't prepared for a management lesson. He fidgeted a moment and answered, "Uh, well, my goals are to put the guy in jail and then write my report, I guess,"

"You guess? Have you thought about all reasonable alternatives?" The Lieutenant wisely asked.

"Alternatives to what?" the officer responded, obviously confused. "I just want to know what code violations to put into the spaces of my report, that's all."

"It would be too easy for me to sit here and tell you, but then you wouldn't learn anything. I suggest you research the information and then make the appropriate entries."

"Sure, Lieutenant. Thanks."

The officer walked down the hall and I poked my head out of my office and motioned for him to come inside.

"What a jerk," Les said. "What was that all about?"

"Here," I said, handing him a piece of paper with the codes written on it. "I heard. I should have just given them to you in the first place. Sorry about that."

"It's okay," he said. "Thanks." He continued walking back to the report room shaking his head in amazement.

Too often, people who are promoted to managerial positions ignore the fallacy of their preeminence, that they walk amongst the mere mortality of their former brethren. They begin talking management-ese, a language far advanced for ordinary simpletons and inferiors like the young officer, an affliction also common amongst those in the law profession. Instead of saying things like, 'What were you doing there?', they asked, "What caused your presence in the location of the occurrence?', or instead of saying, "There's a meeting in the squad room at 3:00 PM,' they say, 'Your attendance at the Chief's conference scheduled in the department's briefing facility at 1500 hours is required. Failure to comply with this directive may result in disciplinary action.' Instead of the Lieutenant telling the officer what he should have: 'I don't know the codes offhand. Let's go look them up together,' he blew him off with management-ese, a cultural barrier between management and labor, thus hindering effective relations.

Of all things, management was a harbinger of good tidings. Chief Rendle and his flunky, Schultz, called me for "an unscheduled conference in the Chief's quarters," a meeting in the Psycho's office for those not schooled in management-ese. He also "requested the presence of my immediate subordinate to attend the meeting." I brought my underling, Kevin, to the Chief's office.

"I just got a call from Agent Battlestone of U.S. Customs," the chief said with utmost importance, pausing a moment. I thought the pause was for me to say, 'Gee, I'm impressed. YOU got a call from U.S. Customs? Why would you desire my unworthy presence to tell me that?' An absurd thought crossed my mind. I thought I saw a smirk cross the Chief's face which immediately made me think that Barney Fife had bypassed Sheriff Andy Taylor of Mayberry to become the new Sheriff, or our new Chief.

Barney, rather, the Chief, not getting any response, went on. "They arrested a guy at the border trying to smuggle some kilos of heroin." Another pause. My bitterness was hard to stifle. I thought I was now supposed to say, 'Wow, that's great! They do an awesome job down there, don't they, Chief?'

"And?" I asked, impatiently.

"The guy's telling the agents he's wanted for a murder here. Do you or your men know anything about that?"

"We might be able to shed some light," I answered. "You forgot one important thing."

"What's that?"

I looked at Kevin, who tried to avoid my glance, then back to the chief. "The name. What's the guy's name?"

"Oh, yeah. Let's see," he looked down at his notes. "Raul Ortiz." Well, blow me down! I had to think fast, real fast. Kevin squirmed in his chair. I can't just tell him about Mary. No one knows.

"Jeez. What a coincidence! We just got information from an informant, although second hand, that he was the guy present when that farm laborer was killed a couple of years ago. Remember?"

The Chief thought about it a minute. "No. Can't say that I do." I quickly explained some of the important parts of the incident, leaving Mary's name out of it. I told the Chief with what little we had, it still might be enough to get a murder warrant and bring the guy back for further investigation. "Well, go ahead and meet with the D.A. and see what you can do. Keep me informed."

"Right, Chief. Let's go, Kevin." We arranged a quick meeting with the D.A. assigned to the Tracy Court and explained a bit more to him. We gave him plenty of good cases earning his trust and respect, so he was pretty much in our corner and went along with most of our plans.

"Well. It's close," he told us. "Might be better if you could identify the informant, though."

Not a chance. "If we can get him back here, and quickly, I think we can get him to talk to us. Think about it. He'd rather tell them he's wanted for a murder than face smuggling charges in Mexico?" I disclosed some more information, telling him it came second hand in an effort to protect Mary.

"Okay. I might be able to get it by a preliminary, but you guys got some work to do."

"It's a deal. Just gimme that warrant and we're gone!" Kevin and I made arrangements to fly to San Ysidro, the border town near San Diego holding Raul Ortiz.

We researched and compiled extensive background information on Raul. He wasn't quite 21, a high achiever in high school, free of any arrests or major brushes with the law. He seemed a pretty decent kid, the youngest in the family, thus, in a position to want to please his parents and siblings, particularly his oldest brother, Jaime. With the family operation the way it was, he got caught up in something in which he had no choice; this was his life, this is the way it was, a common and unfortunate story for many a family's youngest. Our ace in the hole, our only hope, really, was to get him back here quickly and talk with him. We felt he was naïve enough not to invoke his rights to remain silent, therefore, talk with us. Time was our biggest adversary now.

FORTY

"Forty dollars?! A lousy forty bucks? What is this?" I complained loudly to Schultz, the Lieutenant. That was the money allotted for the trip to San Ysidro, money for meals and incidentals on the way and back. The plane fares had been charged to the city. "That's only twenty bucks apiece, for Christ sakes. Who knows how long we'll be gone? Come on, be reasonable,"

"Take it or leave it," Schultz said smugly. "Take it up with the Chief if you want."

"Thanks, Lieutenant," I said sarcastically, snatching the two twenties from his hand.

"Don't forget to sign this." He handed me the city voucher, verifying the disbursement. Things got worse from there.

Time formed an alliance with death to play more tricks on me, to vaunt their derision of my existence. They formed an unholy alliance with that evil beater of old men in dungeon-like jail cells, Chief Psycho, G. R. Rendle. I stressed the importance of time, maintaining our success rested with our proven ability to talk with people, and it would never be put to the test more than now. I was wrong to take my job so seriously. I thought precisely because of that, our departure was delayed to the point that it may be a deliberate attempt to undermine me. Some would call it an obstruction of justice. The arrest of Raul Ortiz occurred on a Friday. We weren't able leave town until the following Tuesday due to bureaucratic hazards, the paperwork, vouchers, and other such drivel. I stayed in constant contact with Customs Agent Battlestone who told me Ortiz was aware of our impending arrival, but hadn't had any visitors yet.

We arrived only to find Ortiz's family was there, who reached him shortly before we could. "Damn it, Kevin! Damn it to hell! If they've gotten to him, we're screwed." The court proceedings in San Ysidro lasted until early afternoon before we were finally able to meet with Ortiz. When I first saw him in the morning, before he made his appearance, he looked like a scared little kid. A guy we presumed to be his attorney conferred with the agents then with Raul who was immediately swarmed by his family.

There he was! Arrogant and vain as had been portrayed; Jaime Ortiz. I felt for my weapon, thinking of a time and place I could kill him. Once Raul was released from custody of the court and remanded to me, his family again surrounded him as he strained to get a look at me, assuming I was the cop who was to transport him back to Tracy to face the murder charge. Jaime then left the courtroom, "mad-dogging" me on the way out, a term Mexicans used for staring each other down, a sign of disrespect. As he kept looking at me, I mouthed the words 'You're dead, punk,' feeling all Dirty Harry-ish. His eyes widened as I said it and he nearly ran into the swinging courtroom door on his way out. Kevin and I took Raul to the holding cell of the courtroom and signed for his property, which consisted of a watch, a nice ring, and a little cash. I introduced ourselves and made small talk about the flight, home, and such, then casually informed him of his constitutional rights.

"You understand those, don't ya?" I asked, downplaying it in hopes that in his nervousness and anxiety, my words wouldn't make much sense.

"Yes, sir. I understand. I invoke my rights to remain silent until I'm able to consult with an attorney," he said spuriously. Invoke? Consult? Tell me this guy wasn't coached. Kevin and I looked at each other in despair. Anything he said couldn't be used against him, and then I thought, 'against him'---that was my strategy.

We were forced to wait a bit longer before we could take him with us, so he had to wait in the holding cell until then. The Customs agents took us to the border town of Tijuana for lunch, which we felt obligated to buy since their professional courtesy and help were much appreciated. There went the last of our forty bucks!

Raul's manner reminded me of my own when I was in that car when the marijuana and bennies were found belonging to my friends. I felt badly for him, doing my best to relax him so he wouldn't be intimidated by us. In time, he loosened up and we talked about girls, boxing, everything but the killing. We flew back to the San Francisco airport continuing to make small talk. It was nearing five o'clock. Raul was a mere child, a kid deprived of his innocence making me think more and more of my youth.

Kilos of heroin! The guy would rather face a murder charge in the States than be locked up in a Mexican prison. Many guys his age didn't make it out alive, or if they did, they were never the same, which is the true aim of punishment. In that short time together, I got to like him and he respected us. It was almost as though three friends were out for some fun instead of transporting a murder suspect into custody. At the airport parking lot, we took the handcuffs of him, then Kevin stopped at a small market just outside San Francisco.

"I'm thirsty," he said.

"Me, too. How about a beer, Raul?" I asked.

"A beer? Yeah, that sounds good," he answered.

"Be right back," Kevin reached for his wallet and went inside.

I decided to play on Raul's emotions in hopes he would at least talk to me about what he knew. I knew he couldn't incriminate himself, and if he did, I couldn't use it anyway. I thought he'd talk and give me the names of the other people present during the shooting, and from there, I'd take my chances. Kevin came back and walked over to my window.

"Hee, hee. Uh, I don't have any money." I gave him my last five.

We sat in the car and sipped the cold beer. "Let me tell you something, Raul," I began. "I know you invoked your rights," repeating the words his attorney, no doubt, told him to use. "Whatever you say can't be used against you, and I understand that. But, you don't look like a bad guy, and I don't think you're capable of killing anybody. And you know what?" His eyes widened as he took a small sip of beer. "I think your brother killed that guy. Ain't I right?" I asked while he took a larger swallow of the brew.

My plan seemed to take hold. He took another sip of his beer and looked at me, as though to acknowledge a bonding between us, not as a cop to a crook, but as two Mexican men to each other, the same as if we sat in a bar and shared a beer. I treated him with respect, and I expected the same from him and he knew it. Of course, I was using him, but under the circumstances, I had to. A dead man's life was at stake.

"I'm hungry. Can we stop someplace to eat?" he asked.

"Good idea. I could use a bite, too." Kevin drove around looking for a McDonald's.

"Look at these, Raul." I reached into my jacket pocket and retrieved some photos, photos of the dead man, bloated and blackened by his burial in the river. I let him look at those and just flashed the autopsy pictures in front of him, knowing they probably make him throw up. He became somber, looking as if he were about to cry.

"Can I have another beer?" He asked with a quivering voice.

"This man had a family, Homes," I said, appealing to his culture, "he had people who cared for him. You've got a mother and father. They love you. What do you think Juan's (the dead man) family is thinking? What if your parents saw you like this?" I quietly said, showing the pictures again. He kept looking at the death pictures in disbelief. He wanted to talk. I could tell it, he wanted to tell someone, but he was scared, scared of his parents, scared of his brother, scared of the world. I know what he felt like; I could empathize with his turmoil.

"I told you, what you say can't be used against you. You have an attorney. You can tell him we talked, but I can't use anything against you, right Kevin?"

"He's right, Raul. We know you were just there. You don't know how we know, but we know." Kevin saw the familiar golden arches. "Okay, here's McDonald's. What do you guys want?" He started to get out of the car, then stopped. "Oops. Almost forgot. No money."

"Me, neither. I gave you my last five," I reminded him.

"I got some money. I'll pay," Raul offered.

"Thanks, Raul. We'll pay you back once we get to town," I told him. Kevin went to the trunk to get Raul's wallet. Raul took out a ten and gave it to Kevin. "We'll keep the receipt and pay you back," I reassured him.

"I ain't worried about it, eh. Get what you want and get me something." We sat in the McDonald's parking lot munching our burgers and fries. Good!

"I didn't kill him!" Raul suddenly exclaimed. "I didn't pull the trigger, it wasn't me! I didn't know. I just thought we were going to beat him up for stealing from us. I didn't even know Jaime brought a gun. I'm telling you the truth," he pleaded.

"I know you are, Raul. I know you are. Just take it easy. Try to remember everything," I coaxed.

"Got any beer left?" Kevin popped the top and gave him the last one.

"All I really want to know, Raul, is who else was there? You don't have to mention your brother."

"Yeah. They'll tell you I didn't kill him," he said with some hope. He talked the rest of the two hours' drive home. He gave us the names of Mary and the other two, whom he said were illegals, a man and a woman, but are now in Sacramento. He said once they learn of his arrest, they'll probably split back across the border.

We arrived at the department and booked him in jail on the murder warrant. We went back to our office and gave each other high fives, whooping it up, feeling ecstatic. All we had to do was find Mary, tell her she's been implicated in a murder and she'd be compelled to testify. It wouldn't be like she came forward or anything. She could even be subpoenaed as a hostile witness so the family wouldn't feel like she betrayed them. We also had to track down the other two before they went back to the black hole, Mexico. It was near 10:00 PM, plenty of time to stop by our watering hole, The Old Douglas Market, for some philosophizing and planning.

The next day, we met with the D.A. and explained what we were told. He was quite emphatic in his words. "The word I get is this guy's family wants to push this through trial as fast as possible. They may even have Raul take the full rap. You guys better get on this like yesterday." We worked day and night and with the help of Sacramento P.D., we finally tracked down the names of the two Raul gave us. We found their house, a tidy little shack in south Sacramento, geared to the low income and farm laborers who could afford it. We were glad. It looked like someone still lived there.

We knocked on the door…no answer. We kept knocking, someone had to be there. Still no response. We saw curtains move back from the window of the house next door.

"Let's go ask them," Kevin said. We went to the house and an older, Mexican woman answered.

"The people who live there," I said, motioning to the house, "do you know where they are, or when they'll be back?"

The woman, about 60, queried, "Who are you?"

"Police, ma'am," I answered.

"Police? You don't look like cops," as she eyed us suspiciously. "Show me your badges," she demanded.

'Badges? I don't got to show you no stinkin' badges' I almost answered as if almost on cue, bringing to mind Humphrey Bogart's *Treasure of the Sierra Madre*, as we flashed our badges. She seemed satisfied.

"You haven't heard?" she asked in broken English.

"Heard what?"

"They're dead," she said softly, as she hung her head.

"What do you mean, dead?" I asked in utter disbelief.

"Yes. They were killed in a car crash maybe two days ago."

"This is outrageous, this is totally outrageous!" I yelled. My head was spinning, Kevin's too. "They were killed, Kevin, they were set up. They had to have been. This cannot be a coincidence!"

"Yeah, I agree. You want me to check with Sacramento P.D.?" His question escaped me.

"Mary! What about Mary? We better find her first!" We left hurriedly back to Tracy.

I hated this. If I didn't know better, I swear someone was secretly watching me, causing these things to happen, causing this anguish within me. Of course, I knew! I had considered this before, but now, now the reality loomed directly ahead, lying in wait, in collusion with other forces beyond my perception, conspiring, waiting for me. Death!

FORTY-ONE

Like the wisp of a vapor she was, Mary vanished. We couldn't find her. She was my salvation. If I could find her, I'd explain everything Raul said, then she'd be glad to testify and it would set things right. If it wasn't for her, none of this would have been found out. When Raul told customs he was wanted for murder, it would not have checked out because no information had been developed yet, so Mary made the case for us. Days passed, a week, nothing. Her Parole Officer had a hold placed on her, for she hadn't checked in with him either.

The D.A. came to us saying the preliminary hearing was scheduled, and Raul's attorney was ready to proceed. Were we?

"Not much more I can do," I told him. "If we can find that Mary woman, we'd have a much better chance." Mary's name was now a matter of record based on what Raul told us. We couldn't use what Raul told us against himself, but Mary might help put Jaime away.

"I can ask for a continuance, try to buy more time. There may be a little resistance, by I can overcome it. Want me to do that?"

"That'd be great. Thanks," I said, a little relieved. The

continuance granted us a little reprieve, a little more time, a lot more worry.

Mary's name was in the state wide computer as being wanted as a parole violator and a key witness to a homicide. It didn't make me feel any better. If Mary didn't want to be found, she wouldn't be found. Smart woman. As much as I cared about her, I was hating her right now. The next day, I got a call from a Detective in Sacramento.

"How you guys doing with that Ortiz family case?" They were well known up there.

"Not too well," I confided. "Our witnesses are disappearing all over the place."

"I'm not too surprised by that," he said.

"What do you mean? Sounds like you're calling me with some bad news. I need some luck, so please tell me something good."

"That accident your guy called about checks out. Nothing suspicious right now, but we're looking into it. It wouldn't surprise me either if we came up with something, though."

"Speaking of surprises, why don't you surprise me and tell me you've got something good for us."

"I wish I could, partner. Ready for this?" My heart sunk. What else could go wrong?

"The attorney representing your puke ain't much better than the rest of the family. He's pretty well known around here, a guy named Stanley Sherman."

"Is that right?" I asked; standard cop response. "Stanley Sherman, huh? Sounds like some kind of cartoon character, some kind of a wimpy guy with glasses. Am I right?"

"He's a character, alright, but he ain't no cartoon. He's some serious stuff."

"What do you mean?" I was intrigued.

"He's pending indictment for, get this, soliciting murder, receiving stolen property, influencing testimony, and bribing a witness."

"Get out of town," I told the Detective. "You're kidding, right? You can't be serious."

"No shit, partner. I got his rap sheet right in front of me."

I said nothing. Nothing was all I could think. Nothing made any sense.

The Detective went on: "I'm telling you, everything about this family stinks."

"He's a lawyer? How can he still be practicing? Shouldn't he be disbarred or something?" I was in state of utter disbelief. Soliciting murder? Influencing testimony? And now my witnesses turn up dead?

"He ain't convicted yet. You know the law, innocent until proven guilty."

If that wasn't enough, he went on. "There's more. He was charged with attempted extortion, possession of cocaine, possession of a destructive device, some kind of bomb, I guess. He beat the rap on every one of them. Says right here, 'charges dismissed'."

Well blow me down! Was I already dead and sentenced to hell? "Now wait a minute. So with all this on the guy, and my witnesses end up dead in a supposed car wreck, you're telling me there's nothing suspicious? Are you on the payroll, too?"

Fortunately, he laughed. "Well, I said at least right now. We're looking into it."

"Thanks for the good news. Take care."

"You too. Good luck and keep in touch. We're interested in how it goes."

Somebody shoot me right now. I got the information the Detective gave me and checked it on our computer myself. Unreal. Just like he said. The next day, I met with the D.A. "Check this out, dude," I said, handing him the rap sheet.

"You make this up? Is this one of your clown jobs?" He couldn't believe it either. He suspected we were setting him up for a prank, having been victimized more times than he cared to admit. My unit was notorious for pulling what we called "clowns," or "clown jobs," little unsuspecting jokes which made the target look like a clown. One time, the other Detective, Tim, made a case from a photo lineup, just a minor offense, a petty theft. The victim had no trouble picking the culprit from a display of six pictures.

The law says you have to have at least five other pictures of people having the same characteristics, age, hair, and physical makeup, in order for the lineup to be accepted for court use. The defense attorney in the case wanted to see Tim's lineup in case there was something he could pick apart, or rather use as a defense. Tim was a good practical joker; nobody was immune from his clown jobs. He told the attorney to come over and he'd have it ready. I later saw him going through the mug shot file and picking out pictures of Blacks, Mexicans, Arabs, a couple of old men and stick them into a file folder along with a picture of the crook, a 25-yr. old white guy.

When the attorney came over, Tim excused himself from the office while I stayed innocently in the background to watch his reaction, reading a newspaper to hide my face, occasionally peeking over it to see him. Classic! The guy did a double take when he looked at the lineup photos, looking around to make sure he wasn't set up while I tried my hardest to stifle my laughter. He looked happy because some idiot cop completely bungled the lineup. Tim came back into the office.

"You through? Got what you need?" Tim innocently asked.

"This is your lineup? You used these to show the victim?"

"Yep, she had no trouble picking him out." I was amazed Tim could keep such a straight face, but then I shouldn't knowing how many times he clowned me.

"Can you make me copies of those?" The attorney asked him.

"Keep those. Those are duplicates anyway. I've got the originals in my file." The attorney scooped up the pictures, put them in his briefcase and hurried out. His walk told me he thought he had his case won.

"You're crazy, Tim. You're obscene. I ought to have your ass fired," I told him. We laughed for hours. Tim wasn't even going to tell the attorney. He was going to let him take the lineup to court and then make a fool out of him, clown him out bad. I couldn't let that happen, calling the attorney later and telling him he'd been the victim of a joke. He wasn't very happy about it.

I only wish this whole murder case was as much of a joke. The way it was going, I felt like I could already get a job in the Ringling Brothers Circus. I was getting clowned every time I turned around. The D.A. perused the rap sheet of the crooked attorney, shaking his head.

"Let's roll the dice and see what happens," he said, not the least intimidated.

The defense refused to postpone any further and scheduled the preliminary in the local courthouse. A preliminary hearing is a way of determining if the case is strong enough to go to full trial. Evidence is presented, witnesses are examined, everything as in a trial, except there are no jurors. The judge is the sole determinant of whether or not the case will proceed. Those of us involved in the investigation were subpoenaed. Mary was still missing. I was surprised to see one of my detractors at the hearing, the cowardly Boo Hoo, then I remembered he was on duty the night Mary made the call when we didn't find anything, except I didn't remember seeing his name on the witness list. There wasn't anything he could testify to except that we found an empty house, and I didn't see where it would be anything different than what I would say.

I was called to testify and saw the Ortiz family seated near the front of the gallery. "Hello, Raul," I said as I passed him on my way to the witness chair. I then remembered we hadn't paid him back yet for the hamburgers he paid for on the way back from San Francisco. Jaime wasn't there, either. I took my place on the stand and was sworn in.

So that's the guy! His attorney, the shyster, dressed in a black pin-striped suit. If anybody ever fit the caricature of the crooked attorney, this guy was it, even down to the shifty, beady eyes. It was like seeing a burglar in black clothes in a little black mask with eye holes slinking through the night. His looks were deceiving as I didn't take into account how shrewd he was. He had to have been to continue to keep his law license in spite of his criminal record.

The direct examination went as I expected with the D.A. setting up the framework for the statements Raul gave me after invoking his rights. Then it was time for the shyster to begin his cross-examination when a frightening thought entered my mind. He was death! He already solicited someone to kill someone else, he'd been found with explosive devices, he's tried to intimidate and bribe witnesses, and now here he was in front of me—in a court of law, defending a kid from a murder charge—ready to attack me. Without me, there is no case. Who's to say the family wouldn't pay this guy to have someone bump me off. A bomb in my car? A bomb in my apartment, a contract killing? Millions of dollars are gained through heroin trafficking, what would be a fair price on my head, I wondered as I studied him up and down. This stuff was starting to get to me. I was starting to get a bit, how you say, paranoid. I needed to take a deep breath, relax and simply answer the questions.

He slowly walked over to me as I kept my gaze on him while he approached the witness dock, put his hands on the railing and smiled. I noticed his jewelry, an expensive, diamond studded watch, large rings. The guy was doing alright and didn't seem to mind flaunting it.

"All right." He began. "Now officer, it is officer isn't it, or is it Sergeant?"

"Either one will work for me."

"Officer, you told us you initially went down to San Ysidro."

"Yes, sir." His first question was a nothing, yet I was hating him already. After I kill Jaime, I'm going to kill him. Solicit murder, eh, well then solicit nothing! The only one I'm going to solicit is myself.

"And you obtained a...strike that, you had a court order from a judge authorizing his release to you, to be brought back here, in your custody."

"Yes, sir,"

"Which means that you are responsible for his welfare and safety, as long as he is in your custody. Is that right, officer?"

"Yes, that's correct."

He turned and walked from me. "Now, did you contact him before you got the court order?"

"No, sir. Didn't see him at all."

"Okay. So, the first time you saw him was when you went to take possession of him and bring him back." Didn't I just say that?

"Yes, sir. In the holding cell."

"And at that time, did you Mirandize him?" Here we go. He's going to attack me for his statements made after the Miranda warning, his right to remain silent and so forth.

"Yes, sir. That's correct."

We bantered back and forth several minutes over this issue. He was trying to pin me down, but wasn't having much success. The key point in our favor was the amount of time we spent with him when we first picked him up, to the time we got near my town when he decided to talk. It's extremely uncommon for cops and crooks to spend 8 hours together in close quarters after the crook has invoked. What else are you supposed to do except talk? I knew he wasn't getting anywhere when he asked the same question but in different ways. He seemed to resign himself to the validity of the statements, but then his questions took a curious turn.

"Did you, from San Francisco to your jail, did you make any stops?"

"Yes, sir. We made a few stops, bathroom breaks, things like that." Dang! I should have only answered yes. A cardinal rule of testimony is to never volunteer more than you're asked.

"Things like that?" he picked up on it. "What kind of things? Where did you stop?"

"We stopped at McDonald's." He paused, looking away from me.

"McDonald's. Anyplace else?"

"Yes, at a market."

He turned towards me. "What kind of market, officer?"

"Just a market, a small neighborhood market."

"Did the market sell alcohol?"

"Yes."

"Did you buy any liquid refreshments?" He was agonizingly drawing this out. Just get to the point.

"Yes, sir. I bought some beer."

"Some beer. You bought some beer. You were on duty, weren't you?"

"Technically, yes, but we'd been in San Ysidro all day and…" He interrupted me.

"Did you drink beer?"

"Yes."

"Did you offer my client any beer?"

"Yes, I did. I knew he was thirsty and we'd…" He interrupted me again.

"Officer. How old is my client? Strike that…how old was my client when he was in your custody?"

"At the time, he wasn't quite 21."

"Did you make any other stops? Strike that…where was the defendant seated?

"In the back seat."

"I presume he was handcuffed. He was under arrest, correct?"

"Yes, he was, but we took the handcuffs off after we got back to San…"

"He was in the back seat, not handcuffed and drinking a beer. Is that your testimony?"

"Yes." I heard some slight laughter in the courtroom.

"Now, you said you also stopped at McDonald's?"

"Right."

"You bought some dinner, some hamburgers, French fries, whatever…"

"Yes."

"Who paid for it?" Dang, again! I should have paid him back.

"Well. We ran out of money at the market, so Raul offered to pay and we'd pay him back, but we just forgot. I owe Raul about 4 bucks…" The laughter got a bit louder. In the corner of my eye, I saw Boo-hoo get up and leave the courthouse. I also noticed more people in the room as some of the court clerks gathered to watch this fiasco.

"The defendant paid for your meal. Isn't that right?"

"Yes, but I just explained…"

"Okay, the defendant was not handcuffed, you're drinking beer, eating hamburgers and everyone's being all friendly. Is that right?"

"Yes, I already testified he wasn't handcuffed and we were getting along quite nicely…"

He interrupted loudly. "Your honor, the officer is going outside the scope of the question!"

"You asked, counselor. You asked if they were friendly," the judge boldly said. "Finish your answer Sergeant."

"Well, I was saying, yes, we got along quite well all the way back. He wasn't threatened or made any promises, just talk, talking all the way until he…"

"Your honor!" The attorney was getting frustrated.

"That's okay, Sergeant. You answered the question. You may continue counselor."

"Your honor. May I ask the court for a brief recess?"

"The court will take a fifteen minute recess," the judge ordered.

During the break, I asked the D.A. what was going on.

"I don't know," he said. "He's laying the foundation to attack your integrity."

"My integrity? What?"

"Don't worry about it. It's an old strategy. You can't attack the evidence, you attack the officer. You may have left yourself a little open, but I don't think it's anything to lose sleep over. I'll establish your intent upon re-direct." After recess, I took the stand.

The shyster continued. "Now officer, excuse me, Sergeant… that is your rank, is it not?"

"Yes, sir. That's correct."

"Now Sergeant, you are the supervisor of the Detective unit?"

"Yes."

"And as such, your position is to supervise others to adhere to policy and the law?"

"Yes. Correct."

"How old is the defendant, Sergeant."

"At the time, he wasn't quite 21." I could see it coming.

"You allowed him to drink alcohol under age as the supervising officer?"

"Yes, but…"

"And, Sergeant, he bought you hamburgers? From his own pocket?" he interrupted, repeatedly emphasizing my rank.

"Right, but we had no money left, so Raul offered…"

"Sergeant," he stressed. "Yes or no!"

The questioning continued through our conversation with Raul and the information we obtained. He stayed away from the hamburgers and beer, and tried to attack other merits of the case, without much success, I felt. On the stand, my thoughts drifted to Mary. If I only could have convinced her, if I just burned her anyway no matter what. If I had enough money to buy our own burgers, if I just paid him back like I said. If's didn't matter right now. I could only pray that my testimony wouldn't be discredited. The D.A. asked more questions concerning my thought process during our time spent with Raul, but it didn't seem to matter. When I was through testifying, the judge cast me a puzzled look, something he had never done before. It worried me, and I felt a little light-headed.

After court, I called Kevin to let him know how it went. "You know Boo-hoo called the chief?" he asked.

"No, I didn't. So?"

"He told him about the beer we bought Raul."

"Little snitch. He couldn't wait, huh? Ain't no big deal. I figured it'd come out sooner or later. It's not going to cost us the case," I told him, hopefully.

"Okay. I'm just telling you. There's a feeding frenzy going on around here. Just be ready when you get back," he warned.

"Jeez. What's the big deal anyway, Kevin?" I was looking for some moral support.

"You know how these guys are. Just keep your guard up."

"Okay. Thanks. See you tomorrow."

I stopped at a small diner in the middle of town after court for some dinner, which was called The Diner. It was run by a frail, young, balding Greek known as Johnny the Greek, a fabulous cook. He loved the cops and always heaped on a bit more whenever one stopped in for a meal. I sat at the counter and perused the menu. I looked up to see Boo-hoo pull up to The Diner in his patrol car for a break. A reserve was with him. They stopped short of coming in, pretending not to see me, conversing about something. Then they both got back into the car, the reserve casting a glance my way while I caught his gaze. He tried to look right through me and said something to Boo-hoo as they drove away. Quite obviously they didn't desire my company during their break. Johnny the Greek saw me from the kitchen and came out to say hi.

"What's up Johnny?" He always had a grin on his face, even though it seemed he worked 20 hours a day.

"What are you doing, dude." He hadn't been in this country very long and wanted to learn as much English as he could, since the language barrier made him a bit shy. He learned the word "dude", so everyone was a dude.

"Just another day in court, Johnny. Just another farcical day in court."

"Farcical? What's that mean, dude?"

"It's all a big joke, Johnny, just a joke," I sighed, resignedly.

"Lemme fix you some breaded veal." Johnny made the best breaded veal cutlets in town.

"Man, that sounds great. I'll take it."

"Sit, relax. I'll take care of you, dude."

The breaded veal and mashed potatoes were especially good today. I finished my meal then left when I noticed a patrol car parked a half block away. It was near dark, so I couldn't see who it was. As I drove away, the car followed me. I knew it was following me as when I approached the overpass leading out of town, the end of the city limits, it stayed behind me. Suddenly, the overhead lights went on, pulling me over. What the? It was Boo-hoo and his reserve. He slowly approached me.

"Howard? What the hell you doing?" I asked.

"Chief wants me to give you a message. He wants to see you in his office tomorrow morning at 8."

I got out of my car. "Listen, you little punk snitch! What's up with you anyway?" I angrily asked. His reserve approached me, as though we would rumble right here next to the highway. I thought about it for a minute, but his reserve was a big farm boy who could probably take me pretty easily. "Why is he having you stop me? Why doesn't he just call and tell me?"

"Take it up with the chief," he muttered, then returned to his car. I drove home, having moved out of town to the little city near ours, the place where I botched my first undercover drug buy, the city named after hog fat, Manteca. My sound sleep that night didn't portend the following day's shadows.

FORTY-TWO

Mickey's big hand was on the 3 when I arrived at the department, 8:15. I was a bit late, having to make a quick stop at the Quick Stop Market and buy breakfast, a cup of coffee and a package of Sno-balls. Everybody seemed uptight; an air of tension stifled me as I walked through the back door. People weren't as jovial as they usually were first thing in the morning. No cheery 'good-mornings,' no 'nice works' on our cases, unusually quiet. I walked the corridor leading to the Chief's office, stuffing the remains of my first Sno-ball in my mouth and gulping the coffee. His door was closed. I knocked. The Lieutenant, Schultz, opened it as I looked around before I entered. Something told me beware of a booby-trap, for this would have been an opportune time for a clown job. The chief was seated at his desk reading a report. As Schultz opened the door completely, the third of this triumvirate was revealed, Sgt Dumas, ole Peanut-brain.

I seemed to have attracted quite an audience.

"Sit down," Schultz said rather surly. Showing off in front of the chief, eh? I felt like ignoring him, but thought better of it and took a seat, the three of them forming a half-circle in front of me.

"Good morning, fellas. What's up?"

"Who the hell gave you the authority to violate the law when conducting an official investigation?" Rendle began forcefully, suddenly, without even a 'good morning.' Schultz and Peanut-brain looked ready to pounce, Schultz nearly frothing at the mouth. I looked at all three and thought of Muhammad Ali, who once said, "If we can't get along, let's get it on!"

"Obviously we have a problem," I countered without answering his impertinent question. "What's he doing here?" I asked, motioning towards Peanut-brain. I took a bite of my second Sno-ball and sipped my coffee.

"I wanted him here because he was in charge of the unit when the investigation first began." Perhaps it shouldn't have, but the comment angered me. I launched my offensive first.

"Investigation? You call what he did an investigation? He's the one who let it sit for two years, ignoring important details and trying to kiss it off to the Sheriff, until I got to it."

"At least I wouldn't have bought a suspect any beer," Peanut-brain countered, like a little kid who, when his parents are around, tries to act tough knowing he won't get hit in front of his parents. I wanted to hit him.

"That's an intelligent comeback, Dumas," I told him. "Is that what this is all about?" I asked the chief. He had his face on, the face that said, 'let me impress these guys by showing how obdurate I can be when dealing with an administrative problem,' the problem being me.

"Once again, you've damaged the reputation of this department. And I think it's only the tip of the iceberg of what's going on back there," he said, referring to my Detective unit.

"The tip of the iceberg? What the…what are you talking about? Have you seen our latest stats? Have you even checked the clearance rate? Good God, Chief, what are you talking about?" I looked at the three of them and my confusion gave way to fear. I was in the midst of three blithering, bungling boobs, and nothing I could say would salvage me, so I might as well go down swinging.

"I'm directing the Lieutenant to conduct an internal affairs investigation and, believe me, there will be disciplinary action," the chief exulted.

"What do you mean 'there will be'? Aren't you judging me guilty before you even have the facts? As the Chief, aren't you responsible for upholding the law and policy?" I asked, parroting the shyster's words to me in court yesterday. "Don't you owe it to me to treat me civilly and at least ask me what happened?" The Chief started shaking. I continued as I rose from my chair. "I don't appreciate being insulted and threatened in front of these idiots…"

"Now see here…" Schultz interrupted, but I interrupted his interruption.

"If you think you've got something on me, then go for it, but you damn well better treat me with respect," I said, raising my voice.

The chief, still shaking, said, "You're being insubordinate and threatening!" He was losing control, pounding his fist on the desk. "I will not tolerate it. I've tolerated far too much from you. How's this sound for a beginning?"

I sat down, doing all I could to restrain myself from jumping up and slapping all three in true Stooge fashion. By now, respect went on a complete respite. "Give it your best shot, pal," I disgustedly told him.

"First of all, we have furnishing alcohol to a minor. He wasn't twenty-one yet, right?" The Lieutenant nodded in agreement. "And that's a criminal violation. Now, let's go to the departmental violations." He read from a list. "One! Accepting gratuities. You allowed a suspect, a SUSPECT, to purchase your dinner. Two! Endangering your safety and that of a fellow officer. You did not handcuff your prisoner. Three! Drinking alcoholic beverages on duty. Four! Poor supervisory practices. You exhibited poor judgment with these violations to your subordinate. And we're just starting!" He said triumphantly.

"Wow. You did a good job, Chief, I replied sarcastically." The chief was on a roll.

"Because of what you did, solely without authority, we stand a good chance of losing this case. That defense attorney tore apart your integrity, I understand."

I've heard that one before. "Is that right? Isn't that the same thing you told me about the kidnap-rape, the one you accused me of having the victim as some sort of prize at a bachelor party? How many years is that guy doing? And please tell me, how many complaints do I have in my file from citizens? How many? Does zero sound right? How many do your minions have combined?" I was making him look bad in front of his idolizers. I might as well finish. "But let's get down to the real issue, Chief. You don't want to listen to my side, you don't care that there may have been extenuating circumstances to justify what I did. To you, everything is black and white."

"That's not true," he came back, weakly.

"Oh? You want my hide simply, plain and simple, because you don't like me, because I don't roll over and kiss your ass like these two flunkies…"

"Now see here…" Schultz again protested, repeating his earlier words, and I again interrupted him.

"My success far exceeds anything you ever did Dumas, or you Chief when you were in detectives. Chief Wolfe even honored me as the employee of the year last year, and…" Psycho interrupted, angrily.

"That Chief is no longer here. That is totally irrelevant, don't drag him into your mess!"

"It is relevant, damn it!" I started losing control. "You take exception to that, don't you? Instead of offering me encouragement, instead of working with me, you pull chicken-shit stunts like these policy violations. What the hell's wrong with you guys?"

"Another outburst like that and, so help me, I'll suspend

you on the spot. You don't run this damn department!" Rendle threatened. My rent was due, so I couldn't afford the luxury of a few days off right now.

My mind began whirling and my heart thumped rapidly. I thought about old Sgt. Guevara, how Psycho made subtle references to his perceived incompetency, about his Hispanic background and his cruel comments. I thought about the note on my locker when I was first hired, "Affirmative Action Hire." I thought about him beating up the old Mexican man in the old jail, standing triumphantly over his vanquished. I thought about the administration and its supervisors, with me being the only one of color. I thought about how I was the first Mexican in the history of the department, the first to be hired as a patrolman. I thought about bringing up the race issue, but thought better of it, because if I won an appeal of whatever discipline the Chief was going to administer, and that was a certainty, I wanted to win on the merits of the case, not playing the race card. Stupid me!

"Suspend me? You think I'm supposed to roll over and lick your boot heels because you'll suspend me? I'm already suspended. I've been in a state of suspended animation for the past 18 years, what's another day, three days, a month, a lifetime?" Suddenly, I consciously became aware of my anger. Discipline, morale, duty, dedication, justice. Words, empty, meaningless words. Empty, meaningless men who sat in judgment of me when their judgment meant absolutely nothing. Sometimes a man's pride gets in the way of his own judgment, and what the Psycho failed to understand of his subordinate was how important pride is to those of Mexican descent. My pride was on the line. How much longer would I stand for this circus? Not for long.

"I don't have to sit here and take this. This is complete lunacy. My God, have you guys forgotten who the bad guys are?" I stood up to leave, eyeing each one as trepidation raced through my existence. "Next time you see me, it better be within the parameters of the Peace Officers Bill of Rights."

A feeling of desecration enveloped my being. I felt locked

in a cocoon, locked between a warp of space, time, and infinity, unable to breathe freely, constrained as though shackled in a straight jacket, nailed to a cross. I looked at my three persecutors in front of me---absurd abstractions of men representing law and order, the defender of society and its rules. My mind drifted to a song of my earlier years,

> *My blood's so mad, feels like coagulatin'*
> *I'm sitting here, just contemplatin'*
> *...human respect is disintegratin'*
> *...this whole crazy world is just too frustratin'*
> Eve of Destruction by Barry McGuire

With disgust and nausea, I turned from them and reached for the door.

"Stop! Or you're dead!" The Chief demonically yelled. I froze in my tracks. Did I hear what he just said? Did he have his gun aimed at me? I heard pride can kill. "You walk out that door, it'll be the last time you ever set foot in this department," his voice quivered. He lost control, blowing it in front of his fellow conspirators.

I turned and saw his face, a mask distorted in hatred and loathing. I saw the cruelty and viciousness of a man far removed from altruism law and order was founded upon. I saw the psychotic rantings of a man whose own humanity was lost somewhere in the dark recesses of a disturbed mind. I saw a being unfamiliar with the people whom he held ultimate responsibility in terms measured solely in definitions set forth in policy manuals and codes of ethics. I saw a being I respected less than a lifetime convict or a product of welfare and despair. I saw the same face of the man who crowed over a helpless, beaten old man in the dark dungeons of our old jail cells.

"What are you going to do? Fire me? Without due process?" I asked, challenging him in front of his stooges. He crossed the line. He went too far and he knew it. To their credit, the Lieutenant and Peanut-brain shuffled uncomfortably, as though they were trying to detach themselves from these so-called proceedings. "You'd like to fire me, wouldn't you?" I asked the chief, watching his every move in the event he really went off the deep end and went for his gun. I got the strangest feeling the other two backed away as though anticipating a showdown, waiting for each to draw and fire, like an old Wild West showdown here in the Chief's office. I became conscious of my off-duty weapon at my side. I had finished my Sno-balls, leaving my left hand, my gun hand, free.

"With pleasure," the Psycho concluded. I slammed the door and stormed down the hall. Kevin was waiting for me outside my office door.

"Got time for a cup?" he asked.

We sat in The Diner, not saying much. I was feeling pretty blue, but I could still feel my blood steaming, the absurdity of those "charges" haunting my thoughts, like a bad dream. Kevin broke the silence. "What am I supposed to tell them? I'm supposed to go in there at 10."

"You can tell them whatever you want. There's nothing to hide. You can tell them you were following my orders. No sense in taking any more heat for what I did," I told him in earnest.

"You didn't hear me voice any objections, did you? I knew you were doing the right thing. The hell with 'em. Let them fire me if they want."

"Kevin, I'm sorry. I really am. I didn't know this would lead to all this nonsense. I don't really understand it myself, but this is my predicament. It's me the chief wants, and I gave him plenty of ammunition. I don't want anything to happen to you. You just tell them you were following my orders, okay?"

Kevin was much less animated than I was during his meeting, but certainly not intimidated. He told me later they wanted to bring charges against him for failing to report department violations of a supervisor and dereliction of duty for failing to report a crime, that of furnishing alcohol to a minor. The chief told him he would drop all charges if he turned witness against me, for which Kevin nearly told him to go to hell. It was a good thing he didn't or he'd be on the beach for insubordination.

It's absurd that rules had to be written forcing one to respect one's superiors, that respect had to be mandated and defined in a way to compel compliance. In much the same way the tough con, Baby-Ray, felt disrespected when he was asked to rat on his partner, the chief showed the same contempt with his deal of trying to have Kevin rat on me. The chief could never think that I couldn't look at it as "ratting," that it was Kevin simply telling the truth of what he knew.

Men like the Psycho, whether they be chiefs, administrators, leaders of men in any respect, their sense of perception deteriorates under the guise of their self-perceived worth. They fail to comprehend that integrity is relative, unique to one's environment, background and character. There wasn't a need to disrespect Kevin by offering him a deal. I wasn't about to lie, the facts were in the court records, although distorted by the superficial concerns of a demented man, the dementia of a man who controlled my fate, my executioner. As a Chief, he knew people talked, particularly about things when it comes to serious matters as this. He knew Kevin would tell me of the deal which would add another measure of satisfaction to the chief, knowing he stuck it to me even more.

My discipline became Rendle's obsession. The next several weeks he spent preparing memorandums, documentation, court transcripts, conferring with the City Manager and City Attorney. Perversely, I was beginning to enjoy the negative attention for nothing had really changed. I continued to do my job as always, teasing, laughing, clowning unsuspecting victims, and partying after work. My tribulations became a rallying point for others upset with the inequitable, archaic methods used to instill "a positive work attitude," as defined in the department policy manual.

What bothered me most was having to spend as much

time defending myself as I was trying to get some work done. I exhausted all internal appeals, which were fruitless anyway. Laughably, and I say laughably for I felt it was a sheer waste of time, money and energy, I had to retain an attorney provided me by our membership in PORAC, the Peace Officers Research Association of California. It was absurd to think I needed an attorney within my own department, but such is justice. The attorney felt my case had merit, however, there were built in safeguards. The procedures for internal discipline were that any suspension five days or less could only be appealed to the City Manager, anything over would be reviewed by an independent panel.

Over the years, I had very little to do with the City Manager. He had a latent dislike for me as he believed I had an affair with his wife many years ago, which was laughable, at least to me. When his wife left him, she rented an apartment across the street from me when I lived in town. She often times tried to join our after work get-togethers with her boyfriend, but since he had not reached the legal age of 21, I couldn't let him stay. The scandal was, she was having an affair with a senior high school student, a popular "jock," a football hero at the time. My appeal was a foregone conclusion.

THE BEGINNING

The sea lions barked noisily, their resonance echoing from the waves and the other jagged, jutting outcrop across from the one they basked. The seagulls circled overhead in search of morsels as the brisk ocean breeze whipped against my face, the taste of sea salt from Monterey Bay lightly detectable. Seal Rock on the Seventeen Mile Drive of Monterey was one of my favorite spots to stop and take in the wonder of nature. I spent three of the five day suspension I received here, my own Enchanted Forest, the coast of Monterey Bay. Kevin received two days and spent the time with his family. Raul Ortiz was remanded to the custody of Federal Agents for the smuggling charges because with the absence of an independent witness, the murder charge could not be substantiated beyond a reasonable doubt. The agent I first spoke with about the case, Agent Battlestone, called me later to tell me Raul implicated his brother, Jaime, in an effort to make a deal on the drug charges. Thus, a warrant for murder was issued for Jaime. He would stand trial for the crime, that is, if I didn't find him first. The shyster lawyer continued to practice his craft pending indictment for a myriad of offenses. How long that was to be was anybody's guess, except mine, for he was on my hit list as well.

I received a call at home from a man wanting a recommendation for Mary. She had applied for residency in a halfway house in San Francisco wanting to rehabilitate her life. The caller, who didn't want to give his name, told me she had disclosed a lot of information about what happened in Tracy and my involvement, and that if I didn't want to recommend her, he would understand, no questions asked. Of course I recommended her highly, never asking where she would be housed. It was better I didn't know, but I had a feeling I would run into her again someday soon.

With much sadness, I was reassigned to patrol from Detectives shortly after that episode. Peanut-brain was put back in charge of the unit once again. I felt molested for caring too much, mistaking truth with reality and integrity, misreading the honor code of life and the law. My friend and subordinate, Kevin remained in the Detective unit, a necessity to at least continue some semblance of productivity, and I was glad for him. We formed a lifelong friendship based on trust and loyalty with a mutual respect. He walked with me to the parking lot on my last day in Detectives where we embraced, fighting to hold back tears. He later became subordinate to no one, as he eventually resigned and became a successful businessman in the town he once protected, Tracy, California.

My first night back on patrol, graveyard shift, my mind whirled with thoughts and images of my youth, my adolescence and the absurdity of my world. All that I accomplished, all that I stood for meant nothing. The pride and respect I once revered for the job was reduced to a senseless storm of meaninglessness. I awoke daily to an existence void of purpose and relevancy, nearly dreading my tour of duty, which prohibited me from giving my best to my town and its citizens. I stayed within my room, safe within my room, where *"I touch no one and no one touches me"* (Simon and Garfunkle, <u>I am a Rock</u>). My room entombed me to an existence of emptiness and despair and I found myself wallowing in my own self-pity, slowly realizing my life had no connection to the bizarre rantings of the lunatic fringe governing the enforcement arm of our society.

I cruised through the business district of downtown Tracy, the same district I had driven countless miles and hours, and with my thoughts my eyes caught a glimpse of two shadowy figures fleeing through a back alleyway. My first instinct told me to turn back around and "check things out" as a burglary may be in progress. My second instinct overwhelmed the first and frightened me, for it caused me to do nothing. I didn't care anymore. The Rolling Stones anthem, Gimme Shelter, ran through my mind. *"Gimme, gimme shelter, or I'm going to fade away."*

Death cast its heartless will on many of my town, yet it had the compassion to acquit me, at least for now. He respected me, taunted me, haunted me, yet enlightened me, for I existed; I felt truly alive. Neither death nor his executioners can destroy my spirit, dull my resolve or doom my survival in this hostile universe as I strive to become a being in and for itself. I was happy with whom I am rather than what I was supposed to be for the benefit and judgment of someone else. Authority, position, and power were to be rejected, not respected. The people behind those labels deserved respect only by acknowledging my existence and dignity as an honorable member of humanity. Absolute acquiescence and blind loyalty served no purpose, accomplished nothing for my entirety as a human being. Some would label it defiant and rebellious, while others would call it enlightenment.

I grew up in the streets of this town. I learned of life, death and love in this town. I shed my blood and sweat on the city streets for the people of this town, and I shed tears for people I loved and lost in this town. The people of the town would never know, nor would they ever care that the town broke my heart, yet for all the pain I felt, for all the joy it brought, my soul would forever be flittering through the streets of this town, unseen like the illegal aliens who continue to toil in the fields, restaurants, and hotels, hoping to stay in the town a little longer for a little more money.

During those years, I was able to complete some college courses after the attainment of an Associate of Arts Degree from the junior college in Stockton. The idea of never completing college beyond that was bothersome to me, like a splinter in my mind, so I enrolled at the university in Stockton, the University of the Pacific, determined to finish.

Like Will Cane, the Gary Cooper character in <u>High Noon</u>, I imagined myself throwing my badge into the dirt, or more fittingly throwing it into the river, the Calaveras River where Juan Cortez was cast into a watery grave, like Clint Eastwood at the end of <u>Dirty Harry</u>, but the times were a bit more dignified now, so with dignity, I turned in my badge and walked away from my town into the sunset forever. I was not blue anymore. For longer than I cared to remember, I walked with a meaningful sense of freedom. The shackles of intolerance and ignorance were released from my spirit as I looked to the future. As I looked, I noticed the exquisite blue of the sky which harmonized with a passing of a gull, a gull sent from the sea, and its song told me it was calling for me, leading me from the Fortress of Solitude to continue my search for the Enchanted Forest.

EPILOGUE

"So, here I sit, baring my soul to you; what do you think, Dr. Knighten?"

The professor continued his look of interest. "That's some story—I think you may have something to offer this department. What are you doing now?"

"I joined the little campus police force. I didn't even know the University had a police department until I saw the employment flyer. I figured since it's already what I know, I could do that until I finish my education."

"Tell me," he said with an inquisitive grin, "did all those things really happen?"

"Did they happen? Of course they did. That's only part of it. I didn't want to bore you, so I just touched on the highlights. Think there might be a book in there?"

"You don't really need an education to write a book. Just look at some of the trash that's being printed. My God!" he said, shaking his head. Did he think my story was just as much trash? I wondered.

"You ever hear of Albert Camus?"

"Albert who?" Never heard of him, but my answer spoke for itself.

"How about Jean-Paul Sartre?"

"I heard of Jean-Paul Killey. Wasn't he an Olympic skier or something?"

"Jean-*Claude* Killey," he corrected me.

"Oh. Sorry." Who the heck are these people?

"Richard Wright. Surely you've read or heard of Richard Wright?"

I felt dumb. Should I just agree? "Well, I…that's why I'm here, I guess…"

"But, of course, I didn't mean to imply anything. You're tale, it just sounds so existential."

Yeah. That's it, I thought. Existential. Sounds cool, but what is it?

"I have a class beginning in two weeks. There's still room, for many people tend to shy away from existential literature, although I believe there's a little existentialism in all of us. It's just we don't recognize it, but I think you'll enjoy it. I think your anecdotes can offer much to the class. Interested?"

"Why, yes, I am very much interested."

"Good. Do you mind if I ask you one question?"

"Certainly, sir. Anything." I was intrigued. "Please do."

He leaned forward in his chair and whispered, "Did you actually kill that guy and the lawyer?" His look was serious.

I looked back towards his door, making sure no one was around. "No disrespect intended, sir, but I feel I can trust you. Perhaps that is something we can talk about later, that is, if you don't mind." I smiled and shook his hand then left his office, resolved to enroll at the University. As I stepped onto the lush lawn of the University, the pastoral settings, Burns tower and the rustic buildings of academia told me that this could be my gateway to the Enchanted Forest.

WORKS CITED

Barry McGuire. "Eve of Destruction." Dunhill, 1965.

The Doors. "Horse Latitudes." Elecktra / Asylum, 1967.

The Doors. "Crawlin' King Snake." Elecktra, 1971.

The Eagles. "Heartache Tonight." Elecktra, 1979.

Iron Butterfly. "Soul Experience." Atco, 1969.

Janis Joplin. "Ball and Chain." Legacy, 1970.

Jefferson Airplane. "White Rabbit." RCA Victor, 1967.

Kansas. "Dust in the Wind." Legacy, 1977.

The Rolling Stones. "Gimme Shelter." Abkco, 1969.

The Rolling Stones. "Sympathy for the Devil." Abkco, 1968.

Simon and Garfunkel. "I am a Rock." Legacy, 1966.